USA TODAY bestselling author **Janice Maynard** loved books and writing even as a child. After multiple rejections, she finally sold her first manuscript! Since then, she has written more than sixty books and novellas. Janice lives in Tennessee with her husband, Charles. They love hiking, travelling and family time. You can connect with Janice at

janicemaynard.com
Twitter.com/janicemaynard
Facebook.com/janicemaynardauthor
Facebook.com/janicesmaynard
Instagram.com/therealjanicemaynard

Maureen Child writes for the Mills & Boon Desire series and can't imagine a better job. A seven-time finalist for the prestigious Romance Writers of America *RITA*® Award, Maureen is the author of more than one hundred romance novels. Her books regularly appear on bestseller lists and have won several awards, including a Prism Award, a National Readers' Choice Award, a Colorado Romance Writers Award of Excellence and a Golden Quill Award. She is a native Californian but has recently moved to the mountains of Utah.

Discover more at millsandboon.co.uk

AN HEIR OF HIS OWN

JANICE MAYNARD

WAYS TO WIN AN EX

MAUREEN CHILD

MILLS & BOON

First Published in Great Britain 2021
by Mills & Boon, an imprint of HarperCollins*Publishers* Ltd
1 London Bridge Street, London, SE1 9GF

www.harpercollins.co.uk

HarperCollins*Publishers*
1st Floor, Watermarque Building,
Ringsend Road, Dublin 4, Ireland

An Heir of His Own © 2021 Harlequin Books S.A.
Ways to Win an Ex © 2021 Maureen Child

Special thanks and acknowledgement are given to Janice Maynard for her contribution to the *Texas Cattleman's Club: Fathers and Sons* series.

ISBN: 978-0-263-28307-5

1021

MIX
Paper from
responsible sources
FSC™ C007454

AN HEIR OF HIS OWN

JANICE MAYNARD

For all the health-care workers who have sustained us.
Thank you for your dedication!

One

Cammie Wentworth exited Royal Memorial Hospital via the heavy plate-glass doors and paused on the front walk, exhaling in relief and breathing in the delicious October air. Her favorite month of the year was rapidly becoming her favorite month *ever*. Hard work and single-mindedness were finally paying off.

At twenty-eight, it was about time she found her place in the world. Anticipating the meeting she had just attended with hospital administrators and influential doctors had given her several sleepless nights the past week. She worried they might think she was too young or too inexperienced. After all, her father had created a brand-new charitable foundation and made his only daughter the director.

Some people frowned on nepotism. But in this case—maybe because her father was about to drop a ton of money for a very good cause—the top brass at Royal Memorial had been open and enthusiastic about Cammie's pitch. She was determined to keep them involved and excited.

Being goal-oriented was good in the business world, but unfortunately, her more personal issues were harder to check off the list:

1) Persuade her long-lost brother, Rafe, to come home

2) Explore artificial insemination or adoption and become a mom

3) Erase every memory of Drake Rhodes and his piercing blue eyes

She was working on the first two. A few glimpses of hope kept her going. But that last one was frustratingly impossible. Even after two years, her breakup with Drake felt raw. Thankfully, he was working on the other side of the world for six months in Sydney, Australia. As far as Cammie was concerned, she hoped rabid kangaroos hopped out of the bush and ate him alive.

The bloodthirsty image made her smile again.

Drake was old history. They wanted different things.

Adjusting her shoulder bag, she turned toward the parking lot and ran smack into a hard wall of a man. When she stumbled, warm hands grabbed her shoulders and steadied her. "Sorry," he said. And then they both took a good look at the other. Cammie's shock was astounding.

"Drake?" She shook her head, wondering if the stress of this hospital meeting had tipped her over the edge. "What are you doing here?"

He was as gorgeous as ever, lanky and lean with thick, black hair and a slight swagger in his stance. Her stomach pitched and took a nosedive. Had she conjured him out of her imagination? But no, he was distressingly real.

Her heart, which she had thought mostly healed, cracked again.

* * *

Drake Rhodes was shocked as hell and trying not to let on. Surely fate was testing him. He'd barely been back in Royal for a nanosecond, and already he'd run into Cammie? He couldn't decide if he was angry or excited or both.

"Hello, Cam." Cammie Wentworth was stunning in the unforgiving midday sun. Her skin had the pale translucence of a true redhead, and her long, wavy hair gleamed with highlights of gold. He remembered making love to every inch of her tall, gently curved body.

Green eyes stared at him with suspicion. "I asked you a question."

He shook his head to clear the cobwebs and the memories trapped there. "Ainsley suffered a ruptured appendix."

"Oh, no."

"She's going to be okay, thank goodness. My stepsister has a long history of disrupting my life." He said that last bit with a grin. Cammie knew the story—how Drake had offered to be Ainsley's guardian when she was orphaned seven years ago. Ainsley had been fifteen, Drake only twenty-two. "I was just headed upstairs to see her," he said.

Cammie's face closed up. "Well, I won't keep you."

Drake noticed that she didn't say *nice to see you* or *how have you been?* Cammie wasn't a fan of his—for reasons that were entirely understandable. Even so, the lukewarm response depressed him.

He took her arm. "I'll walk you to your car, and maybe you can tell me why you're here."

Cammie gave him a tight-lipped stare, shaking off his light hold. "It's broad daylight. Ainsley will be waiting for you. I don't need an escort."

"Humor me." He didn't know why he was pushing.

But this might be his only chance to reconnect with Cammie and to see if she had gotten past his cruel rejection.

Cammie's halting confession two years ago about wanting a baby had been like a dash of cold water in his face. What if a condom broke? What if other birth control failed? The thought of having to raise another child scared the crap out of him. Ainsley had required enough parenting for a lifetime. Thank God she was an adult now. He was off the hook.

And yet something in him was glad to see Cammie again.

His ex-girlfriend was clearly trying to ignore him, because she walked quickly—two steps ahead—through the jammed parking lot. Suddenly, she stopped. "I swear, this place is a maze. I thought I parked on this row."

"That big pickup truck at the end is blocking your view. Why don't you try beeping your key fob?"

Cammie grimaced. "Whatever would I do without a big strong man to give me advice?" She pointed and beeped. Yep, they were in the right place. As they rounded the bumper of the obligatory Texas-male vehicle, two things happened at once—Drake heard the unmistakable sound of a baby crying, and he saw something on Cammie's trunk.

Not *something*. A someone. A very unhappy baby strapped into a small car seat. "What the hell?"

Cammie approached her car warily, looking from side to side. "Is this a practical joke?" They scanned the area for the child's mother or father.

Drake frowned, his protective instincts on high alert. "More like the beginnings of a scam. I've heard about situations like this. Somebody shows up asking for money. Or accusing you of kidnapping." Maybe this was why he had insisted on following her. Maybe he was in the right place at the right time.

* * *

Cammie wanted a baby badly. She had seriously thought about the prospect for at least the past five years.

But she hadn't expected one to drop out of the sky. This was just plain weird.

She approached the car and the kid cautiously. The baby screamed louder. Even for a woman with strong maternal instincts, the volume began to make her panic. But she sure as heck wasn't going to let Drake see that she was flustered.

She shot him a look. "I'm serious," she said. "You should go." Quickly, she unlocked her car and tossed her bag on the front seat. Since she had been inside a hospital moments ago, she grabbed sanitizer and cleaned her hands. Then she reached out and began unfastening and loosening all the buckles and straps keeping the infant safe.

Drake stood far too close, his gaze cataloging her every move. "I don't think you should pick it up. There are liability issues."

"Not an *it*," she said. "A baby."

"I can see that…"

The little body was warm. Its face was red. She glanced sideways to see Drake pull his phone from his pocket. "What are you doing?"

He lifted an eyebrow as if questioning her intelligence. "Calling 911?"

"Oh, right. Sorry, I'm a little rattled."

"That makes two of us."

Cammie guessed the baby was a boy. The one-piece pajamas he wore were blue-and-white plaid. A matching cap protected his small head. "Hey, there, munchkin," she whispered, hoping her presence would soothe him. As she scooped him out of his cocoon, she kept up a steady stream of soft, reassuring words. "You're beautiful, did you know that? It's okay for boys to be beautiful, I promise."

Drake snorted but didn't say anything. He was on his phone waiting for an answer.

Cammie cradled the infant against her breast, relieved when the shrieking cries subsided into whimpers. He was warm and solid in her arms. It was impossible to know for sure, but she guessed the child was a month old, maybe six weeks. He had black eyes and black wispy curls. His gaze seemed to lock on to hers, but that might be her imagination.

Whenever she imagined having a baby one day, the baby always looked like Drake. *Dumb, Cammie. Really dumb...*

Now that the immediate crisis was over, she knew she had a very short time to find his family. Babies as young as this one liked to eat often. There was no diaper bag, no note with instructions, nothing. The sheer impossibility of the situation made her think, once again, that someone was pranking her. If so, the joke was in very poor taste.

Fortunately, Drake's phone call bore fruit. The 911 operator was professional and didn't waste any time. With the call complete, Cammie leaned against the car and waited. Drake stood, aloof and quiet. If it had been hotter, Cammie would have sheltered inside the vehicle with the air-conditioning running. Fortunately, the weather was delightful.

Now that the infant had stopped crying, she was able to concentrate on his unmistakable appeal. The tiny boy smelled of baby lotion and all those other wonderful aromas that were part of the package with a newborn. Keeping her attention on the boy made it possible for her to *appear* to ignore Drake.

Finally, she turned to face the man who had broken her heart. "You need to go now. I've got this."

Drake's posture and his level gaze were stoic. "I'm not leaving you."

Unfortunately, the baby was getting squirmy and fussy. Cammie put him on her shoulder, cradled his head and tried walking back and forth. Maybe the warmth of her body and the motion would reassure him. Even so, an empty stomach was not going to be so easily appeased.

Fortunately, the police arrived quickly.

The officer who stepped out of the patrol car was female—a tall, slender Latina with long dark hair and dark eyes. In fact, she could easily have been the child's mother.

Cammie clutched the baby tighter. "Thanks for coming," she said. "My name is Cammie Wentworth. This is Drake Rhodes. We didn't know what else to do but call the police."

"I'm Haley Lopez. Tell me what happened."

The story was short and sweet. Cammie related everything she knew. "I'm afraid he'll be getting hungry any second." Drake didn't interrupt, but he stood close by, his gaze concerned.

Haley nodded. "No worries. I'll line up social services in a jiffy." She moved a few strides away to deal with the call.

While Officer Lopez was on the phone, a second woman stepped out of the cruiser. No badge this time, but she had some sort of credentials hanging around her neck. "Hey," she said. "I'm Sierra Morgan. I've been doing a ride-along with Officer Lopez, hoping to get acquainted with some of Maverick County." Sierra was petite, with long blond hair and green eyes. "I heard something about a baby?"

"He's not mine," Cammie said. "I found him on my car. Have you had a busy morning out on the mean streets of Royal?"

Sierra smiled ruefully, including Drake in her gaze. "Let's just say that an abandoned baby is the most interesting thing we've come across all day."

Drake spoke up. "Are you an aspiring police officer?"

"Oh, heck no," Sierra said. "I'm a journalist for *America* magazine." She pointed at the credentials draped around her neck. "I'm here in Royal to do an article on the upcoming gala and the tenth anniversary of the Texas Cattleman's Club finally admitting women." She wrinkled her nose. "Seriously? Only ten years? That's pretty sad."

Drake nodded wryly. "Change happens slowly around here. If you stay long enough, you'll see what I mean."

Cammie wasn't Drake's girlfriend anymore, but she couldn't deny the curl of jealousy in her stomach. Drake and Sierra were hitting it off a little too well.

Sierra turned back to Cammie. "Here's my business card. You never know—I might end up doing a piece about this little sweetheart."

Cammie took the card reluctantly. *America* was a nationally recognized publication. In a day when magazines were going the way of the dodo bird, *America* was still widely available in print. Nevertheless, Cammie didn't want the baby to be the subject of some gossipy news story. How would Sierra sell it, anyway? No one but local people would be interested.

"Thanks," she said. "But I'm sure there's not much of a tale."

"You never know."

The officer finished her call and returned. She addressed Cammie and Drake. "Sorry. That took longer than I expected. There's been a multicar pileup out on the interstate. If you'll give me a moment to get the car seat in my patrol car, this little boy and I will be on our way." She paused, an odd look on her face. "May I hold him a minute? I love babies."

Cammie handed over her charge reluctantly. "Do you have any of your own?"

Officer Lopez shook her head, staring down at the little boy with a wistful expression. "No, but I do have a few nieces and nephews."

Once Cammie had the baby back in her arms, the officer made a second call to what sounded like the station, updating someone on her situation and whereabouts. Cammie wanted to ask more questions about the social services procedure. She clutched the baby tightly, disconcerted that everything was moving so quickly.

Drake could see that Cammie was uneasy. Two years ago, she'd told him she wanted a baby, but this wasn't it. Besides, he still had a bad feeling about the entire bizarre encounter. Until he had evidence to the contrary, he would assume Cammie needed backup.

He watched her take a deep breath, not looking at him or at the reporter, but at Haley Lopez. "I want to keep him," she said. "Until his mother or father is found."

The officer shook her head. "Sorry. We have a protocol to follow. We utilize foster parents who are certified. I can't just hand him over."

Cammie was pale, almost teary-eyed. "Don't they say possession is nine-tenths of the law?"

Drake felt odd emotions in his chest. Regret. Confusion. Incredulity. First Ainsley, now this.

The universe was clearly offering him a chance to make up for his sins. And the little devil whispering in his ear pointed out how nice it would be to have Cammie close.

He cleared his throat. "Officer Lopez, I'm a licensed foster parent in the state of Texas. I had to jump through the hoops when I took over the care of my stepsister, Ainsley, seven years ago. If Ms. Wentworth is willing, I can go on record as being the kid's foster parent." He shot Cammie a pointed look. "But Ms. Wentworth will have to move into my house and actually care for the child."

Officer Lopez raised her eyebrows. "That seems a lot to ask."

Cammie glared at Drake. "Mr. Rhodes and I know each other." Her eyes were wide, her gaze hunted as she assessed his offer. She chewed her bottom lip, clearly debating her options. "You don't even live here right now, Drake. How would this work?"

He addressed the three women equally, keeping his expression impassive. "My stepsister suffered a ruptured appendix. I've come back to Royal to make sure she's okay. As Cammie knows, the house Ainsley lives in belongs to me. Cammie and the baby are welcome to stay. Ainsley will be in the hospital for several more days. When she is completely back to normal, I'll be returning to Australia. But by then, I'm sure the child's parents will have been located."

Haley Lopez nodded. "I think that can work. I'll need some information from you, Mr. Rhodes. Do you mind stepping over to the cruiser? I'll run your credentials and make sure I have the all clear."

As Drake followed the officer to her car, he kept an eye on Cammie. Her entire attention was focused on the baby. Seeing her again ripped at the scabbed-over guilt he carried. He knew he had hurt her. But what else could he have done? The two of them were polar opposites.

Cammie was soft and maternal and caring. Drake was...well, not that.

There was an old '70s song his mother used to sing. Something about being cruel to be kind. That summed up his broken relationship with Cammie perfectly.

Here was his chance to soften the edges of that pesky guilt. By helping Cammie in this situation, he could absolve himself and hopefully make her happy.

The danger was, he might hurt her again. Equally bad would be to remember how much he had wanted her, even when he broke off the relationship.

Could he keep himself in line? Could he resist the urge to get sucked back into Cammie's orbit of hearth and home?

He never wanted kids. Which meant he couldn't have Cammie.

Being close to her again would be torture.

He gave the officer his Social Security number and birth date and waited while she entered his info and spoke with social services. Soon, the deed was done.

When he and Lopez approached Cammie, she looked up with naked hope on her face. In the past, Drake had been a pro at squashing that kind of hope. But not this time.

Seeing her with a baby in her arms squeezed his heart. This was what Cammie wanted. Though it seemed risky as hell, Drake was going to pay for his sins with a short-term experiment. For once, he would even the scales and make Cammie happy. He owed her this much at least. His libido was all in favor of the tantalizing idea—Drake and Cammie under one roof.

Haley Lopez smiled at Cammie. "Are you sure about this, Ms. Wentworth? Newborns demand an incredible amount of work."

Cammie squared her shoulders. "I want to do it. *Somebody* put this baby on my car. That gives me an odd sort of responsibility. Plus, it will only be for a short time, surely."

The officer nodded. "I think you're right. But don't get too attached. I've seen foster parents grieve."

"I know he's not mine," Cammie said.

Drake touched the child's hair briefly, charmed in spite of himself. "What will you call him? I doubt he'll answer to *hey, you*."

Cammie actually laughed, her green eyes clear and bright when her gaze met his. "Well," she said. "It *is* October. What if I call him Pumpkin?"

Haley Lopez smiled. "I like it."

Cammie shot Drake a challenging glance. "What do *you* think?"

He shoved his hands in his pockets. The urge to touch the baby again was alarming. "Whatever," he said, shrugging to prove that he didn't care one way or another.

And just like that, Cammie's beautiful smile faded.

She turned to the officer. "Am I free to go? I'll give you one of my business cards."

Haley Lopez nodded. "I think you *should* go. As quickly as possible. There's a combo market/pharmacy on the other side of the hospital. They sell premixed formula. It's super expensive, but in this situation, I doubt you have much time." She looked at Drake. "Will you help her get home and settled?"

He fished a key ring out of his pocket and handed one key to Cammie. "Here's a spare. Make yourself comfortable. Mrs. Hampton was there this morning." To Haley, he said, "My housekeeper splits her time between taking care of the house and my ranch on the outskirts of town." Turning back to Cammie, he continued, "Ainsley's bedroom is upstairs. You and the baby are welcome to the guest bedroom on the main floor."

Why did he feel the need to explain why he wasn't going with her? Cammie was the one who wanted to play with the baby. Not him. When neither woman said a word, he shrugged. "I have to go see my stepsister right now. She's expecting me. What if I pick up some food on the way home?"

Officer Lopez nodded. "Divide and conquer. Sounds like a plan."

Drake rubbed the back of his neck, wondering why Cammie's blank expression made him feel like crap. "Text me if you need anything, Cammie. The number is the same. I have a different phone in Australia."

"I'm sure the baby and I will be fine. I appreciate your making this happen."

If her words had been any stiffer, they would have shattered like glass.

Drake felt a tension headache brewing. Was he making a terrible mistake? Was he going to get burned again? It didn't really matter, because he owed her. "I'll see you later," he muttered. Then he strode toward the hospital.

Cammie was heartsick as she watched Drake walk away. Intellectually, she understood that he had to see his stepsister, but despite the truth of the matter, she felt abandoned again. Some stupid part of her wanted Drake to be as excited about the baby as she was.

After the car seat was anchored in her car, she memorized the steps as she watched the officer secure the baby. Haley pointed to the chest strap. "You'll want to loosen this before you get him out."

"Got it," Cammie said, her throat dry. She was tempted to *walk* to the market. It wasn't that far. But the car would be faster, and she was positive it was time for the baby to eat. His little face turned red as he whimpered.

In the store, she didn't waste any time looking for what she needed. She went straight to an employee and asked for assistance.

The woman was super helpful. "These bottles of formula are ready to go. You simply pop off the plastic cap, and the nipples are already sterile."

Thank God. Cammie paid for two six-packs, along with diapers and wipes and new pj's, because that was all she could carry. At the same time, she arranged to have more items delivered to Drake's house the following morning. An infant couldn't demolish more than twelve of these bottles overnight. Or so she hoped.

Back at the car, she turned on the AC and moved her seat back as far as it would go. With the baby cradled in her left arm, she popped open one of the bottles and nudged the nipple against his lips. To her eternal relief, the kid opened his mouth and began sucking greedily.

Though the baby occupied her attention, other thoughts raced in her brain. Drake was back in Royal. He wasn't in Australia. An odd mix of joy and trepidation squeezed her heart. He had offered to let her stay with him.

It was a tiny miracle. Either that or a disaster waiting to happen. She was over him. Wasn't she?

Then how did she explain the excitement fizzing in her veins?

After two ounces, she lifted the baby to her shoulder and was gratified to get a healthy burp. With it came a shot of spit-up on her navy suit jacket. Lesson learned. She was going to need burp cloths.

The little boy went right back to eating when she offered the formula a second time. The bottle wasn't quite empty when his eyes closed, and he conked out.

Cammie sat there holding him, knowing she had

dodged a bullet. What if he had been allergic? What if he was normally breastfed and wouldn't take a bottle?

It didn't take a shrink to see that she was focusing on the baby so she wouldn't have to think about returning to Drake's house. By the time she arrived at the very familiar address, she was exhausted.

Although she had spent plenty of time there in the past, none of it had been in the guest room. She had shared Drake's large, hedonistic bed. The memories made her hot and restless. Laying the baby on the mattress momentarily, she kicked off her shoes and shrugged out of her stained jacket. The silk blouse underneath was sleeveless, so she immediately felt cooler.

Even the guest room had a king-size bed. If she lined the far edge with pillows, she could throw back the covers and let the baby sleep beside her tonight. It wasn't ideal, but until she could get something more suitable ordered, it was the best she could do.

She sank down in a chair, her legs suddenly weak and shaky. Was she out of her mind? She didn't know how to take care of a baby.

The memory of Drake's deep blue eyes as he offered to be the foster parent on record confused her. Why had he done it? They had barely seen each other in two years, and then only at public functions where they both managed to stay on opposite sides of the room. The pain of their breakup had tormented her.

As for Drake...who knew? He was an enigma wrapped in a question. Kind and thoughtful one minute, remote the next.

In the midst of her soul searching, the baby slept peacefully. Where was his mother? His father? Was there a sixteen-year-old girl somewhere who simply couldn't handle motherhood? Cammie was almost thirty, but she

was still scared. This brief experiment might dissuade
her from becoming a single mother. No matter how badly
she wanted a baby of her own, she might discover that
solo parenting wasn't for her.

Because the little boy slept deeply, Cammie decided
this was the time to make one of her famous to-do lists.
It was going to be a doozy. She needed clothes and toi-
letries from her own house. Plus, her computer. Then, of
course, she had to buy something for the child to sleep
in. A bassinet would be fine for the short term. Pumpkin
was small enough that he didn't roll over.

The clothes and blankets and pacifiers would be fun to
choose online. Unless pacifiers were a no-no. She would
have to research that.

Although money was not really a problem, it would
make more sense to order powdered formula and learn
how to mix it. On the other hand, this was a temporary
situation, so maybe to preserve her sanity, the premixed
formula was a worthwhile expense.

Even in the midst of her very practical thoughts, other,
more incendiary considerations intruded. *Drake Rhodes.*
Sleeping just down the hall from her. In the past, they
hadn't been able to keep their hands off each other. To
say they were sexually compatible was like calling the
ocean wet. Drake was a master at giving pleasure, and
she did the same for him.

Over the course of an eighteen-month sexual relationship, they had been as close as two people can be.
But Cammie had been the one to cause a rift. Innocently
enough. One rainy, early-autumn night, when the weather
outside had been dreadful, Drake had built a fire in the
fireplace. They'd ordered in, enjoyed an intimate dinner and then made love in front of the crackling flames.
They had talked afterward, wrapped in each other's

arms on the lushly carpeted floor, swathed in an expensive cashmere afghan. Drake had opened up about his dreams for expanding his financial consulting business…his yearning to travel the world. He had an incredible business mind, and his investing expertise was in high demand.

Cammie had listened, and when he asked *her* a question in return, she'd been honest. She told him that she had always dreamed of becoming a mother. That she wanted a family. Roots. Her own formative years had been turbulent, to say the least, which was why she was drawn to the idea of normalcy.

On that long-ago evening, Drake hadn't said much about her revelation, but gradually over the weeks that followed, she'd felt him drawing away. He'd been busier suddenly. He had traveled more.

Because it happened so slowly, Cammie hadn't connected the dots. She had sensed that things weren't the same between them, but she didn't know why. Until the day he sat her down and told her that he didn't want to get married or have kids.

His words had been gentle, but the pain was no less traumatic. Cammie had fled this very house and never looked back.

Now she was here again. With a baby. Playing at what she had always wanted. This was probably the worst idea she had ever conceived, but she was committed now. And she was too smart to let Drake Rhodes hurt her again.

Two

Three hours after Cammie walked through Drake's front door, she was still nervously awaiting his arrival. What was taking him so long? Was he avoiding her?

She and the baby had come to an understanding. He would tolerate Cammie's clumsiness, and she would protect him from all harm. A couple of times, Cammie could swear he smiled at her. Was that possible? Did babies so young know how to smile? She told herself he did.

At four o'clock, still no Drake. Maybe he wasn't going to come home at all. Maybe he was already regretting his offer to help. Maybe he'd decided to sleep out at his ranch. She told herself a mature woman didn't get her feelings hurt over something so unimportant, but she knew the truth.

Part of her had hoped Drake would enjoy having Pumpkin here for a temporary visit…that the man so opposed to fatherhood would see how sweet it was to have a newborn. She should be embarrassed at her own blind naïveté.

When Pumpkin was ready for another bottle, Cammie felt more confident this time. Soon, his tiny eyelashes fanned his cheeks again. She held him for a few minutes but finally put him down. He needed to sleep on his own.

When her stomach growled, she glanced at her watch. Only then did she realize she had skipped lunch. Drake had promised to bring food, but he hadn't said which meal. Surely, he hadn't stayed all this time at the hospital with Ainsley. There were rules about visiting hours. On the other hand, she knew full well that Drake enjoyed breaking rules.

A shiver snaked its way down her spine. Without the baby to distract her, she was jumpy. For two years she had kept her distance from Drake. Now she was back in his sphere. Too close. Too tempted. Memories washed over her, both exhilarating and painful.

It was her own fault. She could have handed the baby over to Officer Lopez and walked away. But something about the abandoned infant made her determined to keep him in the short term. He wasn't hers. She wasn't delusional.

Even so, she felt responsible.

When she heard the front door open just before five, her heartbeat quickened. Drake was home. Apparently, he wasn't alone, because she heard male voices. Footsteps tromped down the hall. Her host appeared in the doorway.

"Hey," he said.

That single word dried her throat. "Hello."

Drake motioned for the two college-aged kids behind him to enter the room. They carried a large box. Drake looked at Cammie. "I got a bed. I thought that wall over there might work. Is that okay?" His gaze landed briefly on the baby, who slept peacefully.

Her eyebrows shot up as she read the name on the

box. It was a high-end Swedish company that made baby furniture. "Drake. Good grief. We'll probably only have Pumpkin for a few days." This one item must have cost $3,000 or more.

Drake shrugged, his expression hard to read. "Doesn't matter. We can donate it when he's gone. Excuse me. I have to answer a few emails. Give me a yell if there's a problem."

Cammie tidied the room while she watched the two pleasant and competent young men assemble the bed. The blond boards were pale and beautiful, buffed to a pleasing sheen. One of the guys smiled at her. "You've got a beauty here. This particular wood is supposed to be so hard that it barely shows teeth marks."

She wanted to laugh. Poor little Pumpkin was months away from having teeth. "I guess I'll have to choose bedding worthy of such a gorgeous heirloom."

The other workman looked up from tightening a screw on the railing. "Mr. Rhodes already took care of that. We have several more boxes out in the truck. Almost done here. Then we'll bring in the rest."

Cammie's heart sank. She didn't want to be beholden to Drake. Not like this. Was he somehow trying to buy her forgiveness? He'd been nothing but honest with her. It wasn't his fault that she wanted something he couldn't or wouldn't give her.

When the rest of Drake's exorbitantly expensive shopping spree arrived inside, Cammie didn't know whether to laugh or be scandalized. There was a mattress and sheets, a wall hanging and a baby monitor. A rocker in the same wood as the bed came with a lumbar cushion for Mom or Dad. The bed was the type that could convert for a toddler, so Drake had purchased the matching comforter and blanket and pillow.

By the time everything was in place, Pumpkin's new nest was complete, and Cammie was left to wonder where she was going to put all the rest.

At last, Drake returned. He surveyed the new items in his guest room and gave a half nod, the only signal of his approval. "Is he still sleeping?"

Cammie tried a smile, but it felt false. "Yes. But I don't know for how long."

"I had them charge the monitor to a hundred percent in the store before I left. If you can figure out how to work it, we can eat."

"You have food?" she asked, her stomach growling audibly.

For the first time, Drake's expression lightened. "I called Amanda Battle at the diner. She promised to include all your favorites. Pot roast. Mashed potatoes. Her famous broccoli salad. Hot rolls."

"And strawberry pie?"

"And strawberry pie."

He seemed uneasy, being so close to all the baby paraphernalia. "They just delivered the meal. Meet me in the kitchen when you're ready," he said brusquely. "I'll keep it warm."

And then he disappeared again.

Cammie glanced at the baby. He was sleeping on his back. She knew that much was correct. And his little face was serene. "Will you snooze long enough for me to eat dinner?" she asked.

The infant didn't answer.

Unfortunately, Cammie used precious minutes trying to figure out the monitor. But at last, she set the base on the bedside table and tiptoed out of the room carrying the little screen that allowed her to keep a watchful eye on her new responsibility.

She found Drake in the kitchen, as promised. He had shed his expensive sport coat and rolled up the sleeves of his crisp white dress shirt. She saw his tie crumpled on one of the bar stools. Even for a simple hospital visit, he dressed like the successful man he was. His muscular, tanned arms were incredibly sexy. Or maybe that was sexual deprivation talking.

It shouldn't have been a turn-on to watch a man unload a basket of food containers, but Cammie focused on Drake's every move.

He mistook her fascination for starvation. "Grab a plate," he said. "I've set us two places in the dining room."

The kitchen nook had a perfectly serviceable table, though small. Perhaps Drake thought the ambience was too cozy. By the time Cammie had served her plate, he had poured two glasses of wine and carried them into the adjoining room.

Since Cammie knew Drake's housekeeper kept the dining room table set for four all the time, she couldn't be flattered. Even the lit candles were not a nod to romance. Drake entertained often. Clearly, the candlelight was more *sophisticated mood* than a seductive prelude.

He soon joined her with his own plate. For a few awkward minutes, neither of them said a word. Cammie ate too quickly. She'd been almost light-headed with hunger. The stress of the day and the fact that she was probably a little dehydrated made the meal all the more appealing.

When she had cleared half her plate, she looked up to find Drake staring at her. A muscle ticked in his throat. "I should have brought you lunch. I'm sorry."

"Am I making a pig of myself?" She felt the hot flush that crept from her throat to her cheeks.

His gaze darkened to the deep navy of a nighttime sea. "Not at all. You always did have strong appetites."

"Don't do that," she said sharply.

His faux-innocent expression wasn't the least bit convincing. "Do what?"

"Don't bring up sex. That's not why I'm here."

His lips pressed tightly together, rolling inward, his gaze stormy. "I know that, Camellia. You've found another man."

Using her much-hated full name was his way of baiting her. But she refused to play that game. First, she needed to get something out of the way. "Thank you," she said tersely. "For all the baby stuff. It wasn't necessary. In fact, it's ridiculously over-the-top. But I do appreciate it. Pumpkin has everything he needs."

"And what about you, Cammie?" Drake's fingers toyed with a spoon on the table. "Do you have what you need?"

She pretended to misunderstand his innuendo. "I'll have to run home and pack a bag. Maybe after the next feeding. I won't be gone a whole hour. He'll sleep that long."

Her host paled. "Oh, hell no. Make a list. I know my way around your condo. You're not leaving me here alone with that kid."

"He's not that scary. Newborns sleep a lot."

"Doesn't matter. This was your gig. I'm happy to play support team."

"Fine," she said grumpily. The idea of Drake poking around her bedroom now that they were no longer lovers made her uncomfortable. But it appeared she had no choice.

After a few false starts, they finally began a conversation that was impersonal and nonthreatening. She asked Drake what it was like to visit Australia. And then questioned him about the booming movie industry in Australia, because she had read an interesting news story in that vein lately. Later, he said he'd heard about her father's loss…offered his sympathy.

"Thanks," Cammie said. "It's been a hard time for him. Danae was the love of his life."

"Third time's a charm?"

"I suppose. He was crushed when her cancer was diagnosed. And honestly, he did a complete 180 in terms of his outlook. Danae wanted him to be more generous, less of a workaholic. She urged him to give back to the community, convinced him it was the road to happiness. And she begged him to reconcile with Rafe."

"Is Rafe open to that idea?"

"It doesn't seem so. I've sent letters and called him a dozen times over the years. Usually, he never answers me. Once, he simply told me he doesn't believe in looking back. Daddy has written him this time, though, so I'm hopeful."

"Wow. I never thought your dad would do that."

"Danae changed him."

"How is *your* mom?"

Cammie shrugged. "We're still not close. I see her a couple of times a year in New York, but she will never come back to Royal. I think she resents the fact that I wanted to stay here instead of going with her. But I was a kid. Royal was all I knew."

Drake was silent for a moment, his dinner finished. At last, he sighed. "I figured out something when we broke up."

She stiffened. "What do you mean?"

"I never could understand why the baby thing was such a huge deal to you, but I finally understood. It's because your relatives were and are so screwed up. You thought a baby would give you a fresh start. A tabula rasa. You wanted a do-over, a chance to create the perfect family. Am I right?"

The bite of potatoes she'd swallowed turned to a lump in her throat. After a reckless swig of wine, she managed to face him. "Wanting children is a completely normal human emotion. Otherwise, the population would die out."

"I never said it wasn't normal. But you might be trying to get pregnant for the wrong reasons."

She tamped down her fury. "I didn't know you had taken a side gig as a therapist. You don't know me well enough to understand my motivations."

His gaze narrowed. "I knew you pretty damn well once upon a time."

"Maybe."

"Admit it, Cammie. We were a perfect match until you started listening to some mythical body clock."

"We weren't a perfect match," she hissed. "You were an egotistical, self-centered, arrogant jerk, and I didn't see you for who you were until it was too late."

"So the blame is all mine?"

He was angry, too. They had summoned a whirlwind of feelings that should have dissipated by now. The past was the past.

Apparently, Drake was no more sanguine about their breakup than she was.

She took a deep breath, counted to ten. "This isn't a productive conversation. If you won't let me leave you with the baby for a short time, then I'll make a list of what I need. I'll give you my key."

"I still have one," he said curtly, his expression impossible to read.

Her mouth dropped open. Those four words shocked her. She wanted to ask him why, but she didn't want to hear his answer. Perhaps the more important question was, why had *she* never asked him to return her key?

To say they had both forgotten seemed naive in the extreme.

Her stomach tightened with tension. "Pumpkin will be awake soon. I'll go make a list. Will you be in your office?"

"There or the den. You can find me. You know your way around."

He was still trying to provoke her. Instead of responding, she walked out of the room.

Drake took his time driving to Cammie's place. He was angry and frustrated, and he didn't enjoy either emotion. Already, he regretted his impulsive invitation. Having Cammie and the baby in his house was sure to drive him insane.

Maybe he was a glutton for punishment.

Walking through the front door of Cammie's modern, spacious condo had him drowning in emotions. Lust was the big one, but so many more. He could see himself here, vividly. All the nights she had cooked for him. All the relaxed weekend mornings they'd lazed in her bed and made love again and again.

When his body tightened and his sex inevitably stirred, he cursed beneath his breath. He had moved on. So had Cammie. It was for the best.

He pulled open the door of her walk-in closet and was assailed by her scent. Once upon a time, he had tried to buy her perfume, but she told him she preferred simpler fragrances. Lemon. Lavender.

In the midst of shoeboxes and hangers and drawers of belts and scarves and other feminine fripperies, he found himself frozen. Cammie surrounded him. The bright colors she liked to wear. The fuzzy sweaters that outlined her modest breasts. The silky wisp of a nightgown he had bought her in Paris during a romantic trip he'd combined with business. She had been so patient with him. So understanding.

He took a handful of the silk lingerie and held it to his nose, inhaling deeply, remembering. He was hard, hard as stone. Aching for something that was not going to happen. Ever again.

As a man accustomed to running his life *his* way… all the time…what he was feeling now left him gutted. Morose.

With a second curse, he thrust the soft garment away and pulled Cammie's list from his pocket. The suitcase came down from a shelf over his head. He stuffed it with pants and tops and a couple of cardigans. The shoes she'd requested went in another small bag.

Back in her bedroom, he rummaged in her dresser drawers, locating bras and panties. *Hell.* His hands shook. The rock in his stomach made it hard to breathe.

Doggedly, he continued on to the bathroom to retrieve Cammie's travel kit. He opened it to make sure everything was there. Toothbrush and toothpaste were not bothersome. But the birth control pills gave him pause. Was Cammie seeing someone? A red haze obscured his vision.

He had assumed she was grieving for him. Regretting their breakup. Why would she need birth control if she was home alone every night?

The questioned tormented him for the next half hour as he attacked his chores on autopilot. He found her computer on the kitchen table. Shut it down. Packed it up in a stylish leather tote. Eventually, he was satisfied that he had accumulated everything on Cammie's list. He retrieved her mail, set the thermostat.

As he drove back to his house, his brain spun in a million directions. Cammie was under his roof for a short time. Four or five days…maybe a week at most. What did he want from her? Did he have a subconscious agenda when he'd offered to be the baby's foster parent?

Maybe he did. Maybe he was hoping Cammie would find out how hard it was to take care of a kid. Maybe he could convince her to give up on the pregnancy thing. Cammie was young. She had plenty of time. And in the here and now, she could go to Australia with him. They could see the sights in Sydney, wallow in the sunshine. Make love…

By the time he made it back home, he had convinced himself the plan was rock solid. It took him two trips to get everything inside. The house was dark.

He carried the suitcase and the toiletry case down the hall, leaving everything else in the foyer. The guest room door was closed, but a light shone from underneath.

"Cammie?" He knocked lightly.

She opened the door almost instantly. The baby nestled on Cammie's shoulder sound asleep. Cammie looked beautiful but tired. "Did you find everything okay?" she asked, whispering.

"Sure. How are things here?"

She met his gaze with a fillip of challenge. "Fine."

"I'm glad." The lie threatened to stick in his throat. He didn't want Cammie to think mothering was easy. He wanted Cammie to give the baby back to Officer Lopez and play with *him*… Drake.

He set her suitcase and toiletry bag beside the door. "Your computer and other stuff are in the foyer. Is there anything else you need right now? It's the middle of the workday in Sydney. I have several calls to make."

Cammie's gaze was unreadable. "Pumpkin and I are great. Thanks again for doing your part."

His feet seemed reluctant to move. "The fridge is full. Help yourself if you get hungry. Mrs. Hampton shopped yesterday."

"Drake..."

"Yes?"

"I'm sorry we're intruding. And I'm pretty sure you wish you had never said anything. But even so, I'm glad Pumpkin didn't have to go to some strange family."

Drake grinned. "*Technically*, you're a strange family, Cam. You don't have a single connection to this kid. Not at all."

"Except that I found him on my car."

"And that means nothing."

"Why are you being so mean?"

It was a fair question. He hunched his shoulders. "Maybe because I'm trying hard not to seduce you."

She blinked, her cheeks flushing. "You can't seduce me. I'm a grown woman. I can take care of myself."

"And you, my sweet, are apparently not savvy enough to know statements like that are a red flag to someone who has shared your bed. Someone who knows the sounds you make when you come. A guy who remembers every curve of your body."

The flush faded. Now Cammie was pale, her gaze tragic. "Don't do this...please. I spent months getting over you...over us. I won't go down that road again."

"We were a perfect match in almost every way. You know it as well as I do."

"Maybe. But fundamental issues are the ones that tear marriages apart."

"Then don't worry about marriage. Lots of couples

enjoy relationships that have expiration dates. You're young. What's your hurry?"

"It sounds like you were *always* planning to dump me at some point. Is that true?"

Seconds ticked by as the room fell silent. Truthfully? In some deep corner of his heart, he had thought Cammie might be the one. He'd been in no hurry to be serious. He thought they had all the time in the world.

But how could he ever contemplate going back to square one? And with his own baby, it wouldn't be only seven years. Fatherhood would be a two-decade commitment. Two damn decades.

"I wasn't always planning to dump you, Cam. But I also wasn't planning for the future. You and I were great. I didn't want to overthink things."

"It's really okay," she said. "I always believe it's a blessing when couples discover their incompatibilities *before* the wedding. You and I were lucky in that way."

"We weren't incompatible," he snapped. "Not at all." They liked the same books and movies. They were both night owls. Each of them hated cilantro and liked medium-rare steaks. They rooted for the same baseball team, and they loved to travel.

Cammie shook her head slowly. "You need a woman who will be footloose and fancy-free with you. Someone who understands your desire to be unencumbered. She's out there somewhere, but it's not me."

"Thanks for making that perfectly clear," he said sarcastically. "But there's another choice, you know. Recreational sex? Two people who know how to push each other's buttons? Pleasure, Cammie. Sheer pleasure."

The flush returned. For a moment he thought he was making headway.

But she took a step backward. A literal step, as if to

distance herself from temptation. "You're only here in Royal for a short time, and Pumpkin will only need your official status briefly. For you and me to do anything foolish would be just that. We had our time, Drake, and it was wonderful. But it's over."

Three

When Drake spun on his heel and departed the room abruptly, Cammie sank into the nearest chair, her knees rubbery. Having Drake so close was like a biohazard. He affected her in dangerous ways.

He wasn't even trying to mask his intentions or his desires. The man wanted the two of them to tumble back in bed together. Because it was fun.

And he was right, damn him. It *would* be fun. Unless she admitted that *fun* was a misnomer. Fun was a word for things that were lighthearted and entertaining.

Drake was more than fun. When she was in bed with him, the world was bigger and brighter. The fireworks were real. The sex was like riding a perfect wave. Summiting the most challenging mountain. Diving into an endless pool and coming up to bask in sunlight on the surface. He made her feel strong and happy.

Gently, she stroked the baby's hair. Her heart turned

over in her chest, and her womb clenched with yearning. Ever since she was a little girl, she had wanted a baby of her own. College—and a career in communications— had been rewarding. Being asked by her father to head up the new foundation was even better.

But couldn't she have it all? Was that too much to ask?

The early part of the night passed without incident. Pumpkin seemed to be the perfect baby. He ate and slept, and in between, he favored Cammie with happy burbles.

Around 1:00 a.m., things changed.

Clichés were clichés for a reason. Cammie had often heard someone say their infant *had his days and nights turned around.* The expression never meant much to her until now. She dozed for a few minutes after the midnight bottle. But Pumpkin was restless. Eventually, he started to whimper.

She knew he wasn't hungry, so she scooped him up and changed his diaper. She even burped him once more for good measure. But the placid infant morphed into a red-faced, squirmy lump.

Nothing she did appeased him…except for walking the floor. As soon as Cammie put him on her shoulder and paced, Pumpkin was happy. He cooed and smashed his face into her collarbone. She was thankful he was happy, but exhaustion threatened to drag her under. Back and forth. Back and forth.

"It's late," she whispered. "Time for all little boys to be asleep."

Half a dozen times she tried to put him down in his bed. She had a system. Ease him onto his back. Hand on tummy. Gradually lift hand and try to back away.

It might have been comical if she wasn't sleep deprived.

No matter how slowly she removed her hand and straightened, the little boy woke up again and again.

"Please, sweet thing," she begged. "Please go to sleep."

She knew there were appointments on her calendar tomorrow, though at this hour, she couldn't remember what they were. Even if it took a few days for the authorities to locate the child's mother, Cammie had the flexibility in her work to shift things around.

But how long could she maintain a hit-or-miss schedule? Her father's charitable foundation was new. Things were just gearing up. With the gala approaching, Cammie would be busy, really busy.

Maybe Drake was right, though she couldn't bear to hear him say *I told you so*. Maybe Cammie's impulsive decision was neither practical nor possible. Most pregnant women had nine months to figure out a plan for work and babysitters and all the rest.

Cammie had jumped into caregiving without a thought for how it would impact other aspects of her life.

At the moment, she couldn't even summon the energy to be stressed about it. Her brain was numb. Her spine ached. All she wanted to do was sleep.

Sometime around two thirty, Pumpkin got really mad. Scary mad. Cammie grabbed another bottle, but he wasn't interested. He wailed.

How did new parents learn to do this stuff? Cammie had tears in her eyes, too. Maybe Pumpkin's mother had abandoned him because she simply couldn't handle it.

Cammie heard a quiet knock, and then the bedroom door opened. Drake was framed there, bare feet, bare chest, tousled hair.

He had probably been *completely* bare a few moments before. She knew he slept nude. The gray knit sweatpants riding dangerously low on his hips were no more than a concession to modesty. Cammie's modesty. It wouldn't have bothered Drake to enter the guest room stark naked.

He ran both hands through his hair and yawned. "What's wrong with him?"

Her chin wobbled. "Nothing that I can tell. He just won't sleep. I've tried everything." Her voice cracked on the last word.

Drake's sleepy expression softened into rueful sympathy. "I'm sorry. You look fried, Cam. Let me take a turn with him. I'm no expert, but I can walk the halls."

Guilt warred with her survival instinct. Drake had explicitly said the baby was her idea, her project. He'd only furnished the credentials and the house.

On the other hand, if she didn't get some sleep, she wouldn't be able to take care of little Pumpkin tomorrow. "Are you sure?" she asked. Her eyes stung with emotion, and she didn't know why.

"Give him to me," Drake said. "Get in bed and turn out the light." He held out his arms.

Cammie handed over her charge with relief, feeling like the biggest fraud on the planet. For a woman who claimed to want children, she hadn't lasted a single night.

Drake cradled the infant in his arms, managing to look both capable and ridiculously sexy at the same time.

Cammie gnawed her bottom lip. "Come and get me if he won't settle down."

"I will." Drake disappeared with the baby into the hall and shut the door.

For about ten seconds, Cammie nearly changed her mind. Then she climbed beneath the covers on Drake's sumptuous guest bed and passed out.

Drake settled the kid on his shoulder and walked from room to room in his dark, empty house. He'd slept enough that he was wide-awake. Most of the time he didn't need much sleep, anyway, and now jet lag was adding to the mix. Cammie, on the other hand, liked to get a full eight hours. Which made her latest project flawed from the beginning.

He wouldn't tease her about it. A few minutes ago, when he walked into the bedroom and saw her, his heart had clenched with sympathy. She looked beaten. Defeated.

As much as he wanted her to give up the pregnancy idea, he didn't want to see her get hurt. He patted the boy's back absently. "Take it easy on her, kid. She's in your corner."

The baby was awake, sucking his fist. He appeared to be interested in the tour, though whether or not he could actually see much was anybody's guess. Drake didn't turn on any lights. He was hoping the kid might nod off.

This was the first time Drake had taken a quiet breath since flying back to Royal. He'd been worried about Ainsley, and then he'd run into Cammie.

Now, in the middle of the night, he pondered his options. He had only booked a week-long airfare, a day of which had been consumed in flight. He had assumed that his stepsister would be on the mend by then. In six more days, business in Australia would be piling up. Meetings, appointments, consultations. Decisions.

He had good people in place, but everyone always wanted the boss.

If Pumpkin's mother or father or both hadn't been located in the next few days, would Drake be able to fly off to Sydney, knowing that Cammie was sleeping under his roof?

More to the point, would his foster parent status be in jeopardy if he left?

With no one around to see him, he sat down in an armchair and propped the baby on his chest, careful to support his neck. "Tell me, kid. Why do women always want babies? You're an awful lot of work."

Pumpkin wriggled around but didn't answer.

Drake continued the one-sided conversation. "Am I a bad person? Fatherhood isn't for everyone, you know."

No response. Drake touched the silky-fine hair—what there was of it. "I want her in my bed. Now. This week. What do you think about that?"

Pumpkin drooled so much Drake had a wet spot on his sternum.

Drake stretched out his legs and flexed his toes, feeling the pull on the back of his calf muscles. Ordinarily, if he woke up at this hour, he might go for a run. Instead, here he sat with a small weight against his middle.

"If I'm honest with her, maybe she'll come around. Of course, you're not helping. All she thinks about is you. I've been sidelined by another man. I guess you're proud of yourself."

Pumpkin yawned comically. He was so small—how did his little mouth open so wide?

Drake let his body go still, hoping the kid would get the idea. The clock on the mantel ticked away the minutes. Eventually, the boy slept.

Rising from the chair was a challenge, but Drake did it. All he had to do was pretend he was carrying a small explosive. One wrong move…

Fortunately, the baby stayed asleep. Drake eased open the guest room door and carefully laid the little boy on his back in the crib.

Drake held his breath. Maybe his luck would last.

When he glanced at the bed, he knew what he wanted. Cammie was beautiful. Her fiery hair was spread across the pillow. He actually trembled, his breath hitching in his chest. The urge to join her was almost overpowering.

Though he had been the one to end the relationship, it had caused him great pain. He approached the bed, his bare feet making no noise at all on the thick carpet. The fabric of her top was so thin he could see the outline of her nipples through the bra.

He couldn't fondle a sleeping woman. But maybe if she woke up...

"Cammie..." He whispered her name, willing her to open her eyes.

She never stirred. Reluctantly, he knew he had to leave. The monitor on the bedside table would wake her if the baby cried out. Even without the monitor, the two beds were close enough that Cammie would hear the boy if he roused.

Drake stood for far too long staring at what he couldn't have. Cammie needed a certain kind of man in her life. Somebody who would stick around Royal. The kind of guy who mowed grass on the weekends or played a pickup game of football down in the park on Sunday.

Even as Drake tried to conjure up such an image, he frowned. Cammie's father was extremely wealthy. That might make Cammie a target for fortune hunters. Men like that would tell a woman whatever she wanted to hear.

He told himself it didn't matter. It was none of his business.

Cammie had chosen a path that didn't include him.

Cammie woke up in a panic, certain that something was wrong. Faint light sneaked in around the drapes, but she was disoriented. This wasn't her bedroom. Slowly, her racing heartbeat subsided. The sound that had awakened her was a baby's small cry.

Tossing back the covers, she jumped to her feet and grabbed a bottle. Had Pumpkin snoozed this whole time since Drake took him and she conked out? It must be so, because when she picked up the baby, sat in the chair and offered him the formula, he gobbled it down as if he hadn't eaten in days.

She cradled his head. "Good boy. You slept like a champ, didn't you?" How long had he been awake with Drake?

Thinking about the way Drake had looked in the middle of the night rattled her. If she hadn't been so exhausted, she might have tackled him to the rug and insisted he make love to her. His bare torso and flat abdomen were even more tanned and toned than she remembered. Australia must agree with him.

It ate away at her to think he might choose to live in Australia permanently. She didn't want to imagine the town of Royal without Drake Rhodes. As long as Drake was in Texas, there was the slightest chance that she might eventually get through to him. Surely, he wasn't as entrenched in his bachelorhood as he claimed.

Even as she thought it, she knew she had to face the truth. Drake didn't want babies. He probably didn't even want a wife. She would be naive to think she could change him.

Despite all that, she wanted another chance. It was a truth she hadn't fully realized until she saw him striding across the hospital parking lot. How pathetic was that? *He* broke up with her. And she was still holding out hope they might have a future.

When Pumpkin was done eating, Cammie laid the drowsy baby in his bed so she could take the fastest shower on record. When she opened her suitcase, it was a mess. Drake hadn't even attempted to fold anything. With a sigh of exasperation, she pulled out a pair of navy dress pants and a matching yellow-and-navy sleeveless top.

Even if she was not at the office—even if she was babysitting—she sure as heck wasn't going to lounge around Drake's house in sweatpants and a T-shirt. She wanted to remind him of what he was missing.

Her big plan got off to a slow start. When she and Pumpkin made it to the kitchen, Drake was nowhere to be found. A note on the fridge said he had gone to the hospital to visit Ainsley. She hoped Drake's stepsister was improving. He would have told Cammie if Ainsley was still in trouble.

The level of her disappointment at finding Drake not home was way out of line. She had to focus on what was important—Pumpkin. It was up to her to keep the baby healthy and happy until he was reunited with his family.

She juggled him in one arm while she brewed a pot of coffee and made herself toast.

When the doorbell rang, she might have ignored the sound, but it could be someone official, a person with information about the baby. Cammie walked quickly to the front of the house and opened the door. Haley Lopez stood there with an older woman at her side. The beautiful officer smiled. "Sorry to show up unannounced, but this is Ms. Conner from social services. She's required to make a visit and see how you and Mr. Rhodes are accommodating Pumpkin."

"Of course." Cammie stepped back. "Please come in. Mr. Rhodes is at the hospital checking on his sister. But I'm happy to show you the setup."

Ms. Conner smiled. "I'm well aware that you only became involved with the child yesterday. We don't expect miracles."

Cammie laughed ruefully. "You don't know Mr. Rhodes. He tends to exceed expectations."

When Cammie ushered the two women into the guest

room, there was a moment of silence. Ms. Conner looked around the room wide-eyed. "I'm impressed," she said. "But I'm concerned that you might have gone overboard. This child's family will likely be found in a matter of days."

Cammie flushed. "I do understand that. I do. But Mr. Rhodes was determined to make a safe and happy environment for Pumpkin."

Officer Lopez chuckled. "I'd say he succeeded."

Ms. Conner pulled out an old-fashioned spiral-bound notepad. She flipped it open and took a pen from her pocket. "Do you have any concerns, Ms. Wentworth?"

"Concerns?"

"New parents often have a number of questions. Caring for such a tiny infant can be overwhelming." She jotted down something, tore the paper loose and handed it to Cammie. "This is a telephone hotline staffed by volunteers. If you find yourself in any kind of alarming situation, or you're at your wit's end, call that number. No need to feel alone."

Cammie throat tightened. Knowing there were people out there ready to help new moms and dads was touching. "Thank you," she said.

Haley Lopez held out her arms. "May I cuddle him for a moment?"

"Of course." Cammie watched as the other woman cooed and bounced little Pumpkin.

"Is there any progress in finding his mother...or both his parents?" Cammie asked.

Haley grimaced. "We thought we had a lead. A Jane Doe came to the hospital the same night as the multicar pileup on the interstate. But there was so much commotion, we can't trace which ambulance brought her in. Or maybe she came in on her own. She's still unconscious.

But of course, it doesn't make sense that the baby wasn't with her. Unless she abandoned him and *then* was in the wreck. The trouble is, the times don't line up. We know when you found the baby, and we know when the wreck occurred. It doesn't seem possible that anyone involved is connected to Pumpkin."

"Are there other leads?"

"Not at the moment. There's an additional complication. The Jane Doe at the hospital does not appear to have given birth recently. So the doctors are baffled. But don't worry. We have several investigators on the case. They're taking this very seriously."

"I'm not worried for me," Cammie said. "It's Pumpkin I'm concerned about. He's so little. I don't want him to forget his mom or his dad."

Ms. Conner tucked the pad back in her purse. "Children are resilient. And you're here to give him security and comfort in the short term. It's hard for a person to simply disappear in this age of technology. Someone will be found."

After the women said their goodbyes and the house was quiet again, Cammie walked the hall with Pumpkin until he fell asleep. When he was settled, she powered up her computer and answered emails for half an hour. Then she called her father.

For some reason, she didn't tell him about the baby. If things dragged on, she would have to eventually. But for now, she didn't want to hear all the reasons why fostering an abandoned baby was impractical and a hindrance to her career.

Her father might have become more generous after Danae's death, but he was the same difficult man, essentially. He wouldn't like his daughter getting involved in a messy situation like this one. And he would definitely raise an eyebrow to hear that Cammie was staying in Drake's house.

Drake didn't make it home for lunch. Cammie found a container of homemade chicken salad provided by the housekeeper. Eating with one hand was becoming easier. Pumpkin was content to nestle in her arm.

She talked to him a lot. Was that weird? Maybe all moms did that.

Sweet little Pumpkin was fast becoming important to her. As much as she understood that he wasn't hers to keep, it was impossible not to let the tiny infant steal a piece of her heart.

She and the baby were playing on the king-size bed in the guest room when Drake finally returned home. It was midafternoon. No hospital visit lasted that long. It was a good bet that Drake was avoiding her.

Even so, he didn't try to pretend she and the baby weren't there.

She heard footsteps in the hall, and then he appeared in the doorway. "Hey, there," he said, his expression guarded. "How are things here?"

Something about that searing blue gaze always made her weak. "Good." She tickled the baby's foot, not wanting Drake to see how he affected her. "A woman from social services came by for an unannounced home visit to make sure we had everything set up for Pumpkin. Officer Lopez was with her. We passed with flying colors, thanks to your shopping spree."

He ran a hand across the back of his neck as if her comment embarrassed him. "Money makes things easier. I was glad to do it."

"What about you?" Cammie asked. "What have you been up to today?"

She was hoping her question might cause him to

squirm, but he didn't seem flustered. "I spent more time with Ainsley than I planned. She's fighting an infection. Spiking a fever. The docs are trying to pin it down."

Now Cammie herself felt guilty. "I'm so sorry. I didn't know she was worse."

"I don't think she's in serious danger, but they always worry about stuff like this. Of course, she's eager to come home, but they won't release her until she's out of the woods. If the appendix hadn't ruptured, it might even have been outpatient surgery."

"I'll write her a note. You can take it when you go the next time."

"She'd like that. When you and I were dating, Ainsley told me it was the first time I had shown good taste in women."

Cammie laughed. "I always did like your stepsister."

Drake still hovered in the doorway. Maybe he thought getting too close to the baby would give him cooties. "My friend is one of the chefs at the Bellamy," he said. "I've ordered a big dinner for you and me. Someone will deliver it around seven. Do you think Pumpkin might sleep while we eat?"

"I have no idea," Cammie said. "I think he's too young to be on a schedule yet. But if he won't sleep, I can hold him." Drake grumpy expression was comical, though Cammie hid her smile.

"I had in mind something a little more romantic," he said.

Cammie's throat dried. She had to be strong. After a moment, she weighed her words and spoke. "I would enjoy having dinner with you, Drake. But a chaperone is probably a good idea. I'm not willing to do *anything* romantic with you. It's out of the question. The only reason I'm here is because you're a legal foster parent and Pumpkin needs your credentials."

Now Drake's face was wiped clean, no expression at all. He seemed calm, relaxed. "The price for my sponsoring him was to have you under my roof. And you agreed. You can't be entirely surprised if I press my advantage."

Her heart fluttered in her chest. His dogged insistence that there was something left of their relationship both alarmed and exhilarated her. "I didn't think you were the kind of man to force yourself on a woman, Drake Rhodes. Shame on you."

Her reprimand didn't make a dent in his sexy confidence. Nor did the lock of dark hair that refused to stay in place. It fell over his forehead, giving him a rakish air.

His wicked smile sucked all the air out of the room. "Force won't be necessary," he drawled. "When you end up back in my bed, it will be because neither of us can resist. I'm a patient man, Cam. But I can't wait to hear you cry out my name when I make you come."

Four

Drake wanted to laugh at the look of shock on Cammie's face, but he didn't dare. He was playing a dangerous and uncomfortable game. The more he teased and taunted *her*, he more his hunger grew. He'd been awake for hours the night before, stingingly aware that the woman he wanted slept just down the hall.

His impulse to bring the abandoned baby to his house had been just that, impulsive. But he soon realized that his libido had been shouting directions from the back seat. Having the home field advantage when it came to Cammie was too valuable to ignore.

He straightened and gave her his best innocent smile. "I'm going to take a shower. All those hospital germs, you know. After that, I'd be happy to watch the monitor while the kid is asleep. I assume you have work piling up."

Cammie nodded slowly. "Yes. But I thought you didn't want to have anything to do with him."

Drake shook his head slowly, feeling wry amusement. "I think I can manage to glance at a tiny screen. You can trust me, Cammie."

"Okay." She chewed her bottom lip, a sure sign she was agitated.

"Is there a problem?"

"I'm sorry if I was rude about dinner."

"You weren't rude. You merely put me in my place. *No funny business.* I got the message, Cam."

Pumpkin was safely in the middle of the huge bed. Cammie stood and crossed the room until she was so close to Drake their breath mingled. "You're toying with me," she accused. The flush on her cheeks and the fire in her emerald eyes told him she was worked up about something.

He touched her nose with a fingertip. "I've missed you."

Cammie was not wearing shoes. She had to tilt her head back to look up at him. Her eyes were a softer green now. Or maybe he was reading her expression wrong. Maybe he was seeing things that weren't there.

Her shoulders rose and fell in a deep sigh. "I've missed you, too." Her tone was reluctant, as if the admission had been pulled from her unwillingly. She cupped his cheek with her hand.

His heartbeat stilled. "Touching me is probably not smart," he said hoarsely. It was the God's honest truth.

Her thumb traced his chin. Her gaze was troubled. "That was always the problem, wasn't it? Neither of us was smart when we got lost in each other. I still care about you, Drake. Maybe I always will. But I can only be your friend. Yes, I'll have dinner with you tonight. But I won't sleep with you."

He held her hand to his face, feeling the delicate bones in her wrist. *This* was one reason he had gone to Australia. He'd needed to put half the globe between himself and temptation. When he found himself unable to speak, Cammie went on.

"Did you offer to be Pumpkin's foster parent so I would come to your house and sleep with you?" she asked.

He swallowed hard. "No."

"Did you do it because you felt guilty about our breakup and wanted to make me happy?"

He nodded slowly. "Yes."

In a startling move, she went up on her tiptoes and kissed him lightly on the lips. It was a quick kiss, barely any contact at all. But the small caress seared its way to his soul. He caught a whiff of her familiar scent. She broke the contact and stepped back. "I appreciate what you've done. But that's all the more reason for us not to muddy the waters. You're a good man, Drake. You were honest with me. And now we both know where we stand. Why on earth would we want to mess that up by having sex?"

"Because it would be fun?"

"Oh, Drake." She must have thought he was joking, because she laughed softly, her expression affectionate.

"That isn't reason enough?" It sure as hell was for him.

"You have your business and Ainsley and probably half a dozen willing women around the world. Pumpkin and I will only be here for a few days. There's no need to complicate things. I don't want to be at odds with you. I'll be ready to eat by seven," she said.

Drake wanted to argue, though Cammie wasn't wrong. They were finally at a good place. Maybe he would back off for now, but she couldn't ignore the heat between them. It was a living, breathing creature.

If he was patient, the situation might take care of itself.

* * *

Cammie rocked Pumpkin, holding him close. He had taken a bottle greedily. Now he was almost asleep in her arms.

She ought to receive an award for her acting skills. Lying to Drake had been an exercise in desperation. She did want to sleep with him. Desperately. But it wasn't that simple. He was literally a man on the move. If she gave him emotional control of her happiness, he would break her all over again.

Drake wanted a temporary sexual relationship.

Cammie needed far more from a man.

When Pumpkin's head lolled on her arm, she rose to her feet and laid him gently in his crib. "Where is your mother?" she whispered. "Surely she didn't abandon someone as sweet as you." The facts said differently.

In the luxurious bathroom, Cammie freshened up. Her beautiful silky top had a spot of spit-up on it. She wanted to change clothes…wear something more suited to an intimate dinner. But if she was serious about not having sex with Drake, she shouldn't give him mixed messages.

Earlier, he had been as good as his word. For two hours, Drake had kept the monitor with him as the de facto parent on call. Cammie had thus been free to sit at the kitchen table and work without interruption. She had accomplished so much she no longer felt so stressed about her job and her schedule.

Making a face at herself in the mirror, she took a washcloth and removed the dried milk. Then she brushed her hair and twisted it up on top if her head. Why was she so nervous? It was only a meal with a man who used to be important in her life.

Her bravado lasted all the way down the hall but fell apart when she found her host in the dining room. Unlike Cammie, he *had* changed clothes. Dark pants and a pale gray dress shirt with the sleeves rolled to his elbows made him look sexy and relaxed. The fact that his feet were bare emphasized his masculine appeal.

When Cammie entered the room, he looked up and smiled. "Just in time."

She eyed the largesse on the beautiful table. "How many people did you invite?" she asked, teasing him.

"Just the two of us."

Beef medallions in burgundy sauce. Sautéed squash. Asparagus tips. Thin cheddar biscuits. A bowl of beautifully cut strawberries with fresh cream. Cammie sat down and put her napkin in her lap. "Clearly, I ought to patronize the Bellamy more often than once a year. Honestly, during the height of the pandemic I ordered carryout so much, I forgot how nice it is to eat in a great restaurant."

Drake joined her at the table. "This is carryout, too," he said ruefully. "But I didn't think you would enjoy taking a baby to the Bellamy."

"You are so right. I don't imagine my fellow diners would care for it, either."

"Unless Pumpkin slept through dinner."

"There are no guarantees," she said, filling her plate. "This is much nicer."

They shared the meal in harmony for at least twenty minutes. But with each passing moment, Cammie became more convinced she had to ask the question that had haunted her for months. "Drake," she said, taking a sip of her wine for courage.

He looked up, his expression relaxed. "Yes?"

She hated to ruin the mood. "I've been wanting to ask you something. A question I should have asked two years ago."

Now his gaze was guarded. "Then why didn't you?"

"I don't know." She shrugged. "It didn't seem important at the time." Maybe it still wasn't, but with Drake pushing the issue of their sexual relationship, she had to understand why he had ended things before.

He sat back in his chair and crossed his arms over his chest. "Spit it out, Cam. I've never known you to be a coward."

She swallowed hard, her mouth and throat dry despite the wine. "Tell me why you don't want to have babies. I'm not judging you," she said quickly. "And I'm not trying to change your mind. But I don't get it."

Drake didn't look angry, and he didn't look upset. If anything, his expression was resigned. "It's no big secret," he muttered, rotating his head on his neck. He clearly regretted his demand for honesty.

"It is to me," she said quietly. "I'd like to know."

He shrugged. "Ainsley," he said simply. "She cured me."

"I don't know what you mean."

"Think it through, Cammie. Ainsley was fifteen when she was orphaned. No family at all besides me. She was literally on the verge of becoming another teenaged statistic in the system. But she was my stepsister. I couldn't let that happen. So I went through the process, got certified and became a foster parent."

"Okay…"

"A sane person would be grateful, don't you think?"

"And Ainsley wasn't?"

"My God, no. She was furious. Lashing out at anyone in reach."

"And you were the closest target."

"Indeed. I took my college exams early, moved out of the apartment I shared with a friend and came home to

Royal. Bought this house. Let Ainsley fix up her room any way she wanted. I didn't take her in to win any points, but it wouldn't have killed her to say thank you now and again."

"She was hurting."

"I *know* that. And I knew it then. But even knowing didn't make it easier. Fifteen-year-old girls can be hard to handle in the best of situations. Ainsley was a brat. And maybe she had reason to be, but our relationship was hell."

"I'm sorry, Drake. You never talked much about your past with her."

"I was still almost a kid myself when I did the foster parent thing. At twenty-two, I was ready to take on the world. I wanted to travel and have lots of sex and find out who I could be. But I was stuck in Royal."

"Where, by the way, you shot your way to the top of the business scene in no time. You found success early, Drake. And you clearly did a great job raising Ainsley."

"I got lucky in both instances."

"You have an incredible brain and a big heart, even if you don't want to admit it. Surely Ainsley quit fighting you at some point. When you and I started dating, she was super sweet to me."

"You saw the good side of our relationship. Things had mellowed by then. Even so, I can't ever forget the hard years. Until she graduated from high school and went off to college, I thought I might lose my mind. Being responsible for another human being is a huge burden. I did it once. I don't want to do it again."

The tone of his voice and the harsh certainty in his words told her the subject was closed. He went back to eating his meal. By the look on his face, he tasted nothing.

Cammie made herself finish the food on her plate, but

she felt nauseated. This was not a man who was going to change his mind. He'd had a traumatic experience when he was a young adult, and he'd been marked by it.

She summoned a smile, trying to salvage the evening, though she was heartsick. "New subject. Tell me what you're working on in Australia. I have only the vaguest idea."

His body language relaxed visibly. "I'm diversifying my financial consulting business with an entirely different approach in Australia. Actually, Ainsley gets some of the credit for the idea. You probably know she graduated from college in the spring. All she wanted to talk about was how to help her classmates who were floundering. They didn't want to live with their parents, but they couldn't find the kinds of jobs that would enable them to be independent."

"Maybe they wanted too much. Don't most young adults struggle to find their footing? My dad supported me, but he insisted I work a couple of minimum-wage jobs, just so I would understand how hard life can be, even with a college degree."

"You were lucky."

"Yes. So what's this big new approach?"

His grin was boyish and full of enthusiasm. It was also sexy and unfair. Why did he have to be so damn charming? His creativity and determination were two of the qualities that had attracted her in the beginning. He was a fascinating man.

"I'm teaching college kids how to invest," he said.

She stared at him. "You're joking, right?"

"Not at all. They can start with as little as five bucks a week, and if they have the discipline to keep at it, they can potentially retire young and have a sizable nest egg. I'm working on an app to make it even easier."

"And why Australia?"

"I met a guy at a conference. He and I hit it off. When we were brainstorming, we came up with the app idea. He's from Australia, and he says the twenty to twenty-nine age group is over fourteen percent of the population. So we have a big pool of potential customers. Plus, who wouldn't want to spend time in Australia?"

Her heart sank. "Are you thinking about moving there permanently?"

"Maybe. I doubt it. But anything is possible. You'd love it, Cam." He gave her a winsome smile. "I was hoping to convince you to go back with me for a few weeks."

She cocked her head, frowning. "Hoping when?"

"Yesterday. Last night. I've missed you."

"And what about my job and Ainsley and Pumpkin?"

"Problems can be solved. Plans can be changed."

"Maybe in your world. Not mine. You're talking crazy."

He reached across the distance separating them and took her wrist, pressing his fingertip to the spot where her pulse beat rapidly. His usually sky-blue eyes darkened to midnight, the irises almost eclipsed. "I never could think worth a damn when you were around. Tell me you don't remember what it was like between us. I dare you."

That *was* the problem. She did remember. Vividly. "I know what you're saying, Drake. I do. But there's more to life than physical compatibility." Strangely, she couldn't summon the energy to pull away from him. He made her weak. His allure shattered her common sense. She trembled violently.

When Drake rose to his feet and tugged her arm, she stood, too. He rubbed his thumb over her cheekbone, the intimate gesture destroying all the reasons she wanted to keep her distance. "I want to kiss you, Cam." The words were ragged, unsteady.

"Oh…"

"Is that a yes or a no?" The words were teasing, but his expression was grim, his features etched in granite. "Be honest, Cammie. Tell me what you want."

There it was. The chasm. Reason and good choices on one side. A night with Drake Rhodes on the other. But that was crazy. She could kiss him and stop after that. One kiss didn't have to lead to hours of debauchery.

Drake grew frustrated with her silence. She could see it in his eyes. But her lips wouldn't move. Her voice wouldn't work.

Now he took her by the shoulders, his grip firm but careful. "Tell me. What. Do. You. Want?"

It wasn't easy. But it was inescapable. From the moment she saw him in the hospital parking lot, she had wanted this. "Kiss me," she muttered.

The air sizzled in a moment of shock. His fingers tightened on her skin, hard enough to bruise, perhaps. He went entirely still, like a predator waiting for the perfect moment. "Are you sure?" he asked hoarsely. "You have to be sure."

"Oh, for heaven's sake." She put her hands on his cheeks and pulled his head down, dragging his mouth to hers. "I want you. There. I said it. Are you happy now?"

He made a sound low in his throat, a sound that had the hair on her arms standing up in an atavistic recognition of danger. His lips ground against hers, smashing against her teeth, stealing her breath. Joy slammed into her chest, incredulous joy.

Inhaling sharply, she breathed in the essence of him, shivering at how well they fit together. This was bad, really bad.

Drake's body was hard and warm against hers. His hands roved across her back, tugging her closer. Between them, his erection was impossible to miss.

She had imagined a kiss that was filled with poignant regret for things past. A kiss of goodbye. A kiss that acknowledged all the ways a relationship between two such dissimilar people was doomed.

Apparently, Drake had a different agenda. He kissed her wildly, in turns tender and demanding. It was as if the two years they had been apart vanished into the mist.

Leaning into him, she found home. But no, that wasn't true. Drake wasn't her home. He didn't want to be responsible for her. He didn't want to make babies with her.

When he tangled his hand in her hair and loosened it, she knew she was skating into dangerous territory. Something about a man taking down a woman's hair was as intimate as removing her clothes.

Pins scattered on the carpet. Cammie was hot suddenly, too hot, despite her sleeveless top and Drake's top-of-the-line HVAC system.

An insistent voice inside her head told her it would soon be too late. She and Drake were wildly aroused, hungry. And this was no initial encounter. They were each well aware of what came next. Endless, drugged pleasure. Again and again.

He pulled back, his broad chest heaving, his breath ragged. "I want you in my bed, Cammie."

No matter how destructive the impulse was, she couldn't say no to him. "Yes," she whispered. "Yes."

The flare of heat in his gaze was matched by his triumphant smile. She couldn't find it in her heart to care.

He pressed his lips to her forehead. "I should take you here on the table," he said, "so you won't change your mind."

Cammie nipped his bottom lip with her teeth. "I won't change my mind." She wanted to be naked with him, wallowing in the way he made love to her. All virile intensity and demanding testosterone. It was what she had always wanted.

A dark flush rode high on his cheekbones. He stripped off his shirt. "Plan B, Cam. My bed is too far."

With a sleight of hand that startled her and made her gasp, he unzipped her expensive pants and had them down and off in a nanosecond. Next went her top. Now she stood there in front of him wearing heels, panties and a bra.

He went still, his gaze riveted on her barely covered breasts. "You're exquisite, Cam." He touched her nipple, fingering it lightly through a barrier of lace.

Cammie was startled to realize that his hand trembled. Did she really have that power over him? Or was it something they generated together? A drunken, wildly passionate response that had nothing to do with alcohol and everything to do with the desperate way they wanted each other.

"You're right," she whispered. "The bed can wait." Carefully, she unzipped him and stroked his length.

His breath hissed through clenched teeth. "Cam…"

"Yes, Drake?" She smiled, drowsy from the large meal and eager for dessert.

He stepped out of his slacks and kicked them way. His navy boxers barely contained his excitement. When he removed them, Cammie felt like a scandalized Victorian maiden. He was big, and he wanted her badly.

She reached behind her back and unfastened her bra. When she dropped it on the carpet, she saw Drake's Adam's apple shift as he swallowed.

His grin was feral. "Bend over the table, darlin'."

Cammie laughed. "Kinky..." She turned to follow his outrageous command, humoring him, because it pleased her. As she spread her arms, she knocked the baby monitor onto the floor.

Everything in her body froze. Nausea and mortification rolled over her in equal measure. "Oh, no," she cried out.

Drake touched her arm. Not at all sexual. "Easy, Cammie love. Nothing is wrong. He hasn't made a sound."

Cammie was in shock. In her headlong rush to reunite with her lover, she had completely forgotten about little Pumpkin. What kind of person did that? Cammie was supposed to be the woman who wanted a baby more than anything. And yet, when Drake crooked a finger, she lost all reason and metaphorically abandoned the precious little infant in her care.

Wildly, she scrambled to pick up her clothes and the monitor. Tears, hot and dreadful, drenched her cheeks. She felt sick and wounded. With everything in her arms clutched to her naked chest, she faced him. The man who wanted her body but not her future.

"You did this," she said, her heart broken into a hundred nasty pieces. "You wanted to prove to me that I don't have what it takes to be a mother."

He took a step in her direction, his expression tight. "No, babe. Calm down. Nothing happened."

Cammie was humiliated, embarrassed beyond belief. Drake had seen her naked before. That didn't bother her. But the fact that he'd witnessed her failure as a parent—maybe even knew it was happening and didn't care—destroyed her.

"Move out of my way," she said, her voice hoarse.

Drake held out his arms. "Let me hold you, Cam. You're upset."

She narrowed her eyes. "Damn right I'm upset. You used sex to prove a point."

"That's not even rational, honey. We both got caught up in the moment. It was natural and wonderful. Parents have sex, you know."

His joke fell flat. She sucked in a breath and shoved past him. "I'm not a parent, and neither are you. Pumpkin and I will go to a hotel tomorrow."

Drake caught her by the shoulder and whirled her around. His eyes flashed. "You can't do that. *I'm* the one with the foster care credentials, remember?"

"I hate you," Cammie cried.

He crossed his arms over his chest, flaunting his nakedness. "You can try telling yourself that, Cam, but we both know it's not true."

Five

Cammie opened the door to the guest room with exquisite care and sneaked in, like a teenager coming home late and trying not to get caught. She dropped her clothes on a chair and tiptoed across the room to stand by the crib, her pulse finally settling to something approaching normal.

"I'm so sorry, Pumpkin," she whispered. "I didn't really forget about you. Well, maybe just for a minute. But you have to understand. Drake Rhodes is a force of nature. He makes me do crazy things."

The baby slept peacefully, his tiny hands fisted beside his head.

It was getting late. Pumpkin would be wanting a bottle soon. Did she have enough time to take a shower? Surely so.

She wanted to erase every last vestige of Drake's touch from her body. She was *glad* they hadn't actually had sex. Truly, she was.

When the baby didn't stir, she went into the bathroom and shut the door. A hot shower restored some of her equilibrium. She didn't wash her hair. It took forever to dry, and it was a good bet she didn't have that long.

Would Pumpkin do a repeat of last night? Or would he let his temporary mama get some sleep? While Drake had kept watch this afternoon and Cammie worked on her computer, she had taken a few minutes and done some reading about the various stages of newborns. Things could change quickly. It was possible for a child at six weeks to begin sleeping in five-hour stretches.

Cammie could handle that. It was the nonstop crying that was hard. And of course, she didn't know exactly how old the baby was.

There was no point worrying about what might or might not happen.

By the time she was ready for bed, Pumpkin had woken up. Cammie sang to him while he took his bottle. After burps and a dry diaper, she played with him on the big mattress. Thankfully, he lasted only thirty minutes before his eyes closed.

Once he was settled in the crib, Cammie made a beeline for her own bed and climbed under the covers. She was sleepy, but even as she drifted off, Drake was there with her. Kissing her, teasing, ready to make love all night.

Why wouldn't he leave her alone?

Why couldn't *she* forget about what they had once shared?

Please God, let Pumpkin's family be found soon before Cammie did something she would regret.

The next morning followed a familiar pattern. Cammie fed the baby, dressed both of them and discovered that Drake was gone. His bedroom door stood open. The bed didn't look as if it had been slept in.

What happened last night after Cammie fled? Where had he gone? It was silly to worry about a grown man, but her unease continued.

When she went to the kitchen for her coffee, she was embarrassed to see the housekeeper bringing dishes of congealed food from the dining room.

Cammie's face flamed. "I'm so sorry," she stuttered. "I should have dealt with those last night."

The pleasant older woman shook her head. "Nonsense. This is my job. You're supposed to be taking care of that little cutie. Drake told me the whole story." She dried her hands on a towel. "May I hold him while you have a bite of breakfast?"

Cammie smiled. "Of course."

Drake's housekeeper, Mrs. Hampton, cradled the baby in the crook of her arm. "He's precious." She touched a tiny finger. "I had four of my own, but it's hard to remember they were ever so young."

"He's an easygoing baby. I hope they find his mother soon."

Mrs. Hampton shot Cammie a glance. "It's good of you and Mr. Rhodes to look after him."

"Well, he *was* found on my car," Cammie said. "I know there must be a dozen or more good foster parents in Royal, but I couldn't bear to let him go."

"You like babies?"

It was a simple question, not at all judgmental. But Cammie felt defensive. "I do. I want to have at least two of my own someday."

"Any prospective daddies in the picture?"

Mrs. Hampton had been around a long time. She had met Cammie when Drake brought her home as his girlfriend several years ago. So was this a leading question? Was the woman prying? Or was she simply asking?

Cammie leaned against the counter, feigning relaxation, though her mood was unsettled. She took a sip of her coffee to wash down the delicious bite of Danish that stuck in her throat. "No one special at the moment. But I hope he's out there for me. If not, I'll give single parenting a try."

"It's hard," the other woman said bluntly. "My husband was in the army. Deployed all over the world. I was a good military spouse, though at times I couldn't help but resent his freedom. At least he got leave occasionally. I had two little ones in diapers and no life to speak of…nothing but hard, hard work."

"I'm not afraid to work," Cammie said. But suddenly she flashed back to the night before last when Drake had rescued her. She had been at her wit's end with a baby who wouldn't sleep. A single parent carried all the responsibility.

Pushing aside her worrisome thoughts, she held out her hands. "I need to give him a bath," she said. "I have my sink all set up. Wish me luck."

"Do you need a hand?"

"No, but thanks. I think I've got this."

In the guest bathroom, Cammie gave the baby a stern look. "Don't make things too hard for me, kiddo. I'm already scared of dropping you. Give me a break, and we'll both make it through this just fine."

Pumpkin blinked sleepily and drooled bubbles as if to say he knew Cammie was a fraud. *Aren't you the same lady who forgot I existed last night, because you were fooling around with your ex-boyfriend?*

"We're not going to discuss that," Cammie said. "And

besides, I learned my lesson. *You* are the only man in my life from now on."

The bath was not without hazards. Still, Cammie was determined. It probably took twenty minutes longer than it should have, but eventually she had the squirmy baby on the bed—clean, diapered and almost into a soft, warm onesie.

The door to the hall was open. Mrs. Hampton knocked anyway. Cammie fastened two more snaps, careful not to pinch skin. "What's up?" she asked over her shoulder.

"There's someone here to see you, Ms. Wentworth."

"Call me Cammie, please." Cammie picked up the baby and put him on her shoulder. "It's almost time for his bottle."

"It's a young woman about your age—Sierra Morgan? Says she gave you her business card a few days ago?"

Cammie's heart sank. She sighed. "Yes. I've met her."

"I put her in the living room and offered her a glass of tea."

"Thank you, Mrs. Hampton."

Cammie picked up the sweet-smelling infant. "Here we go, sweetheart. Let's hear what she has to say."

Sierra Morgan was as beautiful as Cammie remembered. Petite, long blond hair, green eyes. Though her appearance was soft and vulnerable, Cammie had a hunch the woman was far tougher that she appeared.

That hunch was reinforced when Cammie sat down, and Sierra immediately peppered her with questions. "Hi, Ms. Wentworth. I'm here to do a story about the abandoned baby for the *Royal Gazette*. Have you heard from the child's mother or father? How's the little one doing?"

Cammie held up a hand. "Whoa. Stop right there. First of all, it's Cammie, not Ms. Wentworth. And second of all, what's the deal? You told me you work for *America* magazine."

"I do. And I agree. Last names are pretentious. Please call me Sierra. I'm still preparing the big piece about the upcoming gala and the anniversary of the TCC finally admitting women. Anyway," she said, "this baby thing caught my attention. I spoke to someone at the *Gazette*, and they're willing to run the story with my byline."

"But why you, Sierra? You're an outsider. What is it about this situation that makes you want to get involved?"

Sierra had an odd look on her face for a moment, but it vanished, replaced by determination. "Why not me? Besides, *you* certainly got involved. Far more than I have. I guess most people are suckers when it comes to protecting innocent babies."

"Fair enough." Cammie was a bit taken aback by Sierra's enthusiasm and push to get the story told. Cammie didn't want to give up Pumpkin yet. Though she knew a newspaper article might be the infant's best chance of being identified, she was uneasy about sensationalizing Pumpkin's plight. What if the publicity brought out some of the crazies who liked to benefit from other people's misfortunes?

Sierra picked up on Cammie's ambivalence. "Don't worry. I'm not going to say a word about you and Mr. Rhodes. No one needs to know where Baby John Doe is living at the moment."

"We call him Pumpkin," Cammie said. "He needed a name."

"I like it." Sierra smiled. "Very seasonal." She paused. "But honestly, I'm going to concentrate on when and where he was found and reach out to the community for possible clues. We'll include the appropriate phone numbers for the police department. The story will generate buzz, and that will be in Pumpkin's best interests."

"Maybe." Cammie noticed something odd. Most women couldn't resist playing with a newborn. Sierra hadn't made any move to indicate she wanted a baby cuddle. "Would you like to hold him?" Cammie asked.

This time, Cammie knew she didn't imagine the flicker of *something* in the other woman's gaze…a certain bleakness. Maybe regret.

"Not really," Sierra said with a strained smile. "He's happy. I don't want to spook him. I'd rather concentrate on why I'm here."

Sierra didn't give Cammie time to analyze the reporter's demeanor. She pulled out a notebook and threw out more questions. After the seventh or eighth *I don't know*, Cammie sighed, exasperated. "I swear…you know as much as I do. You were there…remember? I doubt you can make a Pulitzer Prize–winning piece out of a handful of details."

This time, Sierra's smile was the real deal. "Don't worry. I can make a story out of a pencil and a verb. It's in my blood." She stood and slung the strap of her bag over her shoulder. "You still have my card, right?"

Cammie stood as well, bouncing Pumpkin in her arms. "I do."

"Well, then, just shoot me a text if any new information comes to light. We need to reunite this little one with his mama."

The reporter's words were absolutely true. No reason for Cammie to feel threatened. But she clutched the baby a little tighter. "Hopefully, soon," she said, acknowledging if only to herself that she was a fraud. Already, the thought of handing over sweet Pumpkin to someone else made her stomach hurt. The baby was happy with Cammie. Was she a bad person if she hoped the hunt took a little longer?

The afternoon passed quickly. While the baby napped, Cammie ate a packet of peanuts and worked on her computer. The structure of the Danae Foundation was coming along. Although she was not directly involved in planning the gala, her father's money would be an integral part of the night's festivities.

About four o'clock, Drake returned. Pumpkin was asleep. Cammie was working in the den. Drake walked into the room and dropped onto the love seat beside the sofa where she sat. "I'm sorry," he said quietly.

"For what?" She wasn't quite able to look at him. Last night's debacle was too fresh. The memory made her shudder with embarrassment.

He sighed. "I stepped over a line. I'm sorry I tried to pressure you into doing something you didn't want to do."

It would have been so easy to let that statement stand. To let him think everything was his fault.

She shook her head slowly. "That's not what happened. I could have walked out of the room at any time. I didn't. Because I wanted you, Drake. I still do."

His eyes flashed with shock. "But?"

"But I know that passion burns out. Compatibility is the thing that keeps relationships alive."

"Maybe we can agree to disagree."

"Maybe."

After an awkward moment of silence, he motioned to her computer. "Is it rough this week having to be away from work? Are they being accommodating?"

Cammie realized that Drake didn't know her circumstances had changed. "I don't work for the oil company anymore."

His eyebrows went up. "Oh?"

The last time the two of them spoke—before Drake went to Australia—Cammie had still held her position as VP of public relations with one of Royal's big oil companies. It had been an interesting job, and she liked to think she was good at it, but she knew she had made the right decision.

Drake was waiting for an explanation.

She grimaced, wondering if he would judge her. "My father created a charitable foundation and named it after Danae. He made me the executive director."

"Is that what you wanted?" He watched her carefully, as if trying to peer inside her soul. She didn't want him psychoanalyzing her.

"I didn't ask for it, if that's what you mean. But the job has turned out to be very exciting and challenging. I'll tell you a secret, if you swear you won't say anything."

He mimed locking his lips. "You can trust me."

It was true. She could. With everything but her heart. Shaking off the maudlin thought, she tucked her legs beneath her and closed her laptop. "The Danae Foundation is planning a big reveal at the TCC gala in tandem with the club and the hospital. That's why I was there when we ran into each other. A select group of first responders from fire and emergency services as well as hospital workers are going to be inducted as honorary members of the Cattleman's Club."

"Wow. That's pretty forward thinking for such a rigid social pecking order."

"But about time, don't you think?"

"No question." He leaned forward, hands on his knees, clearly interested. "Those people put their lives on the line after the tornado in 2013, and more recently with COVID." He paused. "So where does your dad come in? And the new foundation?"

Cammie smiled, her heart filled with pride. "My father is paying the college expenses for all the children of the people being honored."

Drake blinked. "Holy hell. I've met your father. This doesn't sound like him."

"I know, right? Danae really changed him, both when she was alive and after her death. I'm thrilled, frankly. My father has far too much money anyway. This is the least he can do. I'm hoping his gift will go a long way toward repairing the Wentworth reputation. We could use a little bit of good press."

"No offense, but your dad has alienated more than his share of Royal's citizens."

"Maybe everyone will take his generosity seriously and give him a chance to mend fences and make a new start."

"Let's hope so." Drake seemed dubious.

Cammie wasn't insulted. She knew that people in towns like Royal had long memories and sometimes held on to grudges. Her father had made mistakes. Big ones. But she liked to think Danae had put him on a better path. Maybe, even now, Danae was looking after him from beyond the grave.

Because Cammie was the tiniest bit freaked out about how her father's largesse would be received at the gala, she changed the subject. "I assume you've been to the hospital. How's Ainsley doing today?"

Drake leaned back in his chair and propped his feet on the ottoman. When he laced his hands over his flat abdomen, Cammie shivered inwardly. He was a beautiful man. Intensely masculine. Almost arrogantly confident. Sexy and impossible to resist.

Did she want to have sex with him? He would be leaving soon. Maybe she should go for it. One last time. For closure.

How was that for rationalization?

Her thoughts made her antsy. Was she about to do something stupid?

The object of her obsession looked half-asleep, but he answered her question. "She's fine. Much better, in fact. The doctor says they can probably release her day after tomorrow if all her labs are good."

Cammie's heart sank. Once Ainsley came home, there would be little privacy in this house. He wouldn't be able to spend all his free time trying to seduce a woman he broke up with two years ago.

"I'm glad to hear she's on the mend," Cammie said. "What else did you do today? You've been gone a long time."

For the first time, Drake looked uneasy. "Well…" He stopped, rubbed his chin and sat up. "I had to give some-one a tour of the ranch."

Her gut clenched. "Why?"

He shrugged. "A potential buyer."

Cammie was shocked to her toes. This house Ainsley lived in was only one of Drake's homes. He also owned a huge, fabulous spread outside town. She shook her head slowly. "You love that ranch."

"I do." His jaw was outthrust. Clearly, he didn't want to talk about this, but Cammie was alarmed.

"Then why would you even consider selling?"

"You know that my manager has been running the place for several years now. I've lived temporarily in New York and now Australia. It seems impractical for me to hold on to the ranch. Things change. Life moves on."

Cammie went cold inside. Her fingers gripped the arm

of the sofa. "Does this mean you might move to Australia for good?"

He scowled. "What does it matter to you, Cam? You've been pretty clear about the status of our relationship."

"*You* broke up with *me*. I still care about you, Drake."

"Meaning what?" His tone was challenging. Almost belligerent.

Cammie had thought finding a baby on her car was a watershed moment in her life. But that paled in comparison to this new information. Drake might leave *permanently*. How could she bear it? She took a deep breath and searched for words. "Feelings can't be turned off like water faucets," she muttered.

His expression lightened. "You have feelings? Who knew?"

"Don't mock me," she snapped.

"I wasn't, I swear." His gaze softened. "But you're so easy to tease."

"I don't want you to live in Australia," she whispered.

Now it was impossible to read his expression. He stood and rested one arm on the mantel. "We've barely spoken in the past two years. Why does it matter where I am?"

His gaze was laser focused. He watched her intently. Cammie didn't like it. Why should *he* be allowed to know what she was thinking? But on the other hand, her time was running out. Either Drake would get on a plane, or Pumpkin's family would show up, or both. Cammie would be alone again.

She had a brother who wouldn't come home to Royal, a mother who preferred her life in the big city and an emotionally unavailable father who was grieving. Cammie had an active social life, sure. But it hadn't escaped her notice that one by one, her girlfriends were getting married and *settling down*.

She hated that phrase. It sounded too much like *settling*.

"It matters," she said slowly, "because I liked knowing I might run into you on the street. I liked knowing we saw the same sunrises and sunsets. You're part of Royal, Drake. An important part."

"That makes me sound like a lamppost or a restaurant."

"You know what I mean," she muttered. She had waded so far into this conversation that she couldn't find her way back out.

Six

Drake found himself in quicksand. He had missed Cammie, far more than he was willing to admit. Two years ago, he'd told himself that cutting her loose was the kind thing to do. But his noble gesture, if indeed it was that, had cost him deeply.

"I don't know what you want from me, Cam." It was the truth. He was frustrated in more ways than one, his emotions on edge. He didn't like this feeling.

She sat like a child with her legs crisscrossed now. But she was a woman. A vibrant, sexually appealing woman who still had the power to turn him inside out.

When he didn't say anything else, she picked at a loose thread on the sofa cushion and scowled at him. "Tell me the truth, Drake. If we hadn't bumped into each other in the hospital parking lot, were you planning to find me and say hello?"

The quicksand deepened. He sensed the question was

a deal breaker. But he wouldn't lie to her. "I don't honestly know. I was focused on Ainsley and getting home as fast as I could. I had work things to tie up, too. It probably crossed my mind, but you weren't at the top of my list as I was leaving Australia."

Almost immediately, he regretted his candor, but his answer didn't appear to have upset her. She nodded slowly. "Fair enough."

"What does that mean?"

"It means I'm thinking."

"About what?"

She shrugged. "About whether or not I'm going to sleep with you."

Her matter-of-fact statement was a blow to the chest. He wasn't accustomed to parsing his sexual entanglements so dispassionately. He was more of a live-in-the-moment kind of guy when it came to sex. Come to think of it, weren't most men?

He swallowed against a dry throat. "I'd be happy to weigh in…"

Cammie wrinkled her nose. "No doubt." She cocked her head and stared at him. "Have you changed your mind about not wanting a family?"

The question caught him off guard. "Not even a little." He blurted it out without thinking and was immediately sure that he had destroyed any chance of coaxing her into his bed. Was he stupid?

Cammie stood and crossed the distance between them in two graceful strides. When she was close enough for him to inhale her scent, she stopped. "Okay."

He was befuddled. "Okay, what?"

She placed one hand, palm flat, on his chest. "Yes, I'll sleep with you. We have tonight and tomorrow before Ainsley comes home the next day. Let's make the best of it. Since you're probably moving to the other side of the world, this will be our last chance." She rubbed his lower lip with her thumb. "Kiss me, Drake. Please."

The next few minutes were a blur. He slid his hands beneath her hair, feeling clumsy and desperate. If she changed her mind, he wasn't sure he could bear it. Being in this house with her, so close and yet not together, had tormented him.

When his lips found hers, the air around them sparked. Twenty-four months faded away, Suddenly, it was Cam and Drake again. Perfect. Hot. Erotically charged.

How could a kiss be so deeply arousing when both of them were fully clothed?

He was seconds from stripping her bare when the baby monitor emitted an unmistakable sound. "Damn it…" Drake jerked backward, nearly hitting the mantel with his shoulder. He wanted to howl in frustration. He was hard and ready.

It made him feel the slightest bit better to realize that Cammie was equally flustered. She smoothed her hair where his hands had ruffled it. Her cheeks were flushed. A red scrape on her throat marked the spot where he had nibbled on her. "I'm sorry," she said. "Obviously we'll have to wait until tonight. But anticipation is half the fun, right?"

Her expression said she didn't really believe that.

He ground his teeth. "Go get him. Feed him. Whatever he needs. I'm going for a run. I'll pick up pizza on the way back."

When he stalked out of the room, Cammie didn't try to stop him. She didn't say a word.

Drake changed clothes quickly and exited the house by a back hallway. He didn't want to see Cammie. He felt volcanic. It wouldn't take much to make him say some-thing unforgivable.

He wasn't jealous of a helpless infant. He wasn't.

The route he chose was a familiar one. Occasionally he saw someone he knew, but he cut through side streets to avoid talking to anybody.

He ran, and he ran, and he ran, until his chest hurt and his eyes burned. Knowing he was about to do something selfish made him ashamed. What Cammie offered, he would take, knowing full well he couldn't give her what she needed in return.

Did it matter at all that he had been honest? Were the scales of justice balanced because he hadn't lied?

No matter how many miles he covered, the answers to those questions eluded him.

When he had been gone almost an hour, he forced himself to turn around. Cammie would be hungry. He had promised dinner. Surely, he shouldn't—wouldn't—add to his list of failures.

Leaning against the side of a building, panting, he pulled out his cell and ordered a pizza. Then he sum-moned a rideshare and hoped the driver wouldn't take one look and pass him by. Drake was covered in sweat and still had a stop to make on the way home.

Fortunately, the young man who showed up six min-utes later wasn't inclined to be critical. He was, however, a talker. Drake wanted desperately to lean back and close his eyes, but it wasn't to be. The kid rattled on for the whole trip. Even when Drake hopped out to get the pizza, the monologue started up again as soon as he returned to the neon-green Kia.

Drake paid on the app and added a thirty-dollar tip. It wasn't the driver's fault that his passenger was in a lousy mood.

Back at home, he showered, well aware that the pizza was getting cold. Why didn't he have it delivered? Apparently, his brain was shot.

He dried off, threw on jeans and a soft Henley shirt, and scooped up the box. At least it was still marginally warm on the bottom.

Cammie was in the kitchen with the baby. She had put together a salad and set the dining room table. Her expression was guarded when Drake appeared. "I didn't know what you wanted to drink," she said.

Wine would have been his first choice, but he needed a clear head. "A Coke is fine." When she passed him on the way to the fridge, he caught her shoulder, pulled her close and nuzzled her neck. "I'm sorry I left. I was feeling…" He trailed off. How could he describe his disappointment? It would make him vulnerable to her.

Drake needed to be in control of the situation, didn't he?

Cammie managed to soothe the baby and stroke Drake's hair as if she had been juggling two males her whole life. "I was frustrated, too," she said simply. "But little Pumpkin didn't know he was ruining our fun."

Drake straightened. Had it been something as simple as *fun*? He didn't think so.

Cammie stepped away, and the moment passed.

Over ham-with-mushroom pizza and soft drinks, they talked of random, easy things. The weather. The local football team's winning season. The way Ainsley had waited too long to admit she was hurting. How scared Drake had been when the doctor called to let him know what was going on.

"You know you're a fraud, right?" Cammie said, tempering the words with a grin.

"What do you mean?"

"You talk about how terrible it was to become Ainsley's guardian, how your relationship was toxic. But the moment something happens to her, you drop everything and fly halfway around the world to be by her side. You love her, Drake."

He drained his glass, avoiding Cammie's perceptive gaze.

When he looked up, she shook her head slowly, her expression filled with affection. He didn't want that from her. He wanted mindless, perfect sex.

Cammie must have sensed his discomfort, because she changed the subject. "If you'll hold the baby, I'll clean up the table. I'm not leaving it for Mrs. Hampton again. I don't want her to think we're pigs."

Drake chuckled, taking Pumpkin and nuzzling the baby's head with his lips. "She's my *housekeeper*, Cam. I don't think it's out of line to ask her to clean up the dining room and kitchen."

"Maybe not, but I want to do it anyway."

Suddenly, a memory popped into his head. He and Cammie had been at her place, ready to make love. But Cam had insisted on tidying the remains of their meal. At the time, he hadn't given a flip. The chores could have waited.

His lover had insisted.

Cammie was always the more responsible of the two of them when it came to mundane jobs around the house. She actually seemed to like it.

He'd never given that quirk in her personality much thought until now. Maybe her chaotic childhood had given her a need for order. And maybe he should be more aware and not protest when his wants and needs had to wait.

He rubbed the little boy's back. "You're the man of the hour, kid. I got bumped to second place."

Drake knew the baby didn't understand a word he was saying. Besides, it was a joke.

It was a pleasant evening, so he took the baby outside for a breath of air. Pumpkin seemed interested in the sights and sounds. Birds sang in the maple tree near the sidewalk. A light breeze stirred the branches of the huge live oak.

It occurred to Drake that he might as well deed this place over to Ainsley. That way she would have roots and a home of her own. There was plenty of room in the house for Drake to stay when he came home for a visit.

And what about the ranch? It literally hurt to think about selling it. But if he wasn't going to live here in Royal, why would he keep it? For an investment? Maybe. Still, the way he felt about the ranch had nothing to do with money.

He heard the front door open and shut. Cammie came down the steps to join them. "What does he think of the big ole world?" she asked, smiling.

She seemed calmer suddenly. Happier.

Her mood relaxed some of the tension in Drake's neck. "I think he likes it."

To anyone driving by, they must look like a family. Drake winced inwardly. He handed Cammie the baby. "I'm pretty sure he needs a diaper. I could do it, but you're faster."

She rolled her eyes. "That's the worst excuse I ever heard."

"What can I say? It's not my thing."

Cammie tucked the infant against her shoulder and murmured something to him. The words were so low, Drake didn't quite catch them. She looked sideways at him. "Does *anybody* like poop? It's just one of those things you have to deal with in life. Like the dentist and doing your taxes."

He chuckled. "How about I do your taxes and you handle Pumpkin?"

"Fine," she huffed, pretending to be annoyed. But the light in her eyes told him she wasn't truly miffed. "Are you coming inside?"

"In a minute," he said.

When they were gone, he shoved his hands in his pockets and walked the perimeter of the property. Here in town, the lots were average size. No houses crammed together, but certainly not the acreage he had out on the ranch.

He had grown up in Royal. Gone to school here until college. Returned to finish raising Ainsley and start a business. Ainsley was an adult now. His financial interests continued to diversify and grow. With every passing year, he had more and more reasons to travel the world and fewer to come back to this town.

Could he leave it all? Australia was amazing. He had loved his time there and was eager to get back.

But not without Cam.

The trouble was, she was firmly rooted here. This town, this land, these people. She loved them all.

And she wanted a baby. It was that simple and that complicated.

He shoved the conundrum out of his mind and went inside, counting the hours until the baby fell sleep again. Then Cammie would be in Drake's bed.

He found them in the den. Cammie sat on the rug with Pumpkin on a soft blanket beside her. Drake paused in the doorway, watching them unnoticed.

Cam tickled the baby's tummy. "Are you too little to

laugh for me? I know you are. Where's your mama, little boy? What is she doing? Is she scared? Hurt? Why did she leave you on my car?"

The baby made little burbling sounds, but he didn't answer a single question.

Drake joined them on the floor. He leaned back against the sofa and tugged Cammie into the vee of his legs. "The witness is stonewalling you," he said.

Came leaned her head against his chest and sighed. "Yep. I love taking care of him, but I know he needs his family."

"Did you hear anything from the police today?"

"Same old, same old. Haley Lopez called. They're investigating. Told me to be patient. I just don't understand how it could happen. And why it's taking so long to find the baby's family. It's the twenty-first century. Nobody can go off the grid easily."

"True. But maybe the mother doesn't want to be found. Maybe she planned this for some time."

"I suppose."

Pumpkin seemed happy for the moment, so Drake bent his head and traced the shell of Cam's ear with the tip of his tongue. She groaned and shivered in his arms.

"I want you, Cammie. Quite desperately, in fact."

She half turned in his embrace, searching his face. Her beautiful moss-green eyes sparkled with passion—passion he wanted to stoke. She touched his cheek. "I want you, too, Drake. I've missed you. And don't worry. I know what this is that we're doing. I'm glad we cleared the air."

Her words created an odd, unpleasant feeling in the pit of his stomach. Instead of taking issue with what she had said, he found her mouth and covered it with his. She tasted like pizza and possibilities.

Their tongues dueled lightly. He held her chin in his hand, keeping her faced tipped up to his. The position was awkward. He wanted to feel her soft curves against his chest.

With his free hand, he found her breast. She was wearing another thin top, this time with a flirty short skirt. How had he not noticed that before?

Once he began exploring, there was more good news. Her legs were bare. The only thing underneath the skirt was a pair of undies that were silky against his fingers.

He touched her intimately, all the while deepening the kiss.

His lover whimpered. Even so, it was Cammie who called a halt. She put a hand against his chest and pushed. "It's too soon, Drake. We can wait."

"Not soon enough," he muttered, disgruntled.

Trying to ignore the ache in his rigid erection, he released her and stood. "How much longer till he's asleep?"

"Thirty minutes, maybe more. And I need a shower."

He took her hand and pulled her to her feet. "Will you come to my room? When you're ready? I'll be waiting for you."

Cammie second-guessed herself a thousand times in the next hour. She was both excited and terrified. The memory of how her relationship with Drake had ended was still fresh in her mind. She had cried a million tears. Her self-confidence had shattered. Her heart barely survived.

And now she was going to wallow in his bed, well aware that they weren't a couple. Even knowing how this would end, she couldn't help herself. Being with Drake was what she wanted, no matter how self-destructive.

Pumpkin was in a cooperative mood. He took his bottle easily, burped a couple of times, cooed and played for fifteen minutes, and then zonked out. She laid him in the crib and stared down at him. Was it possible to love someone who wasn't yours?

Sadly, she was walking down that road with two males—one, this baby who would eventually be reunited with his blood kin, and two, Drake, who would soon walk away. Or fly, to be more accurate. Why was she allowing either one of them to have a piece of her heart? If she was smart, she would guard her emotions.

Unfortunately, she had never learned that trick. Her parents and her brother knew how to be aloof, unreachable. Cammie had thrown her love all over the place. Childhood friends, schoolmates, teachers. She had a soft heart, and she expected the best of people. It might not be the safest way to live a life, but she didn't know any other.

It wasn't her fault that she'd been hurt and disappointed over the years.

She wouldn't change who she was, even if she could.

Once she was convinced that Pumpkin was soundly asleep, she took a quick shower. Afterward, she debated what to wear. At home in her closet, she had several sexy, beautiful sets of lingerie. Silky nightgowns. Flirty satin robes. When she asked Drake to pack for her, she certainly hadn't directed him toward those.

Now she was sorry.

Since she couldn't do glamorous tonight, she opted for comfort. She chose an old, soft football jersey in navy and red. One of her high school boyfriends had gone on a college visit and brought it back to her. The teenage beau was long out of the picture, but Cammie had a particular fondness for the jersey.

It hit her midthigh. She brushed her hair and left it down.

Her heart pounded so rapidly, she thought she might be sick. Why hadn't she asked Drake to come to her?

With one last look at the baby, she picked up the monitor and stepped into the hall. The house was silent. Beneath her bare feet, the hardwood floor was cold.

Drake's bedroom was two doors down. First a guest powder room, then the master suite. She knew it well. When she opened the door and entered, the luxurious space was empty. For a moment, she was rattled. Then she saw the ribbon of light beneath the bathroom door.

A few seconds later, before she'd had time to catch her breath, Drake exited, wearing nothing but a damp towel wrapped around his hips.

He smiled when he saw Cammie. "Good timing."

Her throat closed up, making it impossible to speak. To disguise the fact that she was mute, she turned and set the baby monitor on the corner of a beautiful chest of drawers. At the moment, she was standing as far as possible from that massive, hedonistic bed. A taupe duvet, lightly embroidered in gold, covered the mattress.

Drake had turned back the covers on one side, revealing the inviting cream cotton sheets. Large, fluffy pillows rested against the headboard.

One corner of his mouth ticked up in a tight grin. "You look terrified, Cam. Am I that scary?"

She shifted from one foot to the other. "No."

It was an unconvincing lie at best. She held her breath when he crossed the room and took her hands in his. Her fingers were icy cold. His were firm and warm.

"We're still us," he said simply. "Nothing has to be weird."

She searched his face, looking for reassurance. She knew Drake felt *something* for her. Something more than sexual desire. They shared a history. He was fond of her.

It was a terrible time to realize that she was still in love with him. The sudden jolt of awareness made her heart sink. How could she have casual sex with this gorgeous man and not give away her secrets?

Nothing had changed in two years. She had tried to convince herself she was over him…that her wounds had healed. Deep inside, though, on some subconscious level, she had always known. Drake Rhodes was her one and only. She adored him despite the fact he had broken off their relationship. She loved him, even knowing he didn't want her love.

Why else would she have begun to think about in vitro fertilization? Or adoption? If she couldn't have Drake as her husband and the father of her theoretical baby, she didn't want any man in her life.

A child would give her the chance to start a family. A nontraditional family, sure. But was she hurting anyone? No…

Drake must have misunderstood her long silence. He pulled her close, wrapping her in his embrace. The way he held her was both comforting and wildly arousing. How could it be both?

He kissed her forehead. "Talk to me, Cam."

His body was so much bigger than hers. The difference in their heights was pronounced, especially since she was barefooted.

"I'm ready," she said, wanting him desperately.

"It's not a calculus final, darlin'. We're not doing this unless you're all in."

She realized in an instant that his big frame was tense. Beneath her cheek, she could feel his thunderous heartbeat. Could he possibly be as uncertain as she was?

She went up on her tiptoes and pressed her lips to his. "I want to have sex with you, Drake, truly I do."

Seven

Drake didn't believe her, not entirely. But he chose to take her words at face value, even as they gave him pause. The old Cammie would have said *make love*. It was a tiny but important difference.

He knew she didn't love him now. That was part of the price he paid for breaking off his relationship with her. His motives had been altruistic, but he hadn't counted on how much it would hurt to have his sweet Cam look at him with disdain all those months afterward.

She *had* loved him back then, but he had thrown it all away.

These past months in Australia, he'd had plenty of distractions to occupy his attention. Getting a new business off the ground chewed up the hours and days. Royal had seemed like another lifetime.

All that changed when he saw Cammie again. He understood how carefully he had sublimated his desires, how intentionally he had blocked the memories. Perhaps he'd been in blatant denial. Or maybe he hadn't wanted to admit he'd fucked up.

Now, finally, he was so close to getting what he wanted.

Shaking off the past, he stripped off the jersey Cammie wore and scooped her into his arms to carry her to the bed. He knew the exact moment she spotted the pile of condoms on the nightstand. But she didn't say a word.

As he set her gently on the big mattress, Cammie scooted over to make room for him. Drake ditched his towel and joined her. He groaned as he pulled her into his embrace and held her. "You feel so damn good," he said as his body tangled with hers. All arms and legs and beating hearts. She was soft everywhere he was hard.

He kissed her ravenously, ruefully aware that he felt more like a beast than a man. His mood was wild, his control tenuous at best.

When he moved on top of Cam, she wrapped her arms around his neck, smiling up at him, the smile of a siren, a temptress. "You're a hard man to resist."

"If it's any consolation, you came close to turning me into a drooling idiot. You're even more beautiful than before, Cam. Since the first moment I saw you in that hospital parking lot, I've wanted you. Badly."

The intensity of his words seemed to bother her. Her gaze shifted away. "Well, you have me," she said.

"Maybe I'm the one who's scared," he joked. "A two-year break is a lot of pressure. I don't want to disappoint you." *Not like I did before.*

"You know very well that you're good at sex. I'm sure even the women in Australia have figured that out."

Was she fishing? He cleared his throat, not sure how to respond. "I haven't been celibate since we broke up,

Cam. But my sex life is not as…*varied* as you seem to think. And certainly nothing serious."

She held up a hand. "Not my business. Kiss me, Drake."

Something about her demeanor worried him. Was she seriously trying to convince herself this was only sex? He cared about her. A lot. Maybe *showing* her was his only option.

Now that he had her in reach, he found the patience to slow down. He kissed her gently, from her cute nose to the sensitive spot on the arches of her feet and everywhere in between. The intimacy was rich, familiar. Completely alluring. He and Cam had always been like this, their bodies in tune, one person's passion feeding the other.

Cammie gasped and writhed beneath his touch. Her soft moans and the way she arched her back made him feel like he could fly.

He buried his face in her taut belly, inhaling her scent, trembling at the prospect of being inside her again after so long, far too long.

Her nails dug into his shoulders when he stroked her with his finger. She was hot and wet, her body ready for his.

When he would have made her come, she pushed him away. "Not until you're inside me, please."

She didn't have to ask twice. With shaky hands, he rolled on protection. Then he moved between her legs and pressed at her entrance. "I want you, Cam." The words were guttural, forced from somewhere deep. Was *wanting* enough?

When she pulled his hair and lifted her hips, he got the message. He surged hard, making both of them catch their breath. The sensation was exquisite. His eyes burned. How had he lived without this?

Carefully, he stroked deep, resting his weight on his elbows, staring down at her, trying to memorize her face. He kept up the lazy pace until she came apart in his arms. His own climax was not long after. He shouted her name and hammered wildly, wanting to mark her as his.

The world came crashing down on him. He was emotionally and physically exhausted. Everything went black.

When he woke up sometime later, Cammie was gone.

Cammie was pleasantly sore and completely satisfied. See…that wasn't so bad. She could do casual sex. She had just proved it.

When she had heard Pumpkin waking up, she wasn't sure how long she had been asleep. The monitor was set loud enough to rouse her. But Drake never moved.

That was fine. It was actually better this way. She didn't need his help with the baby. After diapering and feeding the boy, she stroked his forehead until the little guy went limp in her arms. By now, she was better at putting him down. Or maybe he was better at sleeping. Either way, this middle-of-the-night feeding went smoothly.

After Pumpkin was settled, Cammie dithered. She didn't quite have the courage to saunter down the hall and climb back into bed with Drake. But she knew he would be pissed if she returned to her own bed.

While she was deciding what to do, Drake appeared in the doorway, yawning.

He kept his voice low. "Everything okay?"

She nodded, feeling off kilter but not unhappy. Being with Drake again had been wonderful. "Yes. He ate and went right back to sleep."

"Splendid." Drake's sexy smile curled her toes. He came to where she stood in the middle of the room and tucked her hair behind her ears, kissing the side of her neck. "Let's not waste a moment."

After they returned to the master suite, the night took on a surreal feeling. She and Drake napped in short snatches, then made love again and again. He was tireless. And hungry. As if she had somehow been depriving him of what he wanted.

When the sun came up, she groaned. Her little charge was once again making his presence known.

Drake lifted up on one elbow. "Go back to sleep, Cam. I can handle a turn."

She shook her head, rattled at the idea of being out of it when the two men in her life were awake. "Oh, no. It's my job. I'll do it."

Her lover leaned over her and kissed her hard. "You'll need your rest for later," he said, the words slurred with fatigue and promise. "Sleep, angel. I'm being completely selfish, I swear."

"Are you sure?" She brushed the hair from his forehead, unable to separate the torrent of emotions she felt.

"Completely." He rolled out of bed and exited the bedroom.

What neither of them had counted on was the fact that Cammie could hear everything happening in the guest suite. When Drake murmured to the baby and soothed the fussy infant during a diaper change, Cammie heard. When he hummed a silly song and settled into the rocker to give the child a bottle, Cammie heard.

Her heart broke into little pieces. How could a man capable of so much care and tenderness be so stubbornly opposed to having a family?

But then again, there was a huge difference between offering temporary foster care and doing the long-haul parenting thing. Despite her pain, she could barely think straight. Sleep claimed her, promising sweet oblivion.

Drake yawned, keeping one eye on the baby, who tried to stuff his fist in his mouth. Pumpkin was growing and changing every day. Drake and the infant were on Cammie's bed, doing nothing in particular.

Cammie needed at least another half hour. Drake did, too. But since Cam had handled the middle-of-the-night feeding, it was definitely his turn.

When even sitting up straight was too much, Drake sprawled on his back and slung one arm over his face. Beside him, the baby was happy. Lucky kid.

The world was a much easier place when all a guy needed was milk and naps.

Before last night, Drake had entertained a hazy, half-formed plan where he and Cammie would screw every time the baby slept. But he now saw the flaw in that plan. Babies demanded attention. Drake and Cammie were in bad shape. Sleep deprivation was going to make this a very long day.

He had drifted off for a moment when a small, feminine hand shook his shoulder. "Wake up," she whispered.

"I've been watching him," he said quickly, feeling his face flame. "I wasn't really asleep, I swear."

Cammie grinned. "He's fine. It's a huge mattress. We won't be in any danger of rolling over on him."

Drake scrubbed a hand across his face. "We?"

"Scoot him over and let me in."

"Okay." He felt befuddled. He knew adults weren't supposed to let infants sleep in the same bed with them. But that was during the night—right? Surely a quasi-nap wasn't dangerous.

He moved the baby with extreme care. Then Cammie slid in and pulled the covers over herself.

Drake frowned. "How do we know he's not cold?"

"He's not. That sleeper is very thick and warm. And he has socks on *under* the sleeper. He's fine, I swear. Touch his cheek and his hand if you want to be sure."

Though Drake felt a bit foolish for worrying, he did as Cammie suggested. The baby definitely didn't seem cold. Drake slid closer to Cammie and joined her under the covers. "It seems mean not to cover him up."

"I know. But it's a safety thing."

Drake closed his eyes. His body hummed with arousal, though it simmered at a comfortable level. Right now, he was tired enough to enjoy cuddling Cam.

They drifted in and out, neither of them willing to sleep deeply when the baby was awake. But eventually, Pumpkin slept, too.

Cammie's body was soft and warm. Drake spooned her, lifting the hem of the football jersey she wore to feel her ass. Predictably, his boner grew.

"I have a confession to make," he mumbled, reaching under the jersey to palm her breast.

"Oh?" The single syllable was breathless. Cammie wriggled, nestling her butt into the cradle of his groin more perfectly. Surely, she had to feel his erection.

Drake's forehead broke out in a sweat. "I thought we would probably have sex today every time the kid napped. But I guess that's not practical. We'll have to get some sleep eventually. We sure didn't last night."

Cammie rolled onto her back. Her eyelids drooped. Her cheeks were flushed. "We can sleep when we're dead."

Her naughty grin shocked and elated him. "Hell, yeah."

"But we can't do it right beside him," Cammie said.

She was right. "And we don't want to risk moving him," Drake said.

"And we can't go to *your* room while he's not in the baby bed."

"Well, hell…"

Cam reached under the covers and found his hard-on, stroking him lightly. "Why don't you go grab a condom?" she whispered. "I'll meet you on the floor."

Her suggestion galvanized him. He rolled over her and off the bed. It was a clumsy move, but he was desperate. By the time he returned less than two minutes later, Cammie had found a soft, fuzzy throw and spread it on the floor beside the bed. She was sprawled, buck-ass naked, on her back.

When Drake froze in the doorway, stunned by the erotic display, she held a finger to her lips. "Shh. Don't make a sound."

"Duly noted," he said, dropping to his knees beside her. Though he was as hard as he'd ever been in his life, he paused to appreciate the feast. The thing that pleased him most was Cammie's smile. She looked happy to see him.

Never again would he take that for granted.

He sat back on his heels and stared.

After a span of seconds that felt like an eternity, Cammie blushed everywhere it was possible to blush. "Stop that," she hissed. "Come down here and warm me up."

"Yes, ma'am." They rolled together on the throw, trying to be quiet but failing when Cammie wouldn't stop giggling.

Finally, he put a hand over her mouth. "If you wake the baby," he said, "I'll have to spank you."

Her eyes went wide. She nodded.

Drake didn't move his hand. Instead, he managed protection awkwardly, nudged her thighs apart with his knee and balanced on one elbow. "Not a sound, darlin'."

It was a silly game. She could easily have dislodged the fingers that covered her lips. But Cam played along. Her faux docility ratcheted Drake's chest-heaving hunger.

When he finally managed to get inside her, his heart pounded so loudly in his ears, he felt dizzy. She was completely still, as if moving equated noise. Come to think of it, with Cam, it probably did.

He flexed his hips, gaining another inch. His silent lover made a sound deep in her throat. Barely audible. Rife with need.

He wanted to laugh, but he couldn't. This felt damn serious.

Because he needed to read her expression, he finally uncovered her mouth. Nuzzling the side of her neck, he pumped slowly. "Wrap your legs around my back, Cam. Hold me tight."

She did as he demanded, locking her ankles and making it possible for him to go deeper still. He had blocked this out of his mind. How good it was. How hot and sweet in equal measure.

Cammie wasn't saying anything. But then again, who needed talk when the physical connection was damned near perfection? He kissed her hard. "I can't stop screwing you, darlin'. As soon as we're done, I want you all over again."

She curled one hand behind his neck and pulled him down for another kiss. "I'm not complaining."

The smug, teasing joy in her voice sent him over the edge. Vaguely, he was aware that Cammie found release at almost the same moment. She buried her face in his shoulder, but even so, her muffled cry was audible.

They lay there, panting. Their skin chilled as the sweat dried. At last, he lifted off her, rubbing his face. "Can we get on the bed without waking him?"

"Maybe." She groaned. "I'm getting too old for the floor."

He extended a hand. "I would say I'm sorry, but it would be a lie."

Gingerly, they slipped onto the bed and pulled the covers up again. Cammie rested her cheek against his rib cage, her hand splayed across his abdomen. "That was nice."

Stroking her hair, he tried to summon indignation. "Nice? Come on, Cam. Surely you can come up with a better adjective."

"Don't be greedy." She yawned. "We should grab a few minutes of sleep while we can. I can't guarantee how much longer he'll be out."

Twenty minutes. The answer was twenty minutes. Cammie and Drake had fallen into a deep unconscious state when she heard the baby stir. She tried not to cry.

Her head throbbed, and her eyes were gritty. It was going to be a long day.

Drake woke up seconds after she did. He groaned. "You may be too old for the floor, but I'm definitely too old for all-nighters."

She took a deep breath. "Why don't you shower and get dressed while I feed him? Then you take a turn. And no sleeping in the bathroom."

"Very funny."

When Drake disappeared down the hall, Cammie found her robe and shrugged into it, tying the sash tightly. Her muscles were sore, and her body was tender in surprisingly places. She wanted to smile at the memories, but Pumpkin was not prepared to wait while his temporary mama mooned over the man who had made her body sing.

Cammie grabbed a bottle and carried the baby to the rocker. When she was settled, she offered the meal to him, smiling when he gobbled rudely. Didn't he know it wasn't polite to slurp in public?

Despite how she and Drake had joked about the subject, it wasn't practical for the two of them to fool around all day. For one thing, the lack of sleep would make them zombies. More importantly, Cammie found herself wanting to draw back, to protect herself.

Last night and today with Drake had been both exhilarating and deeply painful. To contemplate what her life could be like with the man she loved was a lesson in futility. Drake had been nothing but honest with her.

He was going back to Australia. For an indefinite time. And if he ever decided to come back to Royal for good, Cammie couldn't marry him even if he asked. Which he wouldn't. She had made no secret of her maternal hopes and dreams.

Drake wanted none of it.

Pumpkin had just reached the end of his bottle when Drake returned, looking handsome and fresh and far more chipper than Cammie felt. His hair was damp from his shower. He was wearing soft, faded jeans with a pale-yellow cashmere sweater that emphasized the breadth of his chest.

Instantly, Cammie felt frumpy. Her hair was a mess. She needed a hot shower to wash away the evidence of her night with Drake.

He took the baby from her without asking. "I'll burp him and walk him. Go do whatever you need to do."

When Cammie stood, Drake pulled her close with

one arm. He kissed her right on the lips with the baby watching. The kiss was long. Lazy. Filled with promise.

Both adults were breathing heavily when it was over.

Cammie stepped back. "I won't be long," she promised.

Drake bounced the little boy gently. "The menfolk will entertain ourselves, right, Pumpkin? And we'll throw together some breakfast."

When they walked out of the room, Cammie gathered clean clothes and headed for the bathroom. Hot, steamy water washed away some of her mental fog. She shampooed her hair and shaved her legs.

Afterward, she used the dryer she found under the sink to restore order to her long hair. Soon it was shiny and soft on her shoulders. She sat down at the counter and applied light makeup. Subtle eye shadow, a quick coat of mascara.

She didn't really know why she was taking such pains except that anyone might drop by the house this afternoon. And though Drake had seen her rumpled and with bed hair, she wanted to present herself in a more flattering light.

When she was done, she followed her nose to the kitchen, inhaling the life-giving aroma of expensive coffee. Drake waved a hand. "It's ready. Will you pour me a cup, too?"

He looked entirely natural with a baby on his shoulder. "Sure."

Somehow, he had managed to butter toast one-handed. He'd chosen to use a cookie sheet in the oven instead of the toaster. A few of the edges were too dark, but Cammie wasn't about to complain. Especially when Drake produced a bowl of strawberries from the fridge to go with their feast.

Her stomach growled loudly.

Drake chuckled. "Somebody burned a lot of calories last night."

He seemed totally relaxed, as if nothing out of the ordinary had happened. But Cam knew better. She had indulged wantonly, despite the risks. Because she couldn't say what she really wanted to say, she chose to keep her face buried in her food.

They ate without speaking after that. Only baby sounds broke the silence in the kitchen.

Cammie could almost see the tension building. Part of it was sexual, no doubt. But there was more. Between them, a host of painful truths danced and mocked.

Soon Pumpkin would be sleepy again.

Suddenly, Cammie couldn't imagine sharing Drake's bed in the cold light of day. Her emotions were raw, her heartbreak too close to the surface. What was she going to say? They had agreed to indulge last night and today. A sort of last hurrah.

The truth was, she was done. The need to get away from Drake was urgent and real.

For once, he didn't pick up on her mood. The man she loved was oblivious to her distraught mental gymnastics. She wasn't allowed to take the baby and leave. Drake wasn't going to move out of his own house.

Cammie was trapped by circumstance and her love for him.

They had almost finished cleaning up the kitchen when Drake's cell phone rang. Cammie took the baby so he could answer.

She watched his face change. And she listened without apology, though the guts of the conversation eluded her.

When he hung up, she cocked her head. "What is it? What's wrong?"

His jolly mood had paled. His expression was hard to read. "That was Ainsley," he said. "The doctor is so pleased with her progress they're releasing her earlier than they thought. Today. After lunch."

"Oh." Cammie's heart sank, even as her common sense told her this was for the best. "That's great news. I know you were worried about her."

He showed his hands in his pockets. "Cam?"

"Yes."

"I thought we had more time to talk and, well, you know."

"It's okay. We had what we needed."

He scowled. "What does that mean?"

"Closure. A chance to end things on a better note."

Eight

Drake strode into Royal Memorial Hospital, trying to ignore the panic-stricken rage swirling in his gut. He desperately needed an outlet for his frustrated anger. In other circumstances, he would have stopped by the gym to go a few punishing rounds with the punching bag.

Closure? What kind of lame-ass word was that? He and Cammie had spent an amazing night together, and now she was talking about *closure*? That was bullshit.

Earlier, after the call from the hospital, Cammie had disappeared with the baby, leaving Drake to wallow in his own dark mood. To go from sexual satiation to the cold knowledge that she was brushing him off made him feel sick. They had been getting along so well.

What was up with her? He would never understand women, damn it.

In the elevator, he inhaled and exhaled, trying to pull himself together. It wouldn't do for Ainsley to think he was upset or didn't want her to come home.

Before he entered her room, he pasted a smile on his face. Then he opened the door. "Hey, my little chick. How ya feelin'?"

Ainsley was still pale, but her grin was genuine. "Not my old self, but definitely ready to get out of here."

He put a hand under her chin and tipped up her face. "You look better. More *interestingly frail* than at death's door."

"Gee, thanks." She stood gingerly and wrapped her arms around his waist. "I haven't said it yet, Drake, but thank you for coming all the way from Australia. It means a lot."

He rested his chin on top of her head and hugged her. "Of course, I came, honey. You're my family."

The nurse interrupted them with a sheaf of dismissal papers in her hand. Once that was taken care of, Ainsley had to be cajoled into a wheelchair. The woman in the blue scrubs was firm. "Hospital policy."

The older woman spent five minutes going over medication details and post-op instructions. Finally, they were allowed to leave.

Drake tucked his patient into the car with care. She seemed to be wilting already. "I'll take you home and get you settled before I go get your prescriptions," he said.

Ainsley shook her head. "That's dumb. We have to pass right by the pharmacy. I'll be fine, I swear. I might even tilt the seat back and take a nap."

Fortunately, Drake was able to get in and out of the drugstore quickly.

Ainsley didn't seem any the worse for the brief wait. When they pulled up in front of the house, she shifted in her seat. "I can't wait to see Cammie and the mystery baby," she said, her expression animated.

Drake stomach clenched. "She's excited about seeing you, too."

He gathered all Ainsley's things from the hospital and ran them up the walk to the front porch. Then he went back to retrieve his patient. As he helped her out of the car, Ainsley batted his hands away. "I'm fine. I can do this."

"Humor me," he said, wrapping an arm around her waist as they approached the house.

The door opened before he could fish the keys out of his pocket. Cammie stood there, framed in the doorway, the baby on her hip. "Ainsley," she said, with a welcoming smile. "I'm so glad you're well enough to be home. From what Drake has told me, it must have been very scary experience."

Ainsley nodded as she entered the house. "I guess it was, but honestly, in the beginning, I was too sick to realize it."

Drake shooed the women deeper into the foyer. "Why don't you two go on into the living room and catch up? I'll carry Ainsley's things to her room."

Cammie frowned, glancing at the staircase. She addressed Ainsley. "I told Drake that the baby and I should give you the guest room, and we'll move upstairs."

Ainsley shook her head. "Thank you, but not necessary. I've been dreaming about my own room, my own bed. And the doctor says the stairs will be good exercise for me as long as I'm careful."

"Enough chitchat," Drake said, the words sharper than he intended. "You two go sit down so Ainsley can rest."

Cammie hovered until Ainsley picked a comfortable armchair. "Can I get you anything?" she asked. "A drink? Something to eat?"

The younger woman curled her legs beneath her, wincing as she moved. "No, thanks. I'm fine. They fed me before I left the hospital."

Ainsley's short, dark hair was styled in a pixie cut. With her blue eyes, she could have been blood related to Drake, though Cammie knew she wasn't. "How are you *really* feeling?" she asked. "I know Drake has probably driven you crazy hovering."

Ainsley laughed. "He does hover at times. I'm doing well," she said. "Sore and weak. But both of those conditions will get better as the days go along. It's just so good to be home. Royal Memorial is great, but I was about to go crazy."

"I'm really sorry you have to put up with houseguests. I hope it won't be much longer before Pumpkin's family is found. I suppose Drake filled you in on all the details?"

"He did." Ainsley cocked her head and stared at Cammie. "Is my stepbrother okay?" she asked. "He seems tense today."

There was nothing Cammie could do about the blush that suffused her face. "As far as I know, he's fine," she lied. "Maybe something at work is bothering him."

"I feel terrible that he dropped everything and flew all the way from Australia." Ainsley's expression was crestfallen.

"You shouldn't," Cammie said. "Drake never does anything he doesn't want to do. He loves you, and he was scared to death when he heard what happened. I think it's sweet that he takes care of you so well. Not that you're not a grown woman," she said hastily.

Drake's stepsister laughed. "You're not insulting me. He *does* take care of me. And I do appreciate it. But he has his own life, and I have mine. I'll be fine when he goes back to Australia."

"He's leaving so soon?" Cammie felt dizzy.

"Well, not tomorrow. I know he rebooked his original flight to add a couple of days. But I told him I'll be perfectly fine on my own. Plus, I've got friends. I'm sure they wouldn't mind taking turns staying here until I'm completely back on my feet."

"Of course." Cammie swallowed. "I promise, Pumpkin and I will be out of your way in no time."

"You're not in the way." Ainsley stared at her. "So, what's going on with you and my brother? I thought the two of you broke up."

Oh, boy. Cammie wasn't prepared for the inquisition. "We did. I'm only here because I wanted to keep Pumpkin until the authorities locate his parents. I'm not qualified, but Drake is. He offered to be the official foster parent on paper. I do the actual baby care."

Ainsley chuckled. "That, I believe." She paused, clearly deciding whether or not Cammie was giving her the whole story. "Drake said he ran into you in the hospital parking lot?"

"Yes."

"That seems like a pretty big coincidence."

"Not really. I had a meeting at the hospital that day. Drake was coming to visit you. He had just flown in." Cammie started to sweat. The last thing she wanted was for Ainsley to find out that she and Drake had hooked up.

Ainsley was clearly not convinced. Cammie was forced to change the subject, but it was an awkward segue. "I haven't congratulated you on graduating from college."

"Thanks," Ainsley said. "I ended up with one of those liberal arts degrees that qualifies me for nothing in particular. But Drake says I should take my time and find a job that makes me happy."

"Don't tell him I said so," Cammie joked, "but he's a smart man."

"He is, isn't he? I'm sorry I gave him such a hard time growing up."

"You were young…and grieving. Drake understood."

"Maybe."

Cammie couldn't tell her the truth—that Drake had been indelibly marked by the conflict with his foster daughter. They related now like sister and brother. And they clearly loved each other dearly. But the harm had been done.

When Drake reappeared, ready to take Ainsley up to her room, Cammie excused herself. "It's time for this little one to eat." She avoided looking at Drake. "I'll see you both at dinner."

Before Drake could stop her, Cammie was gone. He thought he had managed to hide his frustration, but Ainsley poked him in the ribs as they walked slowly up the stairs. "What's going on with you and Cammie?"

"I don't know what you mean." The words sounded wooden even to him.

Ainsley snorted. "Oh, come on, Drake. Either you hate each other's guts, or you want to do the nasty. Which is it?"

"You're a brat," he said. "I think you need a nap."

"Denial isn't healthy, you know."

"Drop it, Ains," he said, managing not to snarl. It wasn't her fault.

She went up on her tiptoes and kissed his cheek. "I'm sorry, Drake. You know I could go to a hotel if I'm cramping your style."

His jaw dropped. "Don't be ridiculous. You're my number one priority." He folded back the covers on her bed. "Seriously. The doctor said you need to take it easy. You don't want to end up back in the hospital."

She pouted. "You're no fun." She kicked off her shoes and climbed into bed with an audible sigh.

Drake pulled the covers up to her chin. "I want you to concentrate on getting well."

"I will." She studied his face, making him squirm inwardly. "But I need you to be happy, Drake. You gave up so much for me. You deserve to have the life you want. Or the woman…" Her arch expression finally made him smile.

"I have a great life, Ainsley. Don't you worry about me."

"I do worry. I love you. And I'm not saying that just because you're the only family I've got. You have a huge heart, but not everyone realizes that. What you did for me practically qualifies you for sainthood."

He sighed, sitting down on the edge of the bed. "Let's not go overboard. And for the record, even though in the beginning my relationship to you felt like an obligation, you grew on me."

"Like a fungus, or maybe a rash?"

"Be serious, Ains." He paused, swallowed, and spoke gruffly. "I love you, too. You wouldn't be any more my sister if we were blood related. You know that, right?"

She was teary-eyed now. "I do. But Drake…"

He lifted an eyebrow and pinched her toe through the covers. "What?"

"Cammie is good for you. Don't let her get away again."

Ainsley's troubled gaze made him restless. His stepsister didn't know that he had basically given Cammie the boot. She would probably kick his ass if she knew.

He managed a smile. "Cammie and I are nothing now. Friends, possibly, but no romance. Maybe you're right. Maybe there's a woman out there for me."

Her face brightened. "And you swear you'll seal the deal when you find her?"

"If I find the perfect woman, you'll be the first to know."

Drake's day went from bad to worse. He hardly saw Cammie at all. She made an appearance at dinner holding the baby, but she ignored Drake for the most part, choosing instead to engage with Ainsley. He was glad to see his stepsister's face have more color and animation, but he was selfish enough to be angry when Cammie shut him out.

The three of them—four if he counted the baby—eventually moved to the living room, where the chairs were more comfortable for Ainsley. Drake had a hunch that Cammie was going to bolt at the first opportunity. But before she could hide out in the guest room, the front bell rang.

"I'll get it," Drake said.

When he opened the door, a uniformed police officer stood there. She smiled. "I'm Haley Lopez."

"I remember." Drake said. "What can I do for you?"

"May I come in and speak to you and Ms. Wentworth for a few moments?"

"Of course." He stepped back, allowing her to enter. "Cammie and my sister, Ainsley, are in the living room."

"I hadn't heard she was released."

"Just this afternoon."

"I'm sure you're relieved."

When Drake and the officer entered the room, Cammie blanched. He introduced Haley Lopez to his stepsister. And maybe it was Drake's imagination, but he thought Cammie clutched the baby more tightly. "Have a seat," Drake said to their tall, beautiful visitor.

Cammie played with one of the baby's tiny fingers. "Do you have news, Officer Lopez?"

"Please call me Haley. Unfortunately, no. But I wanted to drop by and ask both of you a question."

Drake frowned. "We haven't heard anything, either."

"No, it's not that. Our people are still working the active investigation. But since it's taking far longer than any of us expected, social services wondered if you might like to surrender the baby to someone else in the foster parent system. I'm sure you thought this situation would resolve itself in three or four days. It's not really fair to either of you. You both have jobs and responsibilities. Ms. Conner has a family ready and willing to take Pumpkin in and care for him in the foreseeable future."

For a few moments, a long, uncomfortable silence pulsated. Even Ainsley, usually the voluble one, said nothing.

Finally, Cammie spoke. "I suppose it depends on the rules. Mr. Rhodes… Drake…will be returning to Australia in a few days. Will I be able to keep the baby if Pumpkin's official foster parent is not in the country?"

Haley frowned. "Honestly, I'm not sure. I'll have to check."

Cammie nodded. "Well, if it's possible, I'm more than willing to keep Pumpkin longer. I hate disrupting his routine."

"And I can help," Ainsley said. "I'm feeling better every day. Even with Drake gone, Cammie and I would be able to handle it."

"I'm not gone yet," Drake muttered. All three women ignored him.

Officer Lopez jotted something in her phone. "I'll explain the situation to Ms. Conner at social services. It's possible that if you two ladies are willing to continue the baby's care uninterrupted in this same home, we might be able to skate around the fact that Mr. Rhodes has to go back to Australia."

"I could change my flight," Drake said. Already, work was piling up. He was needed in Australia. On the other hand, his career wasn't brain surgery. He was free to make his own choices. And he could work remotely to some extent.

Suddenly, for the first time in hours, Cammie looked straight at him. Her gaze was cool. "You've been generous with your home and your time, Drake. I'm sure Ainsley and I can handle this. If Officer Lopez gets the situation okayed, there's no reason at all for you to change your plans. You can be on that flight to Australia in no time."

Drake was pissed. His stepsister and his former lover were basically ignoring him. Even Officer Lopez seemed to dismiss him.

Why was he feeling so rotten? Wasn't going back to Australia what he wanted? Even so, it felt damned uncomfortable to be forced out the door.

This was still his house. He would leave when he wanted to leave.

The morning after Officer Lopez's visit, Cammie fed Pumpkin, dressed both of them for the day and then tiptoed out of the bedroom. She found Mrs. Hampton in the kitchen stirring up a batch of her delicious apple muffins. After a few pleasantries, Cammie shifted the baby in her arms and said, "Am I the first one up?"

Mrs. Hampton shook her head. "Mr. Rhodes went out for an early run. Miss Ainsley is sleeping in. May I fix you something?"

Relief flooded Cammie's veins. Drake was not happy with her, so she was in no hurry to see him. "Nothing for me, thanks. I have an appointment this morning. I'll drive through somewhere on the way."

"And you're taking the baby?"

Cammie didn't know if the odd note in the housekeeper's voice indicated surprise or disapproval. "I am. It won't be a problem. If you don't mind, please tell Drake and Ainsley that I'll be back sometime this afternoon."

"Of course." The housekeeper pointed at the nearby counter. "I still take the newspaper every day…brought my copy with me. They ran that article about your little man."

Despite the fact that Cammie was in a hurry and *really* didn't want to bump into Drake, she couldn't resist picking up the paper. She scanned the three columns. Sierra Morgan had done an excellent job. The story was compelling and heartfelt without sensationalizing Pumpkin's plight.

"It's good, isn't it?" The housekeeper shot Cammie a glance over her shoulder, waiting for an answer.

Cammie tossed the paper aside with a sigh of relief. "It is. It really is. Hopefully, we'll see progress soon."

Forty-five minutes later, she sat in a nondescript exam room and felt her heart race. This was the only time she had taken the baby out of the house and into the world. Getting him situated in the car seat hadn't been a problem. But perhaps bringing him with her had been a mistake.

This was her second recent visit to the gynecologist. The first had been for testing. Today she was going to find out the results.

When Dr. Nash walked in, Cammie took a deep breath. The other woman was in her late fifties, calm, experienced. And her manner was kind. Cammie needed that.

The ob-gyn pulled up a stool and raised an eyebrow. "Whose baby do you have?"

Cammie flushed, feeling guilty for no apparent reason. "I'm fostering him for a brief time. He was abandoned."

"Is he the one in the newspaper this morning? I read that story. Incredible that they still haven't found the parents."

"I agree. We're calling him Pumpkin. I worry that being separated from his mother at this young age may do him harm."

The doctor shook her head. "If he and his mama are reunited soon, he should be fine."

"I hope so."

The doctor carried a paper chart in her hand. She flipped it open, scanned the contents and smiled. "I'm confused," she said. "You're young. You have no apparent medical problems. You're heterosexual. Why do you want to try artificial insemination?"

Cammie clutched Pumpkin, glad to have a shield. "I want a baby," she said, trying to sound firm.

"I understand *that*," the doctor said. "But why not do it the old-fashioned way? Wine, roses, music?"

For an instant, Cammie's memory shot back to the previous thirty-six hours…or at least the part before Ainsley came home. "I'm not in a serious relationship," she said.

The doctor's gaze was razor-sharp. "But you could be soon. What's your rush?"

It was hard to admit it, but maybe the confession would be therapeutic. "I *was* in a serious relationship," she said quietly. "Two years ago. We broke up when he found out I wanted children."

The doctor grimaced. "A lot of men think they don't want kids. They usually come around."

"Not this man," Cammie said, her throat tight. "He's adamant. And besides, our relationship ended a long time ago."

The doctor leaned back in her chair and shook her head. "I have to point out that artificial insemination comes with its own set of challenges. It's expensive, for one thing, though perhaps in your case that's not a problem. Even so, there's the issue of a sperm donor. Do you have one?"

Cammie's jaw dropped for a moment. Then she quickly snapped it shut. "I do not."

Dr. Nash sighed. "I see couples in my practice who face all manner of roadblocks on their road to conception. They are desperate. You are an anomaly, Cammie."

"So you won't help me?" Tears stung her eyes, but she didn't let them fall.

"Of course I'll help you. I'm a doctor." She reached into her pocket and handed Cammie a business card. "This is a colleague of mine. She counsels couples considering artificial insemination, particularly those who will be using a sperm donor. You might find her expertise helpful."

"I know what I want. I've always known."

"Artificial insemination is not a straightforward process. I encourage you to give this some time and thought before we talk about what comes next."

"I will." Cammie was disappointed but not dissuaded.

The doctor rolled her stool across the small space and gathered several pamphlets from a rack on the wall. "Read through all these first. If you decide you're still interested, I have several book recommendations that go deeper into the subject. Just call my office and they can email you a list."

"But what about all my lab work?"

The doctor smiled ruefully. "By all accounts, you're extremely fertile. Getting pregnant shouldn't be any problem at all."

"Oh. That's good." Again, Cammie's thoughts flashed

to Drake…the man who had been obsessively careful about using a condom. Every time. She juggled the baby and stuffed the pamphlets into her open-topped leather tote. "I'll read everything, and maybe I'll meet with your therapist person. But I don't think I'll change my mind."

"Have you considered adoption?" the doctor asked. "I included a few of those leaflets as well. There are a lot of children out there who need to be part of a family."

"I have. And I might adopt also. But first, I want to get pregnant."

"Fair enough." Dr. Nash made a notation on the chart, stood and went to the door. "See my receptionist on the way out. Schedule another appointment for two months from now. We'll talk again, Cammie."

Nine

Drake went straight to his room and showered after his run. The exercise had done little to blunt his need for Cammie, but hopefully it had given him a modicum of control. The smell of muffins drifted down the hall. A homemade breakfast and a face-to-face convo with the woman driving him crazy? He'd call that a win.

The reality wasn't exactly what he expected.

When he made it to the kitchen, only *two* women were in residence. Mrs. Hampton labored over the stove with an iron skillet. Ainsley sat at the kitchen table reading a newspaper. *A newspaper?*

Drake sat down across from his stepsister. "I didn't know anyone still published newspapers," he said, tongue firmly in cheek.

Ainsley pointed to the headline—Abandoned Baby Sparks Hunt for Mother. "This Sierra Morgan person must be the real deal. It's a great article. I like that she didn't include a picture. That might bring all the crazies out."

Drake's knee bounced under the table. He wasn't going to ask about Cammie. He wasn't. "Are you through reading that?"

She held up one finger. "Almost. Give me a sec."

Mrs. Hampton set a plate in front of him. "Eat it while it's hot," she said.

The food smelled amazing. Hickory bacon, fluffy scrambled eggs, crunchy-topped biscuits with maple butter in addition to the muffins. His mouth watered, but he couldn't bring himself to pick up his fork. He tugged at the newspaper. "You read too slow."

Ainsley surrendered the newsprint with an exaggerated sigh. "You're still a bully."

He tugged her ponytail. "And you're still a whiny baby."

His stepsister burst out laughing. "It's good to have you home, old man. It's been too quiet around here."

Don't ask about Cammie...

He cleared his throat. "How are you feeling this morning?"

"Better."

Don't ask about Cammie...

"Did you take your antibiotic?"

Her gaze narrowed. "Drake…"

He heard the message loud and clear. "Sorry," he muttered. "Old habits."

Don't ask about Cammie...

Ainsley patted his hand. "It's okay. I know you mean well." She picked up his fork and handed it to him. "Eat. Don't let the eggs get hard."

Drake made himself chew and swallow, though the food might as well have been cardboard. All he could think about was the intimate meals he and Cammie had shared recently. The way her face glowed when she looked at the baby. The way her eyes got hazy and unfocused when Drake pleasured her.

He choked on a bit of bacon and had to wash it down with hot coffee that singed his mouth.

When Mrs. Hampton left the kitchen to take a bag of garbage outside, Ainsley frowned at him. "What's wrong with you?" she whispered. "You're weirding me out."

"Nothing's wrong," he said. "I don't know what you mean."

Suddenly, her face cleared. "Oh my gosh. It's Cammie. You're freaking out because you don't know where she is."

He went still, not looking at her. Swallowing another bite. "Do *you* know where she is?" he asked, trying for nonchalance and failing.

"Yes." Ainsley's gaze narrowed. "Mrs. Hampton said Cammie told her she had an appointment. She'll be back after lunch." Ainsley wrinkled her nose. "Damn. I guess the two of you really aren't an item. I pictured her tiptoeing down the hall to your room last night after the baby was asleep. I was hoping for big news. I always thought you two belonged together."

"There's no news," Drake said gruffly. "Let me eat my breakfast in peace."

The morning passed slowly. His office in Sydney was closed, everyone asleep. The time difference had made this trip home problematic.

Since he couldn't do business, he had plenty of time to wonder where Cammie had gone and why. And why hadn't she asked him to take care of Pumpkin while she was occupied? Didn't she trust him?

It made sense that she wouldn't ask Ainsley, who was still recovering.

Mrs. Hampton left at noon, because it was her half day. Ainsley had been on her cell phone all morning talking to friends.

Drake passed the guest suite half a dozen times before he finally entered. He stopped just inside the doorway and stared at the bed, the floor, the baby crib.

How had his orderly life been upended so completely in such a short time? He didn't like this feeling. For one thing, it was messy. He couldn't think about Cammie without thinking about the baby. The truth was, Cammie wouldn't be under his roof at all if it weren't for Pumpkin.

He told himself all he wanted was Cammie in his bed. And he was willing to tolerate the kid to make that happen. The admission painted him in an unflattering light.

Drake wasn't a bad person. He wasn't. He just didn't want to be a dad.

By one o'clock, he was pacing the floor. Ainsley was up in her room. There was no one to witness his black mood. By two o'clock, his anger morphed into worry. Cammie wasn't used to driving with a car seat in the back. What if the baby distracted her? What if she had been in an accident?

When he heard knocking and the front doorbell rang at two thirty, he was tempted to ignore it. He was in no mood for dealing with the public. But in a heartbeat, he realized that it could be someone from social services coming to check up on Pumpkin and the current home situation.

Reluctantly, he made his way down the hall. When he opened the door, shock and relief flooded his chest in equal measure. "You're back."

Cammie looked up from her purse and gave him a rueful smile. Her gorgeous red hair shone with fire in the afternoon sun and danced around her shoulders in the breeze. She tried to tuck one side behind her ear as she balanced Pumpkin on her hip, along with two medium-size shopping bags from the local market. "Sorry. I forgot to dig out my keys while I was still in the car. I decided it was easier to knock."

"No worries." He stepped back, but Cammie's shoe caught the edge of the doormat and she stumbled briefly. "Here," he said. "Give me the baby before you hurt yourself."

"Thanks." As she handed over her tiny charge, Drake's hand bumped her purse straps. Cammie's large leather tote fell off her arm and spilled all over the floor. Lip balm and papers and other feminine items scattered everywhere. When the purse fell, she lost the grocery bags, too. Baby wipes and small formula bottles added to the chaos. Fortunately, nothing broke.

"Good grief," he said. He squatted, baby in hand, and started scooping up what he could reach. Cammie did the same. He froze, his gaze incredulous, as he read the pamphlet in his hand. "You're thinking about artificial insemination? Good Lord, why?"

When he first opened the door, Cammie's expression had been carefree and happy, as if she was happy to see him. He'd felt a connection, a sexual charge. Now she was stone-faced. She finished gathering up the mess and shoved it back where it belonged. "This has nothing to do with you," she said curtly.

His temper boiled. "Ainsley!" He bellowed the summons in the general direction of the staircase.

His stepsister appeared from around the corner. She had apparently been reading in the living room, judging by the book in her hand. "You don't have to shout," she said, grimacing. "I'm right here."

"Will you watch the baby for a few minutes?" he asked. "Cammie and I need to talk. In private."

Cammie scowled. "No, we absolutely don't. And besides, Ainsley isn't supposed to exert herself."

He handed over the sleeping infant. "This nugget hardly weighs anything. Ainsley will be fine."

"I don't want to talk to you," Cammie hissed, her face flushed. Green eyes shot sparks at him.

"Too bad."

Ainsley didn't say a word, but her gaze was wide as she watched the show.

Drake took Cammie's narrow wrist in his hand and started dragging her down the hall. "Outside," he said. "Where no one can hear us."

He expected Cammie to protest, but she didn't put up a fight. At least not physically. The fact that she wasn't saying anything bugged him.

When they burst out into the sunshine, he released her. Cammie folded her arms across her chest with an *I dare you* look on her face.

"Where did you go today?" he asked. "Tell me."

Her chin went up. "To the market."

"And where else?"

"I'm not your stepsister," Cammie said. "I don't have to pay attention to your ridiculous demands."

"Cammie…" He narrowed his eyes and gave her his best intimidating glare.

She didn't seem impressed. "Why does it matter?"

He backed her up against the side of the house, into a patch of shade. Now they were standing so close, he could see the tiny pulse that fluttered at the base of her throat. "I missed you last night," he muttered.

The look in her eyes softened. "I missed you, too, Drake. But this is how it has to be. Ainsley is home, you're leaving and Pumpkin's family will be showing up any day now. Please don't make things difficult."

"I'm not sure I can do that," he said. "Kiss me, Cam."

He would have stopped, of course, if she had protested. But the way she returned the kiss so eagerly and pressed her body to his had him wondering how soon he could get her naked. He ran his hands up and down her back. "You make me burn," he said raggedly. "I can't think. I can't focus on work. I can't even remember why I'm mad at you."

She pulled back, searching his face. "Yes, you can. You saw my pamphlet from the doctor's office."

Cammie was desperate to keep herself from doing something stupid. So she threw gasoline on the fire. Mentioning the pamphlet made the situation both more and less volatile. Drake jerked back, wiping his mouth, his eyes wild.

"Tell me," he said. "Tell me what insane thing you're doing."

"Nothing's for sure yet," she said calmly. "But I want a baby, and artificial insemination is one option."

He scowled at her. "Who is he? Who's the guy donating sperm to your little experiment?"

"No one. Yet. If I decide on that choice, it will probably be someone anonymous. Entirely clinical."

"This is crazy, Cam." He ran his hands through his hair, mussing it, making him look even more appealing.

He was an incredibly beautiful man. Unfairly so. Today he was dressed very casually in jeans and a soft button-up cotton shirt in a blue that emphasized his eyes. From his broad shoulders to his masculine features and his lean frame, he was enough to make any woman's heart give a wobbly little flutter. Because he and Cammie shared a history, she was more vulnerable than most.

She shored up her resolve. "Lots of people go this route to get pregnant. Lesbian couples who want babies. Women whose partners suffer from erectile dysfunction. It's not an outlandish idea."

"But you're neither of those."

"True," she said. "I don't have a partner at all."

She saw him flinch. Perhaps she had wounded his pride, but she was tired of pretending. "I've been thinking about this for months. *You* want to build a business empire. I want to create a family. It's my choice."

He came back to her then, suddenly looking as dangerous as a tiger on the prowl. "Let me give you my sperm," he said. "I don't like the idea of some strange man fathering your child. It's creepy."

"It's *not* creepy. And do you know how ridiculous you sound? No way. You'd never be able to forget that you had a son or daughter walking around Royal."

A shadow crossed his face. For a moment, she saw true vulnerability in his masculine gaze. The glimpse was so shocking she barely knew how to react. Drake Rhodes was an alpha male to the core. He knew what he wanted, and he went after it. Be it business or pleasure, he was the commander of his own destiny. Confident, arrogant. Entirely sure of himself and his decisions.

Often, Cammie had envied his certainty. Her life had never been so clear-cut.

"I have to go in," she said, feeling suddenly exhausted.

"Not yet, Cam." He pulled her into his arms a second time and kissed her lazily. His lips were firm and warm on hers. His arms folded her close, creating a haven of safety and security that was as arousing as it was wonderful. When he set his mind to it, Drake could make a mockery of her resolve. She loved him dearly. Far too much to resist. He wasn't even gone yet, and already she was grieving his loss.

When he slid one big, warm hand under the skirt of her sundress and found her center, she groaned. He stroked her through thin panties, raising her temperature and fracturing her breathing.

Longing, hot and fierce, writhed in her core. "Please," she begged. "Please." Not even sure what she was asking for, she burrowed closer, her cheek pressed to his chest. She felt his lips in her hair.

"Come for me, Cam," he muttered. "Come, my love."

Those last two words hurt, uttered as they were in the pursuit of carnal pleasure. But even knowing the falseness of his ragged demand, she couldn't help herself. She hit the peak, sobbing, drowning in the hot, sweet pleasure.

He held her close as she drifted back to earth. She felt his hand on the back of her head, his fingers combing her sun-warmed hair. Words trembled on her tongue, but she couldn't give them voice. She couldn't beg him to be someone he wasn't.

His voice was low and gravelly when he spoke. "We'll meet in my room tonight, Cam. Please. I understand all the problems. But I don't care. Do you?"

She did—she cared a lot. But he was right. Even knowing the pain that lay ahead, she wanted him. "I'll come," she said. "But we mustn't let Ainsley know. This is her home. You are her family. We'll spend the day and the evening with her."

Drake rested his forehead against hers. "I love your tender heart and the way you care about people."

His words were complimentary, but they cut like knives. He hadn't said he loved *her*. That was a huge difference. "Thank you, Drake." She stepped away and smoother her hair. "The baby will be hungry. I need to tend to him."

"You won't change your mind?"

His intensity both thrilled and pained her. Drake wanted her badly. But only her body. Only that. Not her future. She swallowed against the bitter taste of regret. "I won't change my mind," she said.

As Cammie sat in the rocker in her room and fed the baby his bottle, her thoughts wandered. The doctor's words disturbed her. Why did she need to see a counselor? She knew her own mind. Wanting a baby was nothing new.

She craved that connection, that opportunity to build a family. Though it might not seem so to an outsider, Cammie was alone in the world. Her father was wrapped up in his own interests. Even with the Danae Foundation and his new bent toward philanthropy, he still had little warmth to offer his daughter.

Rafe Wentworth was a brother in absentia, a sibling on paper only. He, too, lived his own life. And Cammie's relationship with her mother had been strained after her father's first divorce years ago.

If anything, Drake was the one person who had shown her what it was like to be cherished and cared for. Even though he had never said the words, and even though she knew his feelings for her were more affection than real love, Drake had supported her, spent time with her and gone out of his way to make her happy. Right up until the day he couldn't do it anymore.

Her desire to get pregnant had been a line in the sand he couldn't cross.

Later that evening, the four of them sat at the dinner table. Ainsley, clearly feeling better, chattered away. She and Drake were discussing an internship she'd been of-fered beginning in the new year.

Cammie held Pumpkin and ate her dinner, content to let the conversation wash over her. Mrs. Hampton had left a homemade lasagna for the evening meal. Drake and Ainsley heated bread and put together a salad. The meal was delicious, but it was the bubble of contentment that fed Cammie's soul.

This was what she wanted, what she had always wanted.

Ainsley inadvertently broke Cammie's warm, fuzzy mood when she questioned her stepbrother. "So be hon-est, Drake. When *is* your flight back to Sydney? I'll be fine. But I don't like surprises."

Join the club, Cammie thought wryly.

Drake looked as if he had swallowed a bad piece of cheese. "Um…" His face flushed. "It's scheduled for day after tomorrow, but I think I'll bump it two more days. Just to be safe. I want to make sure you're on the mend, and I wouldn't mind seeing Pumpkin reunited with his family. I'd hate for all that to go down after I leave."

The shock literally stole the breath from Cammie's lungs. The pain cut through her body without mercy. How she managed not to respond visibly was a mystery.

Inside, she cried. She had known he was leaving soon. But to hear him say it on the heels of their plan to be in-timate tonight seemed…well, cruel.

He shot a glance in her direction, clearly trying to gauge her mood. Cammie would be damned before she would give him the satisfaction. Her smile was bland. "You'll spend a lot of money on flight changes."

Drake shrugged. "Such is life. My crew in Sydney knows my plans are fluid. They want me back, but they'll juggle things in the meantime."

"Well, I'm glad you have staff you can rely on," Ainsley said. "I feel guilty enough about upending your work schedule. And there's no need to add those two extra days. I'm feeling great."

Cammie was pretty sure that *great* was an exaggeration. But it wasn't her place to interfere between the other two. That was a relationship with its own dynamic. She had enough worries of her own.

When she finally made it back to her room to put the baby down for the night, she closed the door to the hall and sagged against it. Tears leaked down her cheeks. Her knees were weak, and her head pounded. The two hours of pretending to socialize normally had required every ounce of her acting ability.

Forty-eight hours. Drake could be gone in forty-eight hours. Maybe ninety-six if he did what he said and tacked on two more days. Honestly, she hoped he didn't do that.

Why torture herself? Maybe Pumpkin's mother would be located overnight, and Cammie would be free.

She went through the motions with Pumpkin and then realized what she was doing. This was dumb. The baby shouldn't suffer because of Cammie's heartache. After she bathed him, she put on his diaper and picked her favorite sleeper to dress him.

Afterward, she fed him and walked the floor, choosing to sing instead of rocking him. She had read that babies needed to learn to self-soothe and fall asleep naturally, but surely not in this case. An innocent infant had lost his mama.

It was nine thirty when his little head lolled on her shoulder. They had fallen into a pattern of sorts. Pumpkin would probably sleep until two or three.

Cammie took a quick shower. She had ordered a soft negligee and robe to wear now that Ainsley was home.

It had been delivered this morning. She clipped off the tags and slid the softy silky gown over her damp body.

Would Drake like the way she looked?

And did it matter?

She picked up her phone and sent him a text.

Is Ainsley upstairs for the night?

Drake's answer was immediate. Yes. I'm waiting for you.

Cammie could almost feel his impatience in those five words. She grabbed the baby monitor, took a deep breath to steady her nerves and opened her door.

This was the end. She felt it in her bones and made peace with the bitter knowledge. After all, this whole interlude with Drake had been nothing but happenstance. An abandoned baby. A chance encounter in a parking lot. A man juggling guilt and duty.

She would take this one final night greedily. Because she was too weak to deny him and herself. If this was all she would ever have of Drake Rhodes, the memories would have to last her a lifetime.

Ten

Drake was buzzing with nerves and caffeine. Earlier, Ainsley had admitted to overdoing things today. She had bid him good night and gone upstairs at eight.

He had been left to walk the floors and wonder when—or if—Cammie would come to him.

It would have helped if he could have gone for another run, but he was afraid to leave on the off chance Cammie would seek him out and he'd be gone.

At nine he locked the doors and turned out the lights—all except the one in the hallway between his room and Cammie's. After that, he showered. Then he paced his bedroom. It was a large space, but not large enough.

He knew he had emails waiting. The office in Australia was open now. But for the first time in months, he couldn't focus. Nor could he summon up any particular interest in his business affairs.

All he could think about was Cammie.

How could she even contemplate becoming a single parent? Didn't she know how hard that would be? How lonely?

His brain shied away from the idea of his Cammie going to a sperm bank and selecting a donor. That process was too impersonal.

Hell, Drake didn't want to become a dad, but even he knew the process would be easier if he and Cammie were in bed together.

In the midst of his tortured thoughts, Cammie opened the door and walked right in. She didn't even knock. When he saw what she was wearing, his tongue felt thick in his mouth. He blinked and searched for words.

"Finally," he said. *Oops. That came out wrong.* He didn't want to sound critical. "I'm glad to see you."

Her small, mocking smile said she recognized his clumsy lack of savoir faire. "I told you I would come."

"What happened to the football jersey?" he asked. "I liked it."

The gown she wore was coffee-colored silk trimmed in cream lace. It was cut low between her breasts in front. When she shimmied out of the matching robe and tossed it on his chair, he saw that the V on the back of the gown went even lower. It revealed the faintest hint of her ass. The fabric skimmed her curves, tantalizing…seductive.

Hell, Drake didn't need to be seduced. Arousal pulsed through his veins and hardened his body. He wanted to snatch and devour. It would be difficult to offer her tenderness, but shouldn't he try?

He reached out and turned off the lights. Now only a single candle burned. It was his one attempt at romance.

There was no shyness about Cammie's posture, no tentative nerves. She came right up to him and put her hands on his shoulders. Her smile was both sweet and challenging. If there were shadows in her gaze, he couldn't see them.

She went up on her tiptoes and kissed his lips softly. Her body nestled against his. "Let's not waste any time."

Curiously, her willingness to jump right in made it easier to keep his vow. "Patience, Cammie." He scooped her up in his arms, feeling the erotic slide of silk beneath his fingertips as he held her. Her hair trailed over his elbow. Bending his head, he nuzzled her cheek. "You look amazing. Too bad I can't let you wear that gorgeous thing in bed."

Her grin was impish. "Can't? Or won't? I spent a lot of money on this."

He dropped her carefully on the mattress. Earlier, he had turned back the sheets and covers. "It was worth every penny," he said, "but I want you naked while I do naughty things to your delectable body."

Her eyes rounded. "I don't know whether I should be excited or scared."

Drake laughed. He ditched his boxers and joined her. "Why not both?" When his body twined with hers, he had to take a jerky breath. He was playing a dangerous game. Both with Cammie and with his own life.

This need he felt should have been simple. Sleep with an old lover. Friends with benefits. Carpe diem.

Instead, he felt like he was drowning. The pleasure was both wonderful and terrifying. He had to get on a plane. Soon. Or he might do something that would change his life irrevocably. Being a good guy seven years ago had altered his entire world. He couldn't do it again. He knew his own limitations.

To silence the annoying voice in his head, he kissed Cammie. She murmured something low in her throat, a feminine sound that made the hair on his arms stand up.

Hearing her pleasure and knowing that he was the one making her purr elated him.

He took the kiss deeper still. Though he had threatened to strip her naked, now he paused to enjoy the feel of her hips and her breasts and the dip of her waist, all of it packaged in warm, silky fabric that beckoned his touch.

Their tongues tangled lazily. He knew her taste intimately. When she nipped his bottom lip with sharp teeth, he was shocked. Cammie was rarely the aggressor in their love play. What was different about her tonight?

Perhaps, like Drake himself, she was trying to squeeze every last drop of carnal pleasure from their last time together. Or was it? He hadn't changed the airline ticket yet. Either way, he felt stuck. Change it—and miss time with Cammie…and Ainsley. Extend it—and get drawn more deeply into a domestic scenario with long tentacles.

Cammie slid her arms around his neck. When she played with his earlobes, his erection lengthened. He sucked in an audible breath.

His lover chuckled. "I love the way your body responds to my touch, Drake. You make a woman feel powerful."

"You *are* powerful, Cam. I'm surprised you don't know that."

His answer seemed to surprise her. The smile disappeared. She searched his face as if he were a puzzle she was trying to solve.

There was no puzzle. He wanted Cammie Wentworth. Always had. And he wanted to make her happy. But that last part was out of his control.

"I think it's time for you to be naked," he said huskily. "Sit up for me."

He shimmied the gown up to her hips as she moved. Then, when she lifted her arms, he pulled the silk and lace over her head and tossed it to the foot of the bed. As he cupped her full breasts in his palms, her eyes closed, and her head fell back.

All Drake could do was wallow in the moment. She was here. In his bed. It was a bit of a miracle. The situation had him feeling rash and impetuous. When he thumbed her soft pink nipples, Cammie muttered his name.

"Drake," she whispered. "Drake."

The yearning in those syllables was impossible to miss. "I'm here, sweetheart. I'm here." He eased her onto her back and slid down beside her.

When he spread her thighs and tried to move on top of her, her eyes flew open in alarm. She put a hand to his chest. "The condom," she said urgently.

Everything inside him pushed toward the goal. Maybe he could be a hero after all. He slid two fingers inside her, feeling how ready she was. Noting how her body wanted his. "Let me give you a baby, Cam," he said urgently. "The old-fashioned way. I'll sign my rights away. I won't interfere. But you'll have that family you've always wanted."

Her gaze went wide and dark, the irises almost swallowed up by her pupils. A single tear squeezed from the corner of her eye and trickled down her flushed cheek. Cammie didn't seem to notice.

She caught his face in her hands, her expression wistful and tender. "That's a lovely offer, Drake. And I do appreciate it. But I can't accept. You would come to regret your decision and to resent me. I can't risk that."

"I wouldn't," he said, but the words lacked conviction, even to his own ears. He wanted to give her the moon and stars and everything in between. But if she wouldn't take his gift, was he any use to her at all?

Cammie pulled his face down for a kiss. Then she ran her hands down his back and cupped his flanks. "Get the protection, my sexy man."

Balanced as he was on his hands, her exploration of his body made his arms weak even as the rest of him pulsed with power and resolve. He was pissed on some level that she was rejecting his very generous offer. But he was too hungry to let a disagreement—even such an important one—derail the moment.

Feeling disgruntled and frustrated, he reached for the packet on the bedside table, took care of business and came back to her. Once again, he tried for tenderness. But he was too far gone, pushed perhaps by the thought he couldn't get out of his head. Cammie, pregnant and lovely, but with a child that wasn't his.

He shut his mind to the images, concentrating instead on the living, breathing woman in his bed. "I need you, Cam. Hard and fast. It's been too long."

"Ainsley's barely been home," she reminded him.

"I don't care. It feels like forever."

He entered her slowly, lifting one of her legs and propping it on his shoulder so he could go deep.

Cammie's gasp reflected what he was feeling. This was as close to heaven as a guy like him could get. The visual was incredible, but no more so than the feel of burying his aching sex inside Cammie. Her body welcomed him, gripped him, made his brow break out in a sweat. "Damn, woman," he croaked. "What are you doing to me?"

After that, he could no longer think. Cammie lifted into his thrusts. When she wrapped her free leg around his waist, his vision blurred. He needed her so badly, he couldn't breathe. His chest labored for oxygen.

He took her again and again, desperate to find what

he was seeking. Dimly, he heard Cam cry out as she climaxed. But he wasn't done. He held back, reining in his own need, bent on proving something to someone.

But in the end, he was mortal. Flawed. Just a man. His orgasm ripped through him from his feet to his hair follicles and everywhere in between. He shouted at the very end, muffling the noise against her shoulder.

Cammie held him as he shuddered in her embrace. He felt her fingers in his hair. In despair, he recognized at that moment that he loved her. But it changed nothing. He was getting on a plane to Australia. Whatever Cammie decided about motherhood would have nothing at all to do with him…

After Drake fell asleep, Cammie contemplated the seismic carnage. Drake had been like a madman. The covers were tumbled and beyond reach of her numb fingers. Now that the fierce coupling was over, her heated skin cooled.

Her lover was a dead weight, pressing her into the bed.

She could have moved him, but that required more effort than she could summon at the moment. The encounter had stunned her.

From the first time she and Drake had become lovers several years ago, there had always been something powerful that happened when they were together in a sexual encounter. She had been fairly inexperienced, so she always assumed that he was simply a very good lover.

But it was more than that.

Now, with the distance of time—and their recent reunion—she understood that they were made for each other; physically, that was. A very strong attraction had survived two years apart and even Drake's stint in Australia.

Why else had she gone back to his bed so quickly? It

was almost as if no time had passed at all. What she felt for him was not going to change. Maybe that's why she needed to talk to a counselor.

The memory of Drake's offer to give her a baby made her eyes sting with emotion. In other circumstances, she would have been elated. But he wasn't having a change of heart about becoming a father. He didn't want to build a family and a lifetime with her. He was literally offering his DNA.

If he but knew, that was absolutely the *worst* idea. For Cammie to have a son or daughter with Drake's deep blue eyes and wavy black hair would be too painful to imagine. She would never be able to escape his presence.

She knew his gesture meant he cared about her. A lot. And that was comforting. But in the end, what Drake wanted from life was not what Cammie could offer him. He wanted to be free.

The baby monitor rested across the room on a small table. At this particular moment, it would have been nice for Cammie to have an excuse to leave. Beneath her fingertips, Drake's skin didn't feel cold at all. How was that possible? Evidently, the life force he wielded was too strong to allow something as simple as a chilly room to affect him.

She kissed his shoulder lightly and prepared to nudge him over onto his side of the bed. When she tried, he roused groggily. "Is it the baby?" he asked.

"No." She slipped from his arms. "I'm going to the bathroom."

Drake was asleep again before she had taken three steps.

In the mirror over the vanity, Cammie studied her reflection. Her warring emotions were right there on her face for anyone to see. First was the smug happiness of a woman who had been well loved. Physical satisfaction. Sexual satiation.

But even in the midst of her momentary bliss, her eyes held sadness. A bleak certainty that Drake wasn't hers. The breakup from two years ago was still intact. Even though she and Drake had used living under the same roof as an excuse to revisit their physical relationship, nothing else had changed.

She was too tired to shower again. Instead, she wet a washcloth and found some of Drake's expensive shower gel to freshen up. There was nothing she could do about the hickey at her collarbone or the red patches on her throat where Drake's late-night stubble had scratched her.

Everything about her body felt his imprint.

When she returned to the bedroom, the candle burned low. Drake was on his stomach now, with both arms flung over his head. The sheet had crumpled down around his feet. For one private moment, she stood there and admired the picture he made.

An artist might have titled it *Masculine Excess*.

When her skin pebbled with goose bumps, she reached for her gown and robe and put them on, tying the sash at her waist. The lovely lingerie made her feel feminine and sexy, but it was the man in the bed who made her feel desirable and whole.

Leaving him was hard.

She sat down on the side of the bed and touched his warm shoulder, her fingers lingering to stroke and pet. "Drake."

It took him a few seconds to wake up. He rubbed the heels of his hands in his eyes. "What are you doing?"

"I'm heading back to my room," she said simply. She leaned down and kissed his warm, firm lips, lingering over the caress when he curled an arm around her waist and wouldn't let her move.

"Don't go," he said, the words ragged and hoarse.

She sat up, despite his efforts to constrain her. "It's for the best. Pumpkin will be awake soon."

"But not yet." He wrapped his fingers around her nearest wrist.

"I'm tired," she said simply. "This was wonderful, but I desperately need to get some sleep. I'll see you in the morning."

He sat up abruptly, seeming unconcerned with his spectacular nudity. "I'll be gone," he said, yawning.

Her heart fell to her feet. She felt sick and dazed. "Gone? I thought your flight was the next day."

In the midst of her internal meltdown, Drake continued to speak. "Not that kind of gone. I have an early doctor's appointment."

She pulled the sheet to his waist, trying to protect her flimsy self-control.

Since the man was the picture of health, she wasn't *too* concerned. But still she had to ask. "Are you okay?"

He smiled and rubbed his thumb over her cheek. "I'm great. It's just a technical thing. Ainsley is the beneficiary on my life insurance policy. Now that I'm living part of the year in Australia, my current company doesn't want to cover me. The new guys require a physical. Since I was here in Royal, I simply made an appointment with my own doctor. It shouldn't take long."

"Ah…" The relief she felt was way out of proportion to the actual situation.

"And do me a favor," he said with a rueful smile. "Please don't mention it to Ainsley. She gets squirrelly when we talk about it. So I don't bring it up."

"Of course." Cammie forced herself to stand, though it was the last thing she wanted to do. "Good night, Drake."

He rolled out of bed and stood as well, cupping her head in his hands, winnowing his fingers through her hair. "Pumpkin is on my side tonight," he said. "Still snoozing." The words were joking, but his gaze was dead serious. "I'm leaving, Cam. Don't cheat us of the time we have left."

You're the one cheating us...

Cammie wanted to yell at him, cajole him, do everything in her power to change the man he was. But if she did that, he wouldn't be the Drake she fell in love with. He had made up his mind. End of story.

Though bitterness tried to take hold, Drake's touch was stronger. "Okay," she said. The word threatened to stick in her throat.

His hands went to the knot at the front of her robe. "Don't be sad, Cammie. I don't want that for you. You should have everything you desire."

Hurt bubbled in her chest. His words were facile, totally ignoring the heart of the matter. How could he say that and not realize he was the problem?

As Drake undressed her and carried her back to the bed, she leaned her head against his chest. From out of nowhere, a thought struck her. Maybe she was as stubborn as Drake. Maybe she had been heaping all the blame for her unhappiness on him unfairly. Maybe she was equally culpable.

This time, Drake didn't rush. The foreplay was slow as molasses. He touched her everywhere, whispering words of praise, telling her all the ways her body pleased him and all the ways he wanted to return that pleasure tenfold.

She wallowed in the tenderness, all the while anticipating the moment when his hunger would overtake this infinitely precious *play*. He looked younger now, more relaxed, sweet and diabolically teasing.

Despite her fatigue and the late hour, he coaxed her latent desire to the surface.

What would happen if she abandoned her plans to have a baby? Had Drake used her desire for motherhood as an excuse to get out of a permanent relationship? Or was there a possibility that he cared a fraction as much as she did?

As he kissed his way from her throat to her navel, she dizzily pondered her revelation. Would he want permanence if parenthood was out of the question? If so, maybe she could have this bliss every night forever.

Drake was a wonderful man. Funny and charming. Intelligent and driven. They could have an amazing life together. Travel. See the world. And Cammie could even run the Danae Foundation from a distance, given technology in the twenty-first century.

Lots of people lived full and amazing lives without children.

She had spent so long being absolutely sure that she *had* to have a baby. Could she change? Could she take a step back and pivot? There were dozens of ways to help children in Royal and around the world. Funding important projects. Donating volunteer hours. The possibilities were endless.

Perhaps it was the late hour. Perhaps she was lightheaded from getting no sleep. But a flicker of hope refused to die.

Still, every time she tried to imagine being childless for the rest of her life, her heart shied away from the thought.

Equally terrible was the very real notion of Drake flying away from Royal and never coming back for anything but fleeting visits.

She loved him. Could she give up her dream for him?

And if she gave up that dream, did Drake love her in return?

He kissed her then, long and deep. Rational thought evaporated. "Drake," she whispered. "Drake…"

Rolling her onto her side, he spooned her and entered her from behind, with her leg over his. This position, though she could no longer see his face, was oddly intimate. He cradled her in his arms, keeping the pace languid.

As he played with her breasts and thrust slowly, she felt tears sting her eyes. What they had was so precious. Couldn't he see that? And seeing it, want to pass it on to another generation?

Her heart was breaking even as Drake stroked her body with his sex and his hands and brought her to a shivering climax. He was seconds behind her, burying his face in her nape as he groaned and found release.

They dozed after that. Pumpkin slept on.

When Cammie finally heard baby sounds on the monitor, thirty minutes had passed.

Groggy and weighed down with uncertainty, she found her nightwear, dressed and hurried down the hall. When she picked up the baby and felt his warmth and weight against her breast, she wanted to howl with frustration and despair.

Already she loved this *borrowed* baby deeply. How much more would she love her own son or daughter? Born of her body or adopted from her heart. Either way, she would give a child all the love and attention and *normalcy* she had missed growing up.

The routines of diaper and feeding were second nature to her now. She rocked Pumpkin, watching for the first faint rays of dawn to sneak around the heavy, expensive drapes. The day would begin whether she wanted it to or not.

The hours would tick by.

Drake's departure would draw near.

Had this small, unknown baby come into their lives to work a miracle, or was all of it a coincidence?

Cammie didn't really believe in fate. But right now, she wouldn't mind a glimpse into the future. So much to gain. So much to lose. And an hourglass where the sand was disappearing far too quickly.

Eleven

Drake didn't see Cammie before he left the house. She was either avoiding him, or the baby had gone back to sleep and Cammie was resting, too.

He was glad, in a way. Last night was etched into his memory. His body felt achy and relaxed at the same time. Sexually speaking, it had been one of the best nights of his life.

Why, then, was he feeling oddly out of sorts this morning?

He had allowed himself plenty of extra time to do a few errands en route to the doctor's office. Which was a good thing, because his Realtor called while he was on the way. Her voice was noticeably excited when she said hello.

"What's up?" he asked, searching for a parking spot on the street. There was never anything in the multi-level garage.

The agent gushed. "You're never going to believe it,

Drake. We've had a cash offer on the ranch. Ten percent over asking price."

The bottom fell out of his stomach. "I see." He put the vehicle in Park and shut it off. Gripping the wheel with both hands, he tried to think of what to say.

His silence obviously confused his caller. "I thought you'd be pleased," she said.

Instead of responding to that comment, he cleared his throat. "How long do I have to think about it?"

"Are you kidding me?" The incredulity in her voice said she was already spending the hefty commission.

"I never actually listed the ranch," he said.

"But you let someone look at it." The retort was sharp and probably well deserved.

"I told you I was conflicted about selling. You were the one who pushed me. I thought the whole thing was pretty casual and unofficial. We never signed stuff."

He had her there. But she was good at her job. She changed tack. "I know this is a hard decision. It would be for anybody. You love the ranch. But you don't even live in Royal anymore, Drake. Don't let sentimentality get in the way of a sound business decision."

Again, he asked, "How long do I have to give them an answer?"

Her silence was longer this time. He fancied he could hear her disgust over the phone line. "Forty-eight hours," she said with a long-suffering sigh. "And they'd like to close in two weeks."

Twenty minutes later—in the physician's waiting room—Drake stewed. Decisions were coming at him hard and fast. Tomorrow he was supposed to board a flight to Sydney. He'd just had a text from Cammie telling him that social services approved Pumpkin's care with Cammie and Ainsley as long as they stayed in the same house.

So Drake could leave tomorrow with no qualms, no guilt.

He grimaced, feeling as if his entire life in Royal was being stripped away all at once. He loved this town, loved the life he had known here. And as much as he might try to deny it, he loved Cammie Wentworth. So why then was he walking out the door?

When the nurse called him back and checked his vitals, she raised an eyebrow. "Your blood pressure is up. Not bad, but unusual for you."

"I had a phone call right before I came in," he said, shrugging.

"I hope not bad news."

The woman was making small talk. Being polite. But Drake answered anyway. "Just one of those fork-in-the-road things," he said ruefully.

She made a couple of entries on his electronic chart. "I understand. Stress can make the BP go up. But you're here for an insurance physical, so we'll let the doctor check it again before you go."

Drake had come by for blood work a few days ago. Today was only a formality. He would hear the results and get the forms signed. He concentrated on deep breathing. The last thing he wanted was to get turned down by this company, too. He was healthy as a horse. All he needed was to protect Ainsley's future.

Like in most medical establishments, Drake had to wait. It made him antsy, but he checked email and tried to stay calm so his BP would hit the normal range.

When the door finally opened, Dr. Brad Stockton walked into the room. He shook Drake's hand. "Good to see you, Drake."

"You, too." He and the doc had known each other since they were kids. "So, any surprises in the bloodwork? Your nurse said my blood pressure was a little high today. I told her I was stressed."

Brad grabbed a cuff and wrapped it around Drake's arm. "We're all stressed, aren't we? We live with it." He pumped and listened. Finally, he unwound the cuff and set it aside. "You're in the normal range. Barely. Nothing to cause problems with the insurance stuff. But it's my job to tell you to chill out. Find a hobby. Take some time off."

Drake managed a smile, thinking about his erotic overnight activities. You'd think that would count for something. "Duly noted," he said. "Are you signing off on everything else? I need to get this policy in place ASAP."

"Because you're heading back to Australia?"

"Yep." The word stuck in his throat.

The doctor pulled up a stool and sat at the computer. "Whenever I do these insurance physicals, I always check for any red flags that might derail things. In your case, of course, you're young and healthy. So I don't see any problems."

"But?" He could tell Brad was headed somewhere.

His childhood playmate turned around with a grimace. "You know we have access now to electronic pharmacy records."

"Yes." Drake frowned. Had there been some kind of mix-up?

The other man put his elbows on his knees and leaned forward. "Tell me something about your time in Australia. I saw that you were on an antibiotic and steroids."

Drake sighed, relieved. "Oh, yeah. That was several months ago. I was snorkeling off one of the beaches south of Melbourne and cut my leg on some coral. I didn't go to the doctor right away, and it got infected. But no worries. It cleared up beautifully." He pulled up his pants leg, pointing to his shin. "The scar isn't bad at all."

Brad looked closely at the pinkish streak, poked at it carefully and nodded. "That does look good."

"Then why do I get the feeling you're about to tell me something bad?"

"Not bad," the doctor said. "Not necessarily. But the antibiotic they gave you is a very strong one. And you were on it for four weeks. I'm sure they were concerned the infection might spread. Who knows what was in that ocean water? That particular medication is one we don't use much here."

"They told me they wanted to be very careful, because they'd had several cases of flesh-eating bacteria."

"Ah…"

Drake frowned. "But I'm not in any danger now, am I?"

"No. Not at all. It's just that a powerful antibiotic like the one you took can cause male infertility."

Was it Drake's imagination, or did the room shrink and go oddly silent? So what? He didn't want kids. This wasn't bad news, was it?

Brad was a trained professional. He couldn't have missed Drake's shock. "Don't jump ahead on this," he said, his expression kind. "If you and your partner decide to try for a baby, all I'm telling you is that it would be smart to see a specialist beforehand. That way you'll know in advance if you're dealing with any issues."

"Thanks," Drake said. He could barely get the word out.

Fifteen minutes later, he was out on the street, his world turned upside down. He knew he was in shock. His ears were ringing, and he had a hard time unlocking his car.

He couldn't go home not yet. So he drove out to the ranch.

Why had he let anyone think the ranch was up for sale? As he headed past the open gates and down the winding gravel road, several longtime employees who recognized him lifted a hand.

Drake waved back, though he felt anything but carefree. Normally, being here soothed him, pleased him. He'd grown up on this property.

Though he could have stopped at the comfortable and luxurious ranch house, he drove on, deeper and deeper into the massive acreage he owned. Finally, several miles from the main hub of activity, he scaled a low hill, parked the car and got out. A small cottonwood tree offered a patch of shade. Even though the rise was modest, the surrounding land was flat. He could see a very long way.

What he couldn't see was the image of his own future.

The doctor's cautionary advice had been a dash of icy water in Drake's face. Only when he heard the word *infertility* did he realize that his subconscious had been hard at work spinning various scenarios where Drake could keep Cammie in his life and still maintain the status quo.

He'd come up with several ideas. The easiest one was to take her to Australia with him and persuade her to give up on the idea of getting pregnant. But even in his most optimistic moments, he had known that was unlikely.

What he hadn't realized until this very instant was that he'd also been weaving another tale. The one where he took Cammie to Australia with him, but then promised to come back to Royal and start a family.

When had he begun to release his stubborn, long-held ban on babies? Was it the day he rushed home to Ainsley's bedside, knowing how much their bond meant to him? Or when he came face-to-face with Cammie and the abandoned child?

More likely, it had been in the midst of incredible sex. When he had known without a doubt that if he didn't change his mind, he risked losing the only woman who had made him feel invincible.

Though he hadn't changed his flight for tomorrow, deep in his gut, he knew he shouldn't get on that plane without resolving something with Cammie. He loved her. Maybe he had always loved her. During his time in New York, he had come back to Royal frequently.

The months in Australia had a been a different proposition. Royal had seemed very far away. But at night— even on the far side of the globe—he still dreamed of Cam occasionally. His professional life had been going smoothly, but he never felt entirely settled in Sydney. There was always something missing.

Now, he knew the *something* was a *someone*. Cammie.

All along, ever since he had jumped in to take responsibility for the abandoned child and made sure to keep Cammie under his roof and in his bed, his innermost self had been adjusting, growing, seeking new answers.

Some tiny part of him had come to believe that giving Cammie a baby wouldn't be such a bad thing at all.

He had let the idea simmer, occasionally poking at it, studying it, wondering if he really had the mental fortitude to be a dad, this time from the very beginning.

But what now? Even if he told her he loved her, it wouldn't be enough. To say those words to her, knowing what he now knew, meant possibly breaking her heart all over again. What if he couldn't get her pregnant? What then?

Because he couldn't go home, he slid down to the ground and rested his back against the tree. What in the hell was he going to do?

* * *

Cammie and Ainsley had a wonderful morning with Pumpkin. Ainsley even took charge of him for half an hour so Cammie could take a nap. When Cammie stumbled back into the living room and fell into a chair, yawning, Ainsley stared at her in concern.

"Are you okay?" she asked, clearly noting the dark circles under Cammie's eyes.

"I didn't sleep well last night," Cammie admitted.

"Why?"

Lying was not Cammie's strong suit, so she told a half-truth. "I was worried about the baby. About how much longer it will be before they finally locate his family. It shouldn't be like this."

"You love him, don't you?" the younger woman said, her blue-eyed gaze filled with sympathy.

Cammie shrugged, feeling weepy but trying to pull herself together. "How could I not? Honestly, when I brought him here, I thought it would be twenty-four or forty-eight hours at most. Now I've had time to really get to know him. He's so small, but he has his definite likes and dislikes."

"Just like a man," Ainsley said, grinning.

"Do *you* ever think about having children?"

Ainsley rubbed the baby's head, her expression reflective. "Occasionally. But I'm only twenty-two. I've got time."

"Will you tell me about you and Drake?" Cammie asked. "He never really talked much to me about your shared past."

"The man doesn't like to reveal his emotions, you know."

"I do know," Cammie said.

Ainsley put the baby on his back in her lap and let him

curl his tiny fingers around her pinkies. "Drake's mom died young of cancer."

"Yes."

"And my dad died of a heart attack when I was thirteen. Even now, my hazy memories tell me that Mom wasn't too sad he was gone. From what she said over the years, he was a very hard man to be married to... maybe even abusive, though I hope not. Anyway, my mom didn't stay single long. She'd only been a widow a year, and then boom...she was getting married to Drake's dad."

"Did you all live at the ranch?"

"Yes, though Drake was away at college most of the time," Cammie said. "When our parents were killed in the car accident, suddenly, I was alone."

"You and Drake both..."

"I suppose that's true. But he was the same age I am now. He could handle himself."

Cammie pushed, feeling protective of the man she loved. "Still, it was traumatic for him, too."

"Of course," Ainsley said. "I didn't mean to imply it wasn't. But no one was going to send him off to strangers. I know most foster parents are wonderful. But I had heard stories, and I was terrified."

"How soon did you know what Drake was going to do?"

"Almost right away. After the funeral, we were both sitting in the kitchen at the ranch. The house was quiet. No one was around. Suddenly he told me he would get licensed as a foster parent so that I could stay with him."

"What did you think of the idea?" Cammie asked.

"At first I was glad, but soon he started acting like a real parent, and I resented that. I resented *him*. I was a total pain in the ass, Cammie. I've heard him say he doesn't want kids because of what he went through with me. He makes it sound like a joke, but I know it's true. I made his life hell for several years. You don't know how much I regret that."

Cammie didn't know how to respond to the raw, pained confession. "Well," she said slowly. "It was a long time ago. And you have a great relationship now. That should count for something."

"Maybe. I don't know. Sometimes I think I broke him." Her comical face punctuated the half-serious statement.

Cammie laughed, as Ainsley intended. "You didn't break him. Drake is fine. He has a great life and a challenging, exciting job. But tell me, why didn't you and he continue living at the ranch?"

Ainsley sighed. "I think it was just too damn sad with his dad and my mom gone. Drake offered to buy a house in town so I would be closer to school, and I said yes. We've been here ever since. He comes and goes between trips."

"Did you know he's thinking about selling the ranch?" Cammie wanted to see if she got a reaction.

Ainsley's head shot up, her expression alarmed. "He wouldn't do that."

"I don't know. He showed it to somebody last week. He told me so. I assumed he might settle in Australia permanently."

"But he loves that ranch."

"That's what I said."

The two of them sat there for a moment, not speaking. Cammie didn't know what thoughts were running through Ainsley's mind. But Cammie's were clear. If Drake really did sell the ranch, she would know her chances of ending up with him were gone.

If he had no more ties to this town, he would have no

reason to stay. With Ainsley an adult now, Drake could reclaim his life.

Pumpkin began to fuss.

Ainsley let him suck on her finger. "Can I go with you to change him? And could I give him his bottle?"

"That's dangerous, you know."

"What do you mean?" Ainsley's eyes widened.

"Soon you'll be as attached to him as I am, and then we'll both go to pieces when he leaves."

"I'll take that chance," Ainsley said, looking down at the baby with a soft smile. "Isn't it better to have loved and lost and all that?"

Cammie wasn't sure the sentiment was true. She remembered what it was like to lose Drake. Now, soon, she would have to go through the pain all over again.

Her life would have been far easier if she had never met him.

In the guest room, she and Ainsley laughed and played with the little boy as they got him ready for his nap and his feeding. Pumpkin was more animated now.

Cammie watched with a smile as Ainsley settled in the rocker. "He changes every day," she said. "I can already see his personality."

Ainsley rocked slowly and held the bottle at the correct angle. "I feel so bad for his parents. They must be grief-stricken. Even if they abandoned him on purpose, because they couldn't care for him, that must have been agonizing."

"I know." Cammie stretched out on the bed, content to watch Drake's beautiful and capable stepsister feed the baby. Her eyes drifted shut again.

That was a mistake. Even though she hadn't been in *this* bed last night with Drake, the memories of the moments they had shared in his room played behind her

eyelids in vivid color. His big, masculine hands stroking her skin. The way his tousled hair made him look
more carefree. The glint of heated sexual intent when he
smiled at her.

She missed him already. It had only been a few hours,
and she *missed him already*. How needy and self-destructive was that?

Once again, she thought about her options. What would
he say if she offered to postpone her baby plans and come
to Australia with him? He had actually suggested that
very thing early on. Surely he hadn't changed his mind.

Of course, she couldn't leave with him tomorrow. She
had responsibilities to the foundation and to her father
and to all the men and women who would benefit from
the announcement at the gala.

And honestly, if Drake went back to Sydney alone,
what were the chances Cammie would really follow him?
Wasn't it more likely that the connection would simply
fade away? Their current sexual relationship was one of
convenience. It probably wouldn't survive a separation.

Still, the thought of cutting all ties was impossible to
contemplate.

Unfortunately, as good as Pumpkin had been all morning, he was now extremely fussy. Maybe he was overly
tired. Ainsley walked him first, then Cammie. The baby
fell asleep again and again but jerked awake if he was
moved.

Finally, at almost one o'clock, he gave up the fight.
Cammie laid him in the crib and held her breath. Ainsley
approached the bed cautiously. "Is he out?" she whispered.

"I think so."

The tiptoed toward the door. Cammie grabbed the
monitor. In the kitchen, both of them exhaled in relief.

Ainsley immediately started rummaging in the refrigerator. "I'm starving," she said, pulling out leftover roast beef and opening a loaf of bread.

"Leave out a couple of slices for me, too," Cammie said. Ainsley was a very comfortable person to be around. Cammie liked her immensely. Maybe, even with Drake gone, the two women could be closer friends.

Cammie had known Drake's stepsister back when Cammie and Drake were dating, but not well.

When they finally sat down to their meal, Ainsley shot Cammie a sideways glance. "So do you really not have a thing for Drake anymore?"

"Does it matter?" Cammie asked wryly.

"I think it does. Maybe you could persuade him to come home for good. I know he's having a good time in Australia, but when you're born and bred in Royal, it sticks with you. I can't imagine him turning his back on his heritage."

"I told you. He's probably selling the ranch."

"Maybe. But even so, this is his town. It's part of his DNA. Wouldn't it be fun if the two of you passed that DNA on to another generation?"

"You're dreaming," Cammie said. "You admitted it. Taking care of you in your *difficult* years cured him of any desire for fatherhood."

"True." Ainsley took a sip of her soft drink and wrinkled her nose. "But I think he hangs on to that just to keep women from getting close to him."

"I *was* close to him," Cammie said bluntly. "And he broke up with me when he found out I wanted kids."

"Ouch." Ainsley seemed abashed. "I just assumed the two of you drifted apart."

"Nope. Your sainted stepbrother cut me loose. The thought of having a baby with me scared him spitless."

Twelve

Drake stood just outside the kitchen door, unashamedly eavesdropping. He hadn't eaten lunch yet. He could have joined the two women. But the thought of food made him ill. To hear Cammie put reality into words so succinctly twisted the knot in his stomach even tighter.

She was right. He *had* been scared. It wasn't so much that he didn't want to have kids. The truth was, he was *scared* to have kids. He had spent many sleepless nights over the last seven years wondering if he was screwing up his stepsister's life.

That uncertainty had dogged him at every turn. For a man who was confident and focused in every other aspect of his life, his rocky relationship with his stepsister had pained him. He felt like their difficulties were entirely his fault.

How could he go through that again with a baby? What did he know about raising children? They weren't like horses and cows. A son or a daughter needed more than food and water. A child needed love and nurturing and attention.

Drake was pretty sure he was a failure at all those.

Finally, when enough time had passed and the conversation in the kitchen turned to innocuous topics, he walked into the room.

Even though his stepsister and his lover had been talking about a television show and nothing more intimate, they both looked guilty. Had they guessed he'd been in the hall for some time?

Drake pasted a carefree smile on his face. "Any news about Pumpkin?"

Cammie blushed, as though she couldn't look at him without remembering last night. "No," she said. "Haley Lopez promised to keep me in the loop, but apparently there's nothing to tell."

"You want a sandwich?" Ainsley asked.

He ruffled the ends of her hair. "No, thanks." He reached in the fridge for a bottle of water. "What about Sierra Morgan? Have we heard anything else from her?"

Again, Cammie shook her head. "She really wanted to do a follow-up story, but there's the same problem—no new information."

"I don't get it," Ainsley said. "What about security cameras and all that *NCIS* stuff? How did *no one* see what happened?"

"It was the middle of a huge parking lot," Drake said, sitting down across from Cammie and adjacent to his stepsister. "Whoever did this was careful not to get caught."

He could see that the conversation was bothering Cammie, so he changed the subject. "Ains," he said. "I need to talk to you about something important. Why don't we go to my office?"

His hideaway was a small room on the back of the house. He rarely used it anymore, but it was outfitted with all the necessary tech gadgets.

Ainsley gave him on odd stare. "I have no secrets from Cammie," she said.

Drake frowned, feeling as if the two women in his life were ganging up on him. "Maybe I do," he said.

Cammie jumped to her feet. "I'll leave you two alone. You have things to discuss."

Drake grabbed her wrist. "Good grief. Sit down. I was kidding. If Ainsley doesn't care, then I don't."

"Stay, Cammie," Ainsley said. "I might need reinforcements."

"You're making a big deal about nothing," Drake said. "All I wanted was to get your opinion about selling the ranch."

Both women were silent. Tight-lipped.

Finally, Ainsley sighed. "It's your property. I don't have a say."

"Is that true?" Now Cammie glared at him as if he was throwing Ainsley out on the street.

"Technically, yes," he said. "My father never changed his will before he died. Not intentionally, I'm sure. He was always busy, and financial details weren't his priority. But as it happens, everything came to me at their deaths. I've made sure that half of it is Ainsley's, of course."

His stepsister batted her eyes at him. "My hero." She made a face as she spoke to Cammie. "Why should I inherit a ranch that's been in the Rhodes family for generations? My mom was only married to Drake's dad for a year. I'm fine."

Then she looked back at Drake. "Seriously. It's your decision."

"But?" He lifted an eyebrow."

Cammie frowned. "Why is there a *but*?"

Drake saw the shadows under her eyes. He should feel bad for putting them there, but he was having a hard time concentrating on anything but the memory of Cam's naked body. That was the sole reason he had asked to speak to Ainsley in private.

He laughed. "There's always a *but* with Ainsley. She has opinions about everything. Many opinions."

"You're mean," Ainsley pouted.

"But you're not denying it. Go ahead," he said. "Speak your piece."

Ainsley stood and went to lean against the sink, facing Drake and Cammie. She crossed her arms, looking fierce. "Selling would be a mistake. I don't know if you're having some kind of midlife crisis, but this is dumb, Drake."

"I'm not even thirty," he protested.

Cammie snickered.

Ainsley went on. "You've always loved the ranch. And I'm pretty sure you regretted buying this house when we could have both been living there."

Drake leaned his chair back on two legs. "Maybe that's true. But things have changed. I've changed."

It surprised him when Cammie spoke. Her gaze seemed to see through his walls. "How?" she asked. "How have you changed? You're still closed off and a loner. Neither your stepsister nor I know what you're thinking most of the time."

Drake flinched, feeling the need to defend himself but not knowing what to say. An uncomfortable silence reigned in the kitchen.

Ainsley straightened. "I'm still not feeling a hundred percent," she said. "I think I'll go rest and read a magazine. Besides, if you're flying out tomorrow, Drake, I'm sure you and Cammie have things to talk about."

When his stepsister disappeared into the hall and up the stairs, they could hear her footsteps on the floor overhead. Drake exhaled. "She's right. We do need to talk."

Cammie fair skin paled even more. "About what?" She jumped up and began tidying the kitchen, as if she couldn't stand to be too close to him.

He shook his head slowly. "You. Me. Last night."

Now, two streaks of color high on her cheekbones proclaimed that she was either upset or embarrassed or both. "It was good," she said, the words flat.

"Good enough for a repeat tonight?" He wasn't expecting anything of the kind, but he wanted to see what she would say.

Cammie stopped what she was doing and stared at him. "I saw the printout of the flight info you gave Ainsley," she said. "You have to leave the house at 4:00 a.m. I don't think you have time for fooling around."

"I wonder why they call it that?" he said. "Makes it sound unimportant."

"Maybe the word you're looking for is *casual…*or *fun.*"

He stood and took two steps in her direction. Cammie backed up against the refrigerator. Her hands were shoved in the pockets of her faded jeans. She looked young and innocent and incredibly appealing.

It was time for the question he had dreaded. But he couldn't move forward until he knew the truth. "Cam?"

He saw her throat move as she swallowed. "Yes?"

"Can I ask you something about your baby plans?"

A frown line appeared between her eyebrows. "I suppose."

"Why artificial insemination? Why not adopt?"

His question surprised her. He could tell.

She rubbed her forehead as if their sleepless night had given her a headache. "Well, I always hoped I would have more than one child. And I like the idea of adopting a boy or girl who might be a little older…maybe even seven or eight. You know…someone who has been overlooked."

"That doesn't really answer my question," he said. "Why artificial insemination?"

Cammie shrugged, her expression hard to read. "I want to be pregnant," she said. "I want to carry a baby."

Drake shouldn't be surprised. Not really. But could he live with the idea that another man's seed had created a child in Cammie's womb? His feelings were Neanderthal, most likely. But they were his feelings, and he didn't know what to do with them.

"I understand," he said. And he did. The image of Cammie with a rounded belly and a maternal glow tugged at a sore place in his heart.

Perhaps she wanted to change the subject, or maybe it was just his day for being shocked out of his complacency.

She actually relaxed her wary stance and came to him, sliding her arms around his waist and resting her cheek over his heart. "There's something I've wanted to ask *you*," she said, her voice soft and filled with feminine secrets.

"Oh?" He held her close, feeling his body's inevitable reaction, but concentrating on her words. He couldn't see her face in this position.

Cammie sighed. "You've made me curious about Australia. I'm tied down until after the gala, but what would you think if I came to visit you in Sydney?"

Cammie was so close to Drake there was no way she could miss the way his body stiffened.

He cleared his throat. "Um…"

Her heart shriveled. She'd thought he would be excited. Instead, she felt his shock and something else... dismay?

In a moment of blinding hurt, she jerked away from him. *"It was your idea,"* she said, tears burning her eyes. "But I get it. It's fine to screw around while you're in town. But me following you is not so appealing anymore. You've scratched the itch."

"No, Cammie..."

He held out a hand to touch her, but she slapped it away, a huge sob building in her chest. "I'm so stupid. I keep expecting you to change, but you're the same man who broke up with me two years ago. Go to hell, Drake. Or to Australia. I don't care. But this time, do me a favor. Don't come back."

Cammie fled down the hall toward the back of the house and out into the sun-warmed yard. All around her, autumn frolicked. The day was beautiful, blue-skied and warm. The trees bent in the breeze. Texas was bright and verdant. But her world lay in ashes.

Somewhere deep in her silly, daydreaming heart, she had expected Drake to follow her. When he didn't, the tears came hard and fast. She was so tired of wanting things beyond her reach.

Her brother wouldn't come home despite her repeated pleas. Her father only cared about her organizational skills. Her mother was...well, who knew? Mostly a stranger now. And then there was Pumpkin, who despite everything Cammie had done for him would soon be going away.

What was wrong with her? Why did she offer up her heart only to let it be bruised and battered? Why did she let Drake drag her into his orbit again only to reject her even now when she thought they had been growing closer?

Unfortunately, she didn't have the luxury of wallowing in her self-pity. The baby monitor was still in the kitchen.

She dried her face on the hem of her shirt and marched back inside. Puffy eyes were impossible to conceal, but she had little pride left.

The kitchen was empty, as was the living room. She saw no trace of Drake but found Ainsley in the guest room feeding Pumpkin.

Ainsley's glance was sympathetic, almost more than Cammie could bear. "Drake asked me to look after the baby. He said you needed a moment alone."

"And is he still here?"

Ainsley shook her head slowly. "No. He took his keys and wallet and left."

"To go where?"

"I have no idea," Ainsley said. "I'm so sorry, Cammie. I know he must have hurt you somehow."

Cammie sat down on the edge of the bed. "It's my own fault. I keep expecting him to be someone he's not. And yet I keep coming back for more."

"Are you okay?"

"I will be. I just wish they would find Pumpkin's parents so I could get out of this house." She thumped the nearest pillow with her fist. "I want to go home."

Ainsley shook her head slowly. "No, you don't. Not really. You want to keep this sweet little boy."

"But we both know I can't. Love sucks."

"Now you're just being crazy."

Ainsley's droll comment made Cammie laugh in spite of her mood. "Thanks for covering for me."

"Well, we're a team now. When Drake leaves tomorrow, it will be just you and me taking care of this little sweetie."

Cammie flinched. "So, he's still going?"

"As far as I know."

It was bad enough that Drake was leaving. But to know he no longer cared enough to extend their relationship beyond today was a pain Cammie couldn't shake.

She stood and paced. "How are you feeling? Do your incisions hurt?"

"I'm better every day," Ainsley said. "Are you being nice, or is there a point to your questions?"

Busted. Cammie lifted her shoulders and let them fall, taking a deep breath in the process. She wouldn't let Drake destroy her a second time. "I desperately need to get a dress for the Cattleman's Club gala, and I'm running out of time. Do you think you could handle solo babysitting for a couple of hours?"

"Of course." Ainsley beamed. "This little fella and I will be fine. Go do what you want to do. Take your time."

Cammie changed clothes rapidly and gathered what she would need for her outing. She wanted to go by her place and check on things, but her home was in the opposite direction. That would have to wait for another day.

It wasn't fair to Ainsley to abandon her for very long.

Cammie made two brief stops and finally ended up at a high-end ladies' clothing store that concentrated on bridal and special occasion gowns. Fortunately for Cammie—probably because it was the middle of the afternoon on a weekday—the shop was empty. The single employee greeted her new customer warmly and jumped into action, gathering stacks of dresses for Cammie to try.

After the first dozen, Cammie was discouraged. She put on her own clothes again and came out of the fitting room. "So far I'm zero for twelve."

"Not to worry. We have plenty more."

With Cammie's red hair, some colors didn't work at

all. One dress caught her eye because it was a little out of the ordinary. It was a deep forest green, fashioned close to the body and skimming her hips to the floor. Spaghetti straps supported a low-cut bodice. All over the delicate fabric, tiny, sparkly beads shimmered.

"I like this one," Cammie said. "I'll try it on next. Unless you think it's too fancy for the upcoming gala."

"Not at all," the woman said. "Everybody wants a reason to dress up these days. I've sold dozens of eye-catching gowns. And I think this one is probably going to be perfect on you."

Cammie stepped behind the curtain. The cut of the dress would make a bra impossible to hide. The bodice was lined and stiffened with boning. After stripping down to her undies…again…she slipped the beautiful garment over her head and reached behind, managing to get the zipper up.

The woman who looked back from the gilt-framed, floor-length mirror was almost a stranger. Cammie scooped her hair in one hand and held it on top of her head. Maybe she would try an updo for the night at the Cattleman's Club gala.

The dress was definitely flattering.

But she wouldn't mind a second opinion just to be sure. She pushed the curtain aside and stepped out onto the small platform. "What do you think of this one?"

Everything in the room spun when she saw not the saleslady, but Drake Rhodes. He stood, tall and gorgeous, with his arms crossed over his chest. The store employee was nowhere to be seen.

Drake's expression was serious, his blue eyes closer to midnight than summer sky. In fact, he seemed stunned. "It's absolutely perfect," he said, the words gruff. "You look like a princess."

Cammie resisted the urge to cover her chest with her hands. She had a lot of bare skin exposed. "How did you find me?" she asked.

"Ainsley told me you had gone shopping for a gala dress. Not too many places in town available to do that. Natalie Valentine's shop seemed like the best bet."

"Why?" Cammie asked. "Why are you here?" He hadn't followed her to the backyard when she ran away from him. Why now?

His face was all planes and angles. In his eyes she fancied she saw pain, but that didn't make any sense. His demeanor was grim.

"Will you go out to the ranch with me?" he asked.

On any other day, she would have jumped at the chance. But now it hurt too much. She couldn't keep up the pretense that they were only friends with benefits. She loved the stubborn, frustrating man, and it was tearing her apart.

"I'm almost through here," Cammie said slowly. "But I've been gone too long. I have to get back to the house and relieve Ainsley."

"I've already talked to her," he said. "Mrs. Hampton is there now. The two of them are happy to care for the baby until you and I get back."

Cammie was at a loss. This didn't seem like a casual invitation. But on the other hand, what possible reason could Drake have for taking her to the ranch?

"I think I'll pass," she said. "But thanks anyway." She didn't say *maybe another time*. If Drake was selling the ranch, she would never see it again. That thought was both sad and painful.

She took a step backward, preparing to disappear into the fitting room.

Drake scowled. "Stop, Cam. I know I handled our last

conversation badly. I'm sorry about that. You took me by surprise. I didn't—"

Cammie held up her hand. "No, no, no, Drake." She halted the words tumbling from his gorgeous lips. "I'm the one who should apologize. In the past, I've accused you of being inflexible, but maybe *I'm* the one who needs to bend occasionally. If I truly care about you, and I do, then I need to think about abandoning a few of my non-negotiables. That's why I mentioned Australia. I thought on neutral ground we might find a way to…" *To what?* She didn't know how to end that sentence, so she left it hanging.

Her explanation didn't seem to make things better. In fact, Drake was more grim-faced than ever.

"Cam…" He held out both hands. "Please. I have things to say, and we need somewhere with no interruptions."

What was left to *say*? He was leaving Royal tomorrow. Clearly, he had no interest in her following him to Australia. Still, curiosity was a powerful emotion. That, and the desire to spend a few more precious hours with the man she loved.

"Okay," she said, giving in mostly because she wanted to… "Let me pay for the dress, and I'll meet you outside."

His gaze narrowed. "I'll wait right here. You might duck out the back door."

She turned on her heel and flounced away. Unfortunately, the space she had to cover was three steps at most, so it was hard to make a dramatic retreat.

The dressing cubicle didn't actually have a door that closed. The only barrier between her and Drake was a pair of heavy damask drapes striped in gold and burgundy. Normally, they were tied back with ornate cords.

When closed, anyone who really wanted to might peek through the tiny gaps.

Cammie stripped off the gown, laying it with care across the satin-covered chair. She dressed rapidly, feeling as though Drake might have X-ray vision. Her nipples pebbled at the thought. He was so close and yet so far away.

When she was presentable, she ran a brush through her hair and touched up her lip gloss. Finally, she couldn't delay any longer. As she shoved back the curtains and exited the small area, she saw that Drake had sprawled in one of the comfy chairs designated for spouses or other waiting guests.

He rolled to his feet when Cammie came out. She wondered if he noticed the transformation from prom queen to tomboy. Her clothing—old jeans and a very casual cream-colored sweater—was not what she would have chosen to wear for a heart-to-heart with her lover. Already, she felt at a disadvantage.

Still, why did it matter what she was wearing? Drake had seen her naked, had made love to her again and again. If his regard for her was no more than physical, clothes were the least of her worries.

Thirteen

Drake drove in the general direction of the ranch, winding through town, taking his time before getting out into the countryside. He should have been working his game plan, gently moving the conversation in the direction he wanted it to go.

But all he could concentrate on was how Cammie had looked in that dark emerald dress. Vibrant, sexy. Utterly desirable in every way. He had wanted to take her just like that…to lift her skirts and tumble her over the arm of a chair. The urge had been so powerful, he'd actually felt sweat bead his forehead.

Now, to keep his hands from trembling, he gripped the steering wheel.

He drove on autopilot. The air inside the car was heavy and silent, crushed perhaps by the weight of the deep, arctic crevasse between them. Cammie didn't want to be here, that was for certain.

The ranch gates were not open this time. It was late in

the afternoon. The day laborers would have gone home. His on-site guys would be in the bunkhouse having a beer and getting ready for dinner.

Drake put the car in Park, opened the gate, moved the car and closed the gate. The metal bars were heavy and hard to manage. Cammie didn't offer to help, nor did he ask.

He took the same route he had followed earlier. Only this time, he stopped at the house. Cammie got out and stared at the two-story Texas home where Drake had been reared. There had been spankings aplenty, but he had never doubted that he was loved.

She had her arms wrapped tightly around her as if she was cold. But even with the sun going down, the air was mild. He suspected her unconscious posture was protective.

He faced her across the top of the car. "I'd like to go for a ride. Together. On one horse. Is that okay with you?"

"Sure." She shrugged. There was little enthusiasm in the word.

Instead of going inside, he walked around the house toward the barn. Cammie followed him. Drake had called ahead and asked one of the wranglers to put the big saddle on Drake's favorite stallion.

The horse was waiting, raring to go. He lifted his head and whinnied when Drake approached the stall. "Hey there, old boy. Ready to stretch your legs?"

Fortunately, the vigorous animal was far more excited about the plan than Drake's human guest.

Cammie wrinkled her nose. "Isn't this Diablo?"

Drake checked the cinch automatically. "Yep. But he's older now. He'll behave." He glanced over his shoulder. "Front or back?"

This time, the wrinkle in her brow threatened to become permanent. "Front, I guess. I want to see where I'm going." She pulled an elastic band from her pocket and secured her hair low on the back of her neck.

"Fair enough." Drake swung into the saddle and reached down. "Grab my hand."

In the past, they had done this dozens of times. Cammie remembered the routine. She let him pull her up easily. When she settled between his arms, he picked up the reins. "Here we go."

It was dangerous to ride in the dark. Drake's plan was smashed up against the need to keep Cammie safe. He had a limited amount of daylight.

Because of that, he let Diablo have his head, going from a trot in the barnyard to a flat-out gallop when they exited the fence. Cammie was forced into Drake's chest whether she wanted to be or not.

He inhaled her scent, losing himself in the mad dash, wanting to ride forever with the woman he loved in his embrace. But there were things to be said. When they approached the tree where he had done his heavy thinking earlier in the day, Drake slowed the horse and stopped on top of the rise.

He wound the reins over the lowest branch, helped Cammie down and walked her to the far side of the hill that faced the sunset. There was a stump and a rock. He gave her the stump and sat facing her.

Cammie focused her attention on the colors of the sky. If he had special ordered the moment, it couldn't have been any more perfect. Because his Cam seemed unable to look at him, he saw her in profile.

Strong chin. Cute nose. Smooth brow. Strands of hair that had escaped during their ride, dancing in the breeze.

With the moment now at hand, Drake found his voice frozen.

Cammie turned her head. "Why are we here, Drake?"

He swallowed. "I need your opinion."

"On what?"

"On whether or not to sell the ranch."

That cute but aggravating frown was back. "Why ask me? I'm no finance whiz."

He stood at the edge of forever and saw both ways this could go. "Because I love you," he said gruffly.

Cammie was stunned. And not at all sure she had heard him correctly. For a man who had just professed love to a woman, he looked remarkably miserable.

"We'll circle back to that last bit," she said, refusing to believe him. "Again, I'll ask, why my opinion? Either you want to keep this place, or you don't."

Perhaps she wasn't being very diplomatic, but she was confused. And afraid.

Drake leaned forward, resting his hands on his knees. "When we were dating, did you ever visualize the two of us living here together?"

"Um…" That was a tough one. But he was looking at her so intently, she had to answer truthfully. "We were *dating*," she said. "It was casual."

He refused to be put off. "A year and a half isn't casual. We might not have made any firm plans, but we were more than casual. Surely you thought about it."

"Fine," she said, giving in to his inquisition. "Yes. Once in a while. I did think about it. I could see the two of us growing old here."

"Why did you never say anything?"

"Good grief, Drake. A woman can't wear her heart on her sleeve. And certainly not with a man like you."

He raised an eyebrow. "A man like me?"

"You were a complicated puzzle in almost every way.

I knew you enjoyed the sex, but beyond that, I had no clue what you were thinking. Needless to say, when we finally shared our dreams for the future, it became crystal clear that your bucket list and mine weren't even written in the same language. And then when you dumped me, it was so gradual at first, I didn't see the end coming."

His expression grew darker still. "I made a mistake," he said. "A bad one. I hurt you. I'm sorry, Cammie."

She shook her head slowly, trying to sift through his words. "It wasn't your fault," she said. "You were trying to do the right thing in a bad situation."

"But I made it worse. I didn't know until you were gone how much you meant to me. That's trite, I know, but it's true."

Because I love you. His words echoed in her head. She honestly wondered if she had dreamed them. She did have an overactive imagination. "Drake…" She shook her head slowly. "I don't know what this is about, but it doesn't make sense. We ran into each other purely by chance at the hospital. You were racing home to see Ainsley, who was seriously ill. You said it yourself…reuniting with me wasn't at the top of your list."

He scowled. "You told me I was complicated. Maybe I am. And maybe I'm stupid, too. About women, at least. The subconscious is a powerful beast."

"People don't change overnight. *You* don't change overnight. I get that you're conflicted about selling the ranch, but that has nothing to do with me."

His hands fisted on his knees. She could almost see the control he was fighting to keep. "I told you why. I love you."

He was saying words she had longed to hear, but he was so obviously tormented, she couldn't in good conscience take him at his word. "I offered to visit you in

Australia. To see if there was some middle ground we could find. You practically threw your back out avoiding that idea. I don't understand you."

"I don't understand myself," he muttered. "I've been thinking about the baby thing…a lot. Maybe it wouldn't be so bad."

Cammie leaped to her feet, suddenly unable to continue this conversation. It was tearing her apart. "May we go?" she asked with little finesse. "I'm getting cold."

That wasn't entirely true, but this windblown sunset moment was too beautiful and not beautiful enough. Even if she could believe his words, one of them was going to have to choose. If either was wrong, the relationship was doomed.

Drake rose and untied the horse, not saying a word. The trip back was far slower. Dark piled up quickly when the sun slipped behind the horizon. For the last quarter mile, the horse had to pick his way cautiously.

In the barn, Cammie hopped down. "You'll have to take care of the horse, right?"

Drake shook his head. "No. One of my men is on standby. As soon as I text him, he'll come."

They walked toward the house, close but not touching.

Drake unlocked the door and turned on a light. Someone had laid logs and kindling in the fireplace. With one match, the fire blazed.

Cammie pulled up a small rocker and stared into the flames. Her stomach growled audibly.

Finally, Drake chuckled. "Stay there and get warm. I'll bring the food."

"You don't need help?"

"Nope."

Five minutes later he returned bearing a platter of turkey sandwiches, two water bottles and a bag of chips.

"It's a far cry from the Bellamy, but it was all I could arrange on short notice."

"It looks good." Cammie wasn't going to complain. She had only eaten a sandwich for lunch, and it was late now.

Drake pulled up the chair that matched hers. Their knees were almost touching as they wolfed down the simple meal.

"We should get back," Cammie said abruptly. "I need to check on the baby."

"I just texted Ainsley. Everything is fine." He wiped his mouth with a napkin and stared at her.

"What?" Cammie said. "Do I have mayonnaise on my chin?"

Drake took her plate, stacked it with his and set both on the hearth. Then he leaned back in his seat, his big frame dwarfing the small rocker, and sighed. "When a man tells a woman he loves her, he usually expects some kind of answer."

"Oh." Cammie felt woozy. "You were serious?"

"Of course I was serious. Why would I say it if I didn't mean it?"

The look of indignation on his face almost made her laugh. But the situation was far too serious and fraught with pitfalls. "You've been under a lot of stress," she muttered. "Sometimes people crack."

His jaw went granite hard. Those blue eyes that were her downfall pinned her with a laser gaze. "Do you want to tell *me* something, Cam?"

"Like what?" Anxiety threatened to overwhelm her.

"Do you love me?"

There was so much tenderness in his words, she felt tears burn her eyes. "Of course I love you." She couldn't look at him. "Don't be dumb. Why else would I let you crook your finger and I'd come running after two years apart? A woman doesn't do that just because you're good in bed."

"I see."

When she sneaked a look at him, his lips were twitching. "Don't laugh at me, Drake," she said. "This is serious. I would give up having kids to be with you. I *would*. But what if I get mean and bitchy down the road and start to resent you and ruin our marriage? Adoption wouldn't be much better from your standpoint. We could find an older child so we could skip over the baby years, but Ainsley wasn't even a baby. She was *fifteen*, and look how that turned out."

He scooped her out of her chair and carried her to the comfy sofa nearby. "Did I propose?" he asked. "I must have missed that part." The huge piece of furniture was upholstered in a soft, crinkly velvet that felt both authentic to the house and yet extremely comfortable. The rust-colored fabric echoed the colors in the fire.

When Drake snuggled her close, she felt how fast his heart was beating. And he definitely had a boner. Somehow, that made her feel better.

When he stroked her hair, she felt like crying.

"I want to have babies with you Cammie," he said, his voice gruff with emotion. "I swear I do. And it doesn't matter to me if we adopt or go another route. The important thing is that you believe me. I'm not saying this just to get what I want."

"What *do* you want?" she asked, her words tremulous.

"You," he said simply. "And a family. I've been a selfish, stubborn idiot. I almost lost you because I was so blind. I don't know why I clung to that no-baby thing for so long. I've given it a lot of thought lately, and maybe it was because I was scared, scared I couldn't be a good dad. I'm not used to failing all that often, but being a parent is so much harder than succeeding at business. I think I didn't want to admit how helpless I felt, how uncertain and unqualified. I was afraid to take a chance. But now I realize. You and I together can do *anything*. A baby is a miracle. Little Pumpkin has reminded me of that. And all the trauma with Ainsley was worth it because of the relationship it forged. She and I are solid."

Suddenly, Cammie's pocket vibrated. She wriggled sideways, pulled out her cell and looked at the screen. It was Haley Lopez. After hours.

"Are you going to answer it?" Drake asked.

Cammie couldn't hit the button. "What if they've found Pumpkin's mother? What if they're taking him away tonight?"

She lost it then. From the moment she found a baby on her car and then saw Drake striding back into her life, her world had been turned upside down. Thinking Drake was leaving tomorrow had been the final straw.

She let the call go to voice mail because she was sobbing too hard to speak.

Drake let her cry it out, petting her and whispering sweet things in her ear. About how beautiful she was and how smart and how caring.

Eventually, she ran out of steam. "Sorry," she whispered. "I got your shirt all wet."

His arms tightened around her. "Marry me, Cam. Let's build a family together."

She laid her cheek over his heart. "Yes."

It was such an easy thing to say. Drake jerked when he heard it, as if she had struck him somehow. Surely he wasn't surprised by her answer. Not after this week.

Even so, she felt the tension in him.

"But there's something I have to tell you," he said.

There was an odd note in his voice. Because she was anxious again, she let her words flow, unfiltered. "What? You have another fiancée in Australia? You're not really rich? Or maybe you already have some kids tucked away I don't know about?"

He shifted her so she was sitting beside him. The expression on his face was sober. "Before you commit to a lifetime with me, darlin', you should know. I may not be *able* to get you pregnant."

"Why? What do you mean?" She searched his face to see if he was kidding.

But Drake wasn't joking. "I was snorkeling near Melbourne and got careless. Cut my leg on some coral. Didn't go to the doctor right away. Let the wound get infected. By the time I went in to get it looked at, they were concerned about flesh-eating bacteria."

Her eyes widened. "That's not an urban legend?"

He choked out a laugh. "No. It's a real thing. They put me on steroids and almost a month of a high-powered antibiotic. The doctor this morning told me it can cause male sterility."

"*Can?* But not for sure?"

"He suggested that before I start trying for a child with my partner, I should consult a specialist."

In a sudden burst of clarity, Cammie saw her whole future. "That's fine," she said, unbuttoning his shirt and stroking his collarbone. "Sounds like a challenge to me."

"Cammie?" His voice was strained. "What are you doing?"

"I just got engaged. That calls for celebration sex." She kissed him with all she was feeling, exulting inwardly when his arms came around her and dragged her against his chest.

He kissed her right back. And then some. Suddenly the room was *too* warm.

Drake began stripping her out of her clothes, even as she clumsily tried to help him. Both of them gave up half-way through. He eased her onto her back, his eyes dark with arousal. "I didn't bring any protection."

Cammie rubbed her thumb over his bottom lip. "I don't care if you don't."

Heat flared in his gaze. "This is so damn sexy," he growled.

As he freed his erection and moved between her thighs, she smiled. "Trying to make a baby?"

"No. Making love to my gorgeous fiancée." He thrust deep, forcing a keening cry from her throat.

She wrapped her legs around his back. "I haven't seen a ring yet," she panted. "So it's not entirely official."

"Feels pretty damn official to me."

They were hungry for each other. It had been hours since he touched her like this. Cammie came before he did, crying out. This time was different, though. She felt hope and joy and a blinding certainty that they were going to make it.

When Drake climaxed moments later, his big body rigid and hot above hers, she buried her face in his shoulder.

Wow. She stroked his back, or the part she could reach. His shirt was shoved up to his armpits. Her sweater was in the same shape.

She started to laugh. She couldn't help it.

Drake sat up finally, his expression priceless. "Not the reaction I was hoping for, my Cam."

"Look at us," she said.

When he did, a sheepish wince was his only response.

She straightened her clothes and stood up. "I guess I should listen to the voice message from Haley."

Drake took care of his own attire and yawned. "She's probably working the late shift and is just checking in."

"I hope that's all it is." Cammie's heartbeat skittered as she pressed the button and listened. Relief flooded her as she processed the message. "They haven't found Pumpkin's family yet," she said, looking at Drake with tears in her eyes. "But because the situation is dragging on, the social services lady needs to do another home visit."

"See," Drake said. "Crisis averted."

He took her wrist and reeled her in, kissing her lazily, pointing out without words that the hum of excitement between them was only momentarily banked. "Besides," he said. "You're a tough woman. You've known all along that the day will come when you have to give Pumpkin back. You'll be fine, I promise. I'll be right there beside you when we hand him over. I love you, Cammie. And I'll love our babies, however we have them. I'm sorry it took me so long to realize that I was being an ass."

"I was part of the problem," she insisted. "I was so fixated on getting pregnant, I couldn't admit that I loved you more than I wanted my dream. *You* are my dream," she said. "Babies or no babies. If I have you, I'll be happy."

"Take off your clothes," he said, his expression droll.

"Excuse me?" She lifted an eyebrow.

"Isn't this the occasion for makeup sex?"

"Goofy man. Let's go home to your wonderful bed." She paused, staring up at him with a teasing smile. "And my answer is no."

Shock flashed across his face. "No what?"

"No. Don't you dare sell this ranch."

He cupped her cheeks in his hands and kissed her until her toes curled. "Don't worry, Cam. I've got a very good imagination. I'm already thinking about all the ways I'm going to screw you in this house."

"And in the barn. And out under the stars. And—"

He put a hand over her mouth. "Don't tempt me, Camellia." He banked the fire and poured water on it.

Then they walked out to the car. A million stars shone overhead.

Cammie sighed. Had there ever been a more perfect night? Suddenly, she froze, her hand on the car door. "But what about your plane ticket tomorrow and the gala? We didn't figure out what to do."

He tucked her in and joined her in the car, leaning over to kiss her one last time before he started the engine. His smile was a flash of white in the semidarkness. "We covered the important stuff, my love. The rest will work itself out."

* * * * *

WAYS TO WIN AN EX

MAUREEN CHILD

To Patti and Bill Hambleton for so many reasons.
You were there in the darkness and kept a light burning
for me. You held me together when I thought that would
be impossible. You loved him, too, and you help me
smile at the memories.

I'm so grateful for you both. And I love you.

One

"This is the way we've always done things, Serena."

Her mother, Candace, stood in Serena Carey's office and looked down at her. "You're making so many changes, I just don't know how it can all work out. Heaven knows, I don't want to interfere…"

But you're going to, Serena thought. Every year, the Carey Center hosted a fundraiser for their charitable organization, For the Kids. It was the biggest event of the year and donors came from far and wide to be part of it.

And until *this* year, Candace Carey had been in charge. But she'd handed over the reins—in theory—to Serena six months ago. Now it seemed the older woman was having a few second thoughts.

"Mom," Serena said patiently, "everything is handled. You have to trust me on this."

Candace linked her fingers together at the waist and started pacing in slow, elegant steps. Everything Candace did was elegant, Serena told herself, not without a little envy. Then her mother stopped, turned to look at her and bit her lip for a moment before speaking again. "Of course I trust you, Serena. But when we talked about this six months ago, you didn't mention making so many changes. Music. Food. Flowers. Everything is changing and I just don't know if it's the right thing to do." She actually wrung her hands a bit, and that was so unlike the unflappable Candace that Serena felt a little guilty for throwing so many changes at her mother all at once.

"Change isn't always a bad thing, Mom," Serena pointed out. "For example, the cinnamon highlights in your hair are fabulous."

Candace perked up, smoothed one hand over her short, elegant cut. "You're trying to smooth me out, I can tell. And you're very good at it. But, honey, the gala is the biggest event of the year. The children are counting on the money we collect from our donors…"

Serena stood up, came around her desk and took both of her mom's hands in hers. "Do you really think if the flowers are different people won't donate to the charity?"

"There's something to be said for tradition, you know," her mother countered without answering the question. "For example, we've always used the Swing Masters for the music and—"

"Mom…" Serena had known going in that there would be some pushback when she wanted to make changes. Which was the reason, she told herself, she hadn't mentioned those changes six months ago. Remembering that her mother was the one who had started this charity and built it into a real giant, Serena took a breath, then said gently, "The Swing Masters are in their seventies now."

"What does that have to do with anything?"

Age was tricky since her parents were quickly closing in on seventy themselves. But she persisted. "Mom, they're retired. They only get together again now to play for the fundraiser."

"Exactly."

Serena squeezed her mom's hands, then let her go. "The new band can play the old standards, as well as more modern music. I think our donors will enjoy it."

"I don't know…"

Serena had already talked to Leo Banks, the lead guitarist in the Swing Masters, and had been assured that they were perfectly happy to stay retired. So she just hugged her mom and smiled. "Trust me."

"I do, but so many changes all at once…" Candace shook her head and her short chestnut hair swung gracefully at her jaw. And the cinnamon highlights really did look spectacular. "You've hired a roaming photographer, as well?"

"Yes, and you're going to love it." Serena tamped down her impatience. She'd only been back working at the Carey Center for a couple of years, so she was going to have to earn her family's respect and confidence.

Growing up, she'd never been interested in having a career. Actually, she'd never had a plan for her life at all like her siblings always seemed to—well, except for Justin, of course. All she'd really wanted was to find love and have a family of her own. Well, that hadn't worked out so well, had it? Now her marriage was over and she was trying to discover what exactly she wanted for her life. And Serena was slowly learning how to speak up—and stand up—for herself. All her life, Serena had been willing to go with the flow. She hadn't made waves because nothing had really meant enough to her to fight for it.

Serena was teaching herself how to take a stand, because now building a life for herself and her daughter was everything. Working for the family was safe, but carving out her own space in the business was hard. She loved her family, but they weren't used to seeing her give her opinions and, she realized, that was her own fault because she'd always been the easygoing one. The peacemaker. And though she still preferred serenity, that was something she'd never really experience with the Careys.

Even the thought of it made her chuckle internally. Her family would never be called tranquil. And she wouldn't change them for anything. What she had to do was navigate the sometimes churning waters. And she was learning how to do that.

Serena was still too hesitant about speaking her mind, but she was getting better. Right now, she was finding her feet. Figuring out her path. And nobody had ever promised her it would be easy.

"It'll be fun, Mom. The photographer's got some great ideas and a fantastic reputation. People are going to love it." At least she hoped so. Her own future with the family business was riding on the success of the annual fundraiser. Yes, she'd made changes because, frankly, the bash had become a little staid. A little too ordinary. Nothing ever changed, and though people still attended, and they were still able to raise huge amounts of money for the charity, Serena thought the event itself should be more…fun.

Serena had gone over all her ideas with her sister, Amanda, and she'd loved them, too. So Serena wasn't really *worried*. Just…concerned. A little. And her mom's doubts weren't helping anything.

"The photographer is going to wander through the crowd, taking random shots, and then we'll flash the images onto two screens at opposite ends of the ballroom." Serena had contracted with the top photographer in Orange County, California, and trusted the woman would deliver on everything she had promised.

Candace bit her bottom lip.

Serena continued, and the more she talked about it, the better she felt. "Everyone at the gala will get a kick out of seeing themselves and their friends and families up on the big screens. And if anyone wants to buy prints, they can deal with the photographer directly. After the gala, we're going to post the images on our website, as a direct advertisement about what a great time everyone had—which will only increase donations *next* year."

Candace tipped her head to one side, studied her daughter for a long moment or two, then said, "You've done a lot of thinking about this. About all of it."

Yes, she had. Life might not have turned out exactly the way Serena had hoped it would, but she'd discovered that she was good at working with people. She liked pulling plans together and finding a way to make everything mesh. The gala was going to be her first big success—hopefully—and it was nice to have her mother notice.

"I have. Mom, you turned the gala over to me, and I promise I'm not going to let you down. It's going to be great." *Please*, let it be great. If the whole thing flopped, she'd never hear the end of it from the family. Already, her older brother, Bennett, was also questioning every change.

And her mother… Well, Candace had been in charge of the program for decades and had only handed over the reins because she'd believed her husband when he promised to retire. But since Martin was having a hard time letting go, Candace was fighting to regain control. And Serena was going to stand her ground.

This was new for her and she was sure a psychiatrist would have a field day with her motivations. But the truth was, she'd stood by when the man she loved broke her heart. And, God, she didn't even want to remember that she'd silently done nothing while he walked away from her.

Worse, though, was that Serena had allowed that suffocating pain to blind her to the faults of the man she'd married. And she hated knowing that it had taken forever for her to stand up for herself with Robert. But she finally had. She'd gotten a divorce and full custody of Alli and learned that she didn't *have* to be a doormat.

She still wasn't sure if the Carey Corporation was what she wanted to do for the rest of her life, but, damn it, she was here now. And she was going to make her mark and let everyone know that Serena Carey was no longer a pushover. And they had no one to blame but themselves. Because for some reason, since she'd entered the family business, she'd begun picking up some of the Carey family's ingrained competitive streak. Good thing? Bad thing? Who knew?

"I do have some ideas on the catering..."

Serena gave her mom's hand a quick squeeze and lied. Yes, she felt a little guilty, but she needed a break. "You know, so do I, and I've got a meeting with Margot Davis to go over the menu again in a few minutes."

"Oh, good. I'm happy to help with that," Candace said.

"But I think Amanda wanted to talk to you this morning about one of the acts for the Summer Sensation program." She should probably feel guilty for tossing her younger sister under the bus, but she didn't. It was just a small lie. A necessary one, and Serena would no doubt pay for it once she saw her sister.

"Oh." Candace nodded, smiled and said, "Then I'll go see your sister. But I would like to go over the menu for the fundraiser with you, Serena. After lunch?"

Smothering a sigh, she said, "Sure, Mom."

With her mother gone, Serena walked around her desk and dropped into the cream-colored leather chair. Swiveling around, she stared out the window at the greenbelt below the building that wound through the neighboring chrome-and-glass office buildings like a thick ribbon. In the distance, she could see the 405 Freeway and, well beyond that, a blue smudge that was the Pacific Ocean. And right about now, she wished she were standing on the shore, with the wind sliding through her hair and no sound but the pounding of the waves onto the sand.

"But since I'm not..." Serena turned around, picked up the phone and called Margot. "Hi," she said when the caterer answered. "Any chance you could come in now and meet about the menu? I know we were set for this afternoon, but I'd like to get it all ironed out before the rest of the family sees it."

"Absolutely." Margot Davis was as eager for the success of the fundraiser as Serena was. The annual gala at the Carey Center would be the biggest showcase the chef had ever had for her work and it could set her reputation for the future. "I can be there in half an hour."

"Terrific. See you then." When she hung up, Serena reassured herself that everything was working as it should. She had a great band lined up, a terrific new caterer that she'd found through a comprehensive search, a florist who was going to decorate the ballroom with tasteful, beautiful displays. She was in complete control. Nothing was going to go wrong.

Her assistant buzzed in. "What is it, Kelly?"

"There's a Jack Colton here to see you."

And just like that, a perfectly good day turned to crap.

She'd jinxed herself, of course, by thinking about how great things were going. That would teach her.

Scowling at the phone, she said, "Tell him I went to Tahiti."

With a little more warning, it was exactly what she would have done, rather than face Jack again.

The man she'd once loved and hoped to marry. The man she'd watched walk away from her. The man who was still appearing in her dreams, ensuring that she woke up hot and aching and furious with herself that even in her sleep Jack could turn her inside out. Her heartbeat sped up and she took a deep breath, trying to calm herself. It didn't help. Just knowing he was right outside her door made her...shaky.

With any luck, he'd simply go away.

An instant later, her office door opened and there he stood. Serena wasn't surprised. As she remembered it, nothing could stop Jack when he was determined to do something. That fact was both irritating and admirable. At the moment, she was going with irritation.

And, damn it, captivated.

She couldn't take her eyes off him. Was he even taller than he used to be? He stood well over six feet, with too long black hair that curled over the collar of his white shirt, and eyes as deep and dark as a sapphire. He gave her a half smile, closed her office door, then swept the edges of his black suit jacket back to tuck his hands into his slacks pockets. "Tahiti's changed. But you haven't. As gorgeous as ever, Serena."

She refused to be charmed.

"Really?" she asked with a short laugh. "I haven't seen you in seven years and the first thing you say is some lame compliment?"

"Not lame at all," he countered. "You're still beautiful."

"And you're still fast with meaningless flattery." She smiled and shook her head. "I'm not a simpleton, Jack. That's not going to get you very far."

He shrugged that off with another half smile that made her gullible heart do a quick flip. "It's not flattery if it's true."

Now she was annoyed with herself. Seven years since

she'd seen him and one look at him had her pulse pounding in spite of the way he'd ended things between them. Back then, Serena had been so...timid. She hadn't said a word when he walked away from her. Hadn't let him know that he'd ripped her heart out when he left. She hadn't been capable of standing up for herself then. But she'd changed. She wasn't the Serena he remembered. And just because her body was overreacting, it didn't mean she was going to do anything about it. "Go away, Jack."

"But I just got here."

Serena stood up because she wasn't going to stay seated while he stood as tall as a giant. Why wasn't he covered in boils or pimples? Why did he have to look so *good*? "What do you want, Jack?"

"Well, thanks for asking." He pulled his hands from his pockets and strolled across the room, like a man with nothing but time. He glanced around and she followed his gaze, seeing her office as he must be seeing it.

Pale rose walls, with framed photographs of the family dotting one wall. There was a plump, comfortable sofa, two matching armchairs and, on the opposite wall from her desk, a flat-screen TV. A library table held a small fridge and a single-cup coffee maker. The floors were polished oak, dotted with area rugs in faded jewel-toned colors.

"Your office is very like you," he pointed out, and she hated that he knew her well enough to notice. Not that she'd admit that.

"Think you know me, do you?"

"Always have," he said, and his voice seemed to rumble along her spine, sending a shiver she refused to acknowledge right down to her bones. He studied her for a long moment before adding, "Though there's something...different about you, too."

She choked out a short laugh of derision. "Wow, imagine that. I've changed in seven years. Let's see. Marriage. Having a child. Divorce. Joining the family company. Yeah," she said, nodding thoughtfully. "I suppose I am different."

"Touché," he said and bowed his head briefly in acknowledgment.

Steadying herself, Serena simply said, "I don't have time for this, Jack. Why are you here?"

"Right to business," he countered. "That's different, too. I don't remember you being interested in the Carey company."

She hadn't been. Then. "Like I said. Changes."

"Okay then, business. For starters, I want to buy a table at the fundraiser."

Well, that was a surprise. She hadn't seen Jack in years. Not since the night she'd confessed her love for him. He'd left the country the following day to *concentrate on the Colton Group hotel chain. Or to run and hide*, she mentally corrected.

After she'd picked up her shattered heart and taped it back together again, Serena remembered wondering if she was the only woman who'd had a man actually leave the *country* to get away from her.

"Why would you want to do that?" she asked.

"Supporting children in need? Sounds like a good cause to me."

"And you're all about altruism?"

One corner of his mouth tipped up. "Are you this hard on all of your donors?"

Serena locked her fingers together in front of her. "No, you're special."

His lips twitched and she nearly smiled.

"You've been gone for seven years, Jack. How do you even know about the fundraiser?"

"Please. The Carey gala has been one of the biggest events of the year for more than thirty years."

True.

"And," he added, "Bennett told me it was still on."

Serena smiled wryly. "Of course he did."

Jack laughed and walked closer. "I came in today to see him, let him know I was moving back to the States permanently."

Wary now, she watched him. "You are?"

"Yeah." He nodded, keeping his gaze fixed on hers. "I'll still have to travel to Europe for business, but this will be home."

Great. When Jack moved to London seven years ago, it actually helped Serena get over him. She knew he was far from California and she wouldn't be bumping into him all the time, so she could push him out of her mind and heart and keep him there. Then she'd met and married Robert and *mostly* stopped thinking about Jack at all.

Now he was moving back. And since he and Bennett were friends, that meant she'd probably be seeing a lot of Jack. Not that Serena was worried about being around him. She wasn't. Not at all. She simply didn't like to be reminded of mistakes, and having Jack around would be nothing but a constant reminder.

"So," he continued, snapping her out of her thoughts, "I think fifty thousand for a table at your gala is a good way to announce it."

Buying an entire table was certainly generous, but Serena wasn't so willing to make things easy on him. How like Jack Colton to stroll in and expect everything to roll his way. Well, not this time. "That is the usual price for a full table, Jack, but it's late. The gala is in just a couple weeks."

His eyes narrowed on her and Serena almost smiled. Almost.

"So the price of a table's gone up?"

She did smile then. She was about to find out how badly he wanted to make a statement at the gala. "Seventy-five thousand should do it."

Silence strung out between them as he watched her for a second or two before nodding. "All right, Serena. You make a fair point. I did come in late. And it is for a good cause, right?"

"Absolutely." And she had to admit, she was surprised. He hadn't even blinked when she raised the price on him. So did that mean he wanted to impress her? Was that part of the plan? Or was he simply so eager to get back into the life he'd walked away from that price was no object?

He walked closer to her desk and looked down at her. "Then put the Colton Group down for a table and I'll have my assistant wire you the money this afternoon."

Serena sat back in her chair and slowly, casually crossed her legs. "As soon as we've received the money, I'll reserve your table."

Jack laughed shortly. "No trust for an old friend?"

"Is that what we are?" Serena met his gaze and thought of all the things she could say. That they were never friends. That the connection between them had been so blistering hot, it was like trying to live on the surface of the sun. That they'd been lovers within hours of meeting and they hadn't parted until she'd whispered those three words designed to separate the men from the boys. That he'd broken all trust between them when he'd shattered her heart and left her standing alone in the rubble. She could have said all of that and more, but she didn't say any of it. "Friends?"

He shrugged. "If you want to be, sure."

"I have enough friends."

"Funny," he said. "Me, too." Another step closer. "So where does that leave us?"

Her heart pounded in her ears. Her blood rushed through her veins. Breathing was suddenly an effort, and still she looked into his eyes and said simply, "Nowhere, Jack. Exactly nowhere."

He tucked his hands into his pants pockets and strolled leisurely around the room. His gaze swept the framed photos and Serena felt as if he were examining her life. Her world. She didn't like it.

"Not true, Serena," he finally said and turned to face her. "We may not be friends, but for the moment, we will be working together."

She had a bad feeling about this. "What are you talking about?"

"Like I said, I was talking to Bennett about an idea I had that could help both of us and create some real buzz around the donations."

"Buzz?" Serena laughed shortly and pushed her butterscotch-blond hair back from her face. "The Carey Center *is* buzz. So thanks, but the Careys have been handling our own parties and events for a long time. I really don't think we need any new *ideas* from you." Though, apparently, her older brother thought so.

Did everyone in her family think she was incapable of running the gala and making it a success? Now Bennett was sticking his nose in and encouraging Jack to do the same?

His gaze locked with hers. "Don't dismiss it so quickly, Serena. You could at least hear the idea before shooting it down. What I'm proposing will get people talking. It will bring in even more money than usual to the fundraiser."

Okay, she could admit, at least to herself, that she was curious. Because if the gala raised more money than ever before while *she* was in charge, well, the family would have to notice, wouldn't they? She could finally put her own stamp on one corner of the Carey Corporation. And, frankly, it would convince the family—and maybe even herself—that she was capable of whatever she put her mind to. But to do that, she'd have to work with Jack Colton.

Nope. She'd find another way to show the family what she could do.

"Well," she said, moving out from behind her desk, "while it's fascinating that you and Bennett want to *help*, it's not necessary, thanks."

He folded his arms across his wide chest and braced his feet apart as if readying for a battle. Well, if he wanted one, she'd be happy to provide it.

"Bennett likes my idea," he said pointedly. "A lot."

She lifted her chin. "Bennett's not in charge."

One eyebrow arched. "You should tell him that."

"Oh, I will," she promised, already planning what she would say to her older brother.

"Great." He let his arms drop to his sides, then idly tucked his hands into his pockets again. "But first I'll tell you about the idea and then you'll know what you're arguing against."

Serena glared at him. All she really wanted was for Jack to leave. Actually, not entirely true. She wished he'd never been there at all. Because now that he'd been there, in her office, she'd always see him there. Like the ghost of lovers past, he'd haunt her, but she could get beyond that if he would just leave. He wouldn't, though. Not until he was good and ready. She knew that much about him hadn't changed.

Serena also knew exactly what she wanted to say to her brother Bennett, but she couldn't do that until Jack left. And, clearly, the man was going nowhere until he'd told her all about his brilliant *idea*.

"Fine." She hitched one hip higher than the other and tapped the toe of her red heeled sandal against the floor. "Tell me what your *brilliant* idea is."

He held up one finger. "Didn't say brilliant. I said it's a good idea. Plus, it will work for both the Carey Corporation and the Colton Group. It will bring you more donors and more money for the underprivileged kids. That's what it's all about, right?"

She took a deep breath and let it out again. He had a point. "Okay then, tell me."

Jack's mouth curved just a bit and Serena ignored it.

Mostly. It wasn't easy because, oh, she had such memories of that luscious mouth of his.

"All right. I'm going to donate stays at Colton Group hotels in a raffle you're going to run."

"What?" She stared at him, waiting for the punch line. "Donating hotel rooms? A raffle? That's the big plan?"

Frowning at her, he said, "Not just hotel rooms. Five-star hotel rooms. I'm donating twelve one-week stays at any of my hotels—here or in Europe—winner's choice, of course. And those weeks are all-inclusive. Meals. Airfare."

Stunned, Serena thought about what he was offering and had to admit that he was right. This kind of prize offering would certainly bring more people out. For the chance to win one of twelve one-week stays at a five-star hotel anywhere in the world, people would be willing to buy a lot of raffle tickets.

After a moment, she asked, "Twelve weeks to one winner, or twelve winners?"

He shrugged. "Up to you, since you're *in charge*. But I would think twelve winners would get the donations rolling in."

She tapped one finger against her bottom lip as her brain began to race with possibilities. Boy, she hated to admit that Jack was right. This was a spectacular prize, and she knew their donors would love it and, more important, *compete* for it. That would result in more money for the foundation and more children would be helped. It was a good idea.

Damn it.

"Agreed. Twelve winners would create more…eagerness." Then she tipped her head to one side and looked up at him. "What do you get out of this, Jack?"

He walked a little closer and Serena deliberately stood her ground. He wasn't that attractive, after all. Okay, yes, he was, but she didn't have to let him know she thought so.

"I've spent the last several years updating our hotels." He looked into her eyes. "The reputation that was fading ten years ago has been fixed. I want to get the word out that a Colton Group hotel is the only one worth staying at." He shrugged. "And I figured this was a damn good place to start."

"You never heard of ad space on TV, radio and online?"

His lips quirked. "What can I say? I like the personal touch. Bottom line is, Bennett wants us to work together to plan it out and set it all up to the best advantage for both of us."

"Work together." Nope, repeating the words didn't help her deal with it.

"Problem?"

"Why would there be a problem?" *So* many problems.

"Excellent." He buttoned his suit jacket and said, "So when do you want to start working on this?"

How about *never*?

"I'll get back to you on that after I talk to Bennett." Stalling wasn't refusing. It was just…putting off the inevitable. Forced to work with the man who had once broken her heart? She wasn't a teenager. She could do that. For the children. But, damn it, Bennett should have talked to her before agreeing to this with Jack.

"Fine. He has my new number. Call me when you're ready to talk." He headed for the door, and when he got there, he paused and looked back at her. "It's good to see you, Serena. I knew it would be."

She didn't answer. Apparently, he didn't require one, because in the next moment he opened the door, walked through it and was gone.

Again.

Two

Walking into Bennett's office, Jack had to silently admit that his meeting with Serena had gone better than he'd thought it would. His old friend was on the phone, so Jack took a moment to look around.

Bennett's office was so different from Serena's it was a wonder they were in the same building. The space was huge, maybe twice the size of Serena's, with a better view and floor-to-ceiling tinted windows making up one wall. The furnishings were sparse but starkly modern, with sharp lines, lots of chrome, glass and leather; it was, Jack thought, completely impersonal. He didn't see one damn thing in the room that reminded him of his friend. What had probably happened was Bennett hired a decorator who then got it all wrong and he hadn't cared enough to demand it be changed. That sounded like Bennett.

"Still alive, I see."

He turned, grinned and watched Bennett hang up the phone. "A little bruised, but yeah, breathing."

"Was I right?" Bennett leaned back in his desk chair. "Did she soak you for a table?"

"Yeah, she did. You called that one. Got me for seventy-five."

Bennett laughed. "That's my sister. Cheer up, Jack. It's going to a good cause."

"I don't give a damn about the money."

"Times have really changed for you, then," Bennett mused.

Jack dropped into one of the uncomfortable guest chairs in front of Bennett's desk and looked at his friend. Bennett was one of the few people who knew exactly why he'd left the country—and Serena—seven years before.

Back then, Jack had walked away from Serena because he'd had no choice. He was in no position to give her what she wanted. Hell, everything he'd ever known about marriage had proved it was a prison until one of the caged fought their way free. Love hadn't been a part of his lexicon back then and he wasn't sure it was even now. What was love but some ephemeral notion that came and went as easily as the breeze off the ocean?

So he'd had to leave. Yeah, he knew he'd hurt her. But if he'd stayed and failed at the future she'd wanted for them, it would have hurt her more. Now he was back because he'd done what he'd needed to do. Proved to himself that he was a better man than his father. Proved that he could save the Colton Group hotel chain in spite of the damage his father had done to it. And maybe, he thought, he was better than the old man at other things, as well. Maybe he could have a relationship without letting it all go to crap.

He hadn't come back *for* Serena. But there was no ignoring her, or avoiding her, come to that. Jack was moving back home for good. And Bennett was his closest friend, so he wouldn't be able to maintain that relationship without seeing Serena. But seven years was a long time and they'd both changed a lot. She'd moved on and he couldn't blame her for it. She was a mother now. Divorced from a dick who hadn't deserved her any more than Jack had.

So even though everything in him had wanted to reach for Serena, he hadn't. He'd lost that right, and judging from the reception she'd given him, he wouldn't be welcome. Although, he mused, he'd expected more ice from her. Had she changed so much that she was able to actually hide her real feelings now? Back in the day, Serena had worn her heart out in the open for everyone to see. Today, he'd had the impression there were millions of thoughts racing through her brain and he wasn't privy to any of them.

But, damn, he couldn't help wanting her. That particular ache had never gone away completely.

So, better that they both get used to being around each other right from the jump.

"Yeah," he said thoughtfully. "Things have changed. Made a ton of changes to the company, got rid of a lot of dead wood at the top, and now the Colton Group is bigger and healthier than ever."

"Your mom still happy with her new husband?" Bennett asked.

"Yeah. John's great for her. Treats her like a queen, and they live in an apartment in Paris that Mom loves. She's happy and settled, so I'm moving back home."

"Good news," Bennett said. He walked across the office to the coffee bar. "Want one?"

"Sure. Black." Jack stood, then walked over to join him. "Serena wasn't exactly thrilled to see me."

Bennett held up one hand. "Nope. I told you seven years ago. No details."

Laughing, Jack took the offered coffee. "Seriously? It's been seven years and you still don't want to know what happened? Still sitting this out?" He took a sip of coffee, then said, "Most brothers are more protective of their sisters."

"Oh, I'm protective," Bennett assured him, but shook his head at the same time. "But I learned my lesson with Amanda ten years ago. Got involved then and only made things worse. So when you and Serena broke up, I stepped back."

Jack nodded. "Whatever the reason, I appreciate it."

"Oh, hell, I didn't do it for you." Laughing, Bennett said, "I did it for my own sake. The mess with Amanda and Henry Porter might have turned out differently if I hadn't gotten involved. But just so you know, that doesn't mean I won't do it again if I have to."

Jack studied his friend for a long minute before he simply said, "Understood."

Hell, he'd known that coming home again wouldn't be easy, but seeing Serena again, feeling the ice of her, hadn't been pretty, though he'd known she wouldn't exactly greet him with open arms. Still, she hadn't thrown anything at him, so maybe he should consider that a win.

"Working with her won't be a problem?"

Jack looked at him and lied. "No. Not at all." Then, in a sudden change of subject, he added, "While I'm here. What do you think about working up a package between my hotel and your restaurant?"

Confusion shone in Bennett's eyes. "You mean besides the prizes you're offering at the benefit?"

"Yeah." Actually, Jack had been doing a lot of thinking about these things. "This is separate from the gala."

Bennett frowned, but motioned with one hand for Jack to go on.

With Serena pushed to the back of his mind, where, he told himself, she should stay, Jack said, "The Colton Dana Point hotel is going to have a big reopen by the end of the month. I've been renovating—"

"Yeah, I've seen the construction crews on my drive to work."

He laughed. "Yeah, well, they're nearly done. Just putting some finishing touches on and the decorators are wrapping things up on the penthouse level this week." Jack took a sip of coffee and wandered to the windows overlooking the greenbelt. It was a nice enough view, but too many office buildings for his tastes. That was why he'd moved his headquarters to Newport Beach, where he could watch the ocean from his office.

When he'd lived in Europe, he'd always managed to get a view of the Atlantic, but the Pacific was home. And looking at it reminded him of how far he'd come and, now that he was home again, how much more he still had to accomplish. Jack had vowed to take the family company to the top of the food chain and he wouldn't stop until he had. He'd watched his father nearly destroy the very thing that he and his mother had depended on. Jack would never again trust his mother's well-being or his own to anyone but himself.

The idea he wanted to run past Bennett wasn't designed to be a game changer at all, but Jack figured it was a good way to reintroduce the Colton hotels to Orange County. Turning to face Bennett, he said, "I'm thinking that we offer our guests coupons for dinner at your restaurant and having you offer coupons for my hotel. Gain both of us some business."

Bennett leaned against the coffee bar and thought about it. Hell, Jack could practically see the wheels turning in the man's head. "You know the Carey restaurant is a five-star operation."

"So's my hotel. What's your point?"

Bennett snorted. "Are you talking a permanent sort of arrangement?"

"Not thinking that far down the road, actually," Jack said. "I see this as a trial period for now. I'm thinking we can offer a one-night stay at our hotel and a dinner for two at your restaurent. Hell, your restaurant's in Laguna, just a short drive from my hotel, so it would work out well for both of us. And maybe we'll both get guests we might not have otherwise."

"It's an intriguing idea," Bennett mused. "Why don't we talk about it over lunch?"

"At your restaurant?"

"You know a better one?"

"Well," Jack said, "I have been gone for seven years. Maybe there is a better one now."

Bennett grinned. "There isn't."

"Just what I wanted to hear."

"One thing we don't talk about," Bennett said as he set his coffee cup aside. "Serena."

Hell, Jack didn't even want to think about Serena at the moment, so that stipulation worked for him. Besides, what was between him and Serena should *stay* between him and Serena.

"Agreed," he said tightly.

"What is this? Reunion Romance Spring?" Amanda Carey's voice hitched higher and Serena shushed her sister.

She glanced around the Carey Center Pavilion, then back to Amanda. "Can you keep your voice down?" It probably wouldn't help, since the acoustics in the pavilion were every bit as exceptional as those in the concert hall itself.

While the Carey Concert Hall was the star of the Carey Center, the pavilion was rented out for wedding receptions, family gatherings and, in this case, the annual gala. The room itself was cavernous, with some of the same decorative points used in the concert hall. Lots of glass and gold and chrome, with a gleaming polished oak floor and overhead chandeliers that made that floor sparkle like a jewel. The walls were mostly floor-to-ceiling windows, which afforded views of the gardens that surrounded the building. And now, in the heart of spring, the trees were in full bloom and the roses were just coming into their own.

The night of the gala, those accordion-style windows would be opened to the night air, allowing the scents of the garden to swamp the pavilion, adding another layer of romance to the night. For the gala itself, part of the room would be used for dancing, while high-top tables dotted the rest of the space. There would be chairs scattered throughout for people to rest when they needed to, but usually, people wandered, visited and danced the night away.

Today, she'd come here with Amanda to lay it all out in her mind, along with the changes she'd put into place. Of course, the flowers, the catering stations and the tables and chairs weren't there, but in her mind's eye, Serena could see it all as it would be.

Of course, the gala plans weren't uppermost in her mind at the moment. "This is not a romantic reunion, and for heaven's sake, keep it down."

"Lower my voice?" Amanda said, laughing. "Sure. My reaction is what's weird here." Shaking her head, Amanda walked to the closest accordion window group and opened it to let an ocean breeze slide inside. "Suddenly I'm wishing we could have a glass of wine in the middle of a workday."

"Probably better this way," Serena said. "After talking to Jack, I'd need a bottle or two, and that would solve nothing."

"Fine. No wine." Amanda stepped outside and lifted her face to the sun. "If it's not a big romantic reunion—and let me tell you, they're very nice—"

Serena rolled her eyes. Ever since Amanda and her Henry had reconnected, and now become engaged, she never missed the chance to tell her sister all about how happy she was. Not that Serena begrudged her or anything, but this wasn't about Amanda.

"So, tell me why he's here."

"How do I know?" Serena gave up even the pretense of normal.

Serena followed her sister outside and crossed her arms over her middle as if giving herself a comforting hug. Naturally, it didn't help. Ordinarily, she loved the gardens at the center. Serena couldn't keep a plant alive, so being there with the scents and colors was sort of soothing, and definitely calming on a typical crazy Carey family day. But today she wasn't feeling it.

Her stomach felt as jumpy as the jittery beat of her heart. Sighing, she said, "Amanda, it was so weird to just look up and see Jack standing there in my doorway. And worse? He says he's moving back to California permanently."

"Yes, but what I want to know is, how's he look?"

Serena's eyebrows lifted. "Really? That's what you want to know? What he looks like?"

"Shoot me," her sister quipped. "I'm shallow that way."

Serena huffed out an exasperated breath. "How do you think?"

Amanda sighed. "Probably great."

"Bingo." Somehow, he'd managed to get even more handsome over the last seven years. Back when she loved him, Serena had thought he was the most gorgeous man she'd ever seen. A sardonic smile, a flash in his beautiful eyes and just a hint of recklessness that drew her in even when it shouldn't have. Today, she'd seen all that and more in him.

That fact was extremely annoying.

"Too bad he didn't develop a limp or something," Amanda mused.

Serena smiled. It was nice to know her sister and

she were on the same page here. "Just what I thought. But, sadly, he didn't. Now he's back and says he's only going to Europe on business trips now."

"Okay..." Amanda sat on one of the decorative iron benches scattered throughout the gardens. Draping one arm along the back, she looked up at her sister. "But just because he's moving back here doesn't mean you have to be around him."

Serena dropped down beside her. "He's one of Bennett's best friends."

"True."

"And he bought a table at the gala."

"Okay, well, that makes a statement. He spent fifty thousand just to see you."

"Not just to see me," Serena corrected. "And it was seventy-five, actually. I charged him extra. I shouldn't have, but—"

"Are you kidding?" Amanda gave a delighted laugh. "You should have charged him even more."

"Thanks." Good to have family on your side when you needed them, Serena thought. But it still didn't solve her problem. "He's going to be there. At the gala. In my life. Driving me crazy."

"You're not still in love with him, are you?"

"Of course not," she assured Amanda. "That would make me a complete fool. He walked out on me the minute I told him I loved him." And she hadn't said a word. Hadn't fought back or forced him to tell her why he was leaving. She'd simply stood there and taken it. Well, she wasn't that quiet, timid woman anymore. "I got over him. Married Robert. Had Alli. I totally moved on, so why on earth would I still care about Jack?"

"You shouldn't."

"Exactly." She nodded to herself and stiffened her spine. She was long since over the man she'd once loved so desperately. Even remembering her feelings at the time now embarrassed her. She'd been so sure the night she told him that she loved him. So positive that he would say those words back to her. That they would plan a future together.

And then none of it had happened.

She'd watched his eyes and seen the distance that had sprung up in those dark blue depths almost instantly. Serena had known that this wasn't going to be the fairy-tale ending she wanted so badly. He'd kissed her, told her he couldn't be what she wanted and left so quickly it was a wonder he hadn't left a Jack-sized hole in her front door. And she'd been so damn shattered by that action she'd married the first jerk who'd come along. Robert O'Dare had been a terrible husband, but at least with him, she'd finally discovered her spine. She had Jack to thank for that, as well.

And until today, she hadn't seen him again. She didn't want to remember the rush of heat that had swamped her or the quick jump of her heartbeat when he walked into her office so unexpectedly. Except for the occasional guest spot in her dreams, Jack had been invisible for seven years. She'd been married—granted, to a man who had made her life a misery—and she had a child. Alli was the light of her life. Basically, in the last seven years, Serena had watched her life crash and burn. Then she'd rebuilt it from the ashes, and now she was finally on a path that was one she'd forged herself.

She didn't need or want Jack Colton to push himself back into her life and throw everything off balance again.

"So you didn't get excited when you saw him?"

"No." *Yes.*

"Uh-huh." Amanda studied her manicure for a second or two. "I don't believe that for a second."

"Well, you could pretend and help *me* pretend."

"What's the point of that?" Amanda shook her head, gave Serena a one-armed hug and sat back to look at her again. "We both know that Jack Colton is your kryptonite. So it's better if you just admit it going in and then promise yourself that you're going to ignore it."

"Doesn't sound better to me," Serena admitted. "How can it be good to say yes, he still does it for me, but I'm not going to do anything about it?"

"Because then it's just your willpower against the sexual pull."

"Uh-huh." Serena stared her sister down. "Right. So I should ignore that pull as well as you did with Henry?"

Frowning, Amanda muttered, "That's different."

"Sure it is."

Just last month, Henry Porter, Amanda's long-lost love, had appeared again after being gone for ten years. And like metal filings to a magnet, the two of them were drawn together, in spite of their shared past, and now they were engaged.

Serena was happy for her sister, but Amanda was right, too. Their situations couldn't be more different. Fighting a sexual pull was going to be a full-time job, since she and Jack would be seeing a lot of each other, and she had no doubt it would be the most difficult one she'd ever done. But she couldn't fail. Couldn't risk letting her life be destroyed again. Especially by a gorgeous man who knew how to push all her buttons.

"Okay, fine. The situation is different. But," Amanda added, "sounds like Jack's here to stay, so you're going to have to find a way to deal with him."

"Do I?" Serena pushed off the bench, took a few steps, then whirled around again. "Just because he's back in the States doesn't mean we have to see each other." Thinking about that, she mused aloud, "Although he is friends with Bennett, but then, how much time does Bennett spend with his friends? He's more obsessed with the business than Dad is."

"Speaking of Dad," Amanda interrupted, "not that I'm finished talking about this, but Mom stopped in to see me this morning after she left you."

Serena sighed. "I'm sorry about sending her off to you. But, really, I'd had enough *help*."

"No problem, really. Well," she hedged, "not much of one. But the thing is, Mom says that Dad backed out of their trip to San Francisco."

Rolling her eyes in exasperation, Serena said, "Mom didn't take that well, I'm guessing."

"You could say that," Amanda told her. "Mom says she's going on the trip alone and staying at a different hotel than their usual so that if Dad does decide to follow her, he won't be able to find her."

"This is starting to feel like a soap opera."

"Starting to?" Amanda pushed her hair back when the breeze blew it across her eyes. "If Dad doesn't keep his promise to retire soon, I don't know what's going to happen."

"Great. This is just great."

"Honestly," Amanda said, "I shouldn't be happy about that, but I sort of am. At least it means three days of peace."

"Does it? All it really means is that Dad will be bugging us, not Mom."

"Good point." Amanda nodded and sighed. "Okay, back to Jack."

"No." Serena shook her head, set her hands at her hips and took a deep breath. "I'm done with Jack. What we had ended seven years ago. Nothing can change that." She lifted her chin, squared her shoulders and said, "I've got my job, my house, and most especially, I've got Alli. I'm fine. I like my life just as it is, and I don't need Jack in it."

"Right. So you're just going to be supermom and never be with another man?"

"How's my track record with men?" Serena asked, not needing an answer. "Jack left me. Robert married me to use me. Does it sound like I should be out choosing *another* man? No," she answered before Amanda could. "That way lies madness. Besides, I like standing on my own. I'm a mom. I make the decisions for Alli and I don't have any interest in letting a man in on that."

"Right." Amanda stood up, dropped her hands on her sister's shoulders and stared into her eyes. "Okay, sweetie, here's the thing. You need more than Alli and your job. You always have. You're the one who always dreamed of being a wife and a mom."

"I know, but things change." It was true. She'd never wanted the competitive world of the Careys. Yet here she was now, taking her place in the family business. And, damn it, she was good at the job, too. She was finding her niche. So if that much had changed, what else was possible? Maybe one day, she'd be the CEO of the Carey Corporation. She could unseat Bennett and wouldn't that be fun?

Even as she considered the possibilities, Serena dismissed them. "No," she said, with a firm shake of her head. Maybe she wasn't totally in love with the corporate life, but… "I always wanted family, I give you that. But I realized something a couple of months ago."

Amanda sighed and smiled. "Okay, let's hear the epiphany that's going to keep you a vestal virgin."

Serena laughed. "The virgin ship sailed a long time ago. All I've really discovered is I don't need another man in my life, because I've already got family."

"Sweetie…"

"No, hear me out." Serena looked around the garden, noticing two of the gardening crew working in the distance. The glass on the concert hall gleamed in the sun, a soft breeze carried the scent of the ocean, and here she stood in the middle of it all with her sister. Things could be worse. "Working at the company, I have time with my sister, my brothers—when Justin bothers to show up—and my parents, as irritating as that can be sometimes."

"It's not the same thing as having your own family," Amanda said softly. "I was busy burying myself in the family business, too, remember? Then Henry came back into my life and I realized what was missing."

She gave her a smile. Amanda just didn't understand that for Serena that longing was over. She'd wanted it, briefly had it, then lost it all. Now there was more than just her heart to worry about, and she wouldn't risk Alli caring for a man in their lives only to lose him and have her heart broken, too.

"I'm glad you and Henry are together again and that you're engaged and all set up for a happily-ever-after," Serena said, meaning every word. "But it's not for me." Amanda opened her mouth to speak, but Serena cut her off. "Don't look so stricken. I'm fine. I'm actually happy. For the first time in my life, I'm making my own happiness. I'm finding out that I'm good at my job, I have my family, and most important, I have Alli."

Her daughter was the one good thing that had come from her short-lived and unlamented marriage. Her ex had turned out to be a horrible human who'd only married her to worm his way into the Carey family's wealth. He'd cheated on her almost from the first, though she'd been the clueless wife. So wrapped up in her own vision of what she and Robert were, she missed all the signs that were, in retrospect, so obvious.

And by the time she'd discovered the truth about Robert, Serena was pregnant. With Bennett's help, she divorced him, got Robert to sign a document relinquishing all rights to their child and began the task of building a life for her and her daughter.

Now life was nearly perfect and would only get better as she got stronger. Why would she want to risk it all on the chance of maybe, at some point, possibly being in love?

Nope.

"So what you're saying is, you're just going to devote yourself to work and your daughter?"

"Is that so bad?"

"No, but it's what you used to complain about. How Dad and Bennett and *I* were too focused on work."

"Yes, but—"

"And counting on Alli to make you happy outside of work puts a lot of pressure on her, doesn't it?"

"Of course it would, but I'm not doing that." Was she?

"Not yet," Amanda said. "But eventually, if you don't have another outlet besides work, you will."

Frowning, Serena stared off into the distance, letting her sister's warning slide through her mind. Maybe that could happen. But it wouldn't. Not to her. "You're grasping."

"No, I'm not, but maybe you should."

Shaking her head, she asked, "What are you talking about now?"

"I'm talking about you doing a little *grasping* once in a while. Jack showing up is handy, but if you don't want to restart things there—"

"And I don't."

"Fine. All I'm saying is find a guy. Date. Have a complete life."

That was annoying. "For starters, I already have a complete life, and since when are you a big believer in having a man means completion?"

"I'm not. I'm saying it's what *you* have always thought."

"And that's what led me to Robert, and now I'm over it." She started back inside the pavilion. "Can we move on?"

"Can you? Good question," Amanda mused.

It was, wasn't it?

Three

"I can't believe you're doing this."

Bennett Carey looked up from the paperwork strewn across his desk. "I don't see why not. It's an excellent addition to the gala, and if the Carey Corporation owned spectacular hotels, I'd offer them up, too." He sat back in his chair, steepled his fingers in front of him and tipped his head to one side to study her. "The idea's a good one and you know it. Jack gets some great publicity for the new hotels and we get the added bonus of extra donations to the fundraiser. Work with Jack to set it all up in time."

Serena just stared at him. Oh, she would work with Jack…because clearly she had to. And like she'd told Amanda, she was completely over him. But that didn't mean she wasn't going to confront Bennett about setting her up without even *warning* her what he was going to do.

Bennett bent his head and went back to work as if she'd already hurried from the room to carry out his orders. "Work with Jack."

"Yes."

"And you didn't think you should talk to me about this?"

"Seriously?" He dropped his pen to the desktop and looked up at her again, impatience clear on his features. "It was seven years ago, Serena. You've been married and divorced. You have a daughter. Are you actually trying to tell me you're not over Jack Colton yet?"

"I didn't say that," she argued. "Look at you. You're still furious with Henry Porter and it's been ten years, not to mention he's now engaged to Amanda."

He scowled at her.

"And of course I'm over him. I just don't want to work with him."

"Get over that, too," he advised.

"I'm touched, Bennett, by the brotherly concern."

He dropped his pen, sat back in his chair and stared up at her. "Oh, I'm concerned—that you're acting as if you can't handle your job when it comes with a little conflict."

"Ha!" Her laugh was short and sharp. *This* was what she was fighting against. The you-can't-do-it thing from her own brother, for heaven's sake. Partly her own fault since she'd spent so many years avoiding the very business she was now devoting herself to. But times changed. *She* had changed and she would make them all see it, sooner or later. "I can't handle my job? Since when? You haven't had any complaints about the work I'm doing, have you?"

He stared at her. "No. Of course not."

Nodding, she took a step closer to his desk. "That's right, you haven't, and yet the first thing you say is that I can't handle my job when it comes with a little conflict. Well, in case you haven't noticed, the Carey family is filled with conflict and I do just fine, thanks."

"I didn't say you couldn't handle it," he said slowly. "I said you were *acting* as if you couldn't handle it. Big difference."

Maybe he had a point.

"Fine. My point is, I simply don't think it's necessary to import conflict."

Bennett grinned. "Good one. Look, Jack's a good guy. You guys had issues. Fine. It's done. This is a good idea for both of our companies. Make it happen, Serena. After all, you don't want Jack to think you can't handle being around him, right?"

She hadn't considered that and scowled at her brother. "Low blow, but I get your meaning. Fine. I'll handle it. But if anything like this comes up again…"

"A warning. Agreed."

"That's all I want." Well, not *all*. But close enough for now.

That evening, Serena picked Alli up from the company day care and took her to the Summer Sensation auditions at the Carey Center. Every year, the Carey Center held a series of summer concerts that was very popular. But this year, they were adding a new element. They were holding auditions for a contest called Summer Stars. And every act that auditioned would be recorded and added to the Carey Center website, where the public could vote for their favorites. At the end of the contest, the winner would be awarded a chance to shine for one night during the Summer Sensation concert series.

The response from the public had been overwhelming and now they were holding open auditions every night at the center. Like a television reality show, there were some people who had no business being on a stage, and a few others who were born to be stars. Even Serena had gotten caught up in the magic and the dreams and went to the auditions most nights.

Sitting in the Carey Center with her family, watching people chase their dreams, was…wonderful. She admired them all. Even those with no talent, only the ambition to be rich and famous. Because every one of them had put it all on the line to try for what they wanted.

"Can I sing, too, Mommy?"

She looked down at her daughter and smiled into those big blue eyes. Amazing that just being with her little girl could make the worst day better. "Sure, sweetie. We'll sing in the car all the way home, okay?"

Alli clutched her doll a little tighter and did a sort of hopping step beside Serena as they made their way down the center aisle to where her family was sitting. The sound of those joyful little steps was almost lost in the cavernous glory of the Carey Center.

This building was designed to celebrate the arts and no one did it better.

There were three levels of seating, fronted by glass railings that rippled like waves on the ocean. Those rails were wrapped around an oak stage where the honey-colored wood was polished to a gleam that rivaled a mirror. The stage was seventy feet wide and fifty deep, perfect for a complete orchestra, a huge choir or an intricate ballet.

Every red velvet seat in the house had a wonderful view of the performance, and the ceiling was studded with crystals that looked, with the reflected lighting, like stars on a black sky.

The hall itself sat two thousand, not counting the five private boxes and other VIP seating. Backstage, there were several dressing rooms and a luxuriously appointed performers' lounge, where the stars of the evening could relax before and after the show with their friends and families.

The lobby of the center was elegant, with miles of Spanish tiles and acres of glass and chrome. There was a café for refreshments, a gift shop and a first-aid station, just in case.

For now, though, the center was mostly empty but for the front row, where audition contestants for the night and their friends nervously awaited their turn in the spotlight.

Halfway up the main aisle, Candace Carey waited, beaming a smile at her only grandchild.

"Nana!" Alli shouted in excitement, broke away from Serena and ran the rest of the distance to throw herself at her grandmother.

"Hi, peanut," Candace said, bending down to scoop the little girl up into her arms. Looking over Alli's head, she said, "Serena, it's so good to see you here. We have a couple of exciting performers tonight and I can't wait to hear your opinion."

"Sure, Mom." While Alli and Candace began their mutual-admiration meeting, Serena took a seat behind Amanda, leaned forward and whispered, "Sorry?"

Amanda turned around to face her, glanced at their mother, who was spinning in circles with Alli, and then grinned at Serena. "No reason to be sorry," she said in a hurried whisper. "I actually handed off the auditions to Mom."

"You're kidding!" Okay, she hadn't expected that.

"Oh, no." Amanda shook her head. "I've got so much to do arranging the performances for Summer Sensation— and another one of our regulars is making noises about better compensation—"

"They want more money?" That surprised Serena. Performers at the Carey Center were some of the best paid in the country.

"Oh, no, they want a specific *meal* and snacks set out in the performers' lounge—snacks before the performance and a hot meal after. And not just any dinner, either. They want it catered by the Carey restaurant."

"Wow. Picky. Though," Serena noted with a shrug, "they have good taste. Our restaurant is wonderful."

"True, but I've never had to negotiate steaks in a contract." She sighed a little and continued, "And besides all of that, I've got a brand-new fiancé I'd like to spend some time with." She paused and took a breath. "Anyway, Mom had a couple of good ideas for the Summer Stars competition, and she's looking for something to do because Dad's driving her nuts, so I handed it off to her."

"And she's good with that?"

"Are you kidding? She's thrilled." Amanda glanced at their mom. "She's already working with the web designer to get the audition tapes online. Tomorrow she's meeting with the tabulation experts about setting up the voting. Honestly, Serena, Mom's doing a great job."

Serena wasn't even sure why she was surprised. Candace Carey had raised four kids and helped her husband build the center into what it was today. Just because the woman *wanted* to retire and go on adventures with her husband didn't mean she was incapable of doing the work. "Okay then, I feel no guilt for tossing her at you."

"None at all. I only came tonight to be with her on her first night heading the auditions. But it's not like she needs me."

As if to prove it, Candace held on to Alli and walked down toward the stage. She spoke to the pianist and the cameramen and then headed back up the aisle, with Alli skipping beside her. "Okay, girls, we're ready for our first competitor tonight." She checked her tablet and said, "Jacob Foley, a guitarist, and his sister Sheila, singing."

Amanda winced and Serena couldn't blame her. They'd both sat through several family acts that had been… *Disappointing* was a good word.

"Oh, don't look so appalled," Candace said, a laugh in her voice. "Earlier, I heard them rehearsing backstage, and they were wonderful."

Serena called Alli to her, because if the auditions were truly awful, she'd just take her daughter and go home. Dragging her little girl up onto her lap, Serena whispered, "Shh, let's listen to the music."

"Singing?" Alli clapped her hands.

"We hope so, sweetie," Amanda whispered from in front of her.

"Hush now." Candace fixed her daughters with a

stern stare, then winked at her granddaughter before turning her attention to the stage.

The lighting manager focused a soft pale blue spotlight on the center of the stage. A man, about thirty, holding a guitar and a younger woman carrying a violin stepped into that light and without pausing a moment began to play. It sounded Celtic to Serena and automatically her toe began to tap to the quick, lively music. Alli clapped along, and when the fiddle player lowered her violin and added her voice to the song, it was magic. Serena was completely caught up in the moment, and one look at her mother told her she wasn't the only one.

The music came to an abrupt—almost startling— end and Serena wasn't alone in applauding.

"They were amazing," Amanda said, as they watched the Foley family rush the stage to congratulate the two performers.

"Just wonderful!" Candace gave a happy sigh and laid one hand against her chest for dramatic effect. "Oh, I can't wait to see that performance up on the website. I'm sure they'll get hundreds of votes."

"Mom, I'm so impressed with you—talking websites!"

"Thanks!" Candace grinned. "You know, it's not as confusing as I thought it would be. After all, I don't have to design them. I just have to tell those who do what I want."

"That's great, Mom, seriously."

Candace shot a sardonic look at Amanda. "Yes, I'm sure you're happy, dear. Mom's out of your hair and actually doing well."

Amanda winced. "Out of my hair is a little strong."

"But accurate?"

"Mom…" Serena felt obliged to defend her sister.

Candace laughed and waved one hand. "Oh, relax, both of you. I know when I'm bugging my kids. But it was worth it, because I'm having fun with my new job."

"I'm glad," Amanda said. "And you really are helping me out, Mom. Between the Summer Sensation and planning the wedding, I've hardly got time to see Henry."

On the stage, people were moving things into place, getting ready for the next performance.

"Can't have that, can we?" Candace turned her gaze on Serena. "And what about you, honey? I hear Jack Colton is back."

"Really, Mom?" Serena rolled her eyes. "You, too?"

"Nana, too, what?" Alli asked.

"Me, too, a little nosy, sweet girl," Candace said and tapped the little girl's nose. Lifting her gaze to Serena, she said, "Well, Serena?"

"Well what?" A little exasperated, she countered, "He came in to see Bennett and he had an idea for the gala, so he stopped by my office to see me about it and that's the end of it."

At the front of the hall, the Foleys were still accepting congratulations for their performance and handing over their contact information to the web designer.

"Shouldn't you go and check on the next act to audition?"

"There's time," Candace said with a wink for Amanda. "So are you going to see him again?"

"About the gala? You bet. For anything else, not a chance," Serena assured her. Dipping her head, Serena kissed Alli's cheek. "What about it, sweet girl? Want to stop on the way home and get some ice cream?"

"Yay!" Alli jumped up and raced into the center aisle, where she hopped up and down on tiny pink tennies.

"You guys have fun," Serena said, more than happy to escape any more conversations about Jack. "We're going home."

"Then it seems I'm just in time to walk you to your car."

Serena's heart actually *sank*. Funny, she'd never really understood that expression until that very moment. So slowly it was almost as if she weren't moving at all, Serena turned to face Jack Colton standing beside her brother Bennett.

"This place is even more amazing than I remembered," Jack said, glancing around the concert hall before looking at Serena.

"Well, thank you." Candace spoke up to fill the sudden silence. "It's nice to see you again, Jack. Are you and Bennett here to watch the auditions with me?"

"I am," Bennett said, dropping into the closest seat. "I want to make sure you're not feeling overwhelmed by the job Amanda handed off." He frowned at his sister and she stuck her tongue out at him.

"I'm not overwhelmed. I'm just fine."

"Good, good," Bennett said, pulling his phone out of his pocket and turning it on. "Jack's not here to watch the auditions. He just stopped in to—" He cut off, turned to look at his friend and said, "Why did you stop by?"

"Seemed like a good idea at the time." His eyes were fixed on Serena and she felt the power of that stare right down to her bones. "Haven't seen this place in years, so when you were coming, thought I'd go with you."

"There you have it," Bennett said and settled into checking his email.

He just dropped by? Serena wasn't buying that for a second. But he couldn't have known she'd be there. So what was he up to? And, more important, why did she care?

"Okay, well, Alli and I are heading out," she announced. "You guys enjoy the auditions." She picked up her purse, her sweater and then took Alli's hand as she stepped into the aisle.

"Oh, I'll walk with you," Jack said, and she didn't even stop.

"Thanks, but not necessary."

"What's your name?" Alli asked, looking around her mother to the man walking beside her.

He smiled down at her. "My name's Jack, pretty girl. And you're Alli, aren't you?"

Her eyes went wide. "You know me?"

"I sure do," he said, then smiled at her mother. "Your mommy and I have been *friends* for a long time."

"I like friends," Alli mused with what Serena thought was almost a flirtatious smile. Honestly, Jack appealed to women of all ages. In reaction, Serena quickened her steps up the aisle, hoping that Jack would take a hint and just leave them alone. Of course, he didn't.

"We can be friends, too," Jack said, and he was rewarded with a grin.

"Well, that's very nice," Serena said briskly, "but you really don't have to walk us to my car, Jack. Alli and I are fine, aren't we, sweetie?"

"We're getting ice cream!"

Serena sighed.

"I like ice cream," Jack said.

"You want some with us?" Alli asked.

"I'd love some, if it's all right with your mom."

"'Cause we're friends."

"And friends have ice cream," Serena muttered, knowing when she was beaten. She looked down at her daughter's smiling face and knew there was no way to refuse. For whatever reason, Alli had decided that Jack was going to be her buddy. "Okay, let's go."

Jack smiled. Alli celebrated with a quick dance and Serena wondered how she'd lost control of the situation.

Jack hadn't really expected to spend time with Serena and her daughter. But he wasn't complaining.

The nostalgic ice-cream shop boasted small round tables, tiny uncomfortable chairs and a black-and-white-checked floor. The servers were impossibly cheery, but the ice cream was delicious. The company even more so.

"You two must come here a lot," he said. "The girl behind the counter knew Alli's favorite."

"It's only a few blocks from our condo, so yes," Serena said. "We are here a lot."

"It's good!" Alli said firmly as she took another lick at her cone.

Jack smiled at the little girl, then studied Serena over his chocolate-chip cone and took his time with both. Her honey-colored hair was just shoulder length and her blue eyes were as deep as he remembered. She wore a long-sleeved dark scarlet dress with a tight skirt and some red high heels, and every time her tongue stroked her ice cream, he felt that action pounding in his bloodstream.

He hadn't come back to the States *for* her, but he had to admit to himself just how good it was to see her again. Hell, a part of him had thought that seeing her again would be no big deal. That seven years was long enough to cool any feelings he'd once had for her. He'd thought only to come back home. To be a part of things again.

Now that he'd seen Serena, though, talked to her, he could silently admit that there was still…heat. And want.

Just to watch her eyes flash when she was annoyed. To see that soft smile curve her mouth—even when the smile was directed at her daughter, not him. Hell, the woman could still intrigue him with a glance and he hadn't expected that at all. Nor did he know what the hell to do with it. Once upon a time, all Serena had wanted was to fall in love, have a family and be happy.

And she'd wanted all of that with him.

Seven years ago, all of her dreams had sounded like a life sentence to Jack. And when she'd turned those big blue eyes on him and told him she loved him… Hell, he couldn't leave town fast enough. He wasn't proud of it, but it was something he'd had to do. Not just for his own sake, either, though that was clearly how it had looked to Serena and everybody else. But for her sake, too. He would have made a miserable husband and he had no interest in being a father. So what she'd wanted wasn't in the cards for the two of them, and it was better that he leave quickly so she didn't waste time spinning fantasies about the two of them.

Maybe he hadn't handled it the right way, but he

knew that he'd done the right thing. For both of them. He'd saved his family's company and his mom and Serena. And now Serena had somehow become...*more* than she had been back in the day.

Young Serena had been all dreams and plans, but this Serena had been tested. That had given her a kind of strength her younger self hadn't had. Her eyes were still beautiful, but now he read shadows of pain there. She was a mother, and every time she looked at her child, Jack saw her soften, and he knew that whatever else had happened in the last seven years, that little girl was her mother's heart.

"And then," Alli said, kicking her tennies against the rungs of the chair, "I cried 'cause my magic shoe got dirty, but Miss Ellen cleaned it."

"Magic shoe?" Jack asked, realizing he'd missed most of what had apparently been a very long story.

Nodding, she licked at her ice cream. "Mommy says magic shoes make you happy."

"Ah." He looked at Serena and his eyebrows lifted. "Magic?"

"Gray suede boots are my magic shoes." Primly, she licked at her chocolate-chip cone again and he wondered if she knew what she was doing to him.

He shifted in his seat to ease his discomfort, then concentrated on the back-and-forth between Serena and her daughter. He'd never spent much time around kids, but this one was full of charm.

"Erin's mommy is so happy she made cookies and brought them in today to school."

"Very nutritious day," Serena said wryly. "Cookies *and* ice cream."

"Yes, and maybe more tomorrow. Erin says she's getting a new daddy and her mommy sings at home all the time. And she makes lots of cookies and other good stuff."

"Does she want a new daddy?" Jack asked.

"Oh, yes. Her other one went away like my daddy did, but Mommy says it's okay because we're perfect just us two, but I think I might like a daddy like Erin's getting."

Serena shot Jack a quick look, as if expecting to see pity in his eyes. He didn't give her that, though. Instead, he stared into her eyes and let her see the heat boiling inside him. In response, a flash of that same heat lit up her blue eyes, momentarily. For that one split second, their gazes locked and a soul-searing warmth he hadn't thought to feel again spilled through Jack. When she licked her ice cream again, he damn near groaned.

Then she looked away and focused on her daughter when Alli asked, "When do I get a new daddy?"

"Well, I don't know, baby," Serena said and completely avoided looking at Jack now. And he knew that she was wishing he were anywhere but there at that moment.

Jack, though, was enjoying himself.

"Erin's new daddy made her a castle in their backyard." Alli shot a sly look at Jack. "Can you make a castle?"

Suddenly, he felt as though his measure was being taken by a three-year-old. And, worse, he didn't think he was coming off real well. "I don't know," he admitted. "I've never tried."

"I bet you could," Alli mused.

"We don't have a backyard," her mother reminded her.

Alli sighed and looked at Jack. "We have a roof."

Serena choked out a laugh. "You little traitor. You love the roof garden!"

Sadly, the little girl shook her head. "Doesn't have a castle."

Jack chuckled. "Boy, she's good."

"You have no idea," Serena said, and the dazzle they'd shared a moment ago slipped into a companionable smile from her as if they were sharing a secret. Damned if he didn't enjoy that smile almost as much as the heat. A moment later, though, she must have realized what she was doing, because she allowed the smile to slide from her face. "Now that you're back, where are you staying?" she asked abruptly.

He glanced at her. "At the house."

"Really? You didn't sell it when you left the country?" She stopped, then nodded. "Never mind. I do remember you left in a hurry."

He inclined his head. "Nice hit."

"Thank you."

"But you're right. I guess I did." He took a bite of his strawberry ice cream. "No. I didn't sell the place. Guess I always figured to come back at some point."

Besides, the Colton family home sat on a cliffside in Laguna and had been there for nearly a hundred years. Jack's great-grandfather had built the original house because his wife had always wanted to live where she could watch the sea from her bedroom. Of course, that house had grown and expanded, stretching out across a huge plot of land, and it was more or less a landmark.

The beach community had grown up around the house, though the Colton place maintained a lot of land

and a private beach. The house had been updated across the years and remodeled whenever the mood struck, but its cedar planking and miles of glass were as much a tradition in the Colton family as the Carey Center was to the Careys.

"You should come by sometime. See what's changed."

She laughed a little. "Sure. I'll do that."

"We don't have to be enemies, Serena," he said.

"'Cause we're friends," Alli shouted.

"Exactly," Jack said, smiling at the girl.

Serena sighed and shook her head. "Stop charming her."

"Am I?" he asked.

"Do *you* have a backyard?" Alli wondered.

"Alli!" Serena faced her daughter and said, "Jack is not going to build you a castle at his house."

"But he could if he wanted…"

He had to admire the little girl's never-give-up attitude.

Still, Serena changed the subject quickly. "Did it feel strange to be back? Here, I mean. In California. And the family house."

"Not completely." He studied her. "Being back at the house feels right, but I'll admit I didn't know how facing you was going to go."

Her lips curved and he couldn't tear his gaze from her. "I worried you?"

"Not worry," he said. "Let's say…concerned."

She looked pleased at that admission. "Isn't that a nice thing to say."

"What, Mommy? Is Jack nice?"

"He's being very nice at the moment."

"Because we're friends."

"That's right, baby," Serena said and reached over to swipe orange sherbet off the girl's chin.

As the outsider, Jack watched mother and daughter and felt just the tiniest twinge of…something. He wasn't sure he wanted to identify the feeling, so he let it go and concentrated instead on controlling his purely physical responses to Serena.

"I like Jack," Alli said, capturing his attention.

"Well, thank you," he said, grinning at the tiny heartbreaker. "I like you, too."

"That's great. We're all friends." Serena sighed. "Okay, baby girl, now that we've had ice cream, I think it's time we head home."

Alli tipped her head to one side. "Can Jack come?"

Oh, maybe he should build the girl a castle. She was working on her mother for him and no one could have done it better. He looked at Alli and grinned. A moment later, he looked at her mother. "We do have a lot to do about the promotion at the gala," he suggested.

"But not tonight," Serena countered. "And not at my home."

Couldn't blame her for that, but the twinge of disappointment that pinged inside him was hard to ignore. But, hell, there was always… "Tomorrow?"

At the irritation that bloomed on her features, he only said, "Look, we may not want to work together, but we're going to. It's good for both of us. Our companies. So let's do it right."

"The Jack Colton I remember was impulsive and liked life on the edge and always made spur-of-the-moment decisions," Serena said thoughtfully. "So when did you get so reasonable?"

"When I grew up," he blurted out, then glanced at Alli and softened his tone. "It happens. Even to those of us who fight it.

"And if that's how you saw me all those years ago," he added, "what made you think that I'd be a good husband?"

"Well, I guess I just hadn't grown up yet," Serena said quietly.

Four

When she and Alli walked into their penthouse apartment in Newport Beach, the first thing that came to Serena's mind was *Always have an OCD housekeeper*. It wasn't the first time she'd had that thought. Since hiring Sandy Hall when Alli was a newborn, Serena had had plenty of time to appreciate the woman. Serena's spacious apartment was always perfect and Sandy was always happy to watch Alli. At sixty, the housekeeper was active, opinionated and someone Serena could count on.

Alli took off the moment the door opened, racing for the kitchen, where she knew there would be cookies and milk waiting for her.

Serena thought about stopping her—after all, they'd just had ice cream—but one day of a sugar rush wouldn't hurt her. Walking into the main room, she dropped her purse on the plush rose-colored sectional and poured herself a glass of wine at the bar. She carried the glass with her out to the patio off the main living space and stood in the breeze, looking out at the ocean. No matter what mood she was in when she came home, that view was always enough to smooth her out. And, tonight, she really needed some serious smoothing.

Serena thought back to that one moment in the ice-cream shop, when she and Jack smiled together over Alli and there had been that…connection, which she supposed most parents shared when their kids were being cute or annoying or… But she and Jack weren't parents. They weren't together. So even considering that idea for a second was not going to happen. Ever again. One weak moment was enough to stiffen her spine.

She hoped.

"Thought you might like some cheese and crackers with that wine."

She turned and smiled at Sandy. The woman's natural red hair sported some gray, but her blue eyes sparkled with interest and curiosity. "You read my mind."

"Just one of my many talents," Sandy said and set the plate of snacks on the glass-topped table that was—of course—pristinely clean. "So, you went straight for the wine tonight. Rough day?"

"You could say that."

"Well, whatever it is, it's a new day tomorrow and anything can happen."

Basically, that was what Serena was worried about, but she wasn't going to admit it. Not even to herself. "Thanks, Sandy. And don't let Alli have too many cookies before dinner."

"Do I ever?"

As she walked off, clucking her tongue and shaking her head, Serena laughed. But then her thoughts turned back to Jack and the smile slid from her features. If he was only here for business, why did he insinuate himself into ice cream with her and Alli? Why was he being so kind to Alli, for that matter? Was he trying to use her daughter to get to her? Would he do that? She couldn't imagine the old Jack doing it, but as he pointed out, they'd both done a lot of changing over the last seven years. So, basically, she was left to wonder, *What's he up to?*

There was no way to know. Heck, even when they were a couple, Serena had had a hard time predicting his next moves. If she'd been able to, she never would have told him she loved him and set herself up for humiliation.

"No," she muttered, taking a seat at the table and reaching for a Brie-topped water cracker, "this time is going to be different, because I'm different. I'm not the shy, quiet, trusting little soul I used to be, and in a way, I have him to thank for it."

If he hadn't run from her, she never would have fallen so easily for Robert, who had turned out to be a lying, cheating scumbag. But then she wouldn't have Alli, so, in a way, she owed Jack for her daughter, too. And Alli was worth anything.

Hell, fighting for Alli, standing up to Robert and getting him out of their lives was the first time she'd really felt sure of herself. Knowing that she was doing the right thing, she had been fearless in fighting for her daughter. That whole experience had tempered her.

Made her grow. And in that weird way, she again had Jack to thank for it.

Though none of that meant she was willing to trust the man or his motives.

"Brace yourself, Jack," she muttered, then lifted her wine in a toast.

The following day, Jack was in his office, finalizing a few plans for the Colton Group's newest hotel.

He'd picked up a once-grand building in Florence, Italy, and was now busily transforming it into the jewel it would be in about six months. But there were plans to go over, adjustments to authorize and a contractor to keep in check. The man kept using the language barrier as an excuse for any "misreads" between him and Jack. But that wasn't going to fly for long. Jack had just finished arranging for his project manager—who spoke Italian—to fly over and set things back on track. If the Italian contractor couldn't do the job the way Jack wanted it done, then he would be replaced.

He hadn't built his company into one of the most exclusive hotel chains in the world only to ease off now.

Once he had the Italian situation handled, he opened his email and found one from Serena. Instantly, images of her filled his mind. From seven years ago and from last night. He never would have expected an ice-cream shop to be so filled with sexual tension, but Jack doubted he would ever see a chocolate-chip cone without thinking of Serena, slowly licking that frosty treat.

Frowning, he shifted position in his chair and focused on the email. Safer that way.

Jack—we need to work out the logistics for awarding airfare along with your hotel stays. And I need to know if you're going to be handling most of this with your own assistant or turning it over to me.
Serena

He sat back in the black leather chair, then swiveled it around to look out the window while his mind worked. Whether she knew it or not, that email from Serena had just given him the perfect excuse to back away from getting more entangled with both the Careys and the gala.

Jack didn't mind the grand giveaway he had planned. What he did mind was having to work with Serena to make it happen. Oh, he was pretty sure she was good at her job, because, family or not, Bennett wouldn't have her running her own department for the Carey Corporation if she wasn't.

But working with Serena was bound to bring back memories that were better off staying in the past. Not to mention kindling brand-new fires. Hell, it wasn't as if he'd been pining for her. Sure, he'd thought of her once or twice—how could he not? But he'd moved on a long time ago. Surely, the fact that Serena had been married, divorced and was now a single mom would prove that she wasn't holding on to the past, either. So why was he worried? Because of the damn buzz he felt every time he got close to her.

He couldn't afford to be distracted. Jack needed this to go well. He was putting a lot of faith into Serena and the Carey family fundraiser. If this went well, it would get him the kind of media attention you just couldn't buy.

"Second-guessing this whole giveaway?"

His assistant's voice cut into his thoughts and dragged Jack back to the present. He looked up at her and shook his head. "Oh, hell no, Karen. This giveaway is going to be hugely popular. The great press we get over this will more than compensate for any losses we swallow for the free stays."

Karen was fiftyish, happily married and the mother of five sons, only two of whom were still at home. She was ruthlessly organized, scrupulously honest and had a way of getting things done. She'd only been with him three weeks, but Jack had a feeling she was there to stay. Hell, he only wished he'd had her in England.

"I'll say it is," she said. "One week every month for a year? At any of the Colton Group hotels in the US or Europe?" She shook her head and gave a long sigh. "I might have to buy one of those tickets myself."

Jack laughed. "How about instead you set up an appointment for me with Serena Carey for tomorrow. I want to go over the plans for this whole—" He paused, thought about it and finally said, "I don't want to say 'raffle' because that sounds too small…"

"It does. But the prize certainly doesn't." Karen double-checked her notes, then lifted her gaze to his. "And the most important thing is that a lot of children will be helped by the money raised at the gala. The Careys have always supported children's causes, and thanks to you offering this spectacular prize, this year will be better than ever."

"Hope you're right." He picked up a stack of papers, set them to one side, then grabbed his cell phone. "Take care of that appointment, will you? I'm just calling Bennett to make sure we're all on the same page."

She nodded and left the room, but Jack didn't watch her go. Instead, he punched in Bennett's number, then turned to look out at the ocean. One of the perks of having his office right on the Pacific Coast Highway was the wide, sweeping view. The Pacific was so tame compared to the wild, raw beauty of the Atlantic. And yet the Pacific meant home. Hell, he'd grown up in the Colton house in Laguna Beach, with the sound of the waves lulling him to sleep at night.

California called to him and probably always would. And, yeah, he assured himself, it was *just* California calling to him.

"Jack." Bennett's voice on the line.

"Yeah." He shook his head, told himself to concentrate and said, "I wanted to let you know everything is set on my end. We've got Marketing handling the images of the Colton hotels—that's Europe and US—and I'll deliver them to Serena myself."

"Oh, she'll be thrilled."

"Oh, yeah." Jack remembered the moment he'd walked into her office and the expression on her face. "When I stopped by the auditions last night, she threw herself at me. It was embarrassing. I think she wept."

"Yeah, I remember." Bennett laughed out loud.

Jack's eyes rolled. "Look," he said, "there's nothing between your sister and me. Not anymore. Not for years. I didn't come back for a big reunion. It just worked out that way."

"Hey, none of my business what you two get up to," Bennett said quickly, and Jack could almost see him holding up both hands in a surrender move. "Trust me when I say I learned the hard way to butt out of my sisters' lives."

Jack kept his gaze fixed on the ocean but said, "There's nothing to butt into, but good to know."

"Nothing, huh?" Bennett asked. "And yet after the auditions, you and Serena took Alli for ice cream."

"You hear plenty, don't you?" He frowned at the phone.

"I always do," Bennett admitted. "Oh, and just so you know?"

"Yeah?"

"Whatever happens between you and my sister? That's between the two of you." He paused for a long moment, then said quietly, "But don't hurt Alli's heart. She's off-limits."

"Seriously?" Insulted, Jack scowled out the window at the clear, bright day. "That's what you think of me?"

"Didn't say that," Bennett told him. "It's just a warning. All I'm saying is, we all love that little girl, so don't plan on using her to get to Serena without pissing off every one of the Careys."

"I don't use *anyone*," Jack ground out. "Least of all, kids."

"Then there's no problem," Bennett countered easily. "Hey, had to say something, man. Won't risk Alli."

As the first sting of insult faded, Jack could see his friend's point and allowed himself to be appeased, nodding thoughtfully. All the man was doing was protecting his family. Was it any less than Jack had done when he confronted his father to protect his mother? "Yeah, I get it."

"Thanks."

"Sure." Jack paused for a moment, then suddenly asked, "You busy tonight?"

"Why?"

"Want to grab some dinner?" Hell, it had been a long time since he'd seen his friend. It was time now to rebuild that relationship as well as he'd rebuilt his hotels.

"Sure," Bennett said. "How about seven at the Carey restaurant?"

Jack laughed and shook his head. "There is more than just your restaurant in Orange County, you know."

"None are as good."

Still laughing, Jack agreed. "Fine. Can I get a good steak there?"

"Best steak in California."

"I'll hold you to that," Jack said, grinning. "See you then."

He hung up, then tucked his hands into his pockets and watched the steady, relentless slide of the sea toward the sand. He was back home. His friend was here. His life was here now. It was time to make that life everything he wanted it to be.

All he had to do was figure out how he was going to deal with Serena.

He had one idea that he thought might work, and it would put them on an equal footing.

A few days later, Jack had found his rhythm. California life was very different from being in London. And it wasn't just the weather. He threw open the French doors off his bedroom and stepped out onto the looks-like-oak floor to the railing.

Taking a sip of coffee, he told himself that putting a Keurig in his bedroom was the smartest move he'd made in years. Not having to wait for coffee made every morning just that much brighter. Like today. He stared out at the ocean and listened to the music of the waves sliding into shore. The sky was a deep clear blue that boasted fast-moving white clouds like sails across an endless sea.

"It's good to be back," he told himself and headed inside to get a jump on the day. The Colton Group was climbing to the number one spot in the hotel world and he wouldn't stop until it was all the way there. He couldn't afford distractions, not even one so tempting as Serena—though, damn, she *was* tempting.

Shaking his head, he focused on work, not the woman who was taking up too many of his thoughts lately. Nothing corporate this morning, he thought, already planning his trip to the Dana Point hotel. He wanted to check in with the decorators, make sure they were on schedule for the grand opening in two weeks.

Giving away free stays at his hotel meant he'd damn well be ready to welcome those guests to the kind of five-star treatment that would have them talking about their "win" for years.

He wore black jeans, black boots and a long-sleeved white dress shirt. He grabbed up a black jacket on his way to the stairs and slipped it on. When his cell rang, he reached into his pocket for it, checked the readout and smiled. His day had just gotten even better.

"Hello, Serena. Miss me?"

"Dream on," she quipped, and he laughed. He liked

this more confident, slightly sassy Serena even more than he had liked her back when.

He hadn't contacted her in days. Nothing about the gala, the raffle, the prizes, nothing. He'd wanted her to call him, and it looked as though his patience was finally paying off.

"Okay, then what's this about?" He took the stairs, glancing around at the latest changes made to the Colton house.

Some things remained the same, of course. The stairs and banisters had been hand carved by craftsmen a hundred years ago. The floors were wide plank oak, fitted together by those same craftsmen with such precision there was never a stray squeak heard. The walls were still plaster—now painted a sort of dark sand—studded with rough-hewn beams. There were enough wide windows to make it seem as if the outside was inside, and the surrounding gardens and trees made for picture-perfect views from every angle.

There were antique jewel-toned rugs strewn across the floors like islands of color in a sea of honey, and the furniture had been built for comfort and relaxation. What surprised Jack most about moving back was how much he was enjoying being in this house again. He hadn't been able to sell it because, as he'd told Serena, it had been in the family for far too long.

And while he was in Europe, he'd had caretakers— his housekeeper and her husband, the head gardener, living in the guesthouse for the last seven years.

So now Jack was rambling alone in a house built for a huge family.

But it was, almost surprisingly, home.

"What's this about?" Serena repeated. "You do remember we're supposed to be working together to set up yours and Bennett's big idea?"

He grinned, hit the bottom of the stairs and headed for the double front doors. Also hand carved by some long-lost craftsman that Jack now awarded a silent nod of appreciation.

"Sure, I remember. I also recall you not being very interested in it."

"Interested or not, it's already being advertised on our website, so we need to move on this, Jack."

Amusement faded into annoyance. She hadn't wanted any part of this and now she was calling the shots? "Serena, I'm on my way to the Dana Point Colton hotel to check things out, make sure we're on schedule."

He walked out the front door, down the stone steps and onto the circular driveway. His BMW convertible was waiting for him, black paint and shining chrome glinting in the sunlight.

"Fine," Serena said. "I need a complete list of the hotels you're offering in this raffle."

"All of them," he pointed out as he opened the car door and slid inside. "I told you that already."

"I know you did, but strangely enough, telling Marketing that you're offering up *all of them* doesn't do a lot for the advertising. I'd like a complete list of the hotels, along with descriptions, pictures if possible…"

Jack laughed a little. "That's a lot of information."

"I think we can handle it," she said.

"Yeah, I bet you can." He fired up the engine and it became a low, throaty purr in the background. "Look.

I'm on my way to the hotel now. Once that meeting's done, I'll come to you. What do you say to lunch?"

An ocean breeze ruffled his hair and he picked up a pair of sunglasses off the passenger seat and slid them on while he waited for Serena to speak. It didn't take long.

"I say we can work in the conference room more easily."

He'd expected that. Serena would no doubt do whatever she could to keep them from being alone together. But he wasn't going to let that happen. He wanted some time with her. Maybe more than *some.*

"Suppose we could, but I'll be hungry by then. We can get the work done, as well as eat."

There was another long moment or two of silence and he could almost see her thinking over her options. He kept quiet, waiting.

Finally, she spoke. "Fine. We'll meet for lunch. Where?"

Jack laughed again as he shoved the gearshift into first. "I haven't been in town for seven years, Serena. You choose."

"Right. Okay. La Ferrovia. An Italian place close to our offices."

"I'll find it." He gunned the engine again and said, "Two hours?"

"I'll be there."

When he hung up and steered the car down the long drive, Jack was smiling.

Twenty minutes later, Serena was still wondering how Jack had smooth talked her into lunch when she walked into a family fight in the conference room. Sighing, she was suddenly happy she'd agreed to meet Jack on neutral ground. She walked into the room, took a seat near Amanda and watched Bennett try to referee their parents' latest argument.

"You're spending too much time on this Summer Stars program," Martin Carey said to his wife. "Candy, you're never home anymore."

"I'm surprised you noticed," their mother said, "since you're rarely there yourself."

"But when I do come home, you're always there," he complained. "Until lately."

"Ah, like the faithful family dog, am I?" she countered, cocking her head to glare at her husband. "I run to greet you at the door, bring you your slippers—"

"I don't wear slippers—"

"Irrelevant," she snapped. "I'm not a dog, either, and I'm not going to sit in that big house—just me and the housekeeper—waiting for the precious moments when you deign to show up."

"Now, Candy, you know I've been meeting with clients."

"Yeah, Dad," Bennett said, "but I could have handled that."

Their father swiveled his head to shoot his oldest child the death stare. "I'm trying to help you out while you become accustomed to being in charge."

"And how can he do that," Candace asked, "if you never allow him to *be* in charge?"

"Of course he is," Martin argued. "I'm only helping."

"How long has this been going on?" Serena asked, leaning toward Amanda.

"Feels like forever," her sister said, "but in reality,

the last ten minutes. Bennett's doing his best, but even he can't keep Dad quiet."

Sad but true, Serena thought. Once Martin Carey was fixated on something, nothing short of a nuclear blast would knock him off course. And Martin, though he kept claiming to want to retire…didn't. Their mother, Candace, had had big plans for Martin's retirement. She'd wanted the two of them to do everything they'd put off over the years because of the business and raising their kids. But Martin couldn't let go of the reins and it was driving Candace crazy.

"Dad," Bennett said, and Serena heard the tension and the fight for calm in his voice.

In the best of circumstances, Bennett wasn't the most patient man on the planet. But having spent the last several months caught between their battling parents, he was hanging on by a thread.

"Why don't you and Mom go talk this out at home?" A reasonable tone that Serena almost wanted to congratulate him for.

"We have nothing to talk about," Candace said, lifting her chin and glaring at her husband. "Not until your father agrees to keep his promises."

Serena's chin hit her chest. Honestly, they'd all been suffering through the ongoing war between their parents. Well, all but their youngest brother, Justin, who managed to never be around when the sparks started flying. Serena had long been Justin's champion because she, too, had fought to make a life outside the family company. Though she'd changed her mind and joined the firm, that didn't mean she thought Justin should.

Still, that being said, it would be nice if he were there once in a while to share the heat with his siblings.

"Now," Candace said, "we either continue with the meeting or we call it over."

"I vote meeting," Amanda said with a quick glance at the wall clock.

"Fine," Bennett surrendered. Momentarily, no doubt. "Dad?"

"I'm agreeable."

Candace snorted. The most inelegant sound Serena had ever heard come from her mother. Apparently, they'd *all* been pushed to the breaking point. Honestly, she felt for her mom. Candace wanted to enjoy some time with her husband. The fact that he was choosing his business over her couldn't be an easy thing to swallow.

But she could see things from her father's point of view, as well. He'd taken the Carey Corporation higher than anyone would have thought possible. Of course he would have a hard time walking away from that kind of success.

And it was really hard seeing everyone's position and sympathizing with both of them.

"Serena," Amanda said loudly, to cover any other comments, "why don't you start? Is the catering finalized?"

"Yes." Grateful to be on solid ground, and for the change in subject, Serena opened up her tablet, scrolled to the gala section and then down to catering. "I met with Margot three days ago—"

"And we were supposed to meet to discuss it," her mother said.

She lifted her gaze to Candace. "I've been busy."

"That's no excuse," her father said. "This is a family company and the *family* will make decisions. Your mother deserves better from you."

Candace rolled her eyes. "I don't need you to defend me, Martin."

"I was just trying to point out that Serena should keep her word."

"Everyone should," Candace muttered.

She spoke up quickly to keep her parents from devolving into another argument. "Fine. I'll bring you up to speed tonight, Mom," Serena said, hoping to keep this train on the track. "Margot has some great ideas for the menu, and we'll be having food stations set up throughout the pavilion."

"Will that be enough?" Bennett looked worried.

"No, but that's why we're going to have additional tents set up in the garden with more food stations out there." Serena flipped the tablet around to show them Margot's designs for the stations. "People will be able to wander in and out of the pavilion and not be deprived of food while they do it."

"Sounds great," Amanda said, and Serena gave her a grateful smile.

"What kind of food?" Martin asked.

"The easy-to-carry-around kind," Serena told him. "The gala never holds a sit-down dinner. It would be logistically impossible with as many guests as we're expecting. So there will be all different sorts of finger foods, along with the most amazing little pastries, and I promise you no one will leave hungry."

"Good point, dear," Candace threw in.

Serena would have appreciated that, but she knew her mother had said it mostly to irritate her father.

"There'll be four open bars," she continued and scrolled to the placement designs. "Two in the pavilion and two in the garden. No one will have to wait long for a drink, and servers will be moving through the crowd with appetizers and champagne all night."

Bennett nodded. "Sounds like it's coming together."

"Thanks." Serena almost rolled her eyes but somehow restrained herself. "I've got the flowers arranged, too." Back to her tablet, she found the workup the best local florist had drawn up. "There will be your standard—but beautiful—bouquets near the dais where we'll be announcing the winners of the raffles and where Bennett will welcome everyone to the gala. We'll have individual vases on each of the high tables and more scattered throughout the pavilion and out in the garden."

"Those look fantastic," Amanda said, then wondered aloud, "I wonder if Celeste would be interested in doing my wedding flowers..."

"Don't see why not," Serena told her. "That's a great idea, actually. I'll give you her number."

"Thanks. I'll call her when the meeting's over."

"Which it isn't," Bennett said, speaking loudly enough to carry over his sisters. "I'm sure we're all thrilled that Amanda's wedding will have pretty flowers, but could we stay on topic?"

"For God's sake, Bennett," Amanda snapped. "If you're upset because you've lost a stick, I know where it is."

"Funny," her brother said. "How about you tell us

about the Summer Sensation lineup instead of wedding plans?"

Glad to have the spotlight off her, Serena sat back and listened to her sister outline the troubles she was having with a few of their regular performers. Including the new contract that included steaks and Hasselback potatoes with spinach and Pepper Jack cheese.

"What are they trying to do?" Bennett demanded.

"Trying to work us without asking for more money."

"Well, I think it's very tacky," Candace put in. "And if I remember correctly," she mused, "their performance last year was less than stellar. Perhaps next summer we think about a replacement for them."

"Not a bad idea, Mom," Amanda said.

"You're not still going to be doing this in a year, are you, Candy?" Martin asked, clearly surprised.

Slowly, she turned her head to look at her husband. "Are you planning to still be *helping* Bennett?"

He scowled at her.

"Exactly," Candace said. Then continued with a rundown on the Summer Stars auditions. "I had no idea there were so many talented people out there. Some of them have just been…amazing. I think people are going to have a hard time deciding who to vote for."

"Maybe I should take a look at the website design," Martin said.

"No, you should not," Candace argued, and all three Carey siblings sighed and sat back as the war escalated again.

Honestly, Serena told herself, maybe she had dodged a bullet when Jack left her seven years ago. Watching her parents fight and argue like a couple of children was enough to tell her that even nearly forty years of marriage didn't necessarily mean flowers and balloons every day.

Of course, she'd learned that anyway, with Robert. Now she was standing on her own two feet and she liked it. No one to answer to but herself. No one to worry about making happy. No one to argue with her about how to raise Alli. And no man was going to get in the way of any of that.

Yep. Single was sounding really good. At least it was quieter.

"Has anyone heard from Justin?" Bennett's voice dropped into the room like a hammer blow and immediately got everyone's attention.

"I did," Candace said with one last glare at her husband. "Justin's in La Jolla on business, he said."

"Business?" Bennett asked. "What kind of business does he have in a beach town near San Diego?"

"You know very well that La Jolla is much more than a simple *beach town*."

True, Serena thought. The small town not only boasted some of the best coastline views in California, it was also home to amazing restaurants, gorgeous homes, museums and even sea caves that drew snorkelers from all over to explore their depths.

"Fine." Bennett gritted his teeth. "It's more than a beach town. Why is Justin there?"

"Well, I don't know," their mother answered. "I don't interrogate my children."

"Is that supposed to mean something?" Martin asked.

"Probably. Is the meeting finished?" Candace looked from one to the other of them before finally pinning Bennett with a flat gaze.

"God, yes," her son answered, and Serena felt bad for him. He was in charge with everyone but the parents, who were driving them all a little nuts.

"Enough for one day. Next week, we'll meet again to go over any last-minute needs for the gala." Bennett shook his head as if clearing it of anything that had happened during their meeting. "If anyone needs me, I'm heading out for the day to meet with a client."

"Which client?" their father asked.

"Oh, Martin," Candace said, disgusted.

"I'll race you to the door," Amanda whispered as their parents started arguing again. She got up and headed out.

Serena was right behind her.

Five

Jack knew the moment Serena walked into the restaurant. Not because the owners shouted out a greeting. Not because he heard her laugh with friends.

But because Jack could have sworn that the air electrified when she arrived.

The restaurant was an upscale neighborhood place where regulars were treated like family. The floors were pine planks, the walls were a soft red dotted with pictures of Italy, the owners' family and even a signed photo of Frank Sinatra—which let him know that the restaurant had been around for a long time. Judging by the scents wafting from the kitchen, he could guess why.

Serena came around the corner and he stood up as she approached. His heartbeat jumped into a jagged rhythm just watching her walk toward him. Every nerve in his body fired at the suspicious look in her eyes and his blood burned thick and hot as his gaze swept over her. She wore a short black skirt, those red heels he'd already admired and a navy blue silk shirt with a deep V-neckline. She had her blond wavy hair pulled up off her neck today in some sort of tail that looked both messy and tempting, and her blue eyes were locked on him.

"Hello, Jack."

"Serena." He nodded, then sat down again when she took the chair opposite him. "I like your choice of restaurant."

"You'll like it more after you eat."

When the server showed up, Serena said, "Hi, Barbara. I'll have my usual. And iced tea."

"Unsweetened. Got it." She looked at Jack. "Do you know what you want?"

Yes, he did. But Serena wasn't on the menu. Jack looked at her. "What's your usual?"

"Eggplant parmigiana."

He glanced at Barbara. "Make it two. But I'll have a beer."

"Be right up."

She walked away, and Serena braced her elbows on the table and said, "I don't see the files you were going to bring me."

He laughed as the suspicion in her eyes darkened. "It's a digital age, Serena." Reaching into his shirt pocket, he pulled out a USB key and handed it over. "It's all on there. The hotels, pictures of the suites, the surrounding areas, descriptions. If you need anything else, my assistant will get it for you."

She took the key, nodded, then lifted her black leather bag and tucked it inside. "Okay, thank you. But

I have to say that we could have done a simple handoff at my office or a file transfer."

But then they wouldn't have been here, or they'd have been on her home turf. Advantage Serena. Here they were on even ground. Hopefully, advantage him.

"True, but if we had, we wouldn't be sitting in a restaurant that smells like heaven."

Her lips curved and everything in him wanted to reach across the table and touch her. Just...touch her. Every time that urge, that rush of heat, swamped him, Jack was surprised at the strength of it. Seeing her and being with her again had reawakened feelings he'd thought long dead—or at least comatose. He curled his fingers into his palms to keep from acting on that impulse.

"I swear I can gain weight just taking a deep breath in here."

"If you're fishing for a compliment, not necessary," he said, giving her a slow once-over that should have set her on fire. "You're even more gorgeous than you were seven years ago and that's saying something."

Her eyes went wide and surprised. "Thank you, I guess. But I'm not looking for a compliment."

"From anyone?" he asked, curious. "Or just from me?"

She smiled, took a sip of the water Barbara had set in front of them. Her gaze met his as she said quietly, "Just you."

"Ouch." Jack grinned in spite of the sting of that verbal slap. Then he clapped one hand to his chest. "Direct hit."

Her smile deepened. "You're trying to tell me you have a heart?"

"Oh, I have one," he assured her. He knew that because at the moment his heartbeat was galloping.

"You just don't use it."

"Ouch again." He studied her for a long minute and liked the way her gaze met his and never strayed. Tipping his head to one side, Jack silently compared this new confident, forceful Serena to the quiet, almost shy woman he had known so long ago. She'd changed a lot over the years. But then, so had he.

One thing that hadn't changed? His reaction to her. He hadn't wanted to rekindle a damn thing between them. And yet...

"I don't remember you being quite so outspoken."

She waited to respond until Barbara set her tea and his beer on the table and then left again. Taking a sip of that tea, she set it down and said, "I had to learn a lot of things over the last several years. I've learned to stand up for myself. To go after what I want. To do whatever is necessary to take care of Alli and myself." Her mouth curved briefly as she added, "Nothing stays the same. You should know that, Jack."

She licked her lips and everything in him tightened painfully.

"Oh, agreed." He picked up the frosty beer bottle, took a slow sip, hoping the icy liquid would put out the fire inside. It didn't. Then he studied the label as if looking for something important. "You've done well for yourself. And your daughter."

She gave him an almost regal nod.

"And I'm not saying I don't like the changes, either. I'm just…noticing."

"You don't have to like them, Jack."

He tipped his head to one side and watched her. "I do anyway."

Her lips twitched slowly, reluctantly. "Thank you."

"See?" he said. "We're getting along already."

"Uh-huh." She shook her head and he wished her hair were down so he could watch the heavy blond mass wave with the movement.

Hell, even he was surprised by his reactions to her. A single smile from her burned inside him, sending heat to every corner of his body. Memories awakened in his mind of Serena stretched across his bed. Serena laughing and spinning in a circle while the wind on the cliffs pushed at her hair and the sky blue dress she wore. Serena, lifting her face for a kiss and hooking her arms around his neck to hold on to him and draw him close.

Those memories brought a slow sizzle to his blood, but he had to let them go because this was not the same Serena. As she'd said, she'd changed. But he'd done a lot of changing over the years, too. He wasn't ruled by his hormones anymore. He'd learned to tuck desire away into a small corner of his mind, and he only let it out when he was sure he could control the situation.

Right now? He wasn't sure.

She changed the subject by asking, "So you said you were going to the Dana Point hotel this morning. How's it doing?"

Jack almost thanked her for getting his mind off her and back onto safe ground.

"Looks amazing," he admitted. "I'm not usually a

fan of what the decorators come up with for the hotels." Shaking his head, he added, "We were renovating a hotel in Chelsea—outside London," he explained.

"Yes," she said, laughing. "I know where Chelsea is."

"Right. Sorry. Anyway, when I saw the designs from the *decorator*, it gave me cold chills. Lots of flowing white cloth and white rugs and white furniture and white quartz counters." He shivered in memory. "It was like falling into a marshmallow nightmare."

Serena grinned. "What were they thinking?"

"I don't know," he admitted, pausing for a swig of beer. "She said it was ethereal, meant to welcome guests into a cocoon of relaxation and warmth."

She laughed out loud and he found himself laughing with her.

"Oh, wow. I hope you didn't go with it."

"Please." His laughter slipped away as he said, "No. We went with another decorator who kept the dignity of the old building and gave it the upgrades it needed to become the most exclusive, sought-after hotel in the area. Check the USB key I gave you. You can see how it ended up."

"I will."

Nodding, he continued, warming to his theme. "There are way too many decorators out there who want to go with the *trendy* ideas, forgetting that trends come and go. Have to say, though, the one I hired for Dana Point nailed it. Somehow, she managed to pull together the beach feel, along with luxury, that really works."

"Sounds beautiful," she said.

"Really is. You should come see it." Suddenly, the thought of Serena at his hotel was very appealing. Of course, even more appealing was having her at his house. In his bed. Under him. Over him.

Hell, the fascination with her was deepening by the minute. His attraction to her was stronger than it had ever been and the craving for her was gnawing at him. The more time he spent with her, the more he wanted her. She was strong and he liked that. Sure of herself and it was damned intriguing. Not afraid to give as good as she got and he liked that, as well.

Plus, as he'd told her, she was even more beautiful than she had been seven years ago, and that was really saying something. When she pushed one hand through her hair, it was a sensuous movement that caught his eye and stopped his breath.

Jack's imagination was running wild with all kinds of ideas involving Serena. And the more he entertained those images, the harder it was to breathe past the need.

"You've got a weird look on your face," she said quietly. "What're you thinking?"

"Maybe you shouldn't ask questions you might not want to know the answer to," he said softly.

She only stared at him, a thoughtful expression on her face. "Well, that's vague enough."

"Let your imagination fill in the blanks."

"You sure about that?" she asked.

"Nervous?" he countered.

One corner of her mouth lifted. "Not a bit."

Yeah, he really liked this new Serena. A lot. Maybe *he* was the one who should be nervous.

When their lunch was served, they each got quiet for a few minutes until Jack broke the silence. "This is amazing."

She grinned. "It really is. Mandy and I come here for lunch a lot."

"I know why."

Nodding, Serena sipped at her tea and asked, "So how many hotels have you got listed on that USB key?"

"All of them."

"Uh-huh. All is how many, exactly?"

He smiled. "Thirty-five hotels worldwide and still growing."

Her eyebrows lifted. "Impressive. You've been busy the last seven years."

"I have." An understatement of epic proportions. Those first few years it had been a 24/7 proposition. Constantly working to rebuild a company his father had allowed to fall into ruin. By doing that, the old man had let Jack know that he hadn't given a flying damn how Jack and his mother would live. What they would do when the Colton Group crashed and burned. So Jack had worked his ass off to not only fix what had gone wrong, but to expand their holdings until the Colton Group demanded respect around the globe as it did now. And his mother's future was secure no matter how her second marriage worked out.

"Didn't the Colton Group have twenty hotels back then?"

"Yes. But like you said, things change if you want them to badly enough." He took another sip of beer. "I revamped the standing properties. They all needed a face-lift, so to speak. And once they were finished and profitable again, I spread out. Buying up hotels that had been left to rot and turning them into the kind of hotels that people dream about."

Serena watched him with surprise, and was that…
admiration in her eyes?

"You turned it all around after the mess your father
left behind. Like I said. Impressive."

He stiffened slightly. Jack didn't like knowing that
others were aware of what his father had done to the
family legacy. With his reckless disrespect for actual
work, he'd allowed most of their hotels to fall into dis-
repair and their flagship hotel in London to become a
shadow of what it had once been.

Now it was back, better than ever, and it was because
Jack had given up everything in his life that wasn't
work. Yeah, he'd run from Serena when she said she
loved him. Not only because he hadn't been ready for
anything that even resembled commitment or *forever*.
But because he'd seen "love" up close and personal in
his own damn family.

And what his father called love had left his mother
in tears most days and their family business shattered.
Love hadn't meant a damn thing to his father other
than as a weapon he could use or a weakness to exploit.

So Jack had left, not just because he didn't believe in
love, but because he had no idea what to do with love
when it was offered to him. He had been convinced that
staying with Serena then would have turned out badly
for her, and he wouldn't do that to her.

And to be honest, he'd left because he knew that if
he wanted to save his business, his company, he didn't
have the time to devote to any woman.

Even Serena.

Things were different now. His company was as big
and successful as—maybe even more than—the Carey

Corporation. His mother was happy. His father was so far out of the picture he didn't even rate a mention.

And Serena was...different, too.

Somehow more intriguing, more attractive, more... dangerous to him than she'd ever been. And though Jack insisted that he had changed, too, *love* was still a foreign word to him. An emotion he wasn't sure he knew how to handle—or cherish.

But, he reminded himself sternly, no one was talking about love, were they?

Serena was watching him through narrowed eyes. "You can't possibly be offended because I know what your father did to the family business."

She'd obviously mistaken his silence for anger at the mention of his father's failures. She wasn't completely wrong, either. Though what he'd felt wasn't really anger. It was more shame for the kind of man his father had been. For the choices he'd made that endangered his family. For the fact that the old man hadn't cared about that, either.

No one liked to be reminded of their family's disasters. Hell, he'd been fighting against his father's miserable reputation for years.

"I'm not offended," he told her quietly, "but it's not like I enjoy remembering or knowing that everyone else knows. Would you like to be gossiped about?" he countered.

"Please." She waved that away and took another bite of her side of fettuccine. After she swallowed, she shook her head. "Whatever happens to the Carey family makes the news. Remember? My grandfather having that affair with the actress and my grandmother trying to run them down in Grandpa's prize Bentley outside the Hollywood Bowl?"

He snorted, both at the memory and at her easy acceptance of her family's very public foibles. "Oh, yeah, that's right. Your grandmother said her one regret was missing them when some stranger interfered and pushed the happy couple out of the way."

She nodded. "Gran wasn't the forgiving sort."

"I sense that." He thought he would have liked her.

Serena grinned at him as if she knew what he was thinking. "When it was all over, Gran had the Bentley squashed, placed in her front yard, and had the gardener plant roses around it."

He laughed out loud, imagining it.

Serena laughed, too. Then, shaking her head, she continued, "When my dad took over the company after Grandfather left with the actress—in *her* car, obviously—there was all kinds of public speculation about how he would fail because he wasn't as ruthless as my grandfather." She took a bite of the eggplant, and while she chewed, she thought about it some more. "My mother took out a full-page ad challenging the reporter to prove Dad wasn't ruthless—which seemed a weird tack to take—but he couldn't do it, so he apologized, in print."

"The women in your family are a little scary," Jack mused, enjoying her more and more.

"We are," she said, nodding solemnly. Then a brief bright smile destroyed the solemnity. "You should keep that in mind."

"Believe me when I say I will," he vowed.

"Good to know. Let's see," she mused, staring at the

ceiling before looking at him again. "Oh, my divorce made for great reading when the newspapers and the internet actually printed a *list* of the skanky women my husband cheated on me with."

He winced as he imagined how humiliating that would have been for her. "That's cold."

"And then some," she agreed, then shrugged. "Of course, it made it much easier for my attorney to get me full custody of Alli and for Bennett to pay off Robert so I'd never have to deal with him again."

Nodding, he said, "That's good."

"Very good," she agreed and took a sip of tea. "The last big piece of gossip was when Justin flunked out of college. That was a biggie. Oh, so-called reporters *loved* the story of the black sheep of the Carey family failing."

Okay, she'd made her point. She knew all about bad press. Maybe even more than he did. And not once had the Carey family run and hidden from the gossips or the nosy reporters and the salacious tabloids. They just went on about their business and pretty much said the hell with them. But the Justin thing he didn't understand. "Why's that so big? Hell, a lot of people don't go to college and they do fine."

"Not in the Carey family." Serena gave a wistful smile, then took a bite of her lunch. After a long moment, she added, "For my dad, Justin leaving college was the last straw. The fact that the news seemed to enjoy the downfall of one of us only made things worse. I think my dad's convinced that his youngest son is just a loser." Her gaze lifted to meet Jack's. "And he's not. It's only that Justin's not a books-and-schedules kind of guy."

"I get that," Jack said, with some sympathy. "I'm

not, either. Going to college was like being sentenced to prison. Hell, I couldn't wait to get out."

She smiled, but it was small and brief. "You stayed, though. Graduated."

"I had to." He took a long pull on his beer and said, "You were right. My father nearly lost the whole company because he couldn't be bothered to give a damn." He thought about it for a moment and then told her more than he'd told anyone. "My mother lost her home and that did it for me. The old man didn't care what happened to us, so I had to. I had to make sure my mom was safe. That she'd never have to be worried about losing her home again."

"God, Jack," she said softly. "I had no idea it was that bad."

"Glad to hear it," he said with a half smile. "Good to know gossips didn't report everything. Anyway, I knew that if I was going to save the company, I'd need a degree in business. I got it. Sweat through those classes because I knew what was waiting on the other side. Seven years ago, dear old Dad finally disappeared, taking as much cash as he could with him. So I had to go back. Focus on the company. On saving what I could and reinventing everything else."

"I didn't know."

"And I didn't want to tell you," he admitted.

"I get that, but I still wish you had," Serena said.

"It wouldn't have made a difference, Serena." He looked at her, his gaze locked with hers. "I couldn't give you what you needed from me."

"Well." She sat back and kept her gaze fixed with his. "We'll never know for sure, will we?"

Before he could argue that point, she changed the subject—or rather, went back to the original one.

"Anyway, we were talking about Justin. And the truth is, Justin doesn't have that ambition that you had, pushing at him." She shrugged and pushed a bite of eggplant all over her plate. "I guess he just doesn't know what he wants for himself yet. Except he's made it pretty clear he does not want any part of the Carey Center."

Jack had been headed toward leading the Colton Group all his life, and he couldn't imagine doing anything else. But if he'd had three older siblings to compete against, who knew what he might have chosen? "Where is Justin these days?"

"Last I heard, La Jolla." Serena slid her plate to one side, clearly giving up on finishing the excellent meal. "He doesn't come to family meetings, avoids phone calls and practically moves through the family like a ghost. The only ones he really talks to at all are me and my mom…and lately, more Mom than me."

He heard the worry in her voice and wished he could ease it somehow. He didn't even question that impulse. "How's Bennett with all of this?"

She laughed wryly. "You know Bennett. He *is* rules and schedules. The man wouldn't know what to do with himself if someone told him to *wing it*."

Now Jack laughed at the very apt description of his friend. Hell, he hadn't enjoyed just *talking* to any woman like this in years. Actually, he thought, since the last time he'd seen *her*. Yet this new Serena was so much more than her younger self. She really had come into her own and he admired that.

Plus, there was something to be said for a woman

whose family could be as screwed up as your own. What worried him was that he wanted to do a lot more than *talk* with Serena. Then she spoke up and he focused on the moment at hand.

"How's your mom loving Paris?"

He lifted one eyebrow. "And you know this how?"

"You to Bennett to me."

"Triple play," he mused, smiling. "Mom loves it. Her apartment—and I use that term loosely because it's more like a house on the third floor than an apartment. Anyway, it overlooks the Champs-Élysées, and every morning, so she tells me, she flings open the drapes and stares out at the most beautiful city in the world."

Serena gave him a wide smile. "So she's happy."

"She is." He inclined his head briefly and took one moment to remember the last time he'd spoken to his mother. She practically glowed these days and it was good to see. She'd had enough turmoil in her life, and it was long past time she had a chance to enjoy it with a man who realized just how wonderful she was. "And it's not just Paris making her happy. It's her new husband, John. I admit, when he first started coming around, I had him checked out."

"Of course you did," she said.

He just looked at her. "Thanks for understanding that."

"Jack, she's your mom, and I know how hard it was for her with your father."

She did. He hadn't kept it a secret from her when they were together. Serena had allowed him to be furious. To vent and shout his frustration at not being able to free his mother from the man making her life a misery.

"Yeah, it was bad. But her husband now?" Jack smiled just thinking about his stepfather. "The man's amazing. He makes her laugh. Takes her dancing, brings her flowers and enjoys the same long walks she always has. Thinks my mom is the best thing that ever happened to him and spends every day making sure she's happy."

"Fairy-tale ending," Serena mused. "The world needs more of those."

"Yeah. I guess maybe it does." Which was an odd thing for him to think, much less say. But looking into Serena's sky blue eyes made a man's mind a little... off balance.

More people were trickling into the restaurant and the waitstaff was bustling. As an employer, Jack was impressed. As a man enjoying a semiprivate lunch, he was irritated at the addition of so many more patrons.

"So we're all caught up on personal stuff," she said. "How about we talk business?"

"Oh, I think there's plenty more to talk about before we have to resort to business." Although keeping things on a personal level was getting harder as the restaurant filled up.

"Resort to?" she echoed. "I thought you and Bennett were two of a kind. All business all the time."

"Most of the time." His gaze locked on hers. "But I can take an afternoon off when I'm sitting opposite a beautiful woman."

She laughed and he realized that he'd missed the sound of her laughter. It wasn't shy or quiet or hesitant—not even when she herself had been. When Serena Carey found something funny, she wasn't afraid to show it. Most of the women he'd known over the last several years had that quiet, simpering laugh that always seemed so fake. Another reason he hadn't really been able to forget Serena. She was real.

"Come on, Jack," she finally said when her laughter died and she'd taken a sip of tea. "Empty compliments are too handy. Too easy."

"Why do you assume they're empty?" he wondered. Were the men around here so stupid they didn't see her for what she was?

She took a breath and sighed it out. "Because men aren't lining up to talk to me. Because I have a mirror. Because you always did have way too much charm."

"Thanks for that, anyway." He paused. "I think."

She grinned. "Let's just keep this from going any deeper into the personal zone."

"Don't know if I can," he admitted ruefully. "And that's a surprise to me, too."

Her eyes narrowed on him, and Jack wondered why she was almost *more* attractive when she was being suspicious. What did that say about him? he wondered.

Barbara dropped off the bill, then went away to check other tables.

"You'll just have to try," Serena said and gathered up her purse. Digging into the bag, she came up with her wallet, and Jack stopped her.

"Lunch is on me."

She stopped. "I don't think so. It's not a date, Jack. It's a business meeting."

"You want it to be a date?" Did he?

"I didn't say that," Serena corrected him. "And no. I told you, we're keeping things businesslike between us."

"Right." He reached for his wallet, took out a card and laid it on top of the check. "Well then, let's split it."

"Fine." She got her wallet out.

"No," he said, holding out one hand to stop her. "Not what I meant. I buy this lunch. You pick up the tab on our first date."

She laughed again. "That's not going to happen."

Suddenly, he was determined to get that date with her. Seven years ago, it had been easy. She'd made no secret of how she felt about him. Back then, she'd been as eager as he to be alone together. Nights with Serena had been long and filled with a passion that he'd never found with anyone else.

But as much as he wanted her, should he really open that door again?

Hell yes, a voice in his mind whispered. *Push it open if you have to.*

Being around Serena again had awakened something in him that he'd thought was dead and buried. And Jack wouldn't be satisfied until he'd had another night with her.

Because he had to know. Had to discover if the connection they'd shared so long ago still burned between them. Had to know if this newer, more confident Serena was even more alluring in bed than she had been years before.

He'd done what he had to. Gone away. Built his business. Took care of his mom. Now he was back and Serena was here and there was…something worth exploring. Where it might lead, he didn't know and, at the moment, didn't give a flying damn.

All he knew was he had to have her.

"You remember how much I like a challenge, don't you?"

"Yes, I do." She took a breath, shook her head and said, "I'm not a prize at a carnival, Jack. I'm not something you win. I'm not your latest challenge and I'm not playing games with you."

"Neither am I." Except for a few specific games that were only played in a bedroom. Those he could get behind.

"Good. Then we're on the same page."

"Not likely," he said, because *his* page had her naked and sprawled across his bed wearing nothing but moonlight. That image put a smile on his face that Serena noticed.

"What? Why are you smiling?"

He signed the check when Barbara brought it back, then tucked his card back into his wallet. "Remind me of this moment someday and I'll tell you."

"You have to be vague?"

"Don't have to, no."

"So you just enjoy being an irritation?"

He grinned. "Turns out…yeah."

"Fine." She stood up, slung her bag over her shoulder and said, "I'll go over the list with my assistant, and if I have any questions, I'll call you."

"Looking forward to it."

"Call you about *business*, Jack."

"For now," he said. When she turned and walked away, Jack watched her go, just to appreciate the view. "She always did have a great butt," he whispered.

Six

"The hotels are amazing," Serena told her sister later that afternoon.

She hated that. Hated that Jack had done so well and was now here to make sure she knew all about it. Hated that she'd had such a good time at lunch and *really* hated that he could make her body buzz and burn with that damned slow smile of his.

In Amanda's office, Serena paced like a prisoner counting off the steps of her sentence.

"He didn't have to meet me with the information," she muttered. "Why did he insist on meeting me?"

"Well—" Amanda said.

"Oh, no, he couldn't drop the list off at the office or email it. No, it has to be lunch." Words tumbled from her, one after the other until they were just a stream of consciousness she couldn't rein in and didn't bother to control. "And then he treats it like it's a date. I never said it was a date. Business. That's it. Period."

"What—"

As if Amanda hadn't spoken at all, Serena kept babbling. Worse, she *knew* she was babbling and couldn't stop. "*Then* he says he'll buy lunch and I can pay for the meal on our first date." Shaking her head, she whirled around, stabbed a finger at her sister and said, "Our first date was seven years ago. Right?"

"Right, but—"

"Seven years ago! So how can we have a first date? We can't. That's how." First date. The man had said that on purpose just to get a rise out of her, and here she was, doing exactly as he'd planned. "And I don't want a date with him, no matter what number it is."

"Yeah, you do." Amanda managed to push out an entire sentence this time, and it was enough to stop the steady stream of complaints.

"What?"

Amanda laughed shortly. "Oh, you heard me. Don't pretend you're suddenly deaf." She shook her head and muttered, "Though I may be after listening to that blistering rant."

"Funny." Serena huffed out a breath and set both hands on her hips. "Okay, fine. I heard you. I just don't believe you. How could you even suggest that?"

"Well, for heaven's sake, Serena, look at yourself." Amanda waved a hand in her direction. "Pacing and muttering like a bad actress in an old melodrama. All that's missing is you clutching a string of pearls."

"Thanks very much." She'd have been insulted if

it weren't true. Though she didn't want to admit that, obviously.

Still laughing, Amanda stood up, walked to the coffee bar on one wall of her office and poured herself a cup. "Do you want one? No. Never mind. You're wound tight enough."

"I am not tightly wound, and yes, thanks," Serena said. "Coffee."

Amanda shrugged and poured. "The point is, Jack asking you out on a date—"

"He didn't ask," Serena interrupted. "He proclaimed."

"The horror!" Amanda laughed. "Release the pearls, sweetie."

"Oh, stop it."

"The point is," Amanda repeated, a little louder this time, "you want the date."

"I do not. I—" She stopped talking, sipped at her coffee and quietly fumed at the fact that her sister knew her so well.

"Yeah, you do. Basically, you want *him*. You always have."

Oh, God, her sister had a point. Back in the day, all it had taken was a single look from Jack to turn Serena into a puddle of desire. It was a little lowering to admit that she was still in the same boat when it came to him.

But was she really? Seven years ago, she'd been so wrapped up in Jack she hadn't really thought beyond him. Now she could admit she wanted him while not putting her life on hold to dance attendance on the man. Didn't that make her sort of in charge now? Besides, she hadn't wanted to want him, but it seemed that desire didn't respond to her commands. It just demanded what it wanted. And it wanted Jack.

"Fine. I used to want him." Damned if she'd admit she still did. "But things are different now. I'm older. Smarter. I have a child. And the stretch marks to prove it," she added in a dark mutter.

"None of which makes you impervious to the need for sex." Amanda smiled to herself. "Especially great sex."

"This is not helping." She drank her coffee and burned her throat all the way down.

"It's the only thing that will," Amanda told her as Serena started pacing again. "Go out with him. Go home with him. Have crazy naked sex with him." She shrugged. "Then get over it and move the hell on already."

Serena stopped dead and stared at her sister. "Now you're talking about you and Henry. This isn't about you. This is *me*."

"Pardon me for letting my mind drift a little," Amanda said. "But are you actually trying to tell me you *didn't* have great sex with Jack?"

Erotic images rolled through Serena's mind with a clarity that stole her breath. It was as if every night she and Jack had spent together was now rising up in her mind to torture her with her own memories. His touch. His taste. The way his hands felt on her skin. The look in his eyes as his body entered hers. She remembered it all in vivid detail.

And sometimes in her dreams it was as if she relived it all, only to wake up aching. So, yeah. *Great* didn't begin to describe what she'd had with Jack.

Their connection had been so strong, the chemistry between them so overwhelming that she'd simply assumed they would be together forever. That he felt what she did. But she'd been wrong then, and this time around, she couldn't afford to make the same mistake. She had Alli to think about now. It wasn't only her own heart on the line.

But why even consider that? They weren't talking about hearts and love and forever. Like Mandy had just pointed out, they were talking about great sex and then moving on, right? Could she do it? Could she keep her heart out of the mix entirely and simply use him as he'd once used her? Could she be the one to walk away this time?

"I see you thinking," Amanda mused with a smile curving her lips. "Is that a good sign?"

"Maybe," Serena admitted. Now that Amanda had planted the seed in her mind, she couldn't stop considering it. From all perspectives, of course. It wasn't as if she'd go into anything blind and trusting. Not again.

She stared across the room where afternoon sunlight was washing through the tinted glass. Dust motes danced in the air as Amanda's words rolled through her mind.

"Now you're thinking too much. Stop it!"

Amanda's sharp order shook her out of her thoughts. "You started it."

"I didn't mean for you to run home and make a pro-and-con list, for God's sake." Setting her coffee cup down on the mahogany bar with a sharp click, Amanda put both hands at her hips. "You're my big sister, Serena, but sometimes I swear I feel ages older than you."

"Thank you very much." She didn't care for being told that she was acting like a child. Especially when it was true. "I have more to consider than you did, Mandy, when you started things up with Henry again. There's Alli to think about, remember?"

"Um, not likely to forget my gorgeous niece, but she's not a part of this, right?"

"Exactly. And I want to keep it that way."

"And you can." She sighed. "Neither of you is looking for anything permanent, right?"

"As far as I'm concerned," Serena agreed, "absolutely."

"Then what's the problem?" Amanda threw both hands high. "Go get him, and once you've had him, lose him."

"You make it sound so easy."

"It's only hard if you want it to be," Amanda said.

"And you come by all this wisdom how?"

"Trial and error. Plenty of error." Moving closer, Amanda gave her a hard, tight hug, then stepped back. "God knows I made lots of mistakes where Henry's concerned. And I'm trying to help you avoid doing the same thing.

"It's hard for me to see you getting all wound up over Jack being here. If you don't like how things are, then change them. Take control of the situation, Serena. Don't let him dictate how you feel."

Her words rattled around in Serena's brain for several long moments before she was forced to admit that Amanda was right. She had been allowing Jack to steer this relationship—or whatever it was. He showed up, she was nervous. Or angry. Or excited. Or all of those emotions at once. Why?

She'd learned her lesson about Jack a long time ago, so why was she still behaving as if she hadn't? She'd done a lot of changing over the years—because *she* had decided it would be so. Was this any different?

Heck, couldn't she look at this as her last big test? The final exam on getting over Jack and moving on with a life that was turning out pretty great?

"You know what? You're right."

Amanda blinked, then grinned. "Wow. Where's a recorder when you need one? I'd love to be able to play you saying that to me over and over again."

Serena gave her sister a rueful smile. "Does Henry really know what he's getting into?"

"He does and he's lucky to have me."

"That's very true," she said and reached out to hug her sister. Then Serena took a deep breath, steadied herself and said, "I'm going to do it. I'm going to arrange a date, go back with him to his house and have my way with him."

Amanda laughed. "You sound like a Victorian heroine. You can use the word *sex*, you know."

Serena shot her a sidelong glance. "I'm not going to settle for using the word."

The following day, Jack stopped by the Carey corporate offices with one destination in mind. He hadn't been able to get Serena out of his mind since their lunch date. All night, he'd been haunted by memories that were so stark, so real, that he'd actually been reaching for her when he woke up that morning.

He didn't like being twisted around by his own dreams and it was time to put a stop to it. Jack walked to Serena's office, nodded at her assistant, then strolled through the door and into her office. He liked catching her off guard. He'd expected to see a jolt of surprise in her eyes, but he hadn't expected…speculation.

"Jack." She gave him a smile that was both seductive and secretive. Now he was intrigued.

"Serena. I wanted to go over a few last-minute changes to the hotel lineup."

"What changes?" Serena sat back in her desk chair and stared at him. She was wearing a lemon yellow silk shirt with a wide collar that skimmed over her shoulders. Her honey-blond hair fell in soft waves that made him want to spear his fingers through it.

She looked beautiful. Damn it.

"We're sending the program to the printer this afternoon."

"Then I'm just in time," he said, dipping one hand into his pocket and coming up with a USB key. He walked closer, handed her the black key and said, "Not a big deal. I'm just adding one more hotel to the mix."

She glanced at the key, then up at him. "Which hotel?"

"It's my newest place in Santorini. The infinity pool was finished ahead of schedule, so we're ready to go there." Actually, that hotel was a gem. One of his favorites and it had been a damn wreck when he bought it just six months before. Now it sat on top of a cliff with a view that people would kill for. "I put the latest pictures on that key. Even I have to say they're impressive as hell."

"Okay. I'll get them to our art director and he'll include them when he sends everything to the printer."

"Great." He wandered over to the window, stared out at the view of the greenbelt and more office buildings, and told himself he'd made the right call setting his headquarters in Newport Beach. After a moment, he looked back over his shoulder at her. "Do any more thinking about that *date* we talked about yesterday?"

"Actually," she said, standing to face him, "I have."

He turned toward her. "And?"

"And what about tonight?"

Now it was his turn to shoot her a suspicious stare. "You want to go out with me tonight."

She eased one hip against the corner of her desk, and his gaze swept over her from that yellow silk shirt to the short white skirt and the beige heels that made her legs look amazing. His eyes lifted to hers and he saw that glint of speculation again. He wasn't sure what to make of this change of heart she was showing, but he'd be a fool to turn down the opportunity to get her alone.

"Don't tell me you've changed your mind and now you're not interested," she said, one corner of her mouth tipping up into a tease of a smile.

"Didn't say that." He tucked his hands into his pockets. "I am a little curious what changed for you. All of a sudden you *want* a date, when just yesterday you said it would never happen?"

She shrugged. "A woman's prerogative?"

"Really?" He snorted. "An old cliché?"

"What's the matter, Jack? Don't you trust me?"

"Sure, I do," he said, though even to himself he sounded less than convincing.

"Great." Her smile was wide and bright. "Then we're on," she said and pushed away from the desk.

She leaned over to pick up the USB key and Jack had a second or two to enjoy the view before she straightened up and faced him again. "I'll just get this down to Marketing. Was there anything else you needed, Jack?"

He couldn't take his eyes off her, and that should have sent alarm bells ringing in his head, but it didn't. Instead, all he could see were her big blue eyes, that mass of blond hair and those gorgeous long legs. Hell, he'd come here today hoping to charm her into going out with him, and now she was. Why wasn't he happy about that?

"We are on for tonight, aren't we?" she asked, bringing him up out of his thoughts.

"Yeah." He nodded. "Of course. I'll pick you up—"

"That's all right." She interrupted him with another smile, bright and shining. "I'll come to you. See you at Colton house at seven?"

"That works."

"Great," she said and walked to the door. At the threshold, she paused and looked back at him. "See you then."

And she was gone.

Alone, Jack stood in her office watching the door through which she'd disappeared, trying to figure out just where he'd lost control of the situation. She was being too damned cheerful. Eager, almost. What was happening? What was she up to?

"Hell, why do you care?" he asked himself and listened to his own voice break the silence in the room. Whatever the reason she'd agreed to go out with him, he was going to be grateful for it. He'd wanted her all to himself and he was going to get her. Why should it matter how it happened, as long as it did?

He'd worry about the whys of the situation some other time. Right now, he was going to enjoy the ride, wherever it took him.

Serena looked great and she knew it.

Her hair was loose and waving around her shoulders. She wore a black figure-hugging dress with a deeply square neckline and slim shoulder straps. Black heels completed the outfit, and the tiny black bag hanging off her shoulder held everything she might need.

She pulled up in front of the house, and when she got out of her car, she took a moment to stare up at the place she'd once spent more time in than her own home. Wood weathered by the sun and the ocean air, glass gleaming in the last rays of the setting sun, it looked as if it had simply grown out of the ground on its own. Surrounded by trees and flowering shrubs, it boasted manicured lawns and neatly tended flower beds where brightly colored blooms bobbed and swayed in the breeze.

Serena took a deep breath, dragging in the scent of the ocean and cooling her blood with the chill in the air. Since she'd decided her course of action only the day before, Serena had been sure she was doing the right thing. Have sex with Jack to get him out of her system once and for all. Sounded simple enough, but she'd learned long ago that nothing was simple when it came to Jack Colton.

Still, this time *she* was in charge. She was making the moves and deciding how things would go. This time, she wouldn't be blindsided by love because love wasn't going to be a part of the equation. This was about taking control. This was about feeding the hunger inside her and then, finally, really moving on.

Yet in spite of everything, including that mental pep talk, now nerves began to skitter through her body. Irritated, she squashed that feeling down and told herself to get on with it. Walking up to the wide double doors, she eyed the heavy pewter knocker before simply ringing a doorbell that released chimes inside the house.

She swung her hair back, and smiled when Jack opened the door. His gaze swept over her and she felt that look as if he'd touched her. Serena shivered a little, and he said, "Are you cold?"

"Not even a little," she answered and walked past him into the house.

A few steps into the entryway, she turned to face him. He looked…delectable. His dark hair a little unruly, his blue eyes locked on her and simmering with a banked heat that she felt echoing inside her. He wore a black long-sleeved shirt, black slacks and gleaming black shoes. He looked dangerous and she had reason to know he could be.

Tonight, she didn't care.

"You look amazing," he murmured and closed the door with a careless push.

"Thank you," she said and did a slow turn, enjoying the fire in his eyes when he looked at her.

"Yeah. Amazing," he repeated, his voice even lower than it had been. "So, where are we going on this date?"

Here it was, she thought. What she'd come here for. All she needed was the courage to go through with it.

And looking into his eyes was enough to spur her on. Above those double doors, there was a stained glass arched window, and as the late evening sun poured through the panes, it became slants of jewel-toned lights that gave off a magical air.

Taking one slow step after another, she walked toward him and kept her gaze fixed to his every movement. She saw the flare of heat. The glint of desire, and it kindled the burning embers inside her into a bonfire ready to rage. Nerves disappeared and hunger rose up, rich and thick, inside her. *In charge*, she reminded herself. This time, it was all up to her. "I was thinking that maybe we'd stay here."

"Is that right?"

She laid one hand on his chest and felt the hard hammer of his heartbeat beneath her palm. His eyes flashed. His jaw tightened and his eyes when he looked at her darkened until they became the color of a storm at sea.

"I don't want to go out," she whispered.

"What do you want?" he asked, catching her hand with his and holding her palm to his chest.

Serena tipped her head back until she was looking directly into his eyes, and then she said only, "You, Jack. I want you."

He wrapped one arm around her waist and pulled her tight against him. She felt his erection pressing into her and she knew he wanted her as much as she did him. God, it had been so long since she'd been held. Kissed.

Curling her fingers into the neck of his shirt, Serena pulled Jack's head down to hers and kissed him. Softly at first, almost tentatively. But it took only a second or two for her to dive into that kiss. Her lips opened to him, and when his tongue swept into her mouth, her breath left her body in a rush.

He let go of her hand to wrap both arms around her, holding her to him with arms as hard and tight as iron bands, and still it wasn't close enough. She wanted more. *Needed* more. The kiss deepened further until she couldn't breathe at all and didn't care.

She felt his hand slide up her back to the zipper at the top of her dress, and when he tugged at it, she smiled against his mouth. He pulled on that tiny metal tab until the edges of her dress fell open and he could stroke her bare skin with his palm. Tearing her mouth from his, Serena let her head fall back on a sigh of pleasure.

His touch was the same, she thought. Gentle. Strong. Powerful.

Overwhelming.

"It's a good date so far," he murmured and dipped his head to kiss the base of her throat.

"Best one ever," she said on a sigh and cocked her head to give him easier access.

While he nibbled, she slid her hands up his chest to undo the buttons of his shirt. Once his shirt hung open, she skimmed her palms over his skin, loving the feel of those hard sculpted muscles beneath her hands.

"Believe it or not," he said, lifting his head to look down into her eyes, "I'm going to have to make a drugstore run. I'm not exactly prepared for this…*date*."

Serena smiled up into his eyes, then shrugged her purse strap down into her hand. Lifting the small bag high enough for him to glance at it, Serena said, "I've got you covered. Didn't want to take any chances, so I brought condoms."

"Damn, woman." He grinned at her. "You have a knack for planning every detail of a hell of a date."

"I'm very organized."

"And that's extremely sexy."

"Glad you think so," she quipped, then hooked her arms behind his neck. "So what do you say, Jack? Shall we get this date started?"

In answer, Jack bent down, caught her on his shoulder and then headed for the stairs. "Trust me on this, Serena," he said. "We've already started. And we've got all night to finish."

Seven

Serena felt a thrill sweep through her as Jack took the long winding staircase at a lope with her over his shoulder. She grinned as she slid her hands up and down his back, feeling his muscles bunch and release with his every movement.

Her insides quivered in anticipation and she pushed all thought aside in favor of simply *feeling* what was happening at the moment. She hadn't done that in years and it was…liberating.

"Still with me?" he asked.

"Absolutely."

"Good to know." At the top of the stairs, he took a right and headed down the long hallway. The pictures and photos on the walls were nothing but a hazy blur in the dim light and she didn't care. She wasn't there for a tour, after all. She knew this house. And knew Jack was taking her to his bedroom. That was all she cared about.

Once inside, he kicked the door shut, crossed to the bed and then flipped her over his shoulder to land on the wide mattress. A burst of laughter shot from Serena's throat as she bounced. "That was a smooth move."

He grinned as he took off his shirt. "You want smooth? Baby, I'll give you smooth."

"Give me everything," she countered.

He paused a long moment, looking down at her. "You want to tell me what brought this on?"

Serena stared at him, relishing the moment and the gleam in his eyes. She gave him a smile and asked, "Does it matter?"

He thought about it for a moment, then shook his head. "Not now it doesn't."

He undressed so quickly Serena didn't even get a brief glimpse of the room they were in. All she knew was that the king-size bed beneath her was soft and the man now looming over her was hard—in all the right places.

Jack lifted her foot and slipped off her high heel, then did the same for the other. His thumbs rubbed her insteps and had Serena sighing. "That's amazing."

"Just getting started," he promised.

He dropped her foot and reached out to her. When Serena laid her hand in his, he pulled her to her feet and she took a breath, hoping to steady the jolting beat of her heart. But how could it steady when she was so close to him? When she could feel the tension in his body mounting as her own was?

"Too many clothes," he murmured and finished dragging that zipper down the length of her back. When it was free, he pushed the shoulder straps off and down her arms until her perfect little black dress pooled at her feet.

His eyes widened slightly and she saw fire burning in those dark blue depths. The strapless black lace bra she wore with the matching black thong had done exactly what she'd hoped they would.

"You're full of surprises, aren't you?" His voice was a low murmur.

"I'm glad you like them," she said.

"Oh, *like* isn't nearly strong enough of a word."

She gave him a slow, satisfied smile, then reached to the front clasp of her bra and undid it.

"You're killing me here, Serena." He took a big gulp of air, then covered her breasts with his hands. At the first electrifying touch, Serena gasped and held her hands over his, capturing the closeness and holding on to it for as long as she could.

His thumbs moved over her nipples until a moan slid from her throat. And the sound fired something in Jack that had him tipping her back onto the bed and levering himself over her.

"Whatever brought you here tonight," he said, "I'm glad of it."

"Me, too." She reached up and pulled his face to hers. She kissed him hard, fast, deep, and it wasn't enough. She was a little afraid it never would be.

He broke the kiss and caught her gaze as he hooked his fingers in the slim elastic band of her thong. He pulled it off and down her legs, then cupped her center in the palm of his hand.

"Jack..." She lifted her hips into his touch.

"Just let me have you."

She met his gaze and said softly, "Yes. And I'll have you."

"That's a deal." He kissed her briefly, then slid down the length of her body until he was kneeling on the floor beside the bed. Then he took hold of her legs and pulled her toward him.

Serena's breath caught as she realized what he was planning. The cool silk of the navy blue comforter beneath her was a counterpoint to the heat engulfing her. Every sensation seemed to drop on her at once and tangle together.

The feel of his hands on her legs. The smooth slide of the comforter. The chill in the air. And then his mouth on her core.

Serena jolted in his grasp, but his big hands only tightened on her thighs, pinning her in place. Jack's lips and tongue worked her body into a frenzy that had her mind spinning off into oblivion. She twisted and writhed against him as if she were trying to get away, and that couldn't have been further from the truth.

It had been so long since she'd felt anything like this. So long since she'd allowed herself to simply *be* in the moment.

Serena's thoughts came and went, and she was good with that. There was no time for thoughts when Jack was making her feel so much. Absolutely nothing mattered right now, except what Jack was doing to her. What he was making her feel.

His tongue licked and stroked at her core until she thought she might simply shatter. Serena groaned as he took her higher and higher. She didn't want it to end, but she knew she couldn't hold off much longer. If it were in her power, she would have kept him right where he was, doing magical things to her body forever.

But she couldn't wait. Couldn't keep from feeling the crash of relief hurtling toward her.

So she reached down, threaded her fingers through his hair and held his mouth to her as her body exploded. Again and again, the waves of release washed over her as she cried out his name on a shriek of pleasure that rocked her to her bones.

Struggling for breath, Serena trembled helplessly until Jack came to her, wrapped his arms around her and kissed her until what was left of her mind completely emptied. She lost herself in him as her body immediately rebounded from completion to need in a heartbeat. He cupped her face in his palms and devoured her. It was the only word that could describe how she felt under the onslaught of emotions he was bringing down on her.

When he broke the kiss, she blinked up at him, dazed and confused.

"Your purse. Where is it?"

Frowning, completely befuddled, she asked, "Purse? What?"

"Condoms, Serena," he muttered thickly. "In your purse. Condoms."

"Yes, yes." She shook her head and tried to think. "Dropped it. When you carried me."

"Damn it," he muttered and reeled off the bed. "Oh. It's here. Never mind. Thanks for not dropping it downstairs."

A short laugh shot from her. "You're welcome."

She watched him open her bag, grab the box of condoms and then toss the purse to one side. In a second or two, he had a condom out and sheathed himself.

Serena shifted restlessly, the need already clawing at her again. "Hurry up," she muttered.

He grinned at her. "Don't remember you being so impatient before."

"I don't remember you taking your time, either. Besides, I'm older now," she quipped. "I have less time to waste."

"Right there with you," he said and joined her on the bed again.

In one swift, hard thrust, he pushed his body into hers and she yelped at the invasion. But in the next second, she lifted her legs, wrapped them around his hips and rocked up to meet and match his rhythm. It was easy between them, like a physical memory. Just like seven years before, they moved together as if they were dancing. Each of them reacted to the other as if they were linked mentally, as well as physically.

She stared up into his eyes and couldn't look away from the racing flood of emotions darting across his features. Being with him again was more than she had thought it would be. It was touching her more deeply. Making her feel things she had deliberately let die seven years before. He was at once the same as he had been then and so much more.

A small corner of her mind told her she should be worried about the effect he was having on her, but instead Serena's body hummed with eager anticipation. Dismissing everything but what she was experiencing at the moment, Serena gave herself over to the raging physical need swamping her. She ran her hands up and down Jack's back, scraping her nails along his skin as if marking her territory.

Which was a ridiculous thought, so she pushed it aside instantly.

"Stop thinking, Serena," he whispered. "Just be with me."

"I am with you," she insisted and cupped his face with her hands. "Only with you."

He dipped his head to kiss her, and as he did, her body began that rocket climb to a peak she ached for. She moved with him, against him, and pleaded brokenly for what she needed.

"Let go, Serena," he said, his voice a low hush in her ear.

"No." She shook her head vehemently. "No. Come with me. We go together."

"Then hold on to me, baby, and we'll make that jump."

In just a few minutes, they did. He shouted her name, held her tightly, and when they fell, Serena locked herself around Jack, holding on to him as if determined to never let him go.

Jack rolled to one side, but kept Serena close, tucking her head against his chest as he lay there staring at the ceiling. His breath crashed in and out of his lungs and he felt both energized and relaxed. Mostly, though, he was stunned. When she'd agreed to a date, he'd expected dinner and a few hours of talking and then maybe charming her into his bed.

Serena had flipped all of that upside down and he

was still having a hard time believing it. This was so far from the Serena he'd once known he didn't know what to do with it—beyond enjoy the turnaround. Turning his head to look down at her, he finally asked, "Not that I'm complaining…but what the hell happened here, Serena?"

He felt rather than saw her smile as she trailed her fingertips across his chest. "I made a decision to go after what I wanted."

"Well, it was a great idea."

She pushed up on one elbow and looked down at him. "I certainly think so." Stretching, she nearly purred, "God, I feel fabulous."

"Look pretty good, too."

"Thanks." She gave his flat belly a gentle pat and sat up. "Wow, Mandy was right."

"I'm sorry?" Confusion rang in his tone. "Your sister was right about what, exactly?"

"That there is no substitution for great sex."

"I can agree to that." He watched her as she slid off the bed, stretched lazily, then walked to the French doors and the balcony beyond. Damn, she made a hell of a picture. Her body was riper than it had once been and every new curve looked fantastic on her.

"I always loved this room," she said as she walked, stark naked, into the late evening.

His heart jumped. "Yeah, well, good thing the balcony only faces the ocean or you'd be putting on quite a show."

She looked back at him over her shoulder and shook her hair back from her face. Grinning, she pointed out, "That's exactly what I love about this room. Complete privacy."

"Yeah, unless there's someone out there in a boat with a telescope or binoculars."

Frowning a little—not that he was a prude or anything—Jack got off the bed, yanked on his slacks and carried his shirt with him as he went to join her. Her skin was practically glowing, he thought wildly as he approached her. Her face lit up with her smile and her hair was lifting into a blond dance in the wind brushing past her.

"Come on. Put this on," he muttered, holding his shirt for her.

"Spoilsport," she said, but complied, slipping into the black shirt that was so long on her, it hit her midthigh. "This view is breathtaking."

"Yeah," he agreed, leaning against the railing as he looked at her. "Really is."

Her lips twitched. "I was talking about the ocean and how it looks just as the stars are appearing. Just before the moonlight."

"I was talking about you."

She turned to meet his gaze and her eyes softened. "Now you're being nice," she said. "I'm never sure what to make of you when you're being nice."

He choked out a laugh. "Is it so hard to believe?"

"Hard, no. Just…unexpected."

"Well then, I'm sorry about that."

She shoved both hands through her hair and said, "Wow. Nice *and* an apology."

That stung, but he really couldn't blame her for it, he supposed. He'd left her seven years ago. And he hadn't been *nice* about it, either.

"Don't look so stricken, Jack," she said. "I stopped being mad at you a long time ago."

"I didn't leave to hurt you, Serena," he said, his voice so low now it was almost lost in the rush of wind and the soft sigh of the waves against the shore.

"I know that." She shrugged, and even that tiny movement stirred his blood again. "Now, I mean. I didn't then. You broke my heart."

He'd known that, but hearing it said stabbed a spear of ice through him.

"Looking back," Serena mused, "I can actually see why you left."

"Is that right?" Intrigued now, he said, "Tell me."

She smiled, but it was just a little sad, and that tugged at something inside him whether he wanted it to or not. "Oh, God, when I remember, I can see myself, so eager, so completely in love with you that all I could focus on was the future that my busy little brain had built up for us."

He remembered, too. Her heart in her eyes whenever she looked at him. The way she would lay out their future right down to the color of their kids' bedrooms. Yeah, he wasn't ashamed to admit that it had terrified him at the time. Plus, there was the unhappiness of his family hanging over his head and the absolute *misery* of his parents' marriage as a shining example of what not to do with your life.

Yeah. He'd run. And he hadn't been kind when he left, and though it made him a bastard, he couldn't regret leaving. Only the way he'd done it.

"You're still looking at me like I'm a puppy you accidentally kicked."

His frown deepened. "You're no puppy, Serena, and I want you to know I'm not sorry I left—"

"Okay..."

"But I didn't have to be such a dick about it, either."

She laughed. "This really is an amazing night. Great sex. Apologies. And you being nice to me. All that's missing is some wine." She tipped her head. "Have any?"

God, Serena in this mood was irresistible. He wondered if she knew what she was doing to him, then realized she would have to know. She was looking at him, wasn't she? So that led to another question. One he'd already asked himself. What was she up to? What had prompted this change?

"I think I can manage some wine." He turned for the bedroom. "White or red?"

"Choices, choices," she said, smiling. "White."

He nodded, then left her there on the balcony with the twilight falling around her. Jack made it to the kitchen downstairs in record time, grabbed some glasses, a cold bottle from the fridge and a bag of pretzels—best he could do on short notice—from the pantry. Then he headed back up.

When he walked into the bedroom, he simply stopped and stared at the woman out on his balcony. As the rising moon crept higher, she was as still as a statue and yet as vibrant as any woman had ever been. Life simply pulsed around her and he felt inexorably drawn to her.

For seven years, she'd been a memory that had, occasionally, haunted him, and now that he'd had her again, he couldn't imagine losing her as he once had. Hell, he wanted her again already. Usually, once he'd been with a woman he desired, that itch was scratched and he was ready to move on. But with Serena, it was more. Always had been.

Damn it.

"Are you just going to stand there?" she asked without turning to look at him. "Or are you going to pour the wine?"

Shaking his head, he walked toward her. "You have radar or something?"

"Or something."

Then she did turn to smile at him and *something* inside Jack fisted around his heart. And he wasn't happy about it. He still didn't trust "love." But *love* wasn't on the table, was it? No one was talking about forever. This was great sex and an intimate relationship with a woman he found…fascinating.

He walked toward her, saw that smile of hers and told himself that sex didn't mean commitment. Sex wasn't a promise of a future or that fairy-tale ending she'd talked about the other day. Sex just…*was*. And he wanted more of it. With Serena.

"You look so serious," she said as he approached. "Does this mean your *nice* period is over?"

He set the glasses and the bag of pretzels on the table, then went to work on removing the cork. "I'm always nice."

"Ah. Then I guess I just have to pay closer attention."

He laughed shortly, pulled the cork free and poured each of them a glass of cold, straw-colored wine. Handing her one of them, he saw her glance at the table.

"Pretzels?"

"They were handy."

"I like pretzels." She reached for one and took a bite. Why did that look sexy?

"I'll call for takeout in a while."

"Chinese?"

"Sure." He brushed that aside for the moment just to look at her and try to figure out where they were going from here. "Look, maybe we should talk."

She laughed softly and gave her head a shake, throwing her hair back from her face. "And now for the *after-sex* talk meant to let me down gently?"

God, was he frowning again? Deliberately, he relaxed his features and said, "That's not what I meant to say."

"Okay." A soft chuckle rustled from her throat. "What would you say, Jack?"

At the moment, staring into her beautiful eyes, damned if he could think of a thing.

She took a sip of wine, smiled, then looked at him over the rim of the crystal. "Do you want to remind me that you're just not the marrying kind?"

Jack watched her and tried to figure out what she was thinking. In the old days, he would have known— mainly because she'd have blurted out everything she was feeling at the time. This Serena, though, continually surprised him. He liked it. Well, except for right now.

He sighed a little and briefly turned his face into the breeze sliding in from the ocean before looking back at her. "Serena, this is not what I meant by talking."

"Oh. Okay." She smiled again and tipped her head to watch him. "Maybe you want to tell me that you'll be rushing back to Europe?"

"No." Why was it he was suddenly feeling like a fool when his only plan had been to have a conversation about where this was headed? If anywhere.

"Well, what's left, Jack?"

He took a long gulp of his wine and felt that icy liquid slide through his system. "I just think we should know where we stand. That's all."

"We stand where we have for the last seven years," she said. "Alone." She reached out and briefly laid one hand on his forearm before releasing him and stepping back. "Jack, this doesn't make us a couple. It makes us lovers. At least for tonight."

Another surprise. The Serena he knew was not a one-night-stand kind of woman. He really didn't know what to make of any of this and that left him feeling more than a little off balance. He narrowed his eyes on her as if he could see into her mind if he just worked at it hard enough. "And that's all you're interested in? Tonight?"

"Were you thinking something else?"

Was he? No. Of course not. There was something between them, he knew. But was it more than sex? How the hell could he know that?

"I don't know what I'm saying anymore," he admitted with a scowl. "You're confusing me. Serena, you're not sounding like yourself at all."

"That's because I'm not the same woman you used to know." She took a sip of wine, then turned her face toward the ocean, where waves rolled endlessly toward the shore in a rhythm that was like the heartbeat of the world. "Jack, this isn't just about me. Or you, for that matter. I'm a mom."

"Yeah, I know. Alli's great."

She smiled. "Yes, she is. And I won't have her hurt."

Shocked, he said, "I'd never hurt her."

Serena looked at him. "Not intentionally, no. But if I let you back in and you left again, she might get her heart broken, and I can't—won't—risk that."

"So tonight's it." His fingers tightened on the stem of the wineglass. Disappointment reared up inside him and Jack ground his teeth together to swallow back whatever else he might have said. What would have been the point? How had everything gone from great to crap in just a few minutes?

"Tonight, yes." She looked up at him. "And any other night we might want to share. But sex is all there is, Jack. I don't want anything else from you."

"Well, that's great," he said, with a little less enthusiasm than he might have thought. He took another long sip of wine. "Then we know where we stand."

Jack couldn't believe that *he* had just gotten the speech he'd given way too many women over the years. Hell, it was basically what he'd said to Serena seven years ago. Was this some weird sort of Karma? Or just cosmological payback? Either way, he didn't much like it. Now he had a glimmer of how she must have felt when he'd walked away from her.

"Exactly." She smiled at him, as if he were a kid getting an A on a test, then held out her glass for more wine.

As he poured, he looked into her eyes and saw just what she wanted him to see, he thought. She had changed. A lot. Where he used to see love and anticipation glittering in her eyes, now there was…carefree warmth with no expectations. Where that left them— him—he had no idea.

"So," she said after a sip of wine, "you want to order dinner first? Or should we wait until after we go again?"

Yeah, confusion reigned inside him until he was faced with that particular question. Then he had absolutely no doubts about what would come next. Jack set his wineglass on the table and reached for her.

"After," he said. "Definitely after."

Eight

The gala was inching closer—just a few days away now, and the Careys were closing ranks. Happened every year, Serena told herself a week later. Yes, the last week with Jack had been…illuminating. She hadn't realized just how much she'd missed him. And Mandy had been right. There was just nothing better than great sex.

They hadn't "talked" again since that first night, and she hadn't had him come to her home because she was still worried about protecting Alli from caring for someone only to see him disappear from her life. But every night, she'd been with him. In that wonderful bedroom with a view of the sea. On that fabulous bed with a man who could set her on fire with a single look.

Was she a little worried that she was feeling more for him than she'd planned to? Of course. But that worry wasn't enough to keep her away. For as long as it lasted, she and Jack would use each other, and when it ended this time...*she* would be the one walking away.

Meanwhile, the gala had to be her first priority at the moment. She was going to make sure this year's event was the best one they'd ever held. *Her* name was attached to it this time and she was going to make a statement with it.

So the extra family meetings were just one more hurdle to get past.

"I don't understand, Candy," Martin muttered. "Why are you spending so much time on this competition? You're never at home. I'm eating dinner by myself almost every night."

Serena's mother gave her husband a dumbfounded stare. "Says the man who's a ghost in his own home. Martin, you were supposed to retire. Instead, you're busier than ever. Am I supposed to sit at home waiting for you to drop by however briefly? Not going to happen."

"If we could talk about the gala..." Bennett attempted to steer them back on track, but their parents were on an entirely different train.

"That's not fair and you know it," Martin argued, ignoring their children. "I've got things I have to see to before I can leave the business."

"That's bullshit, Marty, and *you* know it."

The whole table went quiet. Candace Carey *never* swore. The entire family stared at her as if seeing her for the first time, but she was oblivious.

"I've been very patient with you, Marty. But that time is done. If I'm supposed to live a life alone, then it's going to be one I choose."

"Alone? Who said you have to live alone?"

"You do. You're never home."

"You know where I am."

"Yes. Not home." Candace gave her husband a steady stare, lifted her chin and said, "Which is why I've decided to move in with Bennett."

"What?" Bennett sounded horrified and who could blame him? "Mom, you can't move in with me."

"Of course I can, dear. You're never there, either." She shook her head in disappointment. "Just like your father."

"Damn it, Candy."

"Don't you swear at me."

"You swore at me first!"

"How did I get dragged into this?" Bennett demanded. Serena was wondering the same thing.

"Oh, don't burst a blood vessel, Bennett," their mother said, waving his objections away with a flick of an elegantly manicured hand. "Like I said. You're as bad as your father. You're never home. You won't even know I'm there."

"Well, if you'll be alone there," Martin argued, "you can be alone in our home."

"I prefer not," she said primly. Then, glancing at Bennett again, she said, "My bags are packed. I'll be at your home this evening at eight. After the auditions."

For the first time in her life, Serena saw actual *panic* on her older brother's face. If this weren't so weird, it would be funny. Bennett treated his home in Dana Point like the Batcave. As far as she knew, no one in the family had been invited there since he had a tiny house-warming party when he moved in five years ago. For all she knew, he had actual bats hanging from the rafters.

"Mom..." Bennett's voice rang with forced patience. "I'll make dinner."

Beside Serena, Amanda snorted. That was actually more of a threat than an appeasement. Candace Carey hadn't cooked in thirty years. Their housekeeper took care of the kitchen. Serena wasn't much of a cook, either, but at least she didn't pretend to be. Serena did not envy her older brother.

While her parents argued and Bennett looked like a drowning man going down for the third time, Serena thought this would be a perfect time for their youngest brother to stroll in unannounced. Justin would be enough of a distraction that even their parents would be startled into silence.

But, naturally, Justin didn't show up. He never did, and if he had, Bennett would have erupted on him. So maybe it wouldn't solve the argument problem after all.

"Mom!" Amanda's voice cut through the noise and everyone looked at her. When she had everyone's attention, Amanda continued, "Why don't you tell us about the Summer Stars program? Are you having any trouble dealing with the webmasters?"

"Oh, not at all," Candace said, turning her back on her husband to focus on Amanda. "Chad and I came up with a wonderful new design that he's going to implement tomorrow. We have a lunch meeting today to finalize it."

"Who's Chad?" Martin asked.

"We already have the website up," Bennett pointed out unnecessarily.

"Yes, dear, but it lacked…pizzazz."

Serena grinned at the stupefied look on her brother's face.

"Who's Chad?" Martin asked again.

"If we had just held a virtual fundraiser this year like I wanted to in the first place…" Bennett's muttering was half-hearted and Serena felt sure it was because he was still shocked by his mother's determination to move in with him. She really couldn't blame him.

"That was a ridiculous idea anyway, dear," Candace said, with a slow shake of her head.

"Okay, that's all great, Mom," Amanda said, steering the conversation further away from the tension building in the room. "Serena, anything left to do for the gala?"

"Not a thing," she said, hoping she was right about that. "It's all under control. I'm having my final meeting with Margot tomorrow and I think we're going to really shake things up this year."

"Who's Chad?" Martin was still staring at his wife as if she were a stranger.

Serena ignored the undercurrents and went on. "The photographer is in the pavilion today, deciding how to set up his equipment and where it would be best to hang the screens where we'll be flashing the photos."

"And the raffle?" Bennett asked. "What about Jack's idea? How's that coming?"

Jack.

He hadn't been off her mind in days. Ever since she'd decided to finally just go for it so she could put the man firmly behind her—oh, God, there was a mental image for the ages—she hadn't been able to stop thinking of him. Especially since she was spending hours with him every night only to drive home and crawl into an empty bed alone.

"Earth to Serena."

She blinked and looked up at Bennett. "What?"

"The raffle? The big giveaway? Jack Colton? Ring a bell?"

"Several," she admitted, then silently added, *Though not for any of the reasons you brought up.*

"Great," Bennett said. "How about you share some of them?"

Amanda gave her foot a nudge under the table and she was pretty sure she caught a gleam of interest in her mother's eyes. Oh, she didn't want Candace figuring out what was going on. She didn't need family input in a situation she was already blindly stumbling through.

"Sure, Bennett. To business."

"That is the point of this meeting, right?" he asked.

"Yes. Okay then, the giveaway is going to be huge." She really hated that Jack had been right about his idea.

After she and her assistant had gone over the specs and pictures of the hotels Jack was offering as prizes, Serena knew that this hotel raffle was going to be the hit of the gala. And though it irked her to admit it, she also enjoyed knowing that it was going to help her make this gala the best one in years.

Which was also irritating, because she'd needed Jack to put her over the top.

Serena laid it all out for the family, sliding pictures across the table so everyone could see the properties for themselves. "Jack's offering stays at his hotels in the US and in Europe. I think our patrons are going to love trying to win one of the twelve one-week packages."

She looked at Bennett and nodded. "You guys were right. We're going to raise a fortune on the raffle alone."

Nodding, Bennett gave her a brief smile of approval and moved on to their mother. "The auditions still panning out?"

"Oh, yes, we've had some wonderful performers. A few clinkers, too, but God love them. At least they had the courage to go after what they wanted."

"What's that supposed to mean, Candy?" Martin leaned over the table and glared at his wife. "I do go after what I want."

"Yes. As long as it's rooted in the Carey Center."

"Can we not?" Bennett asked, then went on without waiting for an answer. "If that's it for today, I've got an appointment, and if I don't leave now, I'll be late."

"Who's the appointment with?"

"Marty," Candace said, "why do you care? Your son is in charge. You trained him. You taught him. Let him be in charge."

"He is in charge. I'm just asking questions and offering my perspective."

"I don't have time for this," Bennett said, already headed to the door. He stopped when his mother spoke again.

"None of us has time for this." Candace stood up and glared at her husband. "You're hopeless, Martin. You'll never retire. You'll expect me to be at home. Alone. Waiting for you to drop by. Well, I'm tired of being alone, Marty."

All of them stared at Candace, hardly able to believe what they were hearing.

"Which is exactly why I'm moving in with our son."

Bennett's head hit his chest. "Mom…"

"It'll be fine, Bennett. We'll have a wonderful time. Maybe with me there, you'll come home more often than your father does." Then she whirled around and headed out the door. "Come along, Bennett." As they left, the rest of them heard her say, "I'll take the guest room at the front of the house, Bennett. There's a lovely view and…"

"What is wrong with you women?" Martin asked his daughters when the others were gone.

"Nothing is wrong with us, Dad," Serena said. "It's not a battle of the sexes here. It's you versus Mom and I think she's right."

"I'm out of this." Amanda sat back and crossed her arms over her chest.

"It's so wrong for a man to love the company he built up from nothing?" Martin argued, and he threw a frustrated glance at the empty doorway through which his wife had left.

"Maybe it's time to love the wife who helped you do it," Serena said.

"What kind of thing is that to say?" Martin shoved his chair back and jumped to his feet. "Of course I love her. Why would I give a damn about why she's so damn mad all the time if I damn well didn't love her?"

Serena not only heard the frustration in his voice, she could see it all over his face. And she felt bad for him. But at the same time, she wanted to kick him. "Dad, if you don't find a way to let go of the company and grab hold of Mom, you might lose both."

"Damned if I will," he grumbled and left under a full head of steam.

A second or two of silence followed his exit until Amanda turned to her and said, "This is not going to end well."

Jack had had enough of the sneaking-around-only-meet-at-his-place thing he and Serena had going on. He wasn't sure why it bothered him, but it did. She didn't want him at her house. Around her daughter. And that was a thorn digging at him, too.

Hell, Serena was calling the shots in this...whatever it was between them, and that was going to stop today. She'd been in charge long enough and it was damn well time that *both* of them started making the decisions. So, Jack had decided to change things up. Which was why he stood outside Serena's penthouse door holding a giant bouquet of flowers and a teddy bear.

A few seconds after he knocked, the door swung open and he looked down to see a beautiful little girl staring up at him through wide blue eyes. She grinned, clearly delighted. "Jack!"

"That's right—" He broke off when he heard Serena's voice.

"Alli, you know you're not supposed to answer..." Her voice trailed off when she spotted him. "Jack? What're you doing here?"

Serena wore skintight cream-colored leggings with a soft pale lemon off-the-shoulder T-shirt. Her feet were bare and her toes were painted a dark rose. Her hair was loose, and though she wore no makeup, she was still the most beautiful woman he'd ever seen. For a moment, his mouth dried up and his heartbeat hammered in his ears.

Alli reached up and tugged at her mother's shirt. "He's my friend. He came to see me."

Serena sighed and looked up at him. "Jack…"

He grinned at Alli and ignored her mother. "You're right. I did come to see you."

"And you brought me a present!" She bounced a little while she eyed the teddy bear and Jack smiled even wider. He'd never been around kids much, but Serena's daughter had so much charm he couldn't resist her.

"Now, maybe I brought you the flowers and your mom the teddy bear," he said.

Alli laughed in delight. "You're silly."

"I guess I am," he agreed and went down on one knee in front of her. "So I suppose the teddy bear must be for you." He held it out to her and Alli swept it into a huge hug and buried her face in its fur.

When she looked up again, she gave him another bright smile, then threw herself at him, wrapping her free arm around his neck and squeezing. "Thank you, Jack!" She let him go and turned to her mother. "I'm gonna show Teddy my room!"

"Okay," Serena said, but the little girl had already dashed off, chattering to the bear in her arms.

"Well, that was sneaky," Serena murmured.

"Hey, I tried to give you the bear," he said when she turned back to him.

She sighed. "Jack, you shouldn't be here."

He leaned against the doorjamb and let his gaze slide up and down her body, taking the time to relish the view before meeting her gaze again. "Yeah, I got tired of hiding out at my house."

She frowned a little, then squared her shoulders. "I told you when this started that—"

"That you don't want Alli hurt."

"Exactly."

"Bringing her a teddy bear won't hurt her," he said softly.

"No, but if she cares for you and you disappear, she will be hurt."

"I get that," he said, his gaze locked with hers. "But I'm not going to hurt her. I'm not going to disappear."

"You did seven years ago," she pointed out.

"Yeah, well, a lot of things have changed since then, haven't they?"

She was still meeting his gaze, so he saw her eyes flare and he knew she was thinking about everything that had been happening between them since they'd reconnected. Well, hell, it was good to know he wasn't the only one.

"Why don't you let me in and we'll talk."

Her lips twitched. "Another *talk*?"

He gave her a half smile. "Maybe it'll go better than the last one."

"Maybe." Then she looked at the flowers he held. "You remembered that yellow roses are my favorite."

"I remember a lot of things." He handed her the roses, then walked inside when she backed up for him.

"It's a great place," he said, looking around the purely feminine condo. From the rose-colored sectional to the jewel-toned rugs on the wood floor to the landscapes hanging on the walls, it spoke of elegance and a woman who knew what she wanted.

"Thanks. I'll just put these in water. My housekeeper

has the night off, so if you're planning to stay for dinner, it's my turn to call for delivery."

He laughed and took a seat on the massive L-shaped sofa. Draping one arm along the back, he looked up at her and said, "One of us should learn how to cook."

"Why? We both know how to dial."

"Good point." She disappeared into what he guessed was the kitchen, and while she was gone, he took the time to look around. It was what he would have expected from Serena. Quiet. Classy. When he spotted the French doors leading to a balcony, he began to stand to go check out her view.

"Jack!" Alli ran into the room, the teddy bear hooked under one arm and a book in her other hand. "Read me a story!"

He watched her clamber up onto the couch and buried that tiny spurt of…fear? He liked Alli a lot, but he wasn't exactly used to dealing with kids. Still. How hard could it be?

"Sure." He looked at the book. *The Lost Puppy.* "You like puppies?" Stupid question.

"I'm gonna get a puppy."

"Really?"

She nodded so hard, her pigtails flew on either side of her face. Jack smiled because for such a tiny thing, she looked fierce, and he wondered if Serena had been the same when she was a child.

"I thought you wanted a castle like your friend."

She gave him a calculated smile. "She has a castle *and* a puppy."

"Ah." This little girl would go far.

Carrying Teddy with her, Alli snuggled up to his

side, leaned her head on his shoulder and ordered, "Read."

"Right." He opened the book and looked down at the child pressed to his side.

Her breathing was soft and steady, her arm wrapped hard around the teddy bear, and the scent of her shampoo wafted up to him. Her gaze was focused on a book that was clearly her favorite, judging by the worn pages and cracked spine. While he read the story about a puppy trying to find its way home, Alli snuggled closer to him and Jack felt an unexpected hard tug of warmth in his heart.

The little girl, all big eyes and bright smile, had decided she could trust him, and that was a gift he hadn't been given since her mother had done the same and he'd tossed that trust back in her face. Shame briefly flitted through him, but he pushed it aside. There was no changing the past.

He also wasn't sure he deserved Alli's trust, but he was going to make damn sure he didn't abuse it. He wrapped his right arm around her and held her close as she laid her head on his chest and stared at the book with eyes full of wonder. That tug on his heart came harder. Stronger.

He liked it.

And where the hell did that leave him?

He glanced up when he felt Serena's presence, and there she was, in the open doorway to the kitchen. Holding a crystal vase with yellow roses spearing up from it, she was watching him with Alli and her eyes were soft and…worried.

Hell. So was he.

"Mommy! Jack's reading about my puppy!"

"Alli..." Serena smiled at her daughter. "We talked about this. We can't get a puppy right now. We don't have a yard for him to play in."

Jack watched the back-and-forth between mother and daughter, and if there was a bet, he would have put his money on Alli. Who could look into that face and say *no*?

"He can play on the roof with me," the girl said slyly.

"Alli..."

"Jack likes puppies." She turned her face up to him and he was toast. If it were up to him, he'd be running out to the closest shelter to bring her a puppy of her own. But, he reminded himself, it was not up to him.

"It's up to your mom, Alli."

She pouted, her shoulders drooped and she sighed heavily. Oh, yeah, she was very good.

"When Jack finishes the book," Serena said, "it's time for dinner and a bath."

"Can we have tacos?"

Serena sighed, glanced at Jack and asked, "Tacos all right with you?"

"Tacos!" Alli shouted.

"Even if they weren't," Jack said with a grin, "I'd never admit it now."

"You are easy," Serena said, carrying the vase of flowers into the room to set on a table against the wall.

"I've got a soft spot for pretty blondes," he confessed.

She turned slowly around to face him and her gaze locked with his. "For how long?" she wondered.

And that, he thought, was a very good question.

Nine

Two days before the gala, everything went to hell.

"It was perfect," Serena complained, stalking around Amanda's office. She just resisted tugging at her hair. To be this close to pulling off the gala in grand fashion only to watch it explode was infuriating and frustrating and— "It was set. Everything was done. It was going to be great and now we don't have a *band*?"

Amanda perched on the edge of her desk and watched Serena's frantic pacing. "So why did the band back out?"

Serena waved one hand in the air. "Something about being offered a European tour."

"Wow, and they didn't turn that down to play at our fundraiser? Selfish bastards."

Serena stopped, shot her sister a glare and then kept walking. "Fine. Great for them. Sucks for me."

"There must be other bands available."

"Oh, sure. With two days' notice, there's lots of fantastic bands just sitting around, waiting for someone to call." She stopped pacing, put her hands on her hips and took several deep breaths. "I can't believe this is happening." She looked at her sister. "What am I going to do?"

"Well, stop panicking," Amanda said. "That's not helping."

"Do you think I don't know that? You know what else isn't helping? Mom offered to call the band we've used for years." She threw both hands in the air. "*Of course*, the Swing Masters are available! Nobody wants to hire them!"

"Well, that was mean," Amanda said softly. "Accurate, but mean."

"I can't tell Bennett," Serena continued as if her sister hadn't spoken. "I'll never hear the end of it. *And* he might side with Mom about hiring the old band. You just never know what the hell Bennett's going to do."

"True. Plus, now that Mom's moved in with him, he's on edge all the time." Amanda shivered. "Henry called him last night and Bennett started raving about Mom hiring painters to come in and redo his place because, and I quote, *it's too grim*."

"Not grim, really. Just…beige," Serena said. "A lot of beige, as I remember it."

"Yeah. It's more boring than grim." Nodding, Amanda said, "The upside here is she moved in with Bennett and not one of us."

"Points for me not having a guest room."

"And me living with Henry." Amanda got a little starry-eyed, gave a quiet little sigh while her mouth curved in what could only be yearning. Serena snapped her fingers in her sister's face.

"Hey! Back from your daydreams about Henry. I've got problems here."

"Right. Well, hey, maybe Henry knows someone—"

Serena thought about that for a minute and shook her head. Henry wasn't the answer. She'd seen him dance and it looked as though he'd never heard of music. Jack might be the answer, though. Oh, she really didn't want to have to ask him for help. But she only had two days to pull off something amazing. If she didn't have help with this, she'd have to tell Bennett, and there was no way she was going to do that.

"I'll have to ask Jack," she muttered.

"That's a great idea."

"No, it's not." Sighing, Serena considered her options. She'd been getting in deeper and deeper with Jack over the last week or more.

And since the night he'd shown up at her house uninvited, he'd managed to come back twice. Alli was crazy about him. Even Sandy, her housekeeper, was charmed by Jack. It was only Serena holding out now and she had to. Because she'd finally had to admit the truth to herself, if no one else.

The night she came into the room to find Jack reading to Alli and her baby girl curled up trustingly to his side, that one undeniable truth had dropped onto Serena's head like a brick wall.

She was still in love with Jack.

Watching Alli snuggled up to Jack while he read to her about the puppy she was determined to have had touched Serena more than she would have thought possible. Her little girl had never known a daddy, and she had apparently chosen Jack to be the one she wanted. And Serena was torn. She wanted to believe in Jack. To love him completely as she once had. But Alli's heart was even more tender than her own, and how could she take the risk?

Loving Jack was, apparently, inevitable for Serena. But trusting him was something else.

"Hello, Serena. Are you in there?" Amanda quipped.

Serena blinked out of her scattered thoughts and stared at her sister.

Pushing one hand through her hair, Serena said, "Sorry. Mind is just racing and—"

"It's Jack."

"Yes, Jack," she agreed. "I have to ask him for help with the stupid band."

"Not what I meant," Amanda said, smiling. "You're in love with him."

"What?" Serena shook her head and hoped she was believable in her denial. "Don't be ridiculous."

Amanda eased off the edge of the desk and walked toward her. "I'm not. I'm being extremely perceptive. I can't believe I didn't notice before this."

Oh, God. She really didn't need Amanda teasing her about this. "Stop it, okay? Just because you're nuts about Henry doesn't mean everyone else is in love."

"Not everyone," Amanda mused, "just you."

She could keep denying it, but what would be the point? Besides, now that Amanda had noticed, she wouldn't let it go. Really, Serena was lucky no one else had noticed. Especially Jack.

"Fine. I love him. But that doesn't change anything."

Amanda stared at her, baffled. "How are we related? Love changes *everything*."

"No." On this, Serena was very firm. "Okay, yes, I love Jack," and just saying it out loud made it all so real it was nearly terrifying. "But I can't risk Alli's feelings."

"Come on. Jack would never hurt her."

"Not on purpose. Of course not. But when he leaves again, then what? Alli's heart's broken."

"Sure it's Alli's heart you're worried about?"

Serena narrowed her eyes on her sister. "What's that supposed to mean?"

"It means you're sounding like the old Serena, not the new-and-improved version."

"You're not helping."

"I'm trying to," Amanda said.

"I meant with the band situation."

"Screw the band."

"Easy for you to say."

Amanda sighed. "You came a long way over the last seven years, Serena. You went out and took charge of an affair that turned into love and now you've scared yourself. You don't want to go backward with the band? Well, don't go backward with yourself, either."

Serena hated that her sister had a point, but she didn't really have the time right now to think about what Amanda was saying. Once the gala was over and things had settled down, then she'd be able to give plenty of thought to the situation with Jack.

"Look, I get it. And I promise I'll consider everything you said. *After* the gala."

"Fine. Go. Call Jack."

Her head dropped back. "God, I really don't want

to." Sighing, she added, "I'm going to make some more calls. See what I can find on my own."

"You've got two days, Serena."

"Thanks. I know." *Two days.* Not a lot of time and it was ticking past really quickly.

When she left her sister, she went straight to her office only to find Jack waiting for her. Was the universe screwing with her? Or was it sending her a sign? Either way, it was a little unsettling. "Why are you here?"

"Good to see you, too," he said, tucking his phone into his suit pocket. He stood up as she closed the office door behind her. "We had a lunch date, remember?"

"God, I completely forgot." She rubbed the spot between her eyes.

"Headache?" Jack asked.

"You have no idea." She leaned one hip against her desk. In a few minutes, she told him everything. As much as she didn't want to have to ask for help, she knew she needed it. And she actually felt better, spelling it all out for him.

"So, basically, you just need a band for the gala."

"Just?" she repeated, dumbfounded. Had he not been listening? Was the panic in her voice undetectable to him? "*Just?* Yes, I need a band. It's two days away, I can't find a decent band that isn't already booked, and if I don't, the whole thing is going to be a disaster."

He grinned.

She scowled at him. "This isn't funny, Jack."

"No, but not a tragedy, either." He grabbed his phone again and started scrolling through his contacts. "Because *you* have *me*. I know some people who might be able to help."

He stepped away, hit the speed dial and waited for his old friend to answer. When he did, Jack smiled.

"Tom. It's Jack. Listen," he said briskly, "I've got a situation and I need your help." In a few short sentences, he explained the problem to the man, then listened while the other man talked.

Jack watched Serena pace as he answered Tom's questions. She was worried, a little panicked and, clearly, not exactly thrilled to accept help from him.

They'd been together again for more than a week. But there was more than the past week between them. There was chemistry. Magic. And something more that even he could feel. Yet she was holding back. Keeping him in a separate corner of her life where he couldn't interfere in the rest of her world. Hell, he'd be surprised if her family knew they were together again.

And as that thought spilled through his mind, he had to wonder if they *were* together. Sure, they had great sex almost every night, but that was as far as it went. There was no staying overnight. No sharing of everyday stuff. They never made plans together beyond the next night. There was no talk of a future. No pretense of being in a relationship. No trust.

That last word resonated in his mind because he knew that it was his own damn fault that she didn't trust him. She had once, he remembered. Until he'd walked out on her and all of her plans for their future.

She stopped pacing suddenly and turned to look at him, and his heart simply turned over in his chest. It seemed that every time he saw her, there was *more for him to feel*. Serena Carey was still the most beautiful woman he'd ever seen. And in the last seven years, she'd become even more lovely. Everything about her appealed to him. Everything in him responded to her in ways that he never had with anyone else.

He hadn't wanted this and wasn't sure what to do about it now that these *feelings* were swarming through him.

Jack didn't trust feelings. Hell, they'd never done his parents any good. He'd seen love used as a weapon. He'd seen it left to die and wither. His own parents' marriage had been a misery and the one thing he didn't want to do was continue that tradition. So where did that leave him?

"What?" His friend's voice in his ear brought him out of his thoughts and Jack focused on what he was saying. "Seriously? Yeah. It's a benefit for kids and they do really great work. The band canceling at the last minute is going to seriously hurt things for those kids. They really depend on the money raised at the Carey event. Who? Yeah. Okay."

Serena's gaze was trained on him, hope shining in her eyes.

"That's great." He grinned. Tom's brother managed some of the best bands in the world. If anyone could help them out, it would be him. Looked like this was going to work out. "Yeah. I owe you." He laughed and shook his head. "Anytime. Sure. One-week stay at the Tuscany hotel for you and your wife. Least I can do. You got it. Thanks."

He hung up and Serena was on him in a flash. "One-week stay in Tuscany?"

"Seems only fair." Jack shrugged. "He got you a band. They're on a break from their US tour and they're happy to do benefits."

"Oh, God." She stared at him as if he'd lost his mind. "You agreed without even telling me who the band is? How could you do that? Who is it? When will they be here?"

He laughed a little and tucked his phone away. "Yes, I agreed. They'll be here tomorrow to set up for the gala performance. And you're going to approve. I guarantee it."

She closed her eyes and took a deep breath. *"Who?"*

"Black Roses."

Her eyes flew open and her jaw dropped. "Are you serious? They're the most popular band on the planet. How did you do that?"

"Tom's brother is their manager and—" The rest of his answer was lost when she threw herself at him, wrapped her arms around his neck and kissed him, long and hard.

Every brain cell simply went into a coma and he would have dared any man to react differently—if he'd been able to manage a single thought. Instead, he just wrapped his arms around her waist and held her to him, relishing the moment.

When she finally pulled her head back to grin up at him, Serena said, "I can't believe this, Jack. Black Roses? People will be talking about this event for *years*."

"So you're happy?"

"Beyond."

"Happy looks good on you," he murmured, his gaze moving over her face.

"I didn't want to ask you—or anyone—for help," she admitted, still staring into his eyes. "I wanted to handle this mess myself."

"You are."

"No." She shook her head. "I needed help. And you were there. I won't forget that."

"Asking for help isn't failing, Serena."

"I know that. But it's not handling it all yourself, either."

"Nobody does," he countered. "You have an assistant, don't you?"

"Sure, but not the same thing."

"Exactly the same thing." He kissed her forehead. "None of us gets this stuff done without help. Hell, if you could do it all yourself, you wouldn't need an office building filled with employees."

"You're oversimplifying."

"And you're overcomplicating."

"Because I disagree with you?"

"No." He looked down at her. "What's going on with you? A minute ago, you were thrilled. Now… It's not just accepting help, is it?" he asked as the truth began to dawn on him. "It's accepting help from *me*."

"You know what?" Serena stepped back and away from him. "I don't want to argue. I'm grateful for the band, but I've got a ton of minutiae to take care of before the gala, so thank you, but you'd better go."

Jack studied her for a long minute. For a moment there, they'd almost been a team. Then it was gone, and, damn it, he wanted it back. But clearly now wasn't the time for that conversation. "All right. But how about dinner tonight? We can take Alli to the Burger Barn. She loves those strawberry shakes."

"I don't think so, Jack. But thanks." Walking back to

her desk, she seemed to pull inside herself, and he didn't like it. "Like I said, I've got a ton of things to do, so…"

"Fine. Then the night of the gala, I'll pick you up—"

"No, I'll have to be here early, making sure things are as they should be."

"It's not a one-woman show, Serena," he said and hated the tightness in his own voice. He also hated that there was almost a chill in the room from the ice that had suddenly seemed to envelop her. She *really* didn't like the fact that he'd been the one to help her out. Was it so hard for her to accept anything from him? "You don't have to do it alone."

"Oh, I won't. The family always arrives early to check things out." Seated behind her desk, she looked up at him. "Thank you for the band."

"You're welcome." How did things get so stiff and impersonal between them in a matter of seconds? Hell, his lips were still burning from that kiss she'd planted on him, and now she was dismissing him as if it had never happened. "I'll just see you at the gala, then."

She nodded. "Oh, I'm sure we'll run into each other."

He'd make damn sure of it.

The Carey Center was even more beautiful than usual.

As she walked the rooms and the garden area, Serena gave herself a mental pat on the back for pulling this off. She'd taken a chance by shaking things up. New florist. New caterer. The photographer. All of it designed to bring new life to their most important charitable event of the year.

She even had the top band in the world playing for them tonight.

Thanks to Jack. She frowned a little, as she had to admit that without his help this night might have turned out much differently. She could be standing in the middle of a disaster right now instead of feeling triumphant.

As it was, the scents wafting from the food stations were insanely tempting. The flower arrangements were breathtaking, and on stage, Black Roses' road crew were handling the setup of the equipment and running a last-minute sound check.

Servers were all dressed in black slacks, white shirts and red vests and were being given their assignments by the catering service, and the dance floor gleamed like warm honey under the lights.

"Congratulations, sweetie." Amanda came up beside her and gave her a quick one-armed hug. "It looks amazing. I'm seriously going to hire this florist for our wedding."

"Thank God," her fiancé, Henry, said from behind her. "One decision finally made."

Amanda turned and grinned up at him. "Hey, I'm only getting married once. I want it to be perfect."

"If you're there," Henry assured her, "it will be."

"You are so sweet…" She sighed and rested her head on his chest.

Serena felt the tiniest twinge of envy for her sister's happy relationship, then tried to put it aside. Tonight wasn't the time for wishes and hopes.

But she hadn't seen Jack in two days. Alli was asking for him and Serena thought this would be a preview of the rest of her life if something happened and Jack left again. Maybe it would just be best to end it all now. Yes, she loved him. Yes, she would long for him forever. But some risks were too hard to take.

"Serena!" Amanda snapped her fingers in front of her face. "Wake up."

"What? Oh, sorry."

"I didn't tell you how gorgeous you look," her sister said. "I *love* that dress."

So did Serena. A deep scarlet, the dress was a floor-length dream. Narrow shoulder straps supported a bodice that was deeply cut yet managed to look…almost modest. A cinched waist and a flowing bell skirt completed it, and the red heels she wore were already killing her feet.

"I love that color of blue on you."

Amanda did a slow turn and Serena noticed that Henry's eyes burned just watching her. In her floor-length royal blue sheath, Amanda looked like a Greek goddess. And Serena couldn't help but feel another quick prick of envy for the love that her sister and Henry shared. They'd been through a lot and had found their way back to each other. She wondered why that couldn't always happen.

"Uh-oh," Amanda whispered, "the troops are here."

Serena followed her gaze to see Bennett, Candace and Martin approaching. The men were especially handsome in their tailored tuxedos and Candace shone like a candle flame in the deep russet gown that clung to her still-impressive figure.

"Sweetie," Candace said, reaching out to kiss her daughter's cheek. "You did it. Everything is lovely and I'm so sorry I gave you such fits over using the new people. The flowers are divine and I can't wait to taste the shrimp I just passed."

"Thanks, Mom." It really had turned out fabulous, she assured herself silently. Once their guests arrived and the music started, the Carey Center would be pulsing with life and hopefully a sense of fun the gala had lacked the last few years.

"You look gorgeous, Mom," Amanda said.

"I tried to tell her that," Martin tossed in. "But she wouldn't believe me. Wouldn't even let me pick her up at Bennett's house so we could come together."

"We're not together, Martin," Candace pointed out. "Remember?"

Bennett took a deep breath, scrubbed the back of his neck as if attacking the tension knots lurking there and threw a desperate look at Amanda. Leaning in, he said, "You've got to take Mom. I don't know how much more I can handle. She's *cooking*, Mandy."

"Nope. You're on your own. Maybe Serena…"

"No room," she said quickly and was so happy she'd only the three-bedroom apartment. They were all spoken for, so she could dodge her brother's pleas guilt-free.

"Look!" Excitement in their mother's voice had them all looking. "It's Justin!"

Serena watched her youngest brother approach, and she had to admit that, for the rebel of the family, Justin wore a tuxedo as if he were born to. Which, she supposed, he had been. His hair was too long, of course, and his easy, casual stride made him look at ease even though she knew he hated gatherings like this one.

He went right up to Candace, kissed her cheek. "Hi, Mom." His gaze swept over the rest of the family quickly and she noted he didn't spend any time on a greeting to Bennett or their father. Grinning at Serena, he said, "The place looks amazing, sis. Nice job."

"Thanks. I didn't think you'd come."

"Can't miss the biggest event of the year," he said.

"But missing family meetings, that's okay," Bennett put in.

"Where have you been?" Martin demanded. "You're a damn Carey, boy. That comes with responsibility."

"Don't do this now, you guys," Amanda said, throwing a quick look around them to make sure none of the servers or anyone else was paying attention.

"They can't help it," Justin said and gave his older brother a grim smile. "Which is why I avoid the meetings."

"Damn it, Justin—"

"Hush, Bennett," their mother said, and he pressed his lips together so tightly it was as if he were physically holding back the words that wanted to fly out of his mouth.

"Justin, honey," Candace said, laying one hand on his arm, "this is such a nice surprise. Where've you been?"

"Mostly La Jolla, Mom," he said.

"Bodysurfing?" Bennett muttered, and Serena gave him an elbow poke.

"Sometimes," Justin admitted happily. "Mostly, I'm working on something."

"What?" Martin demanded. "The Careys don't have any holdings in San Diego County. What are you *working* on?"

Justin nodded at their father, but kept his expression unreadable. "That's a surprise."

"I'm not a child waiting for Christmas," Martin countered. "What the hell is going on?"

"That's what I came to tell you, Dad," he said, then swept his gaze across all of them. "Tell all of you."

"Let's hear it," Bennett muttered, jamming his hands into his slacks pockets.

"I'm going to have an announcement in a few weeks, so you'll have to wait for the full reveal."

"Perfect," Bennett grumbled.

"That's what you came to tell us," Amanda said. "That you can't tell us something?"

Serena felt bad for her little brother. Justin had always been the one to defiantly carve out his own path. Though she'd admired it from time to time, she also had to admit that he sometimes made things tougher on himself than they had to be.

Why not just tell everyone what was going on with him? Why come to the gala only to announce that he wasn't saying a word about what he was up to for another few weeks? What was the point, other than to stir up Bennett and make their father angry and their mother worry?

"Justin," she said, "you're the youngest, but even you're too old to play games."

He winked at her. "Ever the peacemaker. No worries, Serena. I'm not playing." He looked almost...formidable. "I've got some plans that I'm working on, and once they're ready, I'll tell everyone. But I don't need," he added, shooting a look at his brother and father, "unwanted opinions coming down on me while I get things lined up."

"Fine," Bennett told him. "You don't want to be part

of the Carey Corporation, that's your business. But stop pretending to be. Claiming you'll be at a meeting and then never showing up—"

"Never said I would be." Justin cut him off. "That's you, Bennett. *Expecting* me to be there and then getting pissed off when I'm not."

He had a point, Serena told herself.

"So we're clear on this," Justin said tightly, "until I make this announcement, I'm not going to be around much, so don't expect me to be."

"If you had the slightest respect for—"

Candace cut Bennett off with a look. "The first of the guests are arriving. I won't have this family putting on a show for our patrons. So, listen up, everyone," she said, fixing her stern stare on each of them in turn. "Smile. Be happy. And have a good time with everyone even if it kills you. Understood?"

No one argued with Candace when she used that tone of voice, so they all mutely nodded.

"Good," Candace said with a sharp nod. "And as for you, Justin. If you don't attend meetings, I don't really care. But you will keep in touch with your family. Clear?"

"Yes, ma'am."

"Fine. Now that that's settled, get out there and mingle with our guests, and for the love of God, look *happy* about it."

It had been a while since Candace had given her family that steely look and direct orders, but some things would always work, apparently. Serena watched her family move off to be Careys. She plastered a smile on her own face and put aside thoughts of her mother living with Bennett, Justin having secrets. And mostly, there was Jack. The man she loved but couldn't trust. The man she wanted but shouldn't have.

The one man.

The only man.

Damn it.

Jack spotted her the moment he stepped into the massive ballroom. The murmuring roar of the crowd, the snatches of laughter and the clink of crystal all served as an undercurrent to the music pouring from the stage. Black Roses had toned down their usual stage presence, considering the venue—after all, it wasn't an actual concert, but a chance for wealthy people to get together and donate tons of money to a charitable cause.

By the looks of the crowd, they very much approved.

High on the walls, massive screens flashed with images taken by the wandering photographer and demonstrated just what a success the evening was by the smiles on those featured. On the dance floor, men in black danced with women wearing a rainbow of colors in a dazzle of movement until the whole scene looked like a Jackson Pollock painting.

But once Jack's gaze landed on Serena, she was the only woman he saw. Her hair was golden and that dark red dress against her pale skin seemed to glow, setting her apart from everyone, as if she moved through the crowd with a spotlight attached to her. He watched her pause, smile, chat with people she knew, then move on, checking to be sure everyone was happy and having fun.

He moved through the crowd with a single-minded determination. Two days he'd been without her and he couldn't remember ever being quite so…lonely. He didn't much care for it.

Seven years before, it had been his idea to end things between them. This time, Serena had shut him out, and he liked that even less. He missed her. Missed Alli. He wandered through that big house on the cliffs, listening to the echoes of his own footsteps. His life had become completely entwined with Serena's and he didn't want that to end. So he had a proposal to make and there was no time like the present to do it.

He caught up to her as she was greeting an older couple, the woman draped in diamonds, the man covering a considerable paunch with a well-tailored tuxedo.

"Oh, Jack!" She looked surprised. Had she really believed he wouldn't come?

"You look amazing," he whispered, and he knew from the flash in her eyes that she'd heard him over the noise in the room.

"Thank you. So do you."

He caught her hand in his, then tugged her toward the dance floor. "Dance with me."

"Oh, I should—"

"Dance. The party's going well. There's nothing for you to worry about, so dance."

She took a breath, considered her options briefly, then nodded. "Okay, just one."

He swung her around, then pulled her close, and they swayed with the music. They were a part of the crowd and yet separate from it. Despite the noise and the mass of people, Jack felt at that moment as if they were alone in the universe. Only her blue eyes looking up at him. The feel of her body pressed to his. Her scent, something earthy and intoxicating drifting through him with every breath he took. She felt right in his arms. It was as if everything in the world had suddenly found its balance after being just a little off-kilter for seven long years.

And he knew he didn't want to lose her. Not again.

"What's going on, Jack?" She tipped her head to one side and that glorious hair of hers slid across her shoulders. "You look so serious all of a sudden."

He swept them into a turn, but kept his gaze fixed on hers. "I am serious." He wanted to find the right words. Wanted to find the right time to say what he'd been thinking. But, lost in the moment, Jack couldn't come up with a subtle way to broach his idea. So he blurted it out. "Serena, I want you and Alli to move in with me."

She stumbled slightly, but his grip on her waist only tightened and he held her more closely.

"You what?"

"I mean it. Serena, I've never meant anything more. I'll build Alli that castle she wants—" At her look of astonishment, he amended, "Fine. I'll hire someone to build that castle she wants. We'll get her a puppy. We'll be together. The three of us."

"Jack…"

"Think about it," he said, then corrected himself. "No, don't *think*. *Feel*. We're good together, Serena. You, me, Alli. Move in with me. Give us a chance." The more he thought about it, the better he felt about the idea. They'd be together and she would see that she could trust him again. Eventually.

The music swelled, and Jack steered them around the dance floor while he looked into her eyes, trying to read what she was thinking. But for the first time, her eyes gave nothing away and he found himself holding his breath as he waited what felt like forever for her answer.

"No."

"What?" Stunned, he could only stare at her. "Why the hell not?"

"You almost had me, Jack," Serena said softly, with a shake of her head. "For a second there, I thought— Never mind. But then I realized that all you're offering me is an invitation to play house."

"It's more than that," he argued and wondered how he'd managed to bungle this so completely that she couldn't see how important she was to him. He'd never in his life considered living with a woman. Building something together. Hell, he wanted to be a father to her daughter. He wanted it all. Why couldn't she see that?

She touched his cheek briefly and it felt like a condemnation of sorts. "No, it's not, Jack. There's no commitment. No promise of forever. No proposal. Just move in with you. Bring Alli and we'll pretend we're a unit. A family."

"We wouldn't be pretending," he countered. How could they be having this discussion in the middle of a dance floor while hundreds of people crowded into a massive ballroom all around them? How could she say no to being with him? "You want a proposal?"

"I want a promise," she said.

"Damn it, Serena." He lowered his head, but kept his gaze fixed with hers. "We've both seen terrible marriages up close and personal. How is that an answer to anything? A piece of paper doesn't guarantee happiness, for God's sake, and you should know that. There are no guarantees, if that's what you're looking for."

"I'm not looking for a guarantee, Jack." She took a breath and added, "But how can you keep a promise you never made?" She shook her head again. "You're right, Jack. I had a terrible marriage and you watched your parents implode. But that doesn't mean that the institution itself doesn't work. A marriage is what two people make it, Jack. And they both have to want it to work.

"You don't even want to try, and frankly, I'm not sure I do, either."

"Now you're making no sense." He held her even tighter and still had the sensation that she was slipping away from him. Everything had gone so wrong so quickly. He was watching her, hearing her, and still he couldn't believe what was happening. "You want a proposal but you don't?"

She gave him a slow, sad smile. "I would have preferred you offered me a promise—a chance at forever. But I'm not sure I would have said yes. How can I be?" She stopped moving and the other dancers simply moved around them. "What you're offering me might have won me over seven years ago, but I'm not that woman anymore, Jack. I'm worth more. I expect more. And I won't settle. Not ever again. Not for myself and certainly not for Alli."

"I didn't mean—"

She went up on her toes and kissed his lips briefly. "But now that we have all of this out in the open, I'm happy to keep having an affair with you. Think about it."

When she turned and walked away, Jack simply stood on the dance floor, alone in a sea of swirling, swaying color and sound, and looked like a statue dropped incongruously into the middle of a party.

Well, that worked out fine because he suddenly *felt* as if he were made of stone, too.

The gala went on late into the night, and as he'd suspected they would be, Jack's twelve one-week package giveaways were the hit of the evening. Hundreds of people bought countless raffle tickets in the hopes of winning one of those packages, allowing the Careys to collect half again as many donations as they did every year. The giveaway was the talk of the event, and as he watched Serena present the last of those twelve packages, he felt as if not just the gala was coming to an end.

That scene with Serena played again in his mind and he heard her voice echoing inside him. No. She didn't want to play house. No commitment. No promise.

But the sex could continue.

He should be pleased with that. Why wasn't he? Why did he feel as if he'd missed something? As if she were slipping out of reach while he stood by helplessly?

He didn't like being helpless. Didn't like it at all.

Ten

A week later, Bennett stormed into Amanda's office while she and Serena were congratulating themselves over the successful gala.

"That's it," he proclaimed in a half shout. "I can't take it anymore."

"What are you talking about?" Serena asked.

He looked at her as if she'd lost her mind. "Mom. Of course it's Mom. What else would it be?"

Amanda snorted and he shot her a glare and stabbed his index finger at her. "You can laugh, but she's driving me nuts. She had a *decorator* come to *my* house because she says it's *boring*."

"It is," Amanda said sagely with a nod of her head. "I mean, I haven't seen it since that one glorious party when you first moved in, but I'm guessing you haven't changed a thing. So, how many shades of beige are there, Bennett?"

"That's not the point." He jammed his hands into his pockets and stalked around the room. "My cook's threatening to quit because Mom won't stay out of the kitchen. Suddenly, she thinks she's Betty Crocker!" He stopped and stared at his sisters. "Last night, she made a casserole that was so bad she had to throw the pan away."

Serena bit down hard on her bottom lip to hide her smile. Honestly, it was fun seeing Bennett so shaken. He was always so in control, so locked down emotionally, that this side of him was downright entertaining. Sure, she felt a little sorry for him, but still…

"I can't take it," he repeated and looked at Amanda. "So it's your turn."

"Oh, no, it's not," she said flatly. "I'm living with Henry now."

"Yeah, in a big damn house by the beach. You've got the room, and better, you've got the patience to deal with Mom while she's having this little revolution of hers."

"Little revolution?" Serena stared at him, angry on her mother's behalf. "Dad's the one who caused this situation. Mom's just reacting to it."

"I knew you'd be on her side." Laying a pleading look on Amanda, he said, "You're running the Summer Sensation. Mom's running the Summer Stars program. It would give the two of you plenty of time to work out any kinks."

"There are no kinks," Amanda countered. "But nice try."

"Come on! Help me here." His jaw tightened, his eyes flashed and he blurted out, "Who's the one who went and got your bike back from the kid who stole it?"

"I was eleven," Amanda pointed out with a sardonic twist to her lips. "I think my debt's been paid."

He dropped into a chair, braced his elbows on his knees and cupped his face in his hands. "I don't know how much longer I can last."

"Then talk to Dad," Serena offered. "Tell him to actually resign and that will get Mom back."

Incredulous, he lifted his head and looked at her. "You really think I *haven't*? He's as stubborn as she is and I'm starting to feel like a worn chew toy being pulled on by two pit bulls."

"God, Bennett, I used to think it would be fun to see you shaken out of your rut, but it's just sad." Amanda looked at him and said, "Go away."

"Thanks very much."

She laughed. "Oh, don't get all offended. I didn't mean now. I meant go. Leave town for a few days. Go to your cabin up in Big Bear. Just get out of the line of fire for a while."

He thought about that for a long minute or two, then slowly nodded. "Not a bad idea. At least I'll have some damn quiet and I can order in food from the local restaurants."

"There you go. And without you there, Mom won't be trying to cook," Serena said, "so *your* cook will stop threatening to quit."

"That's good. Okay. I'll give her a week off. With pay," he added. "I can make this work." Standing up, he buttoned his suit jacket, inclined his head toward his sisters and said, "I'll be out of here by tomorrow morning. One week. Don't let the company crumble while I'm gone."

"Wow," Amanda whispered when he left the room. "Never thought I'd see Bennett like that."

"Yeah. Taking a week off work? That hasn't happened in years." Serena looked at her sister and said, "He won't know what to do with himself."

"He'll work anyway, I imagine," Amanda mused. "Just like you would."

"Excuse me?"

"Come on." Amanda gave her a slow smile. "Look at you. You're becoming just like him."

Serena was stunned. This she hadn't expected. She wasn't a workhorse like Bennett. She did her job, but she wasn't obsessive about it. Was she?

"I am not," she argued, thinking that she had a very well-rounded life. "I have a daughter and a life and—"

"And?"

"And there's not a single beige wall in my condo."

Amanda snorted. "Fine, no beige. Everything else, though? The whole work-work-work thing? Hello, Bennett Junior."

"That's not funny."

"Truth rarely is," Amanda said with a smile as she shook her head.

Serena really hated to admit that her younger sister might—key word there, *might*—have a point. But since joining the family company, she had poured herself into the job. Into building a life for herself and for Alli. And maybe she had been a little overeager, but that didn't make her a workaholic, did it?

Serena's mind raced for something else to say and finally came up with only, "So now you're the one with all the answers? Until you and Henry got together again, what were you filling your time with?"

"You have a point, too," Amanda acknowledged, "but the main thrust of that point is that I now *have* a life. You're falling deeper and deeper into Carey corporate structure. Is that really what you want?"

"Of course it is or I wouldn't be doing it." Right? She made her own decisions now and one of them had been to dive into the business. To stake her own claim on the Carey Corporation and she thought she'd done very well in that respect. Serena had devoted a lot of her time to it. She'd had to. She'd worked her ass off on the gala to prove to her family that she could do the job, and now that she had… What?

Serena frowned to herself, and her mind raced with too many thoughts she didn't much like. True, she didn't spend as much time with Alli as she used to, but that was normal. Other moms worked and took care of their kids.

What was the saying? Quality time over quantity? Didn't that make sense anymore? Then she had to admit she'd always hated that saying.

"What I'm trying to tell you is that I have recently discovered that there is more to life than the Carey Corporation. And," she added, "if you're not careful, you're going to fall down the Bennett rabbit hole and end up with no life at all outside this company."

Serena thought about that and was forced to admit her sister might be on to something. At the moment, she was supposed to be in her office working on the marketing strategy for next fall's concert schedule. She was hardly giving herself enough time to enjoy what she'd pulled off at the gala before jumping back into her next project.

Heck, she'd missed putting Alli to bed the night before because she'd stayed late to work over some numbers with Accounting, and... "Oh, my God. You're right."

"I didn't want to be, believe me. Think about it, though," her sister continued. "Before today, when was the last time Bennett went to the cabin?"

She did try. "I have no idea."

"That's because it's never happened. He bought that cabin claiming that he'd spend time there on the weekends. To maintain a life outside the business." Amanda snorted. "He bought that place nine years ago, keeps a property manager to take care of it, and this is the first time he's been in it himself."

Well, that was all kinds of sad. "Okay. I'll think about what you said."

Actually, she didn't believe she'd be able to *stop* thinking about it now that Amanda had dropped those concerns into her head.

"Good. So on to other news." Amanda leaned forward in her desk chair and propped her elbows on the polished oak surface. "How're things with Jack?"

Serena frowned to herself, remembering Jack's non-proposal at the gala and the way they'd left things between them. It had been a week and he hadn't contacted her. So, apparently, if she didn't go along with his plans, he just pulled away completely. Well, fine. Wasn't that what she was trying to protect her and Alli from in the first place?

Serena missed him. But clearly he wasn't missing her, so how could his idea of the three of them living together mean anything? No, she'd done the right thing, she assured herself silently. She had to protect Alli. Had to protect her own heart from another crushing blow.

It didn't matter if she loved him—not if she couldn't trust him.

"It's good," she said finally.

Amanda's eyebrows rose. "Sure. I believe you. That only took a solid minute for you to say."

"Okay, here's the deal." She told her sister about Jack's proposition at the gala and then her reaction.

"Seriously? You had this chat *on* the dance floor in the middle of the gala and then you left him standing there alone?"

Serena scowled at her. "I didn't abandon him in the forest, Mandy. He's a grown man. I think he can find his own way off a dance floor."

"Not what I meant."

Serena didn't care what she meant. "I was proud of myself. Why aren't you?"

"Um, let's think. Since Jack's been back in your life, you've pulled off the event of the year and still managed to leave this damn building before eight o'clock every night. Alli's nuts about him and so are you, and you just tossed it all aside."

"I'm sorry." Serena stood up and glared down at her younger sister. "Yes, it's been fun since Jack's been back. I didn't expect to enjoy being with him, but I do. And, yes, before you ask, I do love him. But I'm not

going to agree to less than I deserve because I love him.
I'm also content with my life the way it is."

"Content?" Amanda shook her head. "That's pitiful.
How many books and movies have you seen that brag
about a *contented* ending?"

"This is real life, Amanda. Content should not be
mocked." Drawing her head back, she almost stuck her
tongue out at her. "Heck, you should be patting me on
the back. He proposes without proposing and I said no.
I took a stand."

"A stand against happiness. Bravo."

Irritated, Serena said, "You know what? I've changed
a lot since Robert tossed a hand grenade into my life.
And I'm glad to know that I can be good on my own."

"Notice you didn't say *happy*."

"I am happy. *Contentment* is actually a synonym for
happy. And more than that, Alli's happy." She threw
both hands up. "We have a terrific life together and I
don't want anything to mess that up. Look, my career
is going well. The family nonsense is quieting down—
except for Bennett and Mom—and I have a gorgeous
lover in my bed." Well, she had, until their talk at the
gala. "I know now that if Jack leaves again, I'll survive.
I love him, yes. But not enough to risk Alli's heart—or
my own, for that matter."

"What exactly are you risking?" Amanda asked quietly.

"Nothing," Serena argued. "That's the point."

"No," her sister told her quietly. "The point is, if you
don't risk failure, you never really win."

"That makes no sense whatsoever."

Amanda laughed a little. "Sure it does. Think about

it." Standing up, she said, "You have to be willing to put your heart on the line, Serena. Otherwise, you're just skimming the surface of a very deep pool and you'll never really be satisfied."

Her voice echoed in Serena's mind until she finally said, "Maybe not. But I'll be safe."

Amanda gave her a sad smile. "Is that really enough for you? Don't you deserve more?"

Jack should have been happy.

Hell, he was free again. There was no commitment holding him back. No one else to think of but himself. Why wasn't he *happy*, damn it? *Because*, a voice in his mind whispered, *being free doesn't mean a damn thing if all it buys you is emptiness*.

Sunlight drifted through the arched transom window over the front door and stretched out in long golden panels on the floor. He wandered through the empty halls of Colton house, and in his mind, he saw the ghosts of earlier generations walking these same floors. They'd lived and loved and built this place to last and it had.

What had he built, he wondered, beyond the bottom line of the Colton Group? Yes, he'd saved the company from his father's disastrous mismanagement, but he was still alone in a big house built for a family.

He stopped, turned around and stared down the long hall that stretched from the kitchen to the wide front doors.

The place was always immaculate and he had a housekeeper to thank for that. But then, there was never much to clean up, was there? There were no child-sized dirty footprints, no toys strewn across the floor. No slamming doors to shatter the quiet and no puppy running and skidding along the polished wood planks.

He was a man alone, sitting on a mountain of success with no one to share it.

"Hell," he muttered, just to ease the quiet in the house, "I tried to share it, didn't I? Offered Serena and Alli a home here. She turned me down. What the hell else am I supposed to do?"

But then, that was a stupid question, wasn't it? He knew what he had to do, but he'd been too cowardly to do it. Like Serena had said, he hadn't offered to make any promises. He'd simply given her a chance for them to live together as separate entities in the same house. Like roommates with privileges. What was wrong with that?

"Damn it, she should be here. They should be here," he said aloud. He missed being with Serena. Laughing with her, talking about their days. He missed the sex, for sure, but not only that.

He missed the smell of her on his pillows. The casually tossed nightgown at the end of his bed. The sound of her in the shower and the squeal she made when he joined her.

Smiling to himself, he walked back down that long hallway, opened the front door and stepped outside. The sea air was cold and slapped at him, but he walked on. Around the house to the backyard that stood as a monument to a great gardener, but showed no signs of life beyond the well-tended plants and the expertly-trimmed grass and trees. Absently, he looked at a wide space of lawn and imagined a child-sized castle there with a blonde princess holding court.

Frowning, he shifted his gaze to beyond the retaining wall, where the ocean was loud and grumbling and the clouds gathered on the horizon looked as dangerous and angry as he felt.

A storm was coming and he would ride it out, alone with the echoes of other generations of Coltons. Instead of curling up on the couch with Alli and Serena and the puppy the little girl wanted so badly. He missed reading that tiny girl the books she loved so much. Missed hearing her laughter and the sly way she asked for what she wanted.

His backyard was empty, but it should have held Alli playing with her puppy while he and Serena watched from the flagstone patio.

And all of that might have happened if he'd been willing to take that final step. Risk it all on a roll of the dice.

He'd held back on making promises because of the damage he'd seen his father inflict on his mother. But, hell, his mom was happy now, in her second marriage. She had suffered the most, yet she was strong enough to take a chance. To put it all on the line and risk everything.

How could he do less?

The following day was Saturday and Serena had plans to spend every minute of it with Alli. Her talk with Amanda had made her think and she didn't like the answers she was coming up with. She had been devoting too much time to the company.

She'd wanted to make her own calls. Stand up for herself and take control of her life. Well, she'd proved she could do that, but what she had to do now was find balance. Her job. Her daughter. Her life. The most important of which was Alli.

They were going to the San Diego Zoo for the day and she wouldn't think about anything else but this precious time with her daughter. So when the knock on her front door sounded, she was more irritated than she might have been otherwise.

She opened it to find Jack standing there looking down at her and the expression on his face was unreadable.

"Well," she said, "I didn't expect to see you."

"I know." He slipped past her into the house as if half expecting her to shut the door in his face. "I need to talk to you. And Alli, too, but that's next. You're first."

She closed the door, turned around and leaned back against it while she watched him. "You'll have to make it fast. We're going to the zoo."

"Fine. I mean, good." Nodding, he pushed one hand through his hair and she took that split second to realize it looked as though he hadn't slept. For the first time since she'd known him, Jack looked...distracted. She had to wonder what was happening, and felt a flicker of worry for him.

God, she'd missed Jack. Her heartbeat thudded in her chest and love for the man swooped through her in a gigantic wave. Was Amanda right about him, too? About opening her heart, taking risks to get what she really wanted?

"Look," he said, splintering her thoughts, "what I said at the gala was stupid."

"Thanks," she said on a short laugh. What was she supposed to do with that? "I think."

"That came out wrong, too," he muttered and took a step toward her before stopping himself again. "You know, I never used to have trouble finding the right words. Hell, I *always* know what I'm doing, saying, thinking."

"Okay… Where are you going with this, Jack?"

"You're the reason my brain keeps tripping me up," he blurted out.

She had to laugh because he looked so frustrated. "Should I apologize?"

"No." Shaking his head, he pushed one hand through his hair and hurried on. "I went to the office yesterday to have this talk there, but I wanted Alli with us, too, and your company day care seems pretty fussy about who they turn children over to."

She smiled wryly. "I'll make sure they get a raise."

He nodded. Still distracted, he muttered, "The hell with it."

"What are you talking about, Jack?" she asked. "Or rather, what *aren't* you talking about? Why are you here?"

He walked to her, grabbed her shoulders and held on as if preventing her from escaping.

"Look, Serena, you deserve a hell of a lot more than me," he said. "I know that. So does Alli. But that's what I'm offering you both. Me."

Her heart actually stopped for one long moment as she looked up into his dark blue eyes. Afraid to believe what she wanted to believe, Serena swallowed hard, held on to hope and asked, "What?"

He held on even tighter, and his thumbs rubbed her shoulders as if he needed the connection. Serena didn't know where he was going with all of this, but her heart-beat was racing. She couldn't take her eyes off him as he continued to speak.

"It's been a week since I've seen you and it's the longest week of my life. Damn it, Serena, I miss you. I miss Alli."

"We've missed you, too," she whispered, know-ing it wasn't enough to describe what she and Alli had gone through over the last week. Countless times her daughter had asked her why Jack wasn't there. Or why couldn't they go see him. And Serena had felt the same way. It had taken every ounce of her self-control to keep from calling him. Seeing him.

"I want you back, Serena," he said tightly, his gaze burning into hers. "I know I said everything wrong at the gala. You had a right to be pissed and I don't blame you for walking away. But I'm here now and… Damn it, I wish I could find the pretty words you deserve, but all I can say is the plain truth. I want you in my life for-ever. I want to be Alli's dad and I'll try really hard not to screw that up."

Her heart simply flipped. Was this really happen-ing? She lifted one hand to her mouth, but couldn't say a word. She didn't want to miss what he might say next. She hoped it would be more than the let's-play-house offer he'd made the last time. "What are you saying, Jack?"

"I'm saying I love you. And I love that little girl, too."

If her heart had flipped before, it was soaring now, making her a little light-headed. In the best possible way. A short choking sound shot from her throat. "I might need to sit down."

"No, you don't," he said, "because you've always known that I love you. I might have been too afraid to say it before, but it was still true."

"Oh, Jack…"

"I've always loved you. Always will. I want the three of us to be a family," Jack continued. "I want to marry you. Make more children with you and get Alli that puppy she wants. The castle, too."

"I don't believe this," she whispered, shaking her head, afraid that she might suddenly wake up from this lovely dream and find herself alone in bed. If that happened, her heart would literally break.

"Well, believe it," he urged. "The Colton house is big and empty, and it deserves to have laughter there again. It needs a family to bring it all the way back to life.

"And so do I."

He let her go long enough to dip into his pocket and pull out a very familiar pale blue jeweler's box. Serena's breath caught in her chest as she realized what was actually happening. The one thing she'd wanted more than anything else in the world was opening up in front of her and she could hardly believe that a day trip to the zoo had been her planned highlight for the day.

He opened the box and a gorgeous emerald engagement ring sparkled up at her. "Oh, Jack…"

He took the ring from its velvet nest and held it out toward her. With his free hand, he tipped her chin up so he could look directly into her eyes. "I love you, Serena, and that's forever. That's what I'm asking you to give me. Forever. I walked away once and lost everything.

"Well, now I'm asking you to believe me and to trust me when I say I will never walk away again. I want to make a promise to you," he said, voice low and earnest, eyes burning into hers. "To Alli. I want that commitment, Serena. I want the future we can build together."

"I can't believe you're saying all of this," she said, looking for the reassurance she needed in the depths of his eyes. When she saw it, the truth nearly buckled her knees.

"Believe it," he said firmly. "Believe *me*. Believe *this*."

He bent his head, kissed her and then looked into her eyes again. "Trust me, Serena. Trust me with your heart and trust me with Alli's. I will never let either of you down."

As if he'd conjured her by saying her name, the little girl ran into the room and skidded to a stop when she spotted him. "Jack! You're here! Are you going to the zoo with us? We're gonna see monkeys and tigers and bears…"

He grinned, picked her up and hooked the tiny blonde on his left arm while he held the emerald ring out to Serena in his right hand. "There's nothing I want more than to be with you two, and I would love to go to the zoo with you," he said, then shifted his gaze to Serena. "Let's ask your mom if I can be with you guys. At the zoo."

"Mommy, *please*." Alli hooked one arm around Jack's neck and leaned into him.

Staying with the zoo analogy, Serena looked from her daughter to the man she loved with all of her heart. In his eyes, she saw everything she'd ever wanted shining back at her. All she had to do was stand up for herself and take what she wanted. Make the decision that would bring them all together. That would create the kind of happiness she'd always dreamed of.

As Amanda had said, if you risked nothing, you never really won.

Heart full, she said, "If we go to the zoo together, I'll still want to keep working at the company..."

"Not a problem. I love my job, too, but we can still go to the zoo." He shrugged. "Sometimes I'd have to go to the zoo in Europe, but you and Alli can go with me."

"What's Europe?" Alli asked. "And when do we go to the zoo?"

Serena rose up, kissed her daughter's cheek, then kissed Jack. Alli laughed in delight. "The zoo with you sounds perfect," Serena said finally and held out her left hand.

Jack slid the ring onto her finger and Alli said, "Ooh, pretty."

Jack smiled at her. "You're prettier."

She cupped his face in her small hands. "Can we go to the zoo now?"

"Yes, we can," Serena said, stepping into the circle of Jack's right arm. "All three of us. Together."

Jack folded his girls close and held on tightly. Then he looked at Alli and said, "How would you like to come live at my house?"

She looked at her mother first, then smiled at Jack. "For always?"

He glanced at Serena, then promised her daughter, "Always."

"With a castle? And a puppy?"

Serena laughed and Jack grinned down at her. "She's a tough negotiator."

"You have no idea," Serena said, laughing.

"I'll learn," he assured her with a wide grin. "How about," Jack said, "you get a castle and a puppy and a new daddy?"

Alli's mouth dropped open and her eyes went wide and astonished. "*You* would be my daddy? For really?"

"For really," Serena said, looking up at Jack. The happiness on her daughter's face echoed the joy in Serena's heart and she knew this was the best decision she'd ever made in her life.

"This is the best day!" Alli crowed, hugged Jack and then asked, "Can we go to the zoo now, Daddy?"

"You bet we can," Jack said, and his voice thickened with the same emotions choking Serena.

"I love you," she whispered.

"I love you more," he assured her, and, in that moment, the three of them became the family they were meant to be.

* * * * *

COMING SOON!

We really hope you enjoyed reading this book. If you're looking for more romance, be sure to head to the shops when new books are available on

Thursday 11th November

MILLS & BOON

THE HEART OF ROMANCE

A ROMANCE FOR EVERY READER

MODERN

Prepare to be swept off your feet by sophisticated, sexy and seductive heroes, in some of the world's most glamourous and romantic locations, where power and passion collide.

HISTORICAL

Escape with historical heroes from time gone by. Whether your passion is for wicked Regency Rakes, muscled Vikings or rugged Highlanders, awaken the romance of the past.

MEDICAL

Set your pulse racing with dedicated, delectable doctors in the high-pressure world of medicine, where emotions run high and passion, comfort and love are the best medicine.

True Love

Celebrate true love with tender stories of heartfelt romance, from the rush of falling in love to the joy a new baby can bring, and a focus on the emotional heart of a relationship.

Desire

Indulge in secrets and scandal, intense drama and plenty of sizzling hot action with powerful and passionate heroes who have it all: wealth, status, good looks…everything but the right woman.

HEROES

Experience all the excitement of a gripping thriller, with an intense romance at its heart. Resourceful, true-to-life women and strong, fearless men face danger and desire - a killer combination!

To see which titles are coming soon, please visit

millsandboon.co.uk/nextmonth

LET'S TALK
Romance

For exclusive extracts, competitions
and special offers, find us online:

- **f** facebook.com/millsandboon
- 🐦 @MillsandBoon
- 📷 @MillsandBoonUK

Get in touch on 01413 063232

For all the latest titles coming soon, visit
millsandboon.co.uk/nextmonth

MILLS & BOON
MEDICAL
Pulse-Racing Passion

Set your pulse racing with dedicated, delectable doctors in the high-pressure world of medicine, where emotions run high and passion, comfort and love are the best medicine.

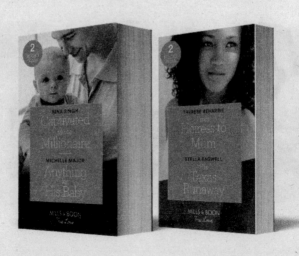